MAXON SPECIAL EDITION

BOOK ONE OF THE ANGELBOUND OFFSPRING SERIES

CHRISTINA BAUER

COPYRIGHT

Monster House Books
Brighton, MA 02135
ISBN 9781945723933
Second Edition

CONTENTS

DEDICATION

For Sharyn Paris,
Who Said, *I Believe*

COLLECTED WORKS

Angelbound Offspring
The next generation takes on Heaven, Hell, and everything in between
1. Maxon
2. Portia
3. Zinnia
4. Rhodes
5. Kaps
6. Mack
7. Huntress

Angelbound Origins
About a quasi (part demon and part human) girl who loves kicking butt in Purgatory's Arena
1. Angelbound
2. Scala
3. Acca
4. Thrax
5. The Dark Lands
6. The Brutal Time
7. Armageddon
8. Quasi Redux
9. Aquila

Angelbound Lincoln
The Angelbound experience as told by Prince Lincoln

1. Duty Bound
2. Lincoln
3. Trickster
4. Baculum
5. Angelfire

Fairy Tales of the Magicorum

Modern fairy tales with sass, action, and romance
1. Wolves and Roses
2. Moonlight and Midtown
3. Shifters and Glyphs
4. Slippers and Thieves
5. Bandits and Ball Gowns
6. Evil Queens and Goblin Kings

Pixieland Diaries

Sassy pixie Calla loves elf prince Dare. Too bad he hasn't noticed her. Yet.
1. Pixieland Diaries
2. Calla
3. Dare
4. Ley Queen

Dimension Drift

Dystopian adventures with science, snark, and hot aliens
1. Scythe
2. Umbra
3. Alien Minds
4. ECHO Academy
This is a completed series.

Beholder

Where a medieval farm girl discovers necromancy and true love
1. Cursed
2. Concealed
3. Cherished
4. Crowned
5. Cradled
This is a completed series.

MAXON

MAXON

*T*ake our picture, and we look like three guys hanging and banging on a beach. We've got lawn chairs, sunglasses, beer bongs, you name it. And the picture'd be right, too, except for one thing.

We're all in black body armor.

Truth is, we're thrax. Demon killers. And we're not partying on the beach. We're staking out an empty stretch of Arizona desert, a magical place called Charybdis. I pop open another beer and ask the big question.

"How much longer, guys?" No need to add 'until the next demon shows up.'

"Two minutes," answers Nizam. Zee's two hundred and fifty pounds of pure warrior with a bald head and mad skills for predicting demon strikes. "You never know with Charybdis, though."

"True enough," I say.

Charybdis is unpredictable as hell, even for Zee. It's the exit point for an underground vortex of supernatural evil that sucks in demons, holds them underground, and then chucks them back out again, right here at this spot. Best demon hunting in the after-realms.

Zee's face lights up with mischief. "You ready for the next fight, Maxon?"

I shake my head. No question where Zee's going with this one. This question always gets Tyberius cranked.

"Don't be a douchebag, Zee," I warn.

"False acc." Zee raises his hands in mock surrender. "I'm just doing the traditional thrax safety check." He speaks his next words super slowly. "So, are you ready, Maxon?"

I look to Ty. "You really up for this?"

Tyberius shrugs. "It's only a safety check."

Clueless, that's my man Ty.

"Fine. I'll play along." I gesture across my torso, showing how I look the same as I always do: Short dark hair, broad shoulders, and a body built for killing demons in hand-to-hand combat. "This is as ready as I get."

"Now, how about you, Ty?" asks Zee. "Wouldn't want to miss anything important, now would you?"

Sure enough, Tyberius starts speed-fidgeting in his chair. He pats down the pockets of his body armor. *Here we go again.* Before every damned fight, Ty always thinks he loses the same thing, thanks to Zee and his crafty safety checks.

"Where are my fireball charms?" asks Ty, his voice rising with alarm. "Where'd they go?"

"Chill," I say. "You'll find them. You always do."

"I don't knoooo-ow," says Zee in a sing-song voice. He has a shit-eating grin on his ebony face. "There's one more minute left."

What a player.

"Damn, damn, damn," chants Ty. He starts tearing through his pockets, the lawn chair, the cooler, and even the sand. I watch him freak out and realize a key fact. Ty could be the poster child for wizards from the House of Striga. He's got olive skin, a pointy face, blondish dreads down to his waist, and a major hard-on for frying enemies with fireballs. Classic.

"Wait a second," Ty pats one of his pockets and exhales. "Got 'em." He bounces from foot to foot, totally pumped for the upcoming battle.

I take a long pull from my beer and watch him fidget some more.

Ty's clearly cranked up. Me? Not so much.

Sadly, my ass feels glued to this lawn chair. At least, my tail's in the game. It's arced into battle stance behind my shoulder. All thrax are part human and part angel, but I've got some Furor demon blood in me, too. That means I've powers across two deadly sins—lust and wrath, the best ones in the bunch—as well as a long black tail with an arrowhead-shaped end. It's great in a fight.

"Thirty seconds," says Zee.

Ty starts the traditional thrax roll call. "Tyberius of Striga, ready to fight!"

Zee rises to stand beside him. "Nizam of Horus, ready to fight!"

With a huge effort, I somehow manage to peel my butt off the chair. The guys look at me like I should say something. Which, let's face it, I should. I am their High Prince after all, and there's a traditional speech that I'm supposed to give before a battle. I cut to the chase instead.

"Let's do this."

"That's it?" asks Ty.

"Yup."

Zee squares his shoulders. "In that case, I'll do the honors."

Damn it. It's worse when one of the guys gives the speech. If Zee does it, he'll launch into how I'm the High Prince Maxon. Fighter of demons. Slayer of hearts. The warrior who killed none other than Armageddon, the King of Hell, when I was just three years old. And now, I'm a grown Prince who's about to lead them all into another epic adventure.

Truth is, I'm not that Prince anymore. Maybe I never was.

I stop Zee before he gets started. "No speeches this time around, man."

"Sure," says Zee, his mismatched eyes wide with shock. "If you say so."

"I do."

Zee still looks confused, and that's fine with me. The guys can't know this, but about a year ago, it's like my life went from color to black and white. Fighting demons isn't a kick anymore. My nightmares are getting worse. And half the time I see a hot piece of ass, my inner lust demon doesn't even wake up, let alone get my body in gear. I'm seriously screwed, and not in a good way.

Time to think about something else.

"How much longer until the next demon?" I ask.

"Ten seconds," answers Zee. He tries to act all calm and cool while his voice breaks with excitement. "And that's five, four, three, two, one."

A circle of sand blackens before us. The air fills with a sickly-sweet smell. Bit by bit, the darkened ground moves in a clockwise motion.

Charybdis is coming to life.

With a low roll of thunder, more dark clouds appear in the sky. Meanwhile, the black sand picks up speed. A twitch of excitement crawls through my nervous system as some battle buzz kicks in. *Finally.*

All of a sudden, the ground stops moving. A small shape appears in the center of the darkened sand. Tiny demons always move fast, so my tail whips out before me, ready to block any quick strikes. Trouble is, the sky's now so dark, it's hard to see what's going on. The creature's nothing but a little white blob. I issue a new order.

"Sun spell, Ty."

Tyberius snaps his fingers and a small bright orb appears in mid-air. At first, this mini-sun blinds me. Seconds pass before I can see anything clearly. Once I catch what's going on, none of it makes any sense.

"Is that what I think it is?" I ask.

"Can't be," replies Zee.

"Oh yes, it can," says Ty.

Sure enough, a small pale creature sits in the middle of the black sands. It might be an albino demon adder, a white maggot monster, or any other breed of small and deadly enemy.

Only, it's not.

I crack a smile. "That's a fucking bunny rabbit, man."

"Hey, who's gonna fight the big bad demon?" asks Ty, his voice dripping with sarcasm. The rabbit hops around, its tiny pink nose twitching up a storm. "You calling the bunny, Zee? You get first dibs since you predicted it."

"Shut your pie hole," snaps Zee. "It could be like, a vicious killer bunny."

"It's a regular rabbit." I give Zee a reassuring pat on the shoulder. Every so often, Charybdis pulls in extra baggage with a huge haul. "The real demon will show itself in a few minutes." I gesture to Ty. "While we're waiting, how about you send the little guy somewhere safe?"

"Sure thing, boss." Ty waves his arm and the rabbit disappears in a puff of purple smoke. Once it's gone, the desert and sky return to their regular state. I focus on Zee.

"When's the next demon due?"

Zee glances between the sand and sky, his mouth making silent calculations. "You were right, M," he says. "It'll be here in two minutes."

Ty's mouth thins to a worried line. "In that case, it'll be a doozy. Everyone got their best gear on?"

"I'm all set." Zee pats his massive breastplate. "What about you, M?"

"Don't worry your pretty bald head about me. I'm covered."

Raising my hand, I summon a small lightning bolt on my palm. The shape twists across my skin, the form all crackling and bright. My chest warms with confidence. I've conjured lightning since I was a little kid. That's how I downed the King of Hell, Armageddon, at the ripe old age of three. My skills have only gotten better over the years.

Ty frowns. "Maybe you should bring something else, too. How about a battle hammer?"

I shoot Tyberius a dry look. *No question what he's hinting at.* I've supernatural powers over regular lightning, but everyone—Ty included—sees that as child's play, partly because I've been wielding the stuff since I was a kid. Everyone's waiting for me to graduate from lightning to igni, which are tiny bolts of power that send mortal souls to Heaven or Hell.

There's a catch, though. For igni to replace my lightning, I need to fall in love. It's called getting Angelbound.

Whatever. That garbage isn't happening any time soon.

"Lightning works fine for me," I keep my voice low and firm. "Change the subject, guys."

"Happy to." Ty bobs his eyebrows up and down. "How about a quick recap of last night?"

I shake my head. Aw, hell. I walked straight into that one.

"Good idea." Zee smiles, his teeth looking all white and predatory in his ebony face. "As I recall, we were all having a good time partying on Earth. Then Maxon left the club early. And what left with him again?" He taps his chin, acting all dramatic-like. "Was it two leggy blondes, perhaps?"

"You know it was," I say.

"So, how were they?" asks Ty. He doesn't need to add 'in bed.'

Both guys stare at me, fixated. When it comes to my love life, they're worse than the paparazzi. I'd like to say that I screwed the girls senseless, but I didn't. They were human nurses who work with vets from Iraq. We started taking about PTSD—why, I don't know—and it was a total mood killer. I took them out for ice cream and drove them home. They said I was a really nice guy. So, I got friend zoned, which was bad enough. Even worse? It didn't bother me.

The High Prince Maxon, a really nice guy.

Shoot me now.

There's no way I'm talking about that disaster, so I dodge the question. "Don't you pack of dicks have anything better to do than talk about who I nail?"

"No," they say in unison.

Thankfully, I don't have to continue with this depressing conversation because the desert sands start to darken once again. Black clouds reappear in the skyline. A low chittering noise fills the air. The ground gently shivers beneath my feet.

Ty lets out a low whistle. "Whatever's coming up, it's a big one."

Zee sets his fists on his hips. "In that case, I'm calling it."

I shoot Zee a thumb's up. "The next kill's yours. You going in solo?"

"I'll give it a try." Zee scans the horizon. "It's not like my battle twin's here." When you have a battle twin, you always fight better as a pair.

In Zee's case, his battle twin is Raj from Kamal, a thrax house that specializes in hunting demons with hawks and tigers. They're also one of the big five houses, along with Striga, Horus, Acca, and Rixa, where I'm from. We do everything together, which makes me wonder.

"Where the hell is Raj, anyway?"

Nizam shrugs. "It's his turn to babysit Uther."

I nod. There's nothing you can say to that. Uth's been working on his new 'phase bomb' for months now. You practically have to kidnap the guy to get him out of his lab. The man's a nut job, but a brilliant one.

Beneath my feet, the ground rumbles and heaves. I suck in an excited breath. Any second now, something demonic's gonna appear.

Only, it doesn't.

For a long time, nothing happens. The desert stays unnaturally quiet. Some small part of me warns that I should be more pumped and battle ready, unless I want to get myself killed. Another part thinks that may be an improvement.

With an ear-piercing shriek, hundreds of little creatures pour out of the sand. These tiny monsters have rodent features, glowing yellow eyes, and blood-red scales. My muscles tense with anticipation. With a great battle cry, Zee launches into the fray, slicing through the tiny demons with his long scabbard. My tail itches to help him.

Let Zee give it a try, Maxon. Don't jump in too early.

While I watch Zee swing away, my mind automatically classifies the kill. These are Rodentia, a cross between rat and lizard demons. By themselves, Rodentia aren't too tough. It's when they move together that things get tricky.

"That's the Scarlet Horde," says Ty. The way he's gripping the fireball charms in his pocket, I know he's anxious to jump in, too. "Class B demons." We rank demons by letter. The higher the letter, the tougher the kill. But Ty's wrong on this one.

"Class A, actually," I say.

"Even better." Ty's mouth twitches with excitement. "Since Raj is a no-show, maybe I should step in and help out Zee anyway. What do you think, M?"

I'm about to answer when a new voice calls out from behind us. "Who says I'm a no-show?" We turn around to see Raj and Uther high-tailing it toward us.

Ty grins. "So you finally got Uth out of his hidey hole."

"Tell me about it," says Raj. "Fucking miracle." Like everyone from the House of Kamal, Raj has cocoa skin, brown hair, and a hunting animal. In Raj's case, it's a black hawk named Jetal.

Uther rakes his hand through his short blonde hair. He has a wrestler's build and no interest in anything other than blowing shit up. "It's not a hidey hole, guys. It's my lab."

I chuck him on the upper arm. "We know that, Uth."

Raj cups his hand by his mouth. "Yo, Zee!" He calls. "Want company?"

Zee mows down a short wall of Rodentia. "Always, my friend."

Acting in sync, Zee and Raj align back-to-back and go to town. Meanwhile, Jetal circles the skies, picking off the odd demon rat, shaking it dead, and dropping it back into the horde. The battle twins move in unison, skewering the mini-monsters with lightning speed. It sure looks pretty to see them fight. Beyond that, I don't get the appeal of having a twin. I've tried it, and other warriors are never fast enough. I end up spending more time trying not to kill my partner than downing demons.

In short order, the horde is wiped out. Little rat-demon carcasses lie scattered across the desert floor. Raj and Zee let out whoops of joy while Jetal hops around the carnage. I'm about to give the 'all clear' when the ground starts rumbling again. Fresh chittering sounds fill the air, but this time, the noise is deafening.

More are coming.

Suddenly, a huge and writhing mass of Rodentia pours out of the desert floor. This time, they're packed in so tight, the tiny bodies make a kind of fountain as they stream onto the sands.

"They're everywhere!" cries Zee.

"We need backup!" calls Raj.

I slowly rise to my feet. Time was, a battle like this would really get my blood pumping. Now, I can't seem to focus. For some reason, I only want another beer. I do have enough sense to grab my baculum, which are a pair of silver rods that can be ordered into the shape of almost any weapon, assuming you want that weapon to be made out of angel-fire. For this battle, I order my baculum into the shape of a long-sword.

What the hell is wrong with me anyway?

After following Uther and Ty into the fray, I start slicing down Rodentia with my baculum and dragon-scale tail. Ty casts fireballs to burn more into little crisps. Uther sits down in the middle of everything and starts fiddling with something in his lap. I battle over to his side.

"Uth, you do realize the rest of us are fighting?"

"Yeah, yeah. My new bomb's almost ready." He holds up a block of gears and wires. "Phase bomb. Will open up a hole into anywhere. We can go straight through the desert floor, even."

My tail takes down a half-dozen Rodentia at once. "Why would we want to do that, Uth?" I keep mowing down mini-demons as Uth gets all gushy about his plan.

"Charybdis sucks in all the best demons and then stores them under-ground." He lovingly presses the bomb against his chest. "Now, we can go right into the heart of it. No more waiting for the demons to come to us, get it?"

I summon a lightning bolt to fry a small cluster of Rodentia into ash. Smells gross, but it's effective. While I battle on, Uther keeps staring at me like a happy puppy who's done an especially neat trick and now wants his bone. *Ah, Uther.* The guy's not what you call a traditional thrax warrior. Never has been, either. His bombs sure work wonders, though... When he can get them to work.

I change my baculum into two short-swords—gotta love how you can change a baculum fire-blade in the middle of a fight—and start taking down Rodentia two-handed. "We've got plenty to kill up here."

"Don't you want to know what Charybdis is hiding? Like, all of it?"

Used to be, maybe I did. Now? Not so much.

I flatten more Rodentia. "Be sure to keep the little buggers off you."

Without looking up, Uther screws something into the bomb with his right hand while lancing a demonic rat with his left. "You got it, boss."

A figure stalks out of the darkened tunnel. He's humanoid and stocky with a rodent face, red-scaled body and long, rat-like tail. I'd know this guy anywhere. He's a Class A job called the Scourge. This demon is what turns a small pack of Rodentia into a massive horde of trouble.

Oh, yeah. My day just got a whole lot better. More of the old kick of battle excitement moves through my veins. Not a ton, but I'll take it.

I stride over to stand before him. "I'm Maxon Vidar Xavion Aquilus, High Prince of the Thrax. Surrender and live."

The Scourge makes a chittering sound, which is then echoed throughout the horde. He speaks past a mouth of long pointed teeth. "Never."

I grin. "Glad you feel that way."

To kick things off right, I slice through the Scourge's tail with my own. Mine's covered in dragon scales. His is a major liability. Plus, losing your backend is a real game changer. You get attached to your tail, and not in the obvious ways. Chopping it off always makes my opponents do something dumb.

The Scourge glares at his bloody tail-stump, howls his lungs out, and then rushes at me with his short-sword. Not a great plan.

Blow after blow comes at me from the Scourge. I block them all with my right arm, which is also covered in dragon scales. It's my own built-in shield and I love it. We trade punches and lunges for a while. It's only a matter of time before this demon slips up again.

Sure enough, the Scourge makes a bad play for my jugular. I grab his short-sword with my bare right hand and fold it in half. Gotta love dragon scales.

The Scourge's big yellow eyes flare red. Now, he's really pissed. Things are about to get fun. I move into fighting stance and start whaling on his head. Then, I follow up with kidney punches to the gut and deep knee kicks to the belly. I've been trained in every kind of martial art out there, plus a bunch of stuff you only learn on the streets. This is one of the few times I get to use it.

At last, I'm really getting into the zone. Adrenaline pumps through me. You'd think I was a junkie scoring a hit, I'm so fucking happy. Sure, my knuckles are sore and the Scourge is down, but I don't give a crap. I'm not stopping for anyone.

That's when the Scourge's rat face turns into someone else's. It becomes long and black with a nose like a knife. Small red eyes lock with mine. I can never forget that face.

Armageddon, the King of Hell.

This freak abducted me when I was three years old. I still have nightmares about it.

"What the fuck are you doing here?" I roar.

Wrapping the demon into a sleeper hold, I start speed-whaling his temple. The skull cracks, and there's no question about it. This bad boy's dead. I drop the carcass onto the ground.

Catching my breath, I scan the battlefield. All the Rodentia are toast. Their bodies cover the desert floor in a solid bloody mass. The guys stand around me, their mouths hanging open. Not good. The fight's long over. I must've been beating up on a dead demon for a while. There's a long pause before anybody speaks.

"What did you mean before?" asks Zee slowly.

"About what?"

"You were talking to the Scourge. You wanted to know what he was doing here?"

A wall goes up inside my mind. On one side, there's the guys. On the other, there's the truth. I'm guarding that wall with everything I've got. No way I'm admitting to seeing Armageddon.

"I don't know, Zee. I was in the zone. Whatever."

"You lost it for a while," says Uther.

My defenses go on high alert. Uther's getting way too close to the truth. What I say next isn't a thought-out thing. More a knee-jerk response.

"Lost it?" I repeat. "You don't get to say that to me. You spent the battle playing with bomb toys instead of fighting like a thrax." The second the words are out of my mouth, I feel like a total ass for saying them. Uth's face gets all red.

And the worst thing is, I was only getting on his case for telling the truth.

Uther was right. I totally lost it. Isn't it bad enough that I don't like fighting or fucking anymore? Now, I have to have flashbacks on the battlefield, too. Man, this crap mood of mine better let up soon. I start giving orders, and that makes everything feel a little more normal. "Ty, cast an incineration spell. We need these carcasses out of here. Then, lock down Charybdis. We're calling it a day."

"Sure thing, M."

While the rest of the guys clean up, I pull Uther aside. "Look, man. I'm sorry about what happened back there. I had no business saying any of that. You're different, and I know you get flak about it. But I want you to hear me right now. I respect the hell out of what you do. You're an important part of the team."

Uther stares at the ground. "If you say so, Maxon."

"Promise me something."

"What?"

"Keep calling me on my shit. You're the only one with the balls to do it."

Uther cracks a smile. "Does that mean my balls are bigger than yours?"

"In your dreams, pal."

Ty jogs over to join us. He does not look happy.

"What's wrong?" I ask.

"I can't get the sealing spell to work."

"What?" I've never heard of Ty being unable to cast a spell, ever. "You sure?"

"I'm telling you, M. Something's immune to my magic."

I jog over to Charybdis. Sure enough, bizarre lights dance under the grains of sand. Everything's in different shades of blue, and none of it's human-made. Doesn't look demonic, either.

What can do something like that?

For the first time in I don't know how long, my pulse skyrockets. Every cell in my body vibrates with life and energy. This is the kind of electric excitement I've been missing for months…the charge that only happens before a really badass battle.

A new opponent is coming.

I can't wait.

2

LIANNA

*A*s I rush through the darkened forest, one thought stays stuck
my mind.

Crap, I'm running late.

That worry, as much as anything, is why I head-butt the flying frog.

"Sorry, Franklin," I say quickly. "Didn't see you there."

Franklin's sapphire skin and gossamer wings shimmer with blue
light. That's typical stuff for a water elemental—brighter skin means
emotions are running high. In this case, Franklin's upset that he's playing
messenger to me, the lowliest of Namare's apprentices.

He can kiss my thrax ass.

"What's up, Franklin?"

The frog hovers by my shoulder. "It took me a fortnight to find you."

"That's why they call it hiding out. If the other apprentices don't care
about getting killed, that's their business." I sidestep another sinkhole.
"Now, if you don't mind, I'm late for battle training."

"With Fisk?" Franklin's basso voice croaks extra low. The tone says 'I
know Fisk is your lover.' Irritation tightens up my neck. Everyone thinks
that I became one of Namare's apprentices by banging Fisk. I'd explain
how I dumped him, but no one listens. Just like they don't retain the fact
that Fisk and I hooked up *after* I got the apprenticeship.

Franklin titters by my ear, and that's when I've had enough.

"Did you come here for a reason, Franklin?"

"I bring dark tidings. Namare's illness is worsening."

Namare's the official leader of water elementals—our monarkki.
There are four monarkki in total, one for each element: Water, air, fire,

and earth. An image pops into my mind; it's my twentieth birthday party. The celebration consisted of me, Namare, and a slice of chocolate cake. That pretty much sums up my family life, right there. My heart clenches with worry. And Namare's getting sicker.

I force my shoulders to straighten. Stay calm, Lianna. Namare's been alive for twenty-thousand years and ill for as long as you've known her. She'll pull through.

"Got it." I work hard to keep my voice level. "What else is going on?"

"I've a new memory for you as well."

"Define new."

"Three weeks."

"Didn't bust your little blue ass to find me, now did you? I'm not *that* hard to locate."

Franklin flitters around in a huff, his chin high in the air. "Do you want what I've gathered or not?"

Collecting memories is the water frog *claim to fame*. They store them on their tongues. Gross, but I've gotten used to it.

"Okay, do your thing."

Franklin hovers by my shoulder. "Wrist or neck?"

"Wrist is fine."

Franklin lands on my forearm. His eyes glow bright blue as his long sticky tongue flicks against my wrist.

After that, everything around me disappears.

Things start off hazy, like I'm standing in a heavy fog. That's pretty standard stuff for a memory transfer from Franklin. At this point, all I know is that this memory's from a Water Valta, an elite guard of the elemental world. Water Valta are all tall, lean guys with pale skin, cropped sea-green hair and blue stone armor that's covered in a pattern of scales. Most have something fish-like about them, too. Some have buggy eyes; others sport gills on their neck. As a group, they're not what you call attractive. Makes me ask the age-old question of my life.

Why couldn't Fisk have been butt-ugly like the rest of the Valta? Then, maybe I wouldn't have gotten myself in such a mess.

The memory comes into clearer focus, jarring me out of my thoughts of Fisk. In the memory, I'm one of about ten Water Valta who line the walls of a swanky penthouse apartment in Tokyo. The furniture is modern and sparse. Large windows overlook the city skyline. Before me, practice mats have been set out for a trio of girls. Everyone calls them the Suzuki three. They're apprentices like me, only they're top of the class. Triplets. Prodigies. Lethal.

A Water Valta steps forward, holding a long stone that glows with blue light. That's the Kristalli of Water. Most of the time, the stone curls around Namare's head as a crown. Every once in a while, she charges it with elemental power, turns it to a dagger-like shape, and lends it to the apprentices for practice.

Every eye in the room is fixed on the Kristalli. Power, energy, and life surround it in an invisible mist. Watching the scene, a sense of joy and purpose electrifies my nervous system. Namare heals the water elemental world with her powers. She builds tsunamis, cleanses rivers, and—drip by drop—slowly transforms deserts into jungles. One day, one of us apprentices will wield that ability, too. Won't be me, but I'm happy I get to watch.

The captain of this Valta troop raises the Kristalli toward the apprentices. He's an older fellow with leathery skin and cropped gray hair.

"I bring this to you from Namare," he says. "Practice well."

The apprentices bow in unison. Aiko, the eldest, steps forward.

"Thank you, captain," she says with a sly smile.

"Anything for you, Aiko." The captain's neck-gills start flexing faster. Whoa, that guy has a serious crush. Must be a Water Valta thing to fall for your apprentice.

Aiko keeps up her eye-lock with the captain while her dainty fingers touch the other side of the Kristalli. The captain still holds onto his half of the stone, totally oblivious to anything outside of Aiko's gaze. The Kristalli flares bright blue. Suddenly, the captain lights up as well. He reminds me of some kind of warrior-shaped Christmas tree.

All Valta are low-level magicians. They amplify or block elemental power. Becoming monarkki takes two steps. First, you take in elemental energy from the last monarkki. That's where the Kristalli comes in. It stores and transfers power. Second, you need to link to your elemental people. The Valta are the ones who make that happen. It's their energy that turns the Kristalli into a crown, literally.

For the captain, that Valta magic is doing something else right now. Namely, it's making him light up like a love-struck dope.

Smiles break out across the room. The captain stays oblivious.

"You look mighty pretty today, Aiko."

"Thank you, kind sir."

The guy gleams even brighter. Around the penthouse, the grins turn into badly muffled chuckles. The captain looks down, noticing his glow for the first time.

"Aiko!" His fish-like mouth falls open in shock.

"Couldn't help it," Aiko says. "I like to see you glow."

The other Valta break out into peals of laughter, as do the apprentices. Aiko finally takes the Kristalli from the captain and sets the stone into the waistband of her karate uniform.

A warm sense of unity and family infuses the space. They're all so casual, so happy, and so totally doomed. I grit my teeth in frustration, wanting to scream through the memory.

Hurry! A charged-up Kristalli is Zephyr's drug of choice. Take the power from the stone and send it back to Namare, now.

But I'm powerless to change anything. The apprentices bow low to each other and begin their warm-ups. They start off with traditional karate kicks, leaps, and lunges. Totally beautiful. Absolutely deadly. And no doubt, they'll soon be dead as well. A weight settles on my soul.

The big mistake here is obvious. I know for a fact that the Suzuki three have been living in that penthouse for the past two months. For apprentices like us, that's asking for trouble.

Smoke clouds the bay windows. The guards stiffen with alarm, grabbing their traditional scabbards from their belts.

The smoke quickly takes form. It's Zephyr, the Monarkki of Air, along with a dozen of his Air Valta. Unlike the older team that protects the triplets, Zephyr's Valta are all young and twitchy. He has a nasty habit of killing off his own people for the smallest infraction. And compared to how he treats the rest of us? His people get off easy.

With an ear-splitting crash, Zephyr breaks through the window. Broken glass showers across the penthouse.

An Air Valta heads straight for me. Or rather, it heads straight for the Water Valta whose memory I'm inside. The Air Valta creates a corkscrew whirlwind that cocoons around my Water Valta's body, holding it in place while choking off any air supply. My Valta tries to twist under the bindings, but he can't move. His breath comes in rough gasps. Dying and desperate, he scans the penthouse.

The remaining Water Valta try to fight off both Zephyr and his guards. Not happening. They're outnumbered and don't stand a chance against a full monarkki without Namare there to help.

The Air Valta quickly restrain everyone in bonds of wind. Zephyr stalks toward the three apprentices. His skin glows in different shades of gray. Like his Valta, Zephyr wears the traditional Roman armor he wore during his lifetime. His face is rugged and crisscrossed with battle scars. A crown of milky-white crystals sits on his head.

Zephyr stalks to the first apprentice in line. "Where is the Kristalli of Water?"

She lifts her chin, defiance clear in her dark eyes. "I don't know."

Zephyr raises his arm, his fist turning into a swirl of cyclone-speed air. He punches the apprentice in the stomach and churns her insides into mush. Her face blanks with a look of shock and pain. After that, she slumps over, dead. My heart tumbles to my toes.

He moves to the next apprentice in line—Aiko. "Do you know where the Kristalli is?"

All the blood drains from Aiko's face. She quickly hands over the blue stone. "Here."

"Wise choice," Zephyr says. He grips the blue Kristalli and sets the end against his upper arm. Small prongs extend from the stone and delve into Zephyr's flesh. Blue light flows out from the Kristalli and into Zephyr's skin. His body quickly fills with sapphire-colored brightness. Letting out a low moan, Zephyr's leans back, his eyes rolling into his head.

A prickly sense of disgust churns through me. Once you become a monarkki, drugs and booze have no effect on you. However, sucking in energy from another elemental class is pretty sweet. Ages ago, Zephyr started crashing practice sessions and killing off the odd apprentice to steal and drain charged Kristalli. Over the years, it's gotten so bad that the guy probably needs a twelve-step program.

Zephyr lets out another moan. Okay, the guy *definitely* needs a twelve-step program.

The Kristalli of Water turns dark. All the practice power has been drained. Bit by bit, the blue light fades from Zephyr's skin as well. With a long sigh, Zephyr pulls the stone away from his arm. Through the memory, my Water Valta gasps harder for breath. Sadness and rage burn through my rib cage. This didn't have to happen.

Aiko steps forward. "You have what you want. Now, kill us or leave."

A sense of awe chills my veins. You have to hand it to Aiko. Facing down Zephyr takes guts.

"I don't have everything that I want," growls Zephyr. "Where are the Kristalli of Fire and Earth?"

A long pause follows. Zephyr killed off the monarkki of Fire and Earth along with all their apprentices. At least Namare was able to hide their Kristalli before Zephyr could drain them. The stones are still charged with elemental power and ready for a new monarkki, but Namare's been too sick to do anything about it. Everyone hopes that her successor will be healthy enough to train new apprentices for the Fire and Earth elementals. They seriously need new monarkki.

Zephyr frowns. "You don't know where they are, do you?"

Aiko flashes him a defiant look. Sometimes, no response is a response. Aiko's not telling Zephyr a thing.

Zephyr tosses the darkened Kristalli of Water onto the ground. "That's unfortunate." He levitates toward the window, ready to leave.

Warm relief washes through me. Maybe Zephyr will take off without a massacre, for once.

Before he goes, Zephyr pauses to issue one last command.

"Kill them all. Slowly."

A weight of sadness settles into my bones. I didn't know the triplets well—or those Water Valta at all—but no one deserves to die at Zephyr's hands.

After that, the memory ends in a flash of light and wind. I'm back in the darkened forest. Franklin's wings still flutter beside me.

"What did you think?" asks Franklin.

Emotions battle it out in my nervous system. Grief. Fear. Anger. I open my mouth to speak. No words come out.

Franklin flies closer to my ear. "Lianna? Did you hear me?"

"Yeah, I heard you. And I know all about Zephyr. Not sure why I needed to see that."

"I should think the lesson is clear. Don't dawdle when you have the Kristalli. Soak in the power right away. Get rid of the stone. To us, it is the storehouse of sacred power. The crown of our monarkki. To Zephyr, it's nothing more than a syringe for his pleasure."

"I always charge up right away." My eyes narrow with suspicion. "But you know that, don't you?"

Franklin pretends to be interested in a nearby fly. He always does that when I catch him lying.

"Yes, I know," Franklin croaks.

"So what's really behind that lesson?"

"When you practice with the Kristalli, you should keep extra guards by you."

And here it is. Because Fisk is the only guy I practice with.

"And you think extra guards would've helped the Suzuki triplets?"

"Yes, an additional ten Valta could easily have saved them all."

"No, hiding out would've saved them." I shake my head in frustration. "This is why I live solo and change my address every two weeks. *That's* protection."

Franklin sniffs. He thinks he knows why I hide out solo. More alone time with Fisk. We're not having that conversation again.

"Any other messages for me?" I ask.

"No."

"You can take off, then."

"I'm not leaving until you understand the importance of that memory."

"Believe me, I get the message. I'm careful." I resume my steady march through the dingy forest. Franklin flutters along at my side. His big frog mouth droops with worry.

"You know I don't like you," croaks Franklin.

"No kidding."

"Yet, I don't want to see you hurt. You've grown on me despite your annoying ways."

I shoot him a half-smile. For Franklin, this is as close as a declaration of love as I'm ever going to get.

"Thanks, Franklin. You've grown on me, too." I gesture to the line of trees ahead. "I'm meeting Fisk for battle practice just past that ridge. Alone. I better go."

"Please be safe, Lianna." The little frog flies away, his tiny legs bouncing with the movement. Even after years of being an apprentice, that sight makes me smile.

I step through the trees to Ghoul Lake G24. Like all the bodies of water I've seen in the Dark Lands, this place is a single sheet of oily sludge. Time was, Namare would cleanse a lake like this with a wave of her hand. Someday, one of her apprentices will do that instead. My pulse quickens at the thought of rejuvenating ponds and invigorating oceans.

Forget it, Lianna. Everyone knows you're the last choice for monarkki. Get your head back into battle training and managing you-know-who.

Right, Fisk.

I scan the shoreline. There's no one around.

I cup my hand by my mouth. "Fisk? Where are you?"

Still no one nearby.

I frown in confusion. Fisk is never late.

Beside me, the air turns blue with condensation. I exhale a relieved breath. Fisk's finally arriving in mist form.

Within seconds, the blue haze consolidates into the shape of a man who's tall and lean with long, sinewy muscles—the classic swimmer's build. Like most water elementals, Fisk's eyes are sea green, large, and haunting. His skin is porcelain with a faint hint of blue, the same coloring as his short, spiky hair. Today, he's wearing a black T-shirt with olive cargo pants. He looks in his early twenties, but you never know with elementals.

"Hello, Lianna."

"Hey, Fisk."

For a long moment, Fisk stares at me like I'm the most beautiful woman in the after-realms. I can't help it; I adore the attention. It's why I started dating Fisk in the first place. I'm a tall and sporty blonde who's more at home in battle gear than ball gowns. Fisk was the first guy to make me feel lovely.

"You're a vision," he says in a husky voice.

"I'm wearing jeans, combat boots, and a Hello Kitty T-shirt. You're such a suck-up."

He winks. "Doesn't make it less true."

My neck starts to redden and I kinda hate myself for that. Fisk and I broke up for some really good reasons. Am I so isolated that one compliment from a hot guy makes me forget our nasty history?

Why yes, yes I am.

Fisk takes a cautious step closer. He's like a panther stalking his prey. "How's your latest safe house?"

"More of a cabin in the woods. It's safe enough."

"You there alone?"

No question where this is going. The first time Fisk and I hooked up, he was staying overnight to 'protect' me.

"Always," I murmur. "I can take care of myself."

Crap. In my head, that response was supposed to come out more kick-ass sounding. Instead, the delivery was a touch desperate. I hope he didn't catch that.

"You don't have to be alone, you know." Fisk moves to stand in front of me. "Invite me over tonight."

Oh, he caught that, all right.

"I can't, Fisk."

"Come now, Lianna. We both know this break-up of yours won't last. We're meant to be together." Fisk leans in closer. His breath cascades gently down my neck. "You'll always be my girl."

And boom—that does it.

All signs of sexy blushing disappear as my hands ball into angry fists. This would be the side of Fisk that bugs the hell out of me. In fact, it's the main reason I broke up with him. The man has no listening skills. After everything I told him, how can he call me by that name?

"You know Silas used to call me his girl. I hate it."

"Ah, but am I Silas?"

"Let me think." I tap my boot dramatically. "No." No, you're not the Class A demon who kept me locked up as his slave for months. *"But you are a tool."*

"That's beside the point." He winks in a way that's meant to be endearing. It's not. "I'm not Silas, and you'll always be my girl."

"Keep calling me 'your girl' and I'm out of here."

He half rolls his eyes. "Saying that only reinforces my point."

"And what's that, exactly?"

"You're threatening to miss out on battle training in order to satisfy a youthful and emotional whim. This is the heart of my argument. You're only twenty years old. That's far too young to know your own mind. You'll come around."

And here's yet another item for the Why I Dumped Fisk file. He constantly treats me like an endearing doll instead of a grown and rather deadly woman. I take a few pointed steps away from him.

"I'm not coming around, Fisk. We've discussed this many times."

"Hey, I've done as you asked. We're taking a break from the relationship."

"It's not a break. We are over. O-V-E-R."

In reply, Fisk leans back and laughs like I'm the most adorable pile of sweetness that he's ever seen. Time was, that laugh always got me gooey and lovey. Before I knew what was happening, I'd forgive Fisk with a long kiss. That was before. Now, I just want to start battle practice and knock his block off.

Multi-colored lights start flickering from the sinkholes, distracting me from my Fisk issues. I do a double-take in surprise. That can't be right. Maybe I got hit with an enchantment or something. It's happened before.

"Do you see that?" I ask.

Fisk's features turn unreadable. "Yes, those lights are elemental magic."

"Is it Zephyr?" The last thing I need is that guy chasing me around.

"No, Lianna." Fisk's eyes widen with sympathy. "It's something else entirely."

A pang of worry goes through my heart. Fisk hardly ever gives me his sympathy eyes. Bedroom eyes, yes. 'You're such a child' eyes, sure. But sympathy? Something huge must be going on.

"What's wrong?"

Fisk scrubs his hand over his face. "I don't know where to begin."

"Just say it. Please."

With a burst of brightness, the lights change. Instead of multiple colors, everything becomes sapphire blue. It's the hue of water elementals everywhere.

It's the shade of Namare.

My breath catches with a realization. Those lights? In that color? It can mean only one thing. The water elementals who live in the earth are weeping. Their bodies give off a light glow at all times—that's so they can see underground—but when they're grieving, the brightness goes off the charts. There aren't a lot of things that would get them so worked up. Losing a leader is one of them.

Please don't let it be Namare. It's too soon. She can't be dying. "Is that what I think it is, Fisk?"

"I'm afraid so. You've never seen this phenomenon before?"

I shake my head.

Fisk gestures to the sinkholes. "These lights are shining through every pit in the after-realms. All non-humans will see it."

"It's really happening, then."

My Namare.

Memories flicker through my mind. First, I recall the beautiful, snow-capped mountains of my childhood home in Colorado. Our isolated log cabin had no neighbors, no phones, and no one to hear us scream when a Class A demon named Silas killed my parents and abducted me. I served Silas for months before Namare saved me. Next, my heart warms as I picture her plump figure and happy, wrinkled face. My throat tightens with grief. She can't be dying.

"Where's Namare?" I ask softly. "I have to see her."

"She's finding a safe place to transfer her power to one of her apprentices."

The words hang in the air, too terrible to be real. "How long until she's ready?"

"A few hours, maybe less. Walker will take you there when the time is right."

I press my fingertips to my temples and think through this news. Walker's a ghoul who appeared in my life about five years ago. He finds me new safe houses to live and train in, which is no small feat considering that I have a homicidal maniac following me around. I nod once to myself. If Walker's in on this, then I trust the process.

"Okay, I can wait." In the nearby sinkholes, the brightness intensifies. I need to focus on something else. "Let's start training."

"As you command."

Leaning over, Fisk rifles through his satchel and pulls out the Kristalli of Water. My breath catches with awe and excitement. Today, I practice with a sample of elemental power.

"Namare charged this up for you." Fisk runs his finger along the length of the Kristalli. A pale blue light dances in its depths. "Let's try summoning the stone, shall we?"

I raise my hand and whisper an incantation. The Kristalli instantly flies onto my palm. The stone feels cool against my skin as I toss it from hand to hand.

"Easy peasy, Fisk."

Go me. We've been working on that move for months.

"Excellent. Now, let's review the process of transferring the power from the stone to the elemental parts of your soul. First, you—"

I grip the Kristalli tightly and whisper another incantation. Tiny prongs of rock dig into my palm. A rush of power hits my nervous system. As elemental energy enters my body, the stone turns dark.

"Another fine effort." Fisk scans me from head to toe. I wonder if more bedroom eyes are coming my way. Nope. Instead, Fisk gives me one of his 'I'm so disappointed in you' looks.

"Out with it, Fisk."

"You've such strength, Lianna. Yet, you haven't the guts to admit that you're mine."

"Wow, are you ever a dick." I move into battle stance and conjure a long icicle in my right hand. It's about the length and width of a short-sword. "Come on and fight me."

Fisk makes a tsk-tsk noise, which only angers me more.

"You sure you don't want to discuss this?" he asks. Fisk snaps his fingers and the Kristalli disappears. It's gone back to Namare, wherever she is.

"I wasn't done with that Kristalli," I say slowly.

Okay, I was totally done with it. I'm just tired of Fisk making decisions for me without asking.

"What a coincidence, I wasn't done with our conversation, either." Fisk folds his arms over his chest. "Still don't want to talk?"

"Positive." I toss my ice weapon from hand to hand. "And I said, fight me."

Fisk keeps staring at me indulgently and not fighting. Every muscle in my body quivers with rage.

"Fine," I say with a snarl. "You asked for it."

Time to use my borrowed elemental powers.

I raise my ice-weapon high, pause, and then jam it deep into Fisk's chest.

At last, the guy snaps out of his funk and into instructor mode.

"That was a terrible strike, Lianna. You hit me at an angle." He points to the top of the icicle sticking out of his sternum. "Now your weapon is cracked and unsuitable if it's required for another volley. You must use frozen instruments only for straight-on impalement."

"Like this?" I conjure another icicle and stick it right into his belly. This one doesn't crack.

Fisk frowns. "That could sting, you know."

"Eh, we both know it doesn't. Ice is water. And water can't cause pain to its own element."

Fisk's mouth hardens into an angry line. He pulls both icicles out of his torso and tosses them into the lake. His flesh instantly closes over. Wish I could do that trick.

"Show me a projectile attack," orders Fisk.

Some serious battle practice. Finally.

Raising my arms, I conjure a wall of bullets made of boiling-hot water. They hover in the air behind my shoulder for a moment. I grin, enjoying the calm before the strike. Lowering my arms, I send the weapons speeding toward Fisk. Loud zings fill the air.

This time, he's ready for me.

At the last second, Fisk's body changes into mist. The bullets pass harmlessly through him. When he reforms, a gloating look fills his big, sea-green eyes.

"You know what you did wrong back there?"

I punch my thigh in frustration. "Yup. I broadcasted my attack."

"Precisely. I had time to change from solid form into mist. The same will be true for Zephyr. Remember, non-solid forms are extremely taxing. No one stays in them longer than absolutely necessary. You need to strike quickly and in unexpected ways. Catch Zephyr in his solid state. That's the only way to injure him."

The word 'catch' gives me an idea. I scan my internal power reserves. I've drained some of Namare's elemental energy, but enough remains for another attack. With a flick of my fingers, I summon a huge block of ice to entrap Fisk up to his neck.

"Like this, you mean?" I ask.

"Well done, Lianna." Fisk laughs, then melts the ice into the lake. "Just don't try something like that right after you gain your monarkki powers. The abilities will be too new and you'll lack the finesse needed for a major attack."

A chill runs through me, and it has nothing to do with the ice I conjured. Namare is dying. Someone will take her powers soon. Fisk guesses my thoughts.

"She could choose you," says Fisk.

"She won't, Fisk. We both know that. And even if she did, I still need Water Valta magic to be crowned. You may like me well enough, but the rest of the Valta don't agree with you."

"Not true. My men do like you."

"They hit on me. There's a difference."

Fisk frowns. It's like the thought of them actually coming onto me never really occurred to him.

Hell, maybe it didn't.

Fisk purses his lips. "And who did this, exactly?"

"All of them. They think I got my apprenticeship because you pulled strings with Namare."

Fisk waves his hand dismissively. "That isn't what happened. You earned this apprenticeship."

"They'll never believe that. They'd rather not have a monarkki than get one who's not qualified." I shake my head. "Not that I blame them. I haven't been training for that long. The other apprentices were selected at birth. They've been working for this all their lives."

Fisk's face turns gentle. "You have a solid chance at being chosen. I wouldn't be here if it were otherwise." He steps closer, and I know that heated gleam in his eyes. He's moving in for a kiss.

Crap, I don't need this right now.

A low hum fills the air, interrupting the moment. I should feel relief at having Fisk's kiss derailed, but I don't. Instead, dread weighs heavily on my spine. I'd know that humming noise anywhere. It's the unmistakable sound of a portal opening, which is how ghouls zap themselves around the after-realms.

My breath hitches. *This is it.* Walker's coming to take me to Namare.

A door-shaped hole appears at the water's edge. Through it steps a tall ghoul in flowing coal-dark robes. He has angular features, short hair, and sideburns. His all-black eyes shimmer with sympathy as he says four words that rock my world.

"Lianna, it is time."

3

LIANNA

*W*alker and I stumble out of his portal and onto a snow-covered plateau high up on a mountainside. A thin layer of clouds hovers below us. The air is crisp, ice-cold, and stings my lungs with every breath. I start to walk forward, but Walker grabs my upper arm.

"Watch out." He points to the ground.

I look down and yow, that was close. I almost stumbled into a deep crevasse. This small clearing is riddled with them. I'm not an elemental, so falling down one of these would've killed me.

"Thanks, Walker."

"All in a day's work," he says with a smile. "This way."

Taking far more cautious steps, I follow Walker toward what looks like a sheet of frozen ice. After all my years of training, I can tell elemental magic a mile away. This thing is no icefall; it's an elemental shield, a sort of force field that monarkki create to keep everyone else out, even other elements.

Namare must be inside along with the rest of the apprentices. My temples tighten with a feeling somewhere between sadness and fear.

"This is where I leave you," Walker says. "I'll see you soon."

I open my mouth and try to say goodbye. Nothing comes out. Walker appeared out of nowhere and became my lifeline, literally. He hounded Namare, saying that Verus, the Queen of the Angels, had demanded that he help me out. Verus is also an oracle, so her request should've easily convinced Namare to loosen her choke-hold rule about 'no outsiders.' It didn't. Walker followed us around for a year before Namare would even talk to him.

Since saying goodbye isn't happening, I opt for a half-smile. At this point, it's the best I can manage.

"You'll do well." Walker wraps me in a deep hug. "This isn't my first time at this kind of challenge, you know. I watched over Myla for years before she came into her powers."

"So they tell me."

Myla is the Great Scala, the only being who can move mortal souls to Heaven or Hell. She's also Queen of the thrax and a big celebrity in our world. Even in our isolated cabin in the middle of nowhere, my parents told me stories about her family.

Walker grips my hands in his. "You remind me of Myla, not a little."

"Is that good?"

"Ah, it's the best."

"Thank you, Walker. For everything." I stop myself before I get really mushy. "Now, get out of here already."

Walker winks, opens a portal, and disappears into it. Once he's gone, I turn to face the ice shield. On the other side of this frozen barrier, Namare waits for me. I know I'm everyone's last choice to take over as monarkki, so it'll be my job to watch her powers go to someone else. After that, she'll die. A shudder of sadness runs down my rib cage.

Don't think about that now. Just be here for Namare.

Steeling my shoulders, I walk straight through the wall of ice. Inside, Namare lies on the snow-covered ground, her body curled into a fetal position. Like always, her skin and hair are in varying shades of blue, only now, there's a grayish tinge mixed in. That means she's losing her life force. Even her once-round form looks slight and frail in her long blue robes. My eyes sting with emotion. She's the last family I have.

"Come here, child," whispers Namare.

I kneel down beside her. "How can I be of service?"

She offers me a sad smile. "You lived. You're here. That's enough for now."

The other four apprentices stand nearby in their robes, looking very official and prepared. Suddenly, I'm feeling rather awkward in my jeans and T-shirt.

"Where are the Water Valta?" I ask.

"Only my apprentices may be present for the transfer of power," says Namare. "The Water Valta will appear shortly afterward." She gestures to the other apprentices. "Join the line."

Nodding, I rise to my feet and walk toward the other apprentices. We exchange sympathetic glances, except for the guy we call Magic Marcus. He's a wiz with the Kristalli and a favorite of the Water Valta. Everyone knows he'll be Namare's pick as successor. Judging by the satisfied look on his face, he knows it too.

Namare hoists herself up on her elbow. The Kristalli of Water glitters about her head as a crown. Namare snaps her fingers and the Kristalli disappears from her brow, only to reappear in her hand as a dagger-shaped stone.

My breath catches. She's about to transfer power.

"You've all been faithful apprentices," says Namare. "I thank you for your diligence and service." With pained movements, she forces herself to sit fully upright. "Today, I will transfer my elemental powers to one of you using this Kristalli." She inhales a shaky breath. "In the end, there was only one candidate for me."

All the apprentices stiffen their stances. My heartbeat skyrockets. Some of these folks have waited a lifetime for this moment. Namare inspects each of us in turn. When she speaks, her voice is unwavering, intense, and full of conviction.

"I choose Lianna."

Shock tingles across my skin. *I didn't hear that right.*

"Did you say Lianna?" asks Marcus.

"That I did," replies Namare. "You're too full of ambition to make a true leader. When it's done right, ruling is about service, not self-aggrandizement."

"But, great mother—" begins Marcus.

Namare's skin flares blue with anger. "Don't question me. Lianna has more strength than all of you combined. She lived through things you can't imagine under—" she stops herself before she says 'Silas.' She knows I don't like advertising that part of my life.

"Lianna is strong," says Namare simply. "That's all that matters."

Marcus makes a point of stretching his arms over his head. The guy is ripped.

"Not that kind of strength, Marcus," snaps Namare. "If you can't respect my wishes, I'll ask you to leave."

Marcus bows his head. "Yes, great mother."

Namare pats the stretch of snow by her side. "Come here, Lianna."

I sit down beside her and wait. My mind scans through what I know happens at this moment. It isn't much. There's one Kristalli for Water. It will act as a conduit to transfer Namare's powers to me. Over the years, I've practiced that transfer. Beyond that, I've no idea what to expect.

I take Namare's hand in mine. Her skin feels papery and cold.

"What do you need me to do?" I ask.

"First, a favor." Her breathing comes in rough wheezes, and my heart cracks with grief.

"Anything, Namare."

"Pass a message to Walker for me. Tell him that Verus's prophecy about you was right. You were meant to become the next Monarkki of Water, and I am grateful that he found me and offered his help. Please give him my deepest thanks."

"I will." I blink away tears.

This is really happening. Namare's dying, and I'm taking her powers. I say the words over and over in my mind. They still don't seem possible.

"Thank you." Namare weakly raises her right hand. "Now, it is time." The Kristalli remains tightly gripped in her fist. The stone is dark; Namare hasn't placed any of her elemental power inside it. She offers me the other side to hold. "Take it, child."

I set my hand on the opposite side.

"There's no power in the Kristalli yet." Namare's gaze finds mine. "Soon, I'll release elemental energy into the stone. Then, it will enter you." Her voice lowers with sympathy. "There will be pain."

"How much?"

"Many apprentices fail this final test."

I know what that means. They implode into water puddles. I shake my head. This is so crazy. There hasn't been a new monarkki in ages. Not water, earth, or fire. Most apprentices were killed by Zephyr before they got anywhere near the stage that I'm at now. And the few who made it? Kaboom.

Namare gently squeezes my hand. "You don't have to become the monarkki, Lianna. Even now, it is your choice."

I straighten my shoulders. Namare asked me to do this, so I'll try my best.

"Thank you for the choice, Namare. I want to do this."

A small smile rounds her mouth. "Very well." Namare stares at the darkened Kristalli. "I thought we had years left together. There's still so much I need to tell you." More blue light leaches from her skin. She looks pale gray. "Now, there is no more time. Are you ready, child?"

"Yes."

That's a total lie. I'm about to pee my pants in terror. I haven't felt this scared since my last nightmare about Silas.

"Open your mind," whispers Namare. "The Kristalli contains the memories of one of the original elements, what we call the Etevin. The experiences of the Etevin of Water will now become your history."

I never learned exactly what happens during the transfer, but I didn't expect memories to be part of it. Still, I suppose it makes sense.

The Kristalli turns a searing bright shade of sea blue. Prongs of stone poke into my skin, transferring energy from Namare to me.

Instantly, every particle in my body feels like it's bursting with energy and life. As more power moves into my soul, my memories merge with someone else's—the Etevin of Water. His experiences flicker through my mind, combining with my own.

It is the beginning of time. I float above the Earth. The planet is an empty thing, dead and cold. Slowly, the tendrils of my liquid thought wind through these vast and empty lands. I erode, cascade, and create. Eons pass as I wear down mountains and exhale atmospheres. I shape vast oceans and tiny raindrops. I divide land from shore.

More time passes. The world grows livable. My liquid journey changes. Rocks brush my belly as I tumble off cliff-sides. Evaporation tickles my spine while I stretch ocean-wide. Flowers soothe me as I rain down on their little petals.

For ages uncounted, the planet remains livable and yet empty. No other consciousness exists outside myself and the other Etevin of Fire, Earth, and Air. Our domains lie limitless and silent.

That is not to last.

Suddenly, life stirs within me. Single cells scurry about in a jumbled rush. From the very start, those tiny clusters sum and summon new consciousness. Millennia pass and their awareness grows. The realms form about them and for them. Soon, I stream through Earth as well as Purgatory, Heaven, Hell, and the Dark Lands. These small conscious creatures call louder and grow larger until they become human, elemental, angel, ghoul, and demon.

And then, these minds begin to suffer. My waters transform into enough tears to fill an ocean of sorrow. I want to ease their agony, yet I know so little of mortal lives. To help them, my energy must be wielded by one of their own. A mortal must join with an elemental. We Etevin choose thrax, hoping their angel blood will give them wisdom. The Tärkein are born, the only race with human, angel, and elemental bloodlines. They will accept our powers.

I enter into an agreement with my fellow Etevin. We create four Kristalli, one for every element. These stones will transfer our abilities to four Tärkein, transforming them into four monarkki. And in turn, those monarkki will create peace.

New visions overtake my mind's eye. I see the resting place of each Kristalli. The Kristalli of Air sits on Zephyr's head as a crown. A fierce, copper-skinned dragon guards the red Kristalli of Fire. An old man made of brown gemstones clasps the Kristalli of Earth.

The memory implants stop and I return to the present. With that, I become aware of only one thing.

Pain.

Agony rips through me as more elemental power presses inside my soul. I'm crammed with seas and clouds, calm pools and waterfalls, veins and raindrops. The hurt seems to go on forever, as does the energy that I gain. Strength flows into my body from the oceans. Resilience rains down into me from the skies. Firmness of purpose enters my mind from glass-blue glaciers.

I become a water elemental.

The torment ends as quickly as it began. I still grasp the Kristalli. Now, the stone is almost dark. The prongs that dug into my skin are gone. The Kristalli is smooth once more. Beside me, Namare lies on her back, panting for breath. The last bit of light disappears from the stone.

Namare waves her hand. With that, the Kristalli of Water disappears.

"The stone's use is over," whispers Namare, her voice hoarse. "I have sent it away for safekeeping." Based on my implanted memories, I know exactly where that is: Inside a vault at the Water Palace.

A new kind of hurt rolls through me. Suddenly, I can sense the pain of all water elementals. There are bodies in need of healing. Rivers that require cleansing. Clouds that must give rain. I have work to do. Every inch of me aches to get started.

I grip Namare's hand. "They need my help."

"I know, child."

Panic empties my mind of rational thought. "So much pain… I can't reach them."

"You will be able to very soon."

My soul aches to connect to my people. "When?"

"After your coronation by the Valta."

Closing my eyes, I make my mind focus on her words. My coronation. Right. The ceremony will take place at the Water Palace as soon as the Valta can be readied. Once the gathering is complete, the Valta will use their collective magic to connect me to all water elementals.

With some effort, I force my breathing to slow. The pain felt by my people fades to a dull ache. It's stays present, but in the back of my mind where it isn't as overwhelming.

"That's better." Namare smiles. "You made it, child. I'm so proud. The power of water truly lives in your soul."

My voice comes out robotic and low. "Thank you, great mother."

Namare's words ricochet about my brain. *The power lives in my soul.* The moment turns crazy and surreal. The icefall disappears and I'm back on the open plateau, wearing a blue robe that matches Namare's. My skin's now covered in moving marks that look like sparkling blue water.

I look around. The other apprentices stare at me, open-mouthed. Namare lies on her side again, panting for breath.

Seconds tick by as everyone continues to stare at me, expectant looks on all their faces. *Maybe I'm supposed to give a speech?* My mind races through stuff to say. Over the years, I paid more attention to battle training than statecraft.

Crap, I'm sure Magic Marcus had a speech ready.

I nip my lower lip in my teeth, trying to come up with something good. Bad things happen instead. Wind whips through my now sapphire-colored hair.

Wait a second. Wind?

A line of smoke curls along the ground, aligning itself into a familiar shape.

Zephyr.

My heart sinks.

It can't be him. Not now. It's too soon.

Dozens of Air Valta surround him.

The apprentices form a loose circle around Namare and me. My mind races through options. I can fight, or I can summon an army of Water Valta.

I'll take the army, please.

Trouble is, I don't know how to summon the Valta yet. My brain speeds through possible incantations while my body stays frozen in shock. Meanwhile, the apprentices kick, leap, and punch at the Air Valta. They're holding the Valta back. That won't last for long, especially considering how Zephyr hasn't even jumped into the fight. Instead, he floats over the scene, a gloating grin on his scarred face. I kneel down beside Namare.

"I need your help," I whisper. "You must summon our Water Valta."

Namare shakes her head. "I used the last of my power to send away the Kristalli. *You* must summon them now."

I freeze with panic. "Look, Fisk and I only covered calling the Kristalli. I have no idea how to summon Water Valta." Hell, it took me months to learn the trick with the Kristalli. Plus, the Water Valta hate my ass in a big way. Namare should summon them.

"There's no time for lessons now," says Namare. "We will make do with what you know."

In which case, we're screwed.

"Can't you turn into mist and escape?" I ask.

Okay, I already know the answer, but I'm pulling for a miracle here.

"I am mortal again." Namare slumps back onto the snow. "I'm sorry."

"Don't worry." *Total lie.* "I got this." *Bigger lie.*

I rise, ready to stand shoulder to shoulder with the apprentices and fight for Namare.

There's no one to stand with.

All the other apprentices are dead. Their limp bodies seep blood into the snow. On a day that's already too full of surprises, this shock hits me hard. These were my peers. Maybe one day we could've become friends, too. I stare around the cold plateau, my mind as frozen as the ice.

Meanwhile, Zephyr stalks toward Namare and me. On instinct, I scoop up her frail body and pull it against mine. She's cold, too cold.

Zephyr's voice booms across the mountainside. "Where is your Kristalli?"

"Not here," I say.

Zephyr pauses before me. He's huge—almost seven feet tall—and radiates evil. "Bring back the Kristalli and charge it with the power of the water element."

I curl Namare closer to me. "No."

There, that'll tell him.

"Namare." Zephyr looms over us. "If you wish a calm passing, tell me the locations of the Kristalli of Fire and Earth."

Namare whispers feebly. "Never."

Zephyr stares at her for what feels like eternity. "I believe you." His eyes narrow into dark gray slits.

With a snap of his fingers, fresh wisps of smoke appear on either side of me. The tendrils instantly weave together into the form of two Air Valta. Dread weighs down my soul. I clutch more tightly at Namare's bony frame. There must be something else I can do here. Nothing comes to mind.

Why didn't Namare choose a different apprentice? Magic Marcus trained to use elemental power for a hundred years. I feel like I know a bunch of party tricks, how to turn into mist, and that's it.

Still, I have to try.

Fisk's battle training runs through my thoughts. I need to break up the Valta's smoke bodies. I can do that.

Whispering a quick incantation, I conjure a sheet of snow. With any luck, it'll smack into the Air Valta and shatter their bodily forms—and their concentration—for a few precious seconds. That's all the time I need to gain an advantage.

However, my powers are too new. I just wanted to create some snow.

Instead I summon a massive avalanche down the mountainside. The ground beneath my feet trembles as a wall of white careens straight towards our little group. An electric current of worry charges through my system.

The Air Valta use my own plan against me. I'm so stunned by the oncoming snow that a Valta easily pulls Namare from my arms. I gasp, trying to reach her again. I don't even get close. Another Air Valta grabs me, pins my arms behind my back, and lifts me from the ground. Rage and panic constrict my throat as the avalanche roars nearer.

What can I do? How can I stop this? I can think of no answers to my questions and Namare's too near death to offer any wisdom. I wait, suspended and helpless, as the avalanche barrels beneath my feet. The onslaught moves like a great white wave, burying the dead apprentices in its wake. My throat tightens with anger and regret. Namare's apprentices deserved a better end.

Once the avalanche is gone, the Air Valta keep Namare and me dangling above the ground. Namare heaves and strains for every breath. I writhe under the Valta's grasp, but can't break free. I can't even change shape or manipulate water, either. The Air Valta's magic easily blocks my too-new powers.

Zephyr floats closer. He stares at Namare, a satisfied smile on his lips. Shivers of fear run down my neck.

"Leave Namare alone," I say. "This is between us."

Or, I'd like it to be.

"No, Namare and I have old debts to settle." Zephyr raises his arms until they're even with his shoulders. Instantly, a cyclone encircles both Namare and her Air Valta guard. Within seconds, the column of fast-moving wind turns brutal in its strength. Bits of Namare's flesh are torn from her body.

A knot of rage and grief forms in my stomach. "She'll be dead soon enough," I plead. "Please, let her go in peace."

Zephyr turns to me and bares his teeth. "Veni, vidi, vici. You know what that is?"

I think my ass off. There must be a way turn this situation around. Sadly, I don't understand whatever Zephyr just said, let alone how to reply. I decide to go for the *Hail Mary pass* of comebacks.

"It means you're letting Namare go?"

"No. It's something my commander said during my mortal life, spoken in the sacred language of Latin. 'I came, I saw, I conquered.'" Zephyr turns to me. "When I was mortal, I burned more human cities than you can imagine. My Roman legion wiped out entire civilizations.

All of them asked for mercy. None received any." His gray eyes turn wild at the memory.

"So killing is what? Some kind of high for you?"

"It's my right," says Zephyr with a snarl. "I've never negotiated with lesser creatures. I won't start now. Once, the Roman Empire ruled. Now, Air is supreme. You give me what I want, when I want it, and you don't whine for favor. If it suits me, I'll kill you quickly. That is the meaning of vidi, veni, vici."

The Air Valta echo his cry. "Air is supreme!"

The cyclone around Namare turns wilder. Bits of bone poke through what's left of her flesh. She throws her head back and howls, the tendons in her cheeks and chin visible as she cries. I strain to break free from the Valta who holds me. All I can think about is tearing Namare loose. The winds rip the last of her flesh from her skeleton. The Air Valta drops Namare's lifeless bones to the ground. I shake with sobs of agony and sorrow.

Zephyr rounds on me again. "Now, it's your turn. Do you know where the Kristalli are?"

"Yes." I keep staring at Namare's skeleton. This doesn't seem real. "I won't tell you, either."

"I have other ways to gain this information, you know. I've some Water Valta in my dungeons. Perhaps they know something of import?"

"They know nothing."

Which isn't exactly true. Some Water Valta know the general location of the hidden Kristalli. Nothing as detailed as what I learned, but if they talked, it could cause some trouble.

I clench my teeth in anger. The Water Valta are pains in my ass. Still, they're my people. "Leave my guards alone. Release them from your dungeons."

"If that's what you wish, then tell me the location of the other Kristalli."

"That will never happen."

"I believe you as well," says Zephyr with a sigh. He motions to his Valta. "Torture the girl as you please, then bring her to my compound."

White hot rage burns across my skin. There's that word again. *Girl.*

"I've got another idea." I say. There's no logical thought behind the two words that come out of my mouth. "Fight me."

Zephyr chuckles darkly. "With pleasure."

I nod toward his Valta. "Get rid of them, then. Or are you afraid to take me on alone?"

"I've had two thousand years to hone my skills," says Zephyr. "You've had two minutes. I've nothing to fear from you." He waves his hand and the Air Valta disappear, including the one who was holding me aloft. I fall to the ground with a thud and a groan. Snow and ice bite into my back. Ouch, that hurt.

Zephyr watches me with interest. "Going to fly away, little bird?"

No question what he means. Now that I'm no longer restrained by the Air Valta, I'd like nothing better than to turn into mist and float out of here. In fact, I'm pretty sure that's what I *should* do. Somehow, I can't. The vision of Namare writhing under Zephyr's powers is too fresh. I'm not going anywhere.

I force myself to my feet. "Ready when you are."

"Good." Zephyr speeds toward me across the frozen ground, his footfalls barely leaving any mark on the snow-covered earth.

Closing my eyes, I summon a cloud of sub-zero mist to form around him. Fisk warned me about major attacks with my new powers.

Narrow the energy flow, Lianna. Only use a little.

After my mistake with the avalanche, I have to be extra-sensitive with this one. If I go all-out, I'll make an ice-block the size of an eighteen-wheeler. I don't want to end up trapped along with my arch-enemy.

I focus my powers, sending a trickle towards Zephyr. A sub-zero mist engulfs him. I order the haze to solidify. Zephyr becomes frozen into a casket-sized block of ice. I exhale a relieved breath.

The wind around me instantly dies. Zephyr remains unmoving inside his icy prison. The silence on the mountaintop turns deafening.

It couldn't have been that easy, could it?

I move in for a closer look, being extra-careful where I step. The ground here is pretty shaky, what with the recent avalanche along with the natural crevasses on the plateau. It would be easy to take a tumble here, and I need to stay upright.

I reach Zephyr's ice prison. Sure enough, the Monarkki of Air remains immobile inside. A thin layer of frost covers his gray body.

Tilting my head, I set my hand on the chilly block of ice. Zephyr's gaze flickers in my direction, his gray irises turning dark with hatred. He's not completely frozen, and that's not good. My ice prison is solid, but I could do better. I need to reinforce the cold. My mind races through options and approaches.

How can I keep this guy imprisoned?

Before I have a chance to figure out a plan, the block of ice explodes. Zephyr howls with anger.

"Foolish girl!"

Panic zooms through every inch of my body. The good news is that it's obvious what I need to do next. The bad news is that it'll probably imprison both of us forever.

Better imprisoned than dead.

Taking a step back, I summon another, stronger cloud of sub-zero mist. This time, I'm giving it everything I've got.

Release all your energy, Lianna. Screw the consequences.

Blue mist engulfs everything. I pump more power into the haze, transforming it into a massive block of ice that's as long as a freighter. A thousand knifes of cold jab into my skin. Ice encompasses both Zephyr and me. Frost covers my eyes, blinding my sight.

I did it. We're both trapped, but I did it.

The huge ice block wavers on the unstable ground. With a low crackle, the snow beneath us falls apart. The world tilts on its axis as Zephyr and I fall down the mountain. I want to scream, but my mouth is frozen shut.

After that, everything turns dark.

4

MAXON

*T*hirty-seven hours... That's how long I've been waiting outside Charybdis. I drum my fingers on the arm of my lawn chair.

Something big is coming, I know it.

Tyberius fidgets in the chair next to mine. "The blue lights stopped hours ago."

I don't bother looking at him because I already know what I'll see: An exhausted guy sitting beside me in the moonlight, his red-rimmed eyes looking at me like I'm nuts.

He's not totally wrong. I may really be losing it now.

"Did you hear me?" asks Ty.

"Yup. And I caught the twelve other times you said it, too." I scrub my hand over my face. My eyes sting with the need for sleep. "I don't care about the reports. I've staked out more demons than you have teeth." I point to Charybdis. "A new kind of battle is waiting in there, you can bank on it."

"How can you be so sure?"

"Because I'm part demon. Goes with the job description."

That's the short answer. The long answer is that I've spent years in demon battle training with the Furor. They taught me how to integrate and focus my wrath powers. Same goes for lust, as well as my tail. Mom has voices in her head; her powers are like separate people in her mind. Thanks to the Furor, my inner demons are all integrated. Because of that control, I get extra abilities. Long story short, I know when a battle is near.

The desert turns silent once more. I go back to staring at Charybdis, and Ty goes back to staring at me.

It's getting on my nerves.

"Something else on your mind?" I ask.

"It's like this." Ty nervously twists another bead on his dreads. "Uther says we need to talk about it, man."

"About what?"

"Armageddon."

Time catches for a second, like the word 'Armageddon' has some special power over the universe. *Aw, hell.* When it comes to me, maybe it does.

"Uther says?" I ask. "So, what? You're hiding behind him now?"

"Maybe I am. Doesn't make it any less true."

I scan Ty carefully. This guy's my friend. All he wants to do is talk. Trouble is, Ty doesn't see the real deal on demon patrol. We only cross paths with the bastards for as long as it takes to slice and dice. Ty has no idea what a Class A job like Armageddon does in his spare time, especially with kids. That shit would blow his mind.

I can't do that to him. "You don't know what you're asking."

Ty exhales a long sigh and looks totally miserable. Now, I feel like an ass.

"Don't get me wrong," I say. "I appreciate what you're trying to do."

"Really?" asks Ty. "Then talk to me. Trust me a little."

"It's not about trust, man." I pat him on the shoulder. "Go back to the Pulpitum. Get some sleep."

"No, I'll stay here. You say another demon's coming, I'll wait."

At that moment, dark clouds roll over the sky, blotting out the moonlight. Before us, the sandy-brown earth of Charybdis turns black. My warrior sense snaps into focus.

This could be it.

I hop to my feet, hoping for a pre-battle adrenaline rush. Nothing happens. A wisp of gray smoke rises from the sand and flies off into the sky. It's weird looking, maybe even magical, but it's not a fight. My shoulders slump with disappointment.

Damn.

"Is this what you've been waiting for?" asks Ty.

"No, it's something else."

A great roar sounds from underneath the sand. The heavy smell of charcoal fills the air, followed by a distinctive three-toned roar. You don't train with the Furor for years without knowing what that means.

Or rather, *who* that means.

"Chimera's coming," I say. A faint kick of adrenaline pumps through my bloodstream. This isn't the battle I've been waiting for. Still, it's a fight against one of the most notorious Furor dragons ever. That's better than nothing.

Ty drops his deadlock and spins around to face me. "*The* Chimera?" He starts searching his pockets for his fireball charm, his features pinched with panic. "Can you take him?"

I bob my head from side to side, weighing the odds. "Maybe, but I won't try too hard."

"Why not?"

"Tempest should kill him, not me."

Long ago, Chimera was the Furor Emperor. His reign started out nice enough. Good laws, great parties, that kind of thing. Soon, Chimera turned out to be a badass sociopath, infamous liar, and self-proclaimed torture artist. Most of all, he was an all-out nightmare to his son Tempest, who's now the Furor emperor and my good friend. Bottom line? It's definitely Tempest's right to kill the old beast.

Bit by bit, a shadowy figure crawls out of the darkened sands. At first, it looks a withered man who's skeletal and tall in his torn black waistcoat and matching breeches.

"So that's Chimera." Ty's eyes get big as saucers. He doesn't get to see many Class A demons outside of Charybdis.

"I need you to summon Emperor Tempest," I say.

Ty shifts his weight from foot to foot, which is his favorite move when he's stalling. "What if I summon Tempest and he doesn't want to some here? Should I to bring the other guys back with me?"

Ty brings up a good point. Tempest is a moody son of a bitch. No one knows what he'll do or why. "Sure, grab the guys."

Ty licks his lips. "Okay if I wait a little before I leave?"

I get what he's up to. Ty's dying to see Chimera for himself. Which is dangerous as hell.

Part of me knows I should order Ty to run anyway, but I don't. Why ruin his parade? He's not fighting Chimera, anyway.

"You get one minute," I say. "After you see the real Chimera, you're out of here."

"Thanks, M." Ty squints at the odd figure. "That's not him *yet*?"

"Nope."

Chimera raises his arms toward the darkened sky. Black dragon scales crawl over every inch of his body. His neck elongates from his shoulders, the vertebrae shifting and twisting like a snake's. At the same time, his face takes on the features of a lizard, with a wide, flat skull and long, lipless mouth.

Now, I should definitely feel some kind of serious battle kick. I mean, I studied Chimera for years in Furonium. This'll be a tough fight. Still, I don't get so much as a drop of adrenaline.

Damn, I am so far gone.

Ty stares at the monster, his mouth hanging open in awe. "So, that's Chimera."

"Not yet."

"Still?"

"Still."

The old man hunches to one side. A second neck sprouts from his shoulder, the length ending in a hooded cobra-style head with long white fangs and bright red eyes. Chimera then leans back on his heels. A third neck sprouts from the center of his rib cage. This one is silver-scaled with an arched skull.

"Now, that's Chimera."

Ty mumbles something that sounds like "humph." More likely, it was a gasp of shock, which is how normal thrax react to a sight like this.

Chimera's three heads sniff the air wildly. He remains in hybrid form —part human and part dragon—so he has to really work at catching a scent.

"You two," Chimera's heads hiss at us in unison. "You're thrax."

My tail sways behind me. "Among other things."

"Ah, you're a Furorling, little man." The three heads smile directly at me. It's the sick grin you give a kitten before you stomp on their spine, if you're the kind of guy who enjoys that kind of thing. And Chimera's definitely that guy.

I turn to Ty. "Summon him," I order. No need to name Tempest here. If Chimera thinks I'm an average Furorling, so much the better.

"You got it." Ty takes off at a run. The Pulpitum isn't far, so Tempest should be here in a few minutes. That'll give me time to play.

Chimera limps closer, his three necks swaying with the movement. "Let me get a good look at you, Furorling."

"Sure," I say with a shrug. "Knock yourself out."

I can't believe my luck. This guy's been stuck underground in Charybdis for way too long. A thrax toddler could pick up on this weak attempt at a sneak attack.

Chimera hobbles nearer and stops inches in front of me. His claw-like hands paw at my chest. The touch makes me want to puke.

"Now," coos Chimera. "What's a Furorling like you doing in thrax body armor?" His heads lean in closer. "Could this be some kind of disguise?" His voices lower to a whisper. "Are we hiding, perhaps? In need of help?"

"Everyone could use a little help," I say.

This is the point in any battle where I remind myself that I have rules. Demons are evil, sure. Not all of them are out of control, though. I don't attack until provoked. Hobbling up to someone and acting like an ass doesn't qualify as starting a fight. Knowing Chimera's reputation, it's only a matter of time before he crosses the line.

A gurgling sound percolates up Chimera's throats, and that's when Chimera crosses the line with a vengeance. All his necks hold sacks of deadly venom. One spews yellow acid. The other's a green-colored paralytic. The last one's an orange, slow-acting poison. The gurgling sound means that he's about to spit one or all of them right in my face. Anger heats my bloodstream.

No time to lose.

Quick as lightning, I move to strike. With my dragon-scale hand, I punch through Chimera's first throat, rip out the venom sack, and toss the small yellow organ to the ground. Meanwhile, my tail tears through the other neck, carving out the blue paralytic and tossing that one aside as well. Chimera can regrow them, but it takes time.

Chimera staggers around, pawing at his necks. The final silver-colored head locks on me, its poisonous venom sack pulsing.

"How dare you?" Chimera's third head asks.

"That was for Tempest," I say. "He'll be paying us a visit soon."

"How like my son to fall in league with a Furorling." Chimera's irises flare demon-red with rage. "You're weak, half-blooded monstrosities, all of you. Only pure Furor have the right to live. I'll piss on your corpse."

My brows rise slightly. "Creative, I'll give you that."

Chimera lunges for me, his arms and heads flailing with effort. His long black tail looks lifeless as it drags behind him. Could be another sneak attack.

And sure enough, it is.

Chimera closes in, clawing at the torso of my body armor. I dodge his jabs while keeping my eye on his tail. It comes to life and makes a grab for my ankles, ready to pull my legs out from under me. Blood pumps faster through my veins as I make my counter-strike.

My dragon-scale hand grips the nose-holes of Chimera's silver head. A crunch sounds as my fingers and thumb snap through the soft tissue. Wielding the skull like a club, I swing it straight into the cobra-style head beside it. At the same time, my tail does another DIY surgery on the remaining venom sack. Once Chimera's fully de-venomed, I flip onto my back, tossing the hybrid dragon over my head. He tumbles backward, rights himself, and stares me down.

This time, there's no hopping around and wailing with fury. Chimera underestimated me before. He won't make that mistake again.

What happens next takes place in a heartbeat but to me, Chimera moves in slow motion as his body balloons in shape. His necks stretch out long as telephone poles. His limbs turn into massive, arched legs.

Seeing Chimera's full dragon form makes my chest tighten with worry. Normally, I'd have killed him in his hybrid state, but I didn't out of respect for Tempest. Now I have three dragon heads after me. Sure, they don't have venom anymore. That doesn't mean they aren't deadly.

Damn, Tempest better get here soon.

Raising my arms, I summon my greatest supernatural weapon—lightning. A huge bolt of white fire crackles down from the darkened clouds. Thunder booms through the quiet night air.

Chimera races toward me. My three bolts of lightning arc straight through his heads, stopping him in his tracks. Tiny whites lines of fire twist through his eye sockets and swirl around his long fangs. The cobra head crumples, unconscious. Meanwhile, the silver head combusts and falls over, dead. That thing's not regenerating, ever.

Two heads out of commission, one to go.

Unfortunately, the lizard head remains awake, alive, and beyond pissed. It turns to me, smoke curling from its nostrils. I know what this means. Attack by fire. Even with only one head on the offensive, I don't stand much of a chance to outrun it. Plus, my body armor can only hold out for so long under flames.

I summon another lightning bolt from the sky. This time, Chimera is ready and easily leaps out of the way. The bolt strikes right in the center of Charybdis instead of Chimera. An ear-piercing crack echoes through the air.

In some recess of my mind, I know this isn't right. I've studied Charybdis for years and I've never heard anything like this. That said, I've never struck it with lightning, either. I don't have time to wonder, though. There's a badass dragon coming after me.

Chimera rounds on me, opens his jaws wide, and unleashes a tidal wave of fire in my direction. My blood pumps so hard with terror and fury, I can hear it roaring in my ears. White-hot flames instantly encase my body. Hunching down, I summon fresh lightning and hope like hell that it'll knock out the last head, too.

Turns out, I didn't need to bother.

At that moment, huge golden shapes appear in the night sky.

Dragons.

This time, it's the Kathikon, the Emperor's personal guard. I exhale a relieved breath. Tempest will be with them, too. A low buzz of excitement zings through my nervous system. Finally, I'm feeling some decent battle rush.

I'm not the only one who spies the newcomers. Chimera glares at the sky, growls, and then shakes out his back. Huge black wings unfold from his spine, stretching out across the desert floor. They begin to beat in a regular rhythm, stirring up sand as Chimera's huge bulk rises into the sky. For a time, the dragons swirl and dive above me. Chimera hasn't lost any of his skill in the air. He evades Tempest and his Kathikon as they chase him across the stars.

Hope they catch him.

I stand there for who knows how long, staring at the dark sky. At some point, the dark clouds roll away and the sands return to their normal shade of brown. I stumble into my lawn chair and find myself staring at Charybdis again. Fighting Chimera should've been the big battle I was waiting for. My gut tells me there's more to come.

An even better fight, actually.

Plus, I don't yet know what created those blue lights. And the sound from Charybdis when the lightning hit it? That cracking noise was like a cage bursting open.

Tyberius returns to my side. His voice fades in and out of my thoughts. I'm pretty sure the guys are with him now, too. They chatter away at me, and I give one-word answers whenever I can. Somewhere along the line, the sun creeps up the horizon. It's morning. Uther hands me a lukewarm beer. Breakfast of champions.

"Thanks, man," I say.

"So, we're still waiting here?" asks Uth.

I roll the bottle between my palms. The movement is calming. "That's the plan."

Uther inhales a long breath, and I know he's about to give me another 'talk to me' speech like Ty did. I'm in no mood to hear it.

Thankfully, he never gets the chance.

Once again, blue lights flicker under the desert sands. Electric excitement zooms through my body. With a low hiss, Charybdis collapses in on itself and the sand disappears in a kind of sinkhole. More blue lights pour out from the earth, reminding me of a sapphire searchlight that reaches toward the sky.

My inner wrath sense goes berserk. Battle fever heats every inch of my soul. I leap to my feet, my limbs humming with so much energy, I wonder if my skin can hold it inside. Looking down, I see the beer bottle stays firmly gripped in my right hand. I twist off the cap and make a silent toast.

To my big battle. At last, you're here.

5

LIANNA

*I*n my dream, I float in total darkness. My mind's a blank, and not a peaceful Zen-like blank, either. More like empty and unsettled. Every so often, I feel like I should wake up and fight someone. It seems pretty important, too. Then, the emptiness overtakes me again. I go back to floating along, deep in sleep.

The next thing I know, a flash of bright light overtakes my dream. Some part of me thinks it could be lightning, and another part suspects magic. No matter what it is, the result is the same. I end up wide-awake, my back pressing against a cold cave floor. It's still dark, only now I'm freezing my ass off and freaking the hell out.

Calm down, Lianna.

What does Namare always say? Make a mental list of what you know.

Item one. My skin is glowing elemental blue instead of dead blue, so I've got that going for me.

Which leads directly to item two. I'm still an elemental.

And item three. For some reason, I'm in the dark and it's freezing cold.

Okay. Could be worse.

Raising my hand, I conjure a luminescent blue mist. A soft light fills the chamber around me. I'm in some kind of underground mini-cave made of black, slimy stone. A pulse drums through the air like a heart-beat. I'm fully encased in this snug place; there's no obvious way in or out.

I'd bet a million dollars I got sucked into Charybdis. *Hey, there are worse things that can happen.* At least there's no sign of Zephyr.

I need more intel than that, however.

Raising my hand, I conjure a waterfall to appear before me. The liquid flares bright blue as it changes into a conduit for communicating with other water elementals. Within seconds, an image appears in the shifting liquid.

It's the Hall of Fountains.

I exhale a breath I didn't know I was holding. This is my throne room, or it will be once I'm crowned monarkki. The circular space is empty. Nothing except tall fountain-walls and a fancy blue throne.

"Hello? Anyone there?"

A child's face appears in the shifting falls.

"Who are you?" asks the young boy.

"I'm Lianna."

"Oh, everyone's talking about you. You took Namare's powers yesterday."

So, I've only been out for a day. Good.

"That's right."

"My Dad calls you the us..usp..."

"Usurper?" No point asking how everyone's reacting to the news of my rule.

"That's it. My Dad says that it's better not to have a monarkki than to have a weak ruler." He lowers his voice. "I mean, look what happened with Zephyr. He should never have been crowned, but the Valta went ahead and did it anyway. All of Dad's friends agree."

"I'm sure they do." I scan his little suit of blue armor. "You're training to become a Water Valta, aren't you?"

He puffs out his little chest. "Yes. One day I'll be Esau the Water Valta."

"I'm sure you will be. Can you do me a favor, Esau?"

"Sure."

"Go find General Fisk. Tell him I wish to speak to him. He'll be in the—"

Esau takes off at a run without waiting for more information. As a Water Valta in training, I'm guessing he knows exactly where Fisk is. It doesn't take long for my magical waterfall to encase a new face. It's Fisk, and he's positively beaming with joy. I smile, too.

"Lianna, is that really you?"

"Yup. Alive and kicking."

He exhales shaky breath. "I'm so glad, my girl."

I make a point to ignore the 'my girl' crack and get right to business. "How are my people?"

"They're not yours yet. Until you're recognized by the Valta, you're just another elemental."

My body turns wary and cold. "Why are you bringing that up, Fisk?"

"No reason. No reason at all."

Sure, there isn't.

"Is it because I'm a usurper and the Water Valta don't want to see me crowned?"

Fisk glances around guiltily. "They aren't quite adjusted to the idea of you. The Wind Valta never wanted to crown Zephyr. Now, look what's happening to them. Zephyr kills them off left and right. They're lucky to make it out of puberty."

"I get it," I say with a sigh. Everyone knows how tough Zephyr is on his people. Even with all the memories Franklin has showed me, I've never seen an Air Valta who looks older than twenty. "Let's ease them into the idea, then."

"What are you thinking?"

"I stop by the Water Palace for a meet and greet. Nothing formal." I scan the stone walls around me. Long black scars mark one stretch of rock. I've seen stuff like that before. It happens when lightning hits a certain kind of stone. "I can turn to mist and get out of here, easy. See you in an hour or so?"

"Give me until tomorrow night."

I let out a low whistle. "That bad, huh?"

"I'm their General, I'll round them up." Fisk's eyes overflow with sympathy. "We found the bodies of the apprentices. Did Zephyr hurt you, too?"

"He tried. We fought for a time." The memory of that battle makes me shiver. "I did a flash freeze on him."

Fisk's mouth thins to an angry line. "I warned you about that," he says in his best teacher voice. The old frustration corkscrews up my spine.

"It's not your place to warn me of such things anymore."

Fisk folds his arms over his chest. "We'll see about that."

A heavy sense of dread weighs down my body. As Namare aged, Fisk became monarkki in all but name. I suppose it's no shock he doesn't want to give up power now. I stifle a groan.

Honestly, it's a total shock. And a pain in the butt. I need to get out of here and think through my options.

Leaning back, I take a second look at my surroundings. The place is old and dark. I got here by falling into the Earth. And there's a giant heartbeat. My first call was definitely on the money.

"I'm inside Charybdis," I say.

Fisk's mouth falls open in shock. "That can't be possible. You wouldn't be awake."

"Can we not fight about this?" I rub my temples with my fingertips. "Wherever I am, I'll get out and find you. I can handle it."

Fisk gives me a look that says he's certain I can't handle anything. What a dick.

"How long have I been down here?" I ask.

"About a day."

The little kid was right. "And Zephyr?"

"Our spies say he's in his Cloud Palace. Brought what could've been a three-headed dragon with him, too. Or it could've been two-headed. Our spies said it was hard to tell."

"Three-headed dragon?" After my stint with Silas, I make it a point to know my Class A demons. "Was it Chimera?"

"Who cares? It's Zephyr you need to worry about." Bit by bit, Fisk's mouth rounds into a satisfied smile. "We did it. We really did it." The way he's staring at me makes me queasy. "Our Kristalli is secured at the Water Palace, my girl. You'll be able to get to it once you're here."

Our? What the? A chill of awareness prickles up my neck.

"I'll see you tomorrow night in the Hall of Fountains," I say firmly.

A needy look glimmers in Fisk's eyes. It's the one he always gets before he launches into a 'give us another chance' speech. "Come to me as soon as you can, Lianna. We need to talk."

"We'll talk tomorrow night." With that, I make the enchanted waterfall vanish. I rub my chin and think through my options. Fisk doesn't want to give up power or me. I need to make it clear who's running the elementals now. However, I can't do that while I'm stuck in this cave.

I scan the rock walls, finding a small crack in the stone. Wisps of fresh air drift out of the hole, along with the burned tang of lightning.

Looks like this is my exit.

I recite a quick incantation that should turn me into mist. Nothing happens. Crap.

You can do this, Lianna. This trick always took a while, even with Fisk around to coach me.

I keep reciting incantations and checking limbs. It's not working. I can only turn a leg or arm into mist. Finally, I get my whole body into the act, which is super-taxing. Makes me crave two things: A glass of water and a nap.

Once in mist form, I wind into the crack and start my ascent to the surface.

I only hope that Zephyr's stays out of commission. The most I want to find on Earth is a few humans to hide out with. After my close encounters with Zephyr and Fisk, I'm in no mood for another fight.

~

I keep floating higher through the earth. Staying in mist form is pulling every ounce of energy from my limbs. The air becomes hotter and dryer as I rise, which doesn't help. To stay strong, I need water nearby.

What I wouldn't give for a Diet Pepsi.

At last, bits of sunlight trickle into the tunnel around me. The passageway widens. Crumbling dirt gives way to cracked layers of rock. The uneven stone surface makes a natural hand ladder to climb my way out. Mist form is no longer a requirement.

I'm almost there.

I change back into my solid state; the shift releases a pop of sapphire light. For a few seconds, I watch the blue patterns dance across my skin. Maybe some day I'll get used to being the monarkki. For now, the sight still takes my breath away. Even so, staring at myself isn't getting me out of this pit, so I start to climb. As I close in on the Earth's surface, it gets even warmer and—cue the angelic choir— there's literally a light at the end of this tunnel. I exhale a relieved breath.

The Earth's surface. I made it.

I climb faster, but pause when I hear human voices.

"The blue lights have stopped again," says a man.

Uh-oh. Someone saw when I switched forms. I'll have to ask Fisk how to hide that next time. These are probably humans and I just scared the hell out of them. I recite another short spell to change my appearance to look like my old thrax self. My lovely blue hair, skin, and robes disappear, to be replaced by my blonde hair, jeans, and T-shirt. This way, I'll be easier for them to accept.

"I know someone's in there," says another voice. "I am Maxon Vidar Xavion Aquilus, High Prince of the thrax. You've exactly ten seconds to declare if you're friend or foe."

I open my mouth to cry 'friend.' No words come out. My mind stays stuck on the name. No way. That can't be *the* Prince Maxon. Son of *the* Myla Lewis, the great Scala and Queen of all thrax. Maxon is the Scala Heir, the one person who'll inherit her powers over igni. My parents never shut up about the guy. What are the chances, really? It can't be right. I pause and consider this turn of events.

Or maybe, my life just got a little weirder.

I frown. Unfortunately, the 'life getting weirder' theory is probably right.

"3, 2, 1," calls Maxon. "Now, you die."

Oh, crap. Was he counting down and I missed it?

I rush up to the surface, scrabbling through the last layer of sand. "I'm a friend. Friend!"

Outside I find a handful of lawn chairs and a huge desert. Five thrax warriors stand nearby, and one of them is definitely Prince Maxon. I mean, he's got a tail and everything.

The lines of Maxon's face are hard and angry. He gestures to the darkened pit behind me. "Is anyone else down there with you?"

"No."

"You're sure? No demons, nothing?"

"Nope, I'm it. And I'm not a demon."

"Great." Maxon turns to the other warriors. "False alarm guys. It's just a girl."

There's that word again. Girl.

My mouth thins to a frustrated line. "You were expecting someone else, maybe?"

"Yes, actually," says Maxon. "We're here for battle, not to rescue illegal tourists. My friends rushed in from Antrum for no reason. Let me guess. You're from the House of Tärkein?"

My hands ball into angry fists. What a pompous know-it-all.

"I am."

"That makes you the ninth one to break security this month alone. And for what? You Tärkein need to feel the elements close up and personal. Well, the fact that your house carries a drop of elemental essence doesn't mean you get free reign to break protocol."

My torso tightens with all-out rage. "What you don't know about me is a lot."

Maxon crosses his arms over his chest. "So, enlighten me."

"That'll take a while, buddy, and it's time I don't have. Look, all I need to know is where the closest humans are. Point me in the general direction and I'll be out of your way."

I need to hide out and get my head together, not deal with this yahoo.

"Answer the question first," orders Maxon. "Who are you?"

"I'm a traveler. Sort of."

"Great." Maxon walks off in a huff.

Screw you, buddy.

A squat guy with white-blonde hair raises his hand. "I'm calling her. This one's mine to fight."

A warm sense of satisfaction rises up my chest. At least, this guy sees me as an opponent instead of a girl.

An ebony man-mountain replies. "You're not calling her, Uther," he says. "The girl is thrax."

And we're back to the g-word. Again.

"Hey, I'll fight a thrax." The Uther guy seems odd. That said, at least he's acknowledging the fact that I exist as a real person.

"You heard Zee," says Maxon. "Leave the girl alone already, Uth. She's harmless."

The girl? Again? And harmless? Waves of rage wash through my body.

My voice comes out low and angry. "Call me girl one more time and we'll have trouble."

At last, Maxon turns to face me. Every line on his face fairly screams 'I can't believe I have to deal with you right now.' The fact that he's all tall, burly, and manly-man hot is not lost on me. And I hate that about myself, really. It's like Fisk all over again. Stupid hormones.

"News flash—you *are* a girl," says Maxon. "And you're alone in the middle of desert without permission. You Tärkein can't sneak cloud-side every time the mood strikes you. Now, I don't know how you got here, but you're going back to Antrum before you get hurt." He lets out an irritated groan. "There's a transfer station nearby, we'll take you there."

I set my fists on my hips. "You're not taking me anywhere."

"Really?" asks Maxon. "What are we supposed to do with you, then?"

That did it.

I raise my pointer finger high. "I know exactly what you can do with me."

He looks at me like I'm half crazy. Hell, maybe I am.

"What's that?" he asks.

"Fight me."

"Come again?"

"Hard of hearing, are we?"

I turn to mist and disappear, only to reappear right before him. Now, I have sea-green hair and matching eyes. Once again, moving blue light plays across my skin.

"I said, fight me."

Maxon's mouth falls open in shock and I have to admit, that's a mighty satisfying sight, right there.

"You're an elemental," he whispers. "I've never met one before."

No kidding. Elementals are experts at hiding. We're like the unicorns of the after-realms.

"You guessed it, genius. I'm the Monarkki of Water." A little exaggeration, since I haven't been crowned yet. Still, Maxon doesn't know the difference. I lean in closer, stopping only when our noses are inches apart. "So fight me."

Some little part of me says I'm nuts, but a lot more of me doesn't care. I'm about to kick Prince Maxon's ass.

MAXON

I blink hard. For fuck's sake. This can't be real. I blink again, just to be sure.

Yup, she's still there.

A thrax girl stands in my way. Minutes ago, she climbed out of Charybdis. Then, she asked to fight me.

In her jeans.

With her Hello Kitty T-shirt.

After that, the chick turned blue. Skin, hair, eyes, everything. That's some weird shit.

No way am I fighting her; I'd crush her like a bug. That said, there's no denying that she's crazy hot. And my body thinks so too, for once. Unfortunately, she's also off limits. Banging anyone from the after-realms only gets the girl a guest spot on Royal Insider. When I was eighteen, that chick Nat even tried to sell them a sex tape. Now, I like my hook-ups human and oblivious. To mortal girls, I'm a one-night stand with lots of fun and no entanglements.

I shake my head. Fight me? Maybe I heard her wrong.

"Let me get this straight," I say. "You're thrax."

"We covered this," she says.

"House of Tärkein."

"Covered that, too."

"And you're asking to fight me. That's it, right?"

"No, you missed the big part. I'm also the Monarkki of Water and I'm not asking."

Her skin flares a brighter shade of blue. Never seen anything like it.

This must be a spell. *House of Striga, maybe?* I've had girls from there pull a few nutty gags before. One snuck into my private chambers by conjuring herself to look like cousin Hildy. Next she climbed into my bed and tried to kiss me. That was disgusting.

The girl tilts her head. "Last chance."

Uther waves his arms frantically. "I told you. It's my turn, man! I'm calling her! I'm calling her!"

"Fine," she says. Something that looks like an icicle sword appears in her right hand. "Let's do this."

Uther eyes the frozen weapon, his mouth quivering with shock. Immediately, he plunks his ass back onto his lawn chair. "On second thought, you can have this one, M."

"That's big of you, Uth."

I slowly look this girl over from head to toe. She's my type, all right. Tall, sporty, and blonde. Or at least, she was blonde until a few seconds ago. *Why am I getting all defensive again?* So, she's trying to pull a scam. The ones who do that all have one goal in mind.

I shoot her my signature smile, the one that shows off my dimples. "You didn't have to go through all this to get my attention, you know."

She rolls her eyes. "Think a lot of ourselves, don't we?"

"I'm not the one running a con to meet some guy."

"You were warned." She raises her ice sword. With a whoosh of movement, her weapon streams toward my chest. On reflex, my right arm blocks it. The icicle's tip shatters against my dragon scales.

Okay, I didn't see that coming.

"Watch out, Maxon!" calls Uther. "Your feet!"

A slow freeze has started creeping up my legs. Raising my arm, I conjure a lightning bolt. With a flash of brightness and the crack of thunder, it strikes the ground, smashing the ice around my limbs into bits.

I look at her more closely. It's like I'm seeing her for the first time.

It must be true.

"You really are the Monarkki of Water."

"You always this fast?" She throws a series of punches rapid fire, which I block just as quickly. I jut my right leg forward, ready to take her out at the ankles.

Before I can make contact, her body turns into liquid. One second, I'm looking at a version of this girl in different shades of blue. The next, everything about her—eyes, hair and robes—becomes clear water. With a splash, she turns into a puddle beneath my feet, only to retake her solid form again, only this time behind me. Her small foot gives me a huge kick in the ass.

I tumble face-first onto the ground. My brain stalls out. I fight demons, not elementals. I mean, who trains to fight someone who specializes in staying out of everybody's way?

The girl wastes no time using my confusion to her advantage. A weight presses into my spine as she leaps on my back. After yanking my hands together, she creates a block of ice around my wrists, holding my arms in place. Another block takes shape around my ankles and tail. Weight lightens from my spine as she steps away. I hear her slapping her palms together.

"That was disappointingly easy, Maxon. Nice friends, too. They always stand around while you get your butt kicked?"

"I haven't given them the go ahead."

"What? Why?"

"Because I'm not done with you."

Flexing my arms, legs, and tail, I burst through my icy bindings. Rolling onto my back, I summon my lightning power. A prison appears around her body, only instead of bars, this cell is made from long lightning bolts spaced closely together. It'll take a long time for her water form to sieve through them. A feverish sense of satisfaction heats my skin.

Now, that should keep her in place.

The girl winks and turns into mist. Her transparent shape easily drifts through the lightning barrier. Once outside her prison, the girl solidifies again. She kicks at my chest with force, slamming me onto the desert floor. Next, she conjures five separate blocks of ice to hold down my hands, feet and tail. While I struggle to get out of them, the girl leaps onto my chest and straddles me. Her arms brace my shoulders while her hips align in just the right way.

Okay, that's pretty hot.

Desire flares through my body. Her blue robes are now hiked up by her waist. That's even hotter. My hands ache to touch her bare thighs.

On second thought, there's no rush to break free here.

"I'd like you to stay put," she says.

"I'm good with that." My voice comes out a little husky. "You're a fine warrior."

"And you're not too bad either, for a *boy*."

I shoot her another award-winning smile. "You're still mad about the girl thing."

She shrugs. "I'm temperamental. Goes with being water." She leans in so close I can smell her scent. Strawberry. *Oh, man. I'm in trouble.*

More heat runs through me. More urges to touch her, too. And the bottom half of my body armor only hides so much. It's time to move. I slam my hands, feet, and tail onto the desert floor, smashing the ice around them. The movement sends the girl off balance, so I easily flip her over. She lands back-first against the sand. I hop upright, raise my arms high and summon a sheath of lightning to surround her. This time, the prison is semi-transparent and one hundred percent solid. She can't turn into mist and slip through.

I kneel down beside her and our gazes lock. Her chest rises and falls as she pants for breath. I frown. This is a desert and she's a water elemental. *Gasping for breath means that I'm hurting her.* Something inside my chest tightens. My eyes prickle with a feeling I don't even know how to name. Suddenly, I can't stand the thought of making her suffer.

This ends now.

"You were right," I say. "I was acting like an ass. I'm sorry." I wave my hand; her prison disappears. The girl hoists herself up onto her elbows. She keeps panting for air, which makes me feel like a dick.

I unclip a small canteen from my belt. "Want some water?"

She stares hungrily, but doesn't move to take the canteen from me.

"What do they call you?" I ask.

"Call me?"

"Your name. I'm Maxon."

"Oh, Lianna. I'm Lianna."

I smile at her. A genuine one, this time. "That's a good name."

Nizam watches us from across the desert. "You all right over there?"

"In thrax sic hunt," I reply.

"What's that?" asks Lianna.

"Code phrase. Means I'm safe." I move to sit beside her, resting my arms on my knees. I twist open the canteen and set it directly into her hands. My stomach jolts when our fingers brush. Her skin is warm and liquid smooth, even if it is blue.

More trouble.

"Here," I say. "Please."

"What is it?" she asks.

"Water. I may be an asshole, but I'm not that much of an asshole."

Lianna inspects me carefully. "Possibly." She sips once and then finishes the rest in one gulp. "Oh, that was good."

"I'm glad." I rise to my feet and wave the empty canteen at the guys. They toss me another. I follow the same routine. Sit down. Open the cap.

Set it in her hands. Feel that sweet brush of her liquid-soft skin. My tail sways happily behind me. My Furor side seems to like her, too. Or at least, it's happy not to be fighting her anymore.

"Thank you," she says. This time, she drinks more slowly. "Much better."

"What are you doing out here?" I ask.

"Looking for humans. There's a city nearby, right?"

"I wouldn't know."

Okay, that's a big fucking lie. There's a little town about a mile from here. I'd tell her that, but then she'll leave. For some reason, I'm not quite ready for that yet.

"Why do you need humans?" I ask.

"I don't particularly. I need a place to get my head together. I've just come into my powers and life is..." She bobs her head from side to side, trying to find the word. "Complicated."

"I know how that goes." I laugh, but there's no humor in it. "Why do you think humans will help?"

"I grew up cloud-side, so I know how to hide with human kind."

"Hide from what, exactly?"

"Zephyr, the Monarkki of Air. He and I don't get along." She leans back, opens her beautiful blue mouth, and pours the last few drops from the canteen onto her pretty pink tongue.

Well, that's about the sexiest thing I've ever seen.

My blood instantly heats. I rise to my feet, the better to mask what's happening to the lower half of my body armor. I offer her my hand. "If you need to hide out, I can take you to Antrum for a night."

"I'd feel safer with humans."

Not safer in Antrum? Where has this girl been? That's when it hits me. "You've never been to Antrum, have you?"

"Never." A sweet blue blush crawls up her neck. "That must sound strange to you."

"Not as much as you'd think. A lot of Tärkein live on Earth. Keeps them closer to the elements." I shoot her another smile. "That settles it. You have to see Antrum at least once. And Zephyr won't get to you there. No one gets past our security systems."

She offers me a sly smile. "The Tärkein do."

"They can escape easily enough. It's getting back inside that's the problem."

Another lie, but a little one. I sneak back and forth all the time. As the High Prince, I'm a special case.

"Come on, what do you say? Want to visit?"

"Thanks," she says slowly. "I'd like that."

"Me too, beautiful." For once, that isn't a total line to get in her pants. Only partial. I extend my arm in her direction. "Need a hand up?"

She slips her palm onto mine. Something in my chest tightens again.

Oh, yeah. I'm definitely in trouble.

7

LIANNA

*D*on't look at him.
    Don't look at him.
Don't look at him.

Crap, I looked. And Maxon caught me at it, too.

Smooth, Lianna. Really smooth.

I know I shouldn't keep glancing at Maxon, but I can't help it. I don't meet a lot of hot guys, and my hormones want a peep show. What sucks is that Maxon's probably another good-looking creep. I mean, what was that nonsense before? I nearly had to tear the guy's head off for him to take me seriously. At least, he's stopped calling me 'girl.'

Still, I can't stop stealing glances and making comparisons. While Fisk is handsome in a spare and elegant kind of way, Maxon is raw power. He's got a few inches on Fisk and he's broader, too, with all sorts of muscles that I didn't even know existed. More than that, Maxon gives off a sense of coiled energy. The way he talks to the guys and they hang on his every word. How he carries himself like he can handle anything. I have to admit he's magnetic, even if he is another jerkoff.

He catches me staring. Again.

Can I be more of a loser?

"You okay?" he asks.

Look away, Lianna.

Look away.

Finally, I look away. Go me.

"Yup, I'm fine."

"Need some more water?"

"No, thanks." For the last few minutes, we've been marching toward the transfer station—'we' being Maxon, his buddies and me—and during that time, I've drained everyone's canteens.

"What's on your mind, then?" he asks.

"Nothing."

He gives me a knowing smile. "You keep looking at me like it's something, beautiful."

I blush so hard, I feel it down to my toes. Does my blue skin now hide that kind of thing? It's something to hope for.

"Well," I tilt my head from side to side, trying to find the right words. "You're not at all what I expected."

"Oh, that." He laughs, and it's a low rumble that I like very much indeed. "Yeah, most people think I'll be a charming little Prince."

"Aren't you?"

"I'm still charming, only now I charm demons out of their lives and to do that, I can't prance around in a crown and watch my language."

I smile. He's got a sense of humor, too. We stare at each other until someone clears their throat.

It's Uther.

"What's up, Uth?" Maxon doesn't break eye contact with me while he talks to his friend. For some reason, I can't look away either.

"We've been standing here for five minutes," says Uther.

I make an embarrassing noise that sounds something like "ack." *Five whole minutes?* Now, I look away and fast. Suddenly, it's very important to straighten the neckline of my blue monarkki robe.

"Right," says Maxon. If he feels uncomfortable, he hides it like a pro. "We're here."

Sure enough, our little group is standing beside a tall gray rock, or it looks that way to humans. To thrax, it's a small, round building made of poured concrete. The words 'Pulpitum XXVII' are carved outside in large letters.

Maxon waves to the guys. "Go on ahead. Lianna and I'll go on to Antrum ourselves."

Ty's mouth falls open with surprise. "Striga has an enchanted hunting cottage. The cloaking spell there is impenetrable. I was talking to the guys. We all think she should stay there."

"Nope. Arx Hall."

All the guys stare at me like I just sprouted extra arms and legs. Maybe even a second head. I know they don't see elementals often—and a monarkki maybe never—but there's something more to it than that. I get the feeling that Maxon doesn't take guests home too often. Girls especially. And that fact is way more satisfying than it has any reason to be.

Reign it in, hormones. No more hot losers.

Zee shakes his head. "Arx Hall is crawling with people. We need to keep a low profile on this. I mean, look at her. She's blue."

"Lianna can change that." Maxon turns to me. "Right?"

"Sure," I say quickly. I whisper a fast incantation so I look like a regular thrax in jeans and a T-shirt. "Do I need to wear something else? I haven't figured out how to conjure different outfits yet."

"Nah, you're fine," says Maxon. "I'll tell Transfer Central that you're a Tärkein that I caught sightseeing on Earth. Happens all the time, and the Tärkein always dress modern when they sneak away."

"Still," says Uther. "She'll cause a frenzy. You don't bring home, you know… Guests."

Ah ha, knew it! I can't help but smile a little bit.

"We'll be fine," says Maxon. "I know hidden passageways to the South Wing."

"The South Wing?" repeats Uther. His stance wobbles as if he'll pass out from shock.

"Yeah," says Maxon.

Now it's Nizam's turn to repeat those three words. "The South Wing."

"I said yeah, didn't I?"

"Those are your private chambers," says the guy with the hunting hawk. "Even we don't go there."

"Come on, guys," says Maxon. "You all make it sound like I'm bringing her into my bedroom or something. The South Wing is huge. A castle in itself. It's not that big a deal."

Uther kicks at the sand with his boot. "I've never been to the South Wing."

"And my hunting lodge would be far more secure," says Ty.

"How about we let Lianna decide?" asks Maxon.

Five sets of eyes fix on me. The urge to run for cover is almost overwhelming. Ever since I can remember, I've avoided crowds and attention. I slow my breathing and do my best to look cool. I should probably stay at the hunting lodge. It's secure and I don't find this Tyberius guy attractive. I should do the safe thing.

My mouth has other ideas, though.

"Arx Hall sounds fine," I say. "I'll stay there."

"See? Arx Hall." Maxon gestures to the transfer station. "Now get."

The guys slowly walk into the Pulpitum. After a minute, a flash of light comes through the station's arched doorway. That must mean they've been transferred to Antrum.

"We're up," says Maxon.

I stare at the darkened arch, a nauseous feeling settling into my stomach. Suddenly, a hunting lodge in the middle of nowhere seems like a much better idea than some castle packed with strangers. I've lived my entire life inside an isolated cabin or in hiding. What if the thrax find out who I am? Will I be mobbed?

Maxon laces his fingers with mine. His skin is warm and a little rough. Really comforting. I decide that since this is a neutral, non-sexy activity, it's totally fine to keep holding his hand.

"Come on," says Maxon. "I'll take you." He grins, shows his dimples and, yeah, I'd follow him over a cliff. He probably uses this move all the time to seduce the unsuspecting. Or in my case, the totally suspecting who can't help themselves anyway. A heavy wind bursts in from nowhere and I couldn't care less. Thoughts of Zephyr feel miles away. Being near Maxon, it's like nothing bad can happen to me. In fact, it's the first time I've felt secure in I don't know how long. Since before my parents died, probably.

We walk into the Pulpitum, hand in hand. The moment we step inside, torches burst to life along the walls. The floor lights up into concentric circles of white on a large silver disc.

A smooth female voice echoes around the chamber. "Greetings, Prince Maxon."

"Hey, Diana. How's life at Transfer Central?"

"Boring until you came along. Who's your guest?"

"Runaway Tärkein." He winks at me, so I don't correct him.

"Another one?" asks Diana. "Wait a minute. I'll pull the alert."

"Hold off on that, will ya?"

"The transfer won't start otherwise."

"Hit the system reboot on your console. You'll have sixty seconds to transfer me with no record."

"I could get in deep trouble for that." The woman lets out a long sigh. "Why can't I say no to you?"

"Cause it's impossible." He smiles and shows off his dimples. "Arx Hall delivery station VI, Diana."

"Just for you." Her voice gets all husky. "Just this once."

I roll my eyes. How about we 'just' stop saying 'just?'

"Wait for my signal." Maxon turns to face me. "Know how a Pulpitum works?"

"In theory, sure."

"But you've never ridden one."

I shake my head.

"Antrum is miles underground. The lit-up circle under your feet is a disc that we'll ride into the Earth. We need to stay at the center and hold on tight."

My mouth falls open. "Hold on to each other, you mean?"

The hint of a smile rounds his mouth. "Yeah."

You can do this, Lianna. Don't act like it's a big deal. Thrax ride these things every day.

Trying to act casual, I slide my arms around his waist and learn a valuable lesson: It's one thing to see that someone's ripped. It's another to touch them through their very stretchy body armor. My skin tingles with awareness.

It's only a body. He's only a guy. I'm sure half of Antrum looks like him. Don't over-react.

"Is this okay?" I ask.

Maxon gives me another one of his rumbling chuckles. This time, I can feel it in my thighs, too.

"That works, yeah." Maxon slides his arms around me. Now, we've got full body-on-body action going, and mine doesn't want to stop with a hug. I have this crazy desire to wrap my legs around his waist, grab his hair, and kiss Maxon for all I'm worth.

Clearly, my hormones and I need to have a little talk. I have bigger things I should be thinking about, like avoiding Zephyr, claiming my crown, and ruling the water elementals.

"On my mark," says Maxon. "Launch in three, two, one."

The disc under our feet tumbles into the ground. Soil, rock, and lava fly by as we lurch deeper into the ground. I lean into Maxon's shoulder and enjoy the ride until a jolt hits us and we stop. I scan the space, seeing that we've arrived in a large brick room. The place looks totally deserted. Piles of wooden shipping boxes are strewn everywhere. Cobwebs drip down from the ceiling.

It takes some serious concentration, but I force my arms to unwind from Maxon's torso.

Clearly, my hormones require way more than a talk. I'm thinking total smack down.

"This dock hasn't taken any shipments for years," says Maxon. "The Pulpitum still works, though. I use it to sneak in and out of Arx Hall." He points to a far wall. "The hidden passages to the South Wing start over there."

Once again, he takes my hand. My heart does a flip-flop in my chest.

Maxon opens a creaky wooden door that leads to a long, thin passage. Together, we sneak through a maze of hidden walkways. Every so often, we step through dark rooms that Maxon calls larders. Basically, they're underground refrigerators without any electricity. Arx Hall has a ton of them, too. Butter, meat, jam, salted fish... The list goes on and on. Finally, the passage empties out onto an ornate wooden hallway. The place is overflowing with pennant crests, suits of armor, and medieval knick-knacks. More torches burn along the walls.

I try to keep a straight face. Inside, I'm more a little shocked. When I see the thrax on Earth, they're always tricked out with the latest demon-fighting armor and gizmos. Down here, they're definitely stuck in the middle ages. I heard about this from my parents but I figured they were exaggerating.

They weren't.

We pause before a huge set of golden doors. Guards stand on either side, both wearing silver armor. In unison, they flip up their visors and stare at me like I came from another planet.

Subtle, guys. Really subtle.

"Your Highness," says the first guard.

"You're home," says the second.

"And you have someone with you," adds the first.

"Listen carefully." Maxon's voice comes out all low and serious. "You don't see me, you don't see her. Got it?"

They both flip their visors down. "Yes, Your Highness."

Maxon pushes open the door. Together, we step inside, straight into another time warp. Instead of the middle ages, I've now returned to the modern era. Everything's done up in some combination of black, white, granite, steel, or leather. There's recessed lighting, funky abstract art, and a huge home theater system. Plus, the kitchen's got every gadget I can think of, and a few that I didn't even know existed.

Whoa.

"Why are you the only one here with electricity?" I ask.

Maxon grins. More dimples. More yum.

"Noticed that, did you?" he asks.

"Hard to miss."

Maxon steps into the kitchen. "I'm a special exception to the middle ages rule. Ty charges a generator for me. Built me some other goodies, too." He opens a huge industrial-grade fridge. "Want something to drink?"

"Water, thanks."

Maxon pulls out a beer and hands me a bottle of water. He leans against the counter, flips off the cap with his tail, and takes a long sip. "I was thirteen when I stopped joining demon patrols. Only Class C jobs wait around for thrax to pick them off. Trouble is, the Class A demons are always the real killers, and they hide out in human cities. I decided to go after them. That means spending months undercover, and nothing says 'I'm really a thrax' like not knowing how to use a cell phone or some shit like that. So, I get every new gadget sent here and practice between missions."

"Your family good with that?"

"Sure. Since I started doing this, demon kills against humans have dropped in half."

An unwanted memory appears in my mind. The only demon I ever met up close and personal. Silas. His rasping voice echoes through my memories as he calls me 'his girl' over and over. I wince, my eyes stinging with remembered pain.

"Hey, you okay?" Maxon step closer. With gentle motions, he rubs his hands up and down my arms. "You said you just came into your powers. Do you need a healer or something?"

"No, it's not that."

He leans in closer. "The politics of ruling, maybe? I suck at that stuff, but I know some experts."

"Thanks, I might take you up on that later." I stare at the floor, my body trembling. I hate that he's seeing me like this. "I've had a big day. Maybe I should get some sleep."

"Sure, you must be beat." Maxon takes my hand again. "Take your pick of bedrooms. I think I have twelve here or something." He pushes open a nearby door. "How's this one?"

I can't focus on much except for the massive white bed against the far wall. All of a sudden, I can't keep eyes open. I'm vaguely aware of stumbling over to the mattress and curling up on top of the covers. I mumble something while Maxon takes off my boots and wraps me in fresh blankets. For the first time in I don't know how long, I feel safe and warm.

My body wants to sleep, but my mind decides that now's the perfect time to go berserk. Questions hit me rapid fire. How do I deal with Fisk? Is there any way to prove to the Water Valta that I won't become another nutjob like Zephyr? What about my people? The dull ache in my chest flares up again. It's the same pain I felt after I first took on my powers because water elementals are out there, suffering. I should be helping them.

My mind keeps running through the same questions and worries until I think my skull will burst. At last, I decide that exhausted is no way to work through my issues. I'm safe and warm in Antrum. For now, the best thing I can do is rest so I have the thinking power to figure this stuff out.

With that thought firmly in head, I finally drift off to sleep.

8

LIANNA

*C*alm down, Lianna. It's only another nightmare.

You're not really thirteen. And you're definitely not Silas's prisoner anymore. You're actually asleep in Maxon's chambers, remember? Open your eyes. Everything will be fine.

Just.

Wake.

Up.

My internal pep talk doesn't work, though. I stay fast asleep. Even worse, my dreams force me down into Silas's underground lair. My conscious self knows the space is actually cold and cramped. But in my dream, it stretches out onto an impossibly large scale. Cages line the walls, each one packed to overflowing with mice and rats. Their frightened, chirping cries echo strangely in the chamber. Huge barrels of bloody goop dot the floor. And in the center of everything lies my old cage. My thirteen-year-old self lies curled in fetal position, a thin blanket clasped tightly around me.

Just like in reality, the dream-me is trying to sleep. It's not happening for either of us.

"Where's *my* girl?" calls a wispy male voice. The way he says 'my girl' is possessive, hungry, and makes my teeth chatter with fear.

Silas is calling for me.

In the way of nightmares, Silas is suddenly there, looming over my cage. I'd guess back in Victorian London, Silas would've been an average-looking middle-aged bloke. He's balding with a bit of a belly and a handlebar moustache. His brown suit perfectly matches his bowler hat.

Sometimes he wears white gloves, only they quickly get soaked with blood.

Silas kicks the side of the cage. "Wake up, my girl. There's work to be done."

The thirteen-year-old me looks up from under my torn blanket. My blonde hair is a tangle; my face is lined with dirt and grease. The little thrax gown my parents made me wear is now a shredded rag. My dirt-encrusted hands grip the filthy blanket closer to my throat.

"What do you want?" I ask.

Silas leans over the cage, his brown irises flaring red with demon-light. "Bring me a mouse. You know the kind I like."

I nod, my jaw clenching with impotent rage. If I bring anything living to Silas, he kills it, using the creature's life energy to power his black magic. It's never easy to give an animal to Silas, but the ones that he wants are especially hard to hand over. He likes animals at the very peak of their life force—just past childhood. It's why he agreed not to kill me until I turned sixteen.

I picture pulling handing another mouse to him and shiver.

Silas pulls my cage door open. The nightmare-version of this sound rattles through my soul. I crawl outside and search through the maze of cages lining the walls. It takes forever to find the right mouse. What in reality was a small basement becomes a complex labyrinth in my dreams. My heart beats faster. If I don't find what he wants quickly enough, Silas will beat me. Maybe he'll figure out how to kill me before my sixteenth birthday, despite the magical deal he made with my parents. They didn't fight back when he murdered them. In return, I have three more years before I join them in death.

At last, I find the perfect mouse. It's gray with a pink nose and based on how it skitters happily about its cage, it's also full of life. The little creature quickly crawls onto my palm and looks up at me with trusting black button eyes. I choke back a sob and go off in search of Silas.

It takes another long, dream-like trek to find Silas at his workbench. As I wander through the maze, I hear Silas sing one of his odd spiritual tunes—this one is something about lords and masters—and it makes my skin crawl with disgust and fear.

He always sings right before he kills.

At last, I reach a tall wooden structure set into the wall and covered with every kind of scalpel, bone cutter, and vise imaginable. It's stuff that humans use for taxidermy, making stuffed animals out of dead ones. Silas takes the practice further with black magic.

Silas gestures to the table in front of him. "What do you think, my girl? My greatest poppet yet."

I take a small step away. "I don't need to see it, thanks."

"Ah, but you do." He flashes me a sallow smile. "Your soul will be inside one of my poppets too, one day."

Which means he won't give up until I look.

It takes an impossibly long time to glance over Silas's shoulder and see what he's working on. It's a rat, or it was one when it was alive. Now small metal clamps run down its back, holding its spine together. Tufts of straw and filthy cotton peep out between the makeshift sutures. The tail is studded with metal barbs, while the eyes are small black stones, oblong and mismatched. Bits of rusted wire have replaced its claws. It meanders across the bench-top in blind circles.

"Almost perfect," says Silas. "Only needs the gift of sight."

On reflex, I hold the shivering mouse closer to my chest. "I think it's fine the way it is."

"That's because you're a soft-hearted fool." He reaches his pale hand toward me. "Give me the mouse."

My arm trembles as I press the tiny creature closer to my chest. "No."

Fast as a heartbeat, Silas scoops the mouse of my hands. The little guy writhes and shrieks in his grip. I bite back another sob.

Silas inspects the mouse. "You've brought a fine one today." He leans in closer to me, inhaling the scent of my tangled hair. The sensation of him this near makes my stomach sick.

"You're already ripe. I could harvest you today, if I hadn't made a binding deal with your parents." He drags out his next words. "I can't wait to claim your life force, *my* girl."

At those words, I flat out panic. Part of me is back with Silas, reminding myself that he can't break a deal sealed with his own black magic. Another part of me knows that in my dreams, he does break the deal, every night. I work like hell to wake myself up. However, both versions of me are frozen in place, unable to do anything while Silas turns away. After pulling out a small hammer, he smashes in the mouse's skull. The frightened creature is now a bloody mess on Silas's bench-top.

Suddenly, the rat's stone eyes move with purpose. Now, it can see.

Silas turns to me, his irises flaring demon red. His face becomes contorted in the way that only nightmares can achieve.

"Think you're free?" he asks. "I'll find you and harvest you. I promised I would."

"You never will," my thirteen-year-old self cries. "Namare will find me. You'll make a deal with her. She'll let you live and you'll set me free."

Silas's face stretches in an odd way. "You'll always be my girl."

"You can't do anything to me. This is a dream."

"I can do anything. I'm a demon. Prepare to be harvested."

Fear zings through my limbs. Turning my heel, I take off at a run into the labyrinth of cages. Silas follows, always one step behind. My mind blanks with terror. Suppose he really can get to me here? What if I finally die in my nightmare? All my thoughts narrow down to one plan.

Find somewhere safe to hide.

My dream-self crawls back inside my cage and cowers into my mangy blanket. Silas's footsteps grow louder.

Once again, I become aware that I'm dreaming, and that I never can stop this particular nightmare. No matter what I do, Silas always finds me, harvesting my soul with a blow of his hammer.

But not this time.

Instead, my threadbare blanket feels warm and safe. I curl deeper under the covers, crying softly.

After that, I wake up.

Blinking hard to clear my head, I find myself back in Maxon's chambers. Heavy arms encircle me. I rub my eyes, trying to make my sleepy mind process what's going on. That's when I realize what's happening.

Maxon is holding me, rocking me softly.

"Shhh, Lianna," he says in a low and soothing voice. "Everything's okay. You're safe."

"What... Why are you here?"

"I heard crying and came in to check on you."

"And I climbed across the bed and right into your lap, didn't I?"

"That you did." He lets out a low rumble of a laugh. "Am I complaining?"

"I guess not." I exhale a long breath. "Thanks."

"Any time."

A droplet of water smacks into my cheek. My hands shake as I wipe it off. "Did a pipe break or something?"

"More like the 'or something.' You summoned a rain storm in your sleep."

"I did not. Really?"

"Yeah."

Sure enough, more water drips down from the ceiling, the curtains, even the light fixtures. Little puddles cover the wooden floor. I close my eyes and make the water vanish. The place is still in need of a good cleaning, though. Already, the scent of mold hangs heavy in the air.

"Sorry about the room."

"Don't apologize," says Maxon. "Even if you trash the place, I've tons more bedrooms." Maxon rubs my back in slow circles. My limbs start to relax. "Did you have a nightmare?"

Nodding, I curl deeper into his chest. It's like my body was made to be held by him. "Of a demon I once knew. I was his prisoner. Namare rescued me."

"What kind?"

"One of the Incarnate."

Maxon lets out a low whistle. "Damn, Lianna. That's Class A. No wonder you have nightmares." His arms tighten around me. "How'd you end up with him?"

For a long time, I sit in his arms, not answering. Dozens of emotions battle it out inside me. Fear, anger, and shame top the list. I don't know if I can tell him about Silas.

There's no pressure from Maxon to talk, only the regular rhythm of his hand on my back. After as few minutes, my mouth seems to move on its own.

"My parents loved nature. We lived in a cabin in the middle of the Colorado mountains. No demons around, at least none that we knew of. Still, Silas found us. One night he came in and threatened my parents. They were good warriors. Silas knew my parents could hurt him, but not kill him outright. So, he offered them a deal. If my parents promised not to fight back, Silas promised not to harvest me until my sixteenth birthday. I was only thirteen then. Mom and Dad hoped I'd find a way to escape."

Maxon kisses my head. "Go on."

"After that, Silas kept me in his basement, making me his assistant until I came of age."

I brace myself, waiting for Maxon to change the subject. When I shared this story with Fisk, he basically bolted out of the room. We never spoke about it after that day.

A long pause follows before Maxon speaks again.

"I get them, too, you know," he says quietly.

I pull on my earlobe, not sure if I heard him right. *Did Maxon just say what I thought he said?*

"What do you mean? You get nightmares?"

"Yeah."

"What do you see?"

Another stretch of silence follows. Anxiety hangs in the air like a physical thing. All of a sudden, I feel like an ass for pushing him to open up.

"You don't have to tell me," I say quickly. "It's not like we've known each other for a million years." *Or even a full day.*

"It's not you. I don't talk about it. With anyone."

"Why not?"

The moment the words are out of my mouth, I wish I could pull them back in. What is it about Maxon that makes me spill whatever's on my mind?

Maxon sighs. "Most people in my world, they think that they know evil. I tell them about me, I shatter whatever they thought. I can't do that to the people I care about."

I nod into his chest. "I get that."

"I thought you would." He starts talking fast, like if he stops he'll never say anything at all. "In my nightmares, I relive something that happened to me as a kid. You know my story, yeah?"

"Sure." Everyone knows how Maxon was kidnapped to Hell when he was three years old. His parents broke in and rescued him.

"The King of Hell, Armageddon, kept me in this metal prison box. When I have nightmares, I'm back in there."

I open my mouth, ready to push for more of the story. Maxon senses my movement and his torso stiffens.

Time to change the subject.

"Thanks for coming in to help."

"Anytime."

The way he says the word is so tender, something inside me snaps. Hot tears roll down my cheeks. Maxon holds me closer. For the first time in I can't remember how long, I cry my eyes out. Minutes pass before I'm able to get my head together again.

"Sorry about that," I say.

"About what?"

"Turning into a crybaby. Not what you expected from a warrior like me, huh?"

He kisses my forehead. "Will you promise me something?"

"What?"

"Don't ever think you're not a warrior because you have nightmares. You have to be plenty strong to face those." He cups my face in his hand, guiding me to meet his gaze. "And your soul is strong as steel, beautiful."

A warm feeling seeps through my chest. That's about the nicest thing anyone has said to me, ever.

"I never thought of it that way. Thanks."

"You should get some more sleep." He tosses a soggy pillow from the bed. "Not here, though."

I look around the destroyed room. Wallpaper sags toward the floor. Furniture is smashed against the walls. The rug stinks of mold. And that's when it happens. I get in one of those moods where I can't stop saying sorry, even though I'm starting to annoy myself. "Sorry again about the room."

"Nah, it's like I told you. I don't care. There's another just like it across the hall." Before I know what's happening, he scoops me up into his arms and carries me away. I debate asking him to put me down, but honestly? It's really nice to be held and carried like this. Every inch of me feels safe and cozy.

Plus, it doesn't last that long. Before I know it, Maxon is setting me down onto the new bed.

"Do you need something else to sleep in?" he asks.

I look down. Gross, I've been wearing the same T-shirt and jeans since forever. "That would be great, actually."

Maxon whips off his T-shirt and hands it to me. "This work? I'll have my staff get you new clothes and stuff by morning."

"They work overnight? Isn't everyone asleep?"

"Not on my team. They know I only need an hour of sleep so they work in twenty-four hour shifts when I'm around. What do you say?"

"New clothes, sure. I mean, thanks."

As I swipe the T-shirt out of his hand, I try not to stare at his bare chest. That's not possible. The guy is seriously ripped.

If Maxon notices my stare, he doesn't say anything. "Bathroom's the second door on the back wall." He sets a candle on my bedside. "I'm going out for a while, too. Light this if you need me. It alerts Ty. He can get to me anywhere."

"Okay." I grip his shirt tightly. It's still warm from his body. "Thanks again for, you know."

Maxon smiles and his dimples reappear. "Yeah, same here." He kisses me on the forehead. "Now, get some sleep, Lianna."

And I do.

9

MAXON

*A*fter I step out of the bedroom, I stare at Lianna's closed door.
What the hell happened back there?

She had a nightmare, I held her, and I talked about Armageddon. Me. No one knows I get nightmares, let alone that they star the King of Hell. Next thing I know, I'll actually tell her what happened.

Damn.

Things with this woman are going too far, too fast. I need to put the brakes on, now. So we got cuddly once. So we shared some secrets. It happens. I'm not getting attached.

With that thought finally straight in my head, I'm able to leave her door. From there, it's a short walk over to my library, which is my favorite room in Arx Hall. The place is pretty old school with its dark oak shelves, leather-bound books, and club chairs. I had Tyberius pimp it out, too. I've got a full bar that's magically restocked with top shelf liquor, along with an enchanted painting that shows demon activity. It's perfect for planning my nightly trips to Earth for kicking evil ass.

Once I'm inside the library, my first stop is the bar. I pour myself two fingers of Macallan '46. I'm only twenty-two, but Tempest is five-hundred-something and a good buddy. He taught me all about whiskey. I take a sip. *Now, that's smooth.*

Glass in hand, I walk over to my enchanted canvas. It's a huge framed painting of a world map. Ty did a solid job on this one, although he insisted on putting in old-fashioned squiggly writing. Whatever. As long as it shows me demons, I told him to go to town.

"Show me the latest," I order.

Like always, my command sets the painting in motion. The brush-strokes rearrange themselves into a new pattern. I sip my whiskey and watch the little bits of color do their thing. Seconds tick by. No surprise, there. This painting always takes a while to warm up.

An older thrax appears in the doorway, dressed in his formal Rixa tunic. "Good evening, Your Highness."

I nod in his direction. "Hey, Edward." He's an older dude with jowls and short gray hair. I'm supposed to address him by some formal title that I refuse to learn.

"It seems that we have an unexpected guest," says Edward.

"Oh, yeah. That's Lianna."

The glint in his mismatched irises says he's dying for some intel. "Should we plan anything special for her?"

"Good question." I lean back on my heels, sip my whiskey, and think. I know what I'd do if the guys were here... *And that would be nothing.* But women? What could they possibly want? I snap my fingers, remembering Lianna and my T-shirt.

"Don't I have someone who gets me clothes?"

"Yes, you have a Mistress of Cloth."

"That's right. Can she scare Lianna up some nice new stuff to wear?"

"The Mistress would be thrilled to do so."

"Cool. Get it here by morning?"

"Of course." He stares thoughtfully at the canvas. "Will you still go hunting tonight?"

"Maybe. Depends what's up." I don't want to leave Lianna, but I don't want to abandon some human to a nasty death by demon, either.

As I down more of my drink, tiny red dashes of paint flicker across the giant map. Each one shows a different Class A on the prowl. Minutes pass and the image gains more definition. Something catches my attention.

"That's interesting."

"Did you say something, Your Highness?"

"Nothing, Edward. That's all for tonight. Thanks."

Edward says something formal and leaves. The guy knows better than to push when I'm in the zone. I step closer to the canvas and watch the fresh brushstrokes and statistics.

There's definitely a major spike of activity in the Colorado moun-tains. Not something I normally worry about, considering the human population there is so low. But now? Colorado's where Lianna's parents were killed. I can't leave that shit alone.

I point to the cluster. "Show me demons in that area."

The canvas repaints a long list of profiles. The word Incarnate pops up.

Bingo.

"Detail on Incarnate."

The painting reforms to show a Victorian-looking male with a bowler hat and handlebar mustache. Stats say he creates little taxidermy demons called poppets. My shoulders constrict with rage. That's him. The fucker that imprisoned Lianna.

"Location."

The image dissolves into more brushstrokes. A lot of Class A jobs have cloaking spells, especially if they've been hunted before. Looks like Silas has been pretty careful, hiding out in outlying places. With any luck, he won't have bothered to cloak his location.

Geographic coordinates appear on the canvas.

That's some luck, all right.

I make a few quick calculations. It's a hike from the nearest Pulpitum to Silas's hideout.

That settles it.

I'm going hunting tonight, and I know the perfect spot.

It's still dark out as I hike up another ridge in the Colorado mountains. The air's crisp and cold, which is good. Keeps my focus sharp. Around me, a light snow falls through the tall pines. Huge white flakes land on my cheeks and black body armor. I check the GPS read-out on my wrist. Silas's lair is only a few clicks to the West.

Not much longer, now.

I scale another trail until a concrete hole opens up in the mountain-side. Steel girders and boxes of building supplies lie busted and decaying in the snow. Looks like some abandoned construction. Military, if I had to guess. The graffiti makes me think it turned into a hang out for wayward kids or drug runners. Maybe both. All those tags are faded now. No one's been here for years.

One guess why.

I step into the darkened concrete hallway. The place is lined with icicles and snow. There's more graffiti, too. Some of it reads 'beware of demons.' I smile.

Definitely the right place.

The hallway winds downward for a bit before opening onto a small concrete bunker with low ceilings. The place is small. Too small to be

Silas's main lair. I wonder where he keeps his number one hideout these days.

I linger in the shadows and stake out the space. A few dead rats lie on the floor. A vat of what looks like blood sits in one corner, beside a dapper-looking guy with a bowler hat and Victorian suit. He doesn't turn to look as I approach.

"Maxon Vidar Xavion Aquilus," he says. "How kind of you to visit. Everyone knows who you are."

I step into a pool of electric light. "And you're Silas. I never knew you from fuck. Now you're on my bad side."

The dumbass still has his back to me. "And why is that?"

"Lianna." I stalk toward him, my tail arced over my shoulder, ready to strike.

Silas swivels around to face me. "Stay your wrath. I have information."

My tail wraps around his neck. "I don't give a shit."

He speaks through rough gasps for breath. "It's... About... Lianna."

I pause. It sure would be satisfying to off this demon right now, but there's no denying that Lianna's in a tough spot. The right intel could save her life. I lean in to Silas, my voice turning low and deadly.

"Give me one good reason why I shouldn't torture that info out of you."

"That will... Take weeks. You don't... Have weeks."

I loosen my hold on his throat. Slightly. "So, what're you saying?"

"We strike a bargain. I give you information on Lianna; you let me live."

Sounds familiar. Silas strikes this bargain a lot.

I glare at the creep for a while. I'd really love to kill him. Still, I can't risk missing good intel.

"Fine. I'll give you an hour's head start. After that, you're fair game if I find you again."

And I will find you again.

"Agreed."

"Now, start talking."

"Making deals is a hobby of mine." Silas turns back to his worktable and starts skinning a rat. "I made one with Zephyr a long time ago. We share information on a certain topic."

No question what topic that is.

"Lianna." I rub my temples, thinking through the implications. "So, if you help Zephyr find Lianna, then he'll let you harvest her life force. That's what you want, isn't it?"

"Her energy is extraordinarily strong." He inhales like he's remembering the scent of a lovely perfume. "And now would be the perfect time to harvest her." He sighs. "Too bad she was turned into an elemental. Now, she's no use to my work." He offers me a sly grin. "Doesn't mean I've lost all interest, though."

A protective rage heats my bloodstream. "Keep talking like that and the deal's off."

Silas goes back to fiddling with his rat. "Zephyr knows you have her in Antrum. He's watching all known exit points. My girl has to crawl out sometime. When she does, he'll be waiting."

My tail bobs menacingly behind me. "What else you got?" I re-wrap my tail around his throat.

"Once Zephyr gets Lianna, he's going after the other Kristalli."

I tighten the hold on his neck. Not enough to stop him from talking, but enough to make my point. "Keep going."

Silas's eyes glimmer with fear, good.

"Zephyr's afraid of Tempest," he says.

"And what does Tempest have to do with this?"

"Zephyr captured one of the Water Valta. He found out where the other Kristalli are hidden. The Kristalli of Fire is in Furonium. Once Zephyr gets Lianna, he's sending all his Air Valta after Furonium."

"And why would Zephyr tell you something like that?"

"I've promised to fight as well. Me and my poppets." He gestures to the skinned rat, and then fixes me with a pointed stare. "Do we still have a deal?"

Damn. I'd so love to kill him. That said, breaking my word is another step toward becoming like the monsters I fight. And I've taken enough steps in that direction already.

"We still have a deal. And you've got fifty-five minutes."

"Excellent." A shower of black dust fills the air. My stomach twists with nausea. I've been around enough demons to know what that means. Silas just cast the spell to lock in our agreement.

"Didn't your mother ever tell you?" asks Silas. "Never enter into a deal with a demon." His face brightens with an evil grin.

And it's that fucking smile that does it. Monster or not, Silas isn't walking out of here without a mark. On reflex, my tail skewers Silas deep in the shoulder. His bones make a satisfying crunch as they snap.

"That," I say. "Was for Lianna."

"Liar." Silas grips his injured shoulder. "You broke your word."

"You're not dead, are you? The deal stands."

"No, you changed the terms," says Silas. "You made things inequitable."

"Tough." As I walk away, a shock of pain tears into my side. I look down to see Silas's scalpel embedded between two seams of my armor. It hurts, but I've had worse.

"Now we're even again," says Silas quickly. "Our deal, you know."

Rage spikes through me. Every cell in my body burns to take Silas down. It takes everything I have, yet somehow, I keep to our deal. I smashed the guy's shoulder and he jabbed me with a scalpel. I'm still ahead. I tear out the scalpel and flick it toward Silas's face. It barely misses his ear and embeds into the concrete wall.

"Fifty minutes, Silas."

He takes off at a run, and I wish I could wait here and track him. After this encounter, Silas won't be dumb enough to go uncloaked. There'll be no more finding him with my enchanted painting. Silas will become tough to track, but he was also right. The information he gave me is time critical.

I have to go warn Lianna and Tempest.

10

MAXON

*B*y the time I walk back into my library, it's late morning. Edward's already there.

"Welcome back, Your Highness."

"Morning, Edward." I head straight for the bar and my magically refilled bottle of Macallan '46.

"I brought coffee," says Edward leadingly. "It's on the credenza."

I pause. "Coffee, eh?"

"Yes, Your Highness." Edward's milky old-guy eyes look at me hopefully. He's always trying to get me to go healthier. You know, stuff like having coffee for breakfast instead of whiskey. I can't say no to him.

"Coffee sounds great." As I head over to the credenza, I thank fuck for the millionth time that I'm part demon. Otherwise, I'd be way dead by now, considering all the crap I do to my body. Staying up for weeks on end. Eating junk, when I eat at all. At least I get lots of exercise while killing demons.

Once I pour my hot cup of java, I head to my writing desk and jot down a quick note on parchment. It's a recap of Silas's news for Tempest. This way, he'll have some time to prepare his troops. I know for a fact that T doesn't know where the Kristalli of Fire is. Otherwise, he'd have pawned it off on someone else ages ago. After sealing up the parchment, I wave Edward over.

"I need you to get this message to Furonium."

All the color drains from Edward's face. "Surely you don't expect me to visit demons?"

I exhale a frustrated breath. "How is it that the thrax adore my mother and yet, you're all terrified of the Furor?"

The whole demon hunter side of the thrax sure dies hard.

Edward collects himself. "Of course, if Your Highness wishes me to go to Furonium, I shall go." A drop of sweat rolls down his cheek.

"Don't get your boxers in a twist. I'm not asking for that. All I want is for you to get a messenger and have them deliver the parchment." I set the envelope into Edward's hands. "This is important. The safety of the Furor is at stake."

Edward nods quickly, a movement that makes his jowls shake. "Yes, Your Highness." He takes off at a jog, or what passes for a jog for Edward. He's really getting up there, even for a thrax. Some of us live for five hundred years.

As I watch him go, I feel a twinge of worry about Furonium. Sure, the Furor love a good fight. That said, no one knows what elementals are capable of, especially a nutjob like Zephyr. I hope Tempest gets my message in time.

I wander over to the library shelves. My battle journals are stored here, and I always take notes on new demons. This morning, I have lots to record about Silas and the Incarnate. Since my logs are stacked on the top shelf, I climb one of the rolling ladders to reach them. With every step, a jolt of pain sears across my chest.

Damn, Silas's scalpel left a sting. Probably poisoned.

I make a mental note to run over and see Ty later. He can clear up even late-stage poisoning with a quick incantation. In the meantime, the leather-bound journal I want is in the top corner of the library wall. That's a stretch away, so I pull the volume out with my tail. As I move the volume to my hand, a sweet voice sounds below me.

"Morning, Maxon."

No question who that is. Lianna.

I smile like a fucking idiot because, let's face it, I am one. I mean, who brings the first new Monarkki of Water in twenty thousand years into the busiest castle in the after-realms? Me, that's who. And all because I couldn't stand the idea of Ty watching over her. Just thinking about his offer, I almost snap the ladder rungs in two.

Since when do I get jealous? I thought it was a breakthrough learning Lianna's name. Most girls never get that far.

"Did you hear me, Maxon?"

Case in point. I've been staring at the journal for two minutes now, smiling my fool face off and not able to say something basic like 'good morning.'

"Heard ya, beautiful." I look down at her and wave. "Be right there."
Lianna's wearing something the Mistress of Cloth picked out. It's a white
sundress that shows off her long, lean body. Since I'm a guy, I picture
what she looks like underneath that thing.

Huh. I think she'd look pretty damn good.

Tucking the journal under my left arm, I use my tail and right hand to
swing my way down, Tarzan-style. Sure, it hurts like hell and yeah, I'm
showing off like a nine year old, but my self-control is crap around
this woman.

I land right in front of her without even wincing from the pain.
Not an easy thing to do, considering how Silas's slice is starting
to sting.

She arches her right eyebrow. "The ladder has steps, you know."

"Yeah, my *Grandma* uses them all the time."

"And she's not a big strong warrior like you."

"Come on, like you'd take the safe way down, either."

She scans the ladder and smiles. "No, I suppose I wouldn't."

"Thought so."

She's like a magnet or something. I can't help myself; I step closer to
her. Lianna gasps a little and I wonder if she makes hot noises like that in
bed. Sure, it's a dumbass thing to think about. I'm not a total moron; I
know I'm playing with fire.

Wasn't it only hours ago that I swore to put on the brakes?

Now that I'm near her again, I'm man enough to admit the whole
'putting on the brakes plan' was bullshit. I step nearer and set my hand
on her hip. She makes another little gasping noise and I'm lost.

Only, I'm not.

Something inside stops me from going further. Maybe it's a spell or
insanity, because I'm not known for my conscience. The bottom line is
this: Lianna's special. She's beautiful inside and out, and she needs a guy
who's as perfect as she is. That's not me. I'm broken. Sure, I'm good in
between the sheets and on the battlefield. But that's it. Lianna deserves
better.

"What are we doing, Maxon?" Lianna tilts her head closer. Her warm
breath moves over my lips.

Damn, she wants this.

I take a pointed step away. "I think we're having coffee. That's it."

"Oh," says Lianna. Her face turns slack with shock and hurt.
Suddenly, I feel like a total dick for sending mixed signals. She clears her
throat. "Sure, coffee sounds good."

We stare at each other again for a crazy-long time. Lianna's the one to get her head together and break the silence. She gestures to my left arm. "What's the book?"

"It's one of my demon battle journals." I toss it onto a red leather couch. "I went out last night and faced a new kind of enemy."

Lianna's voice raises with suspicion. "Anything I need to know about?"

"Definitely." I hate how the playful mood has suddenly gone to hell. I want to put off the Silas conversation for a bit. "How about we go through all that after breakfast? My guy Edward loves to feed me."

"No, thanks." She grins. "I'm not hungry."

"Cause you can't eat or won't?"

"Don't need to, anymore." Her pretty smile fades.

"What's wrong, beautiful?"

"There's a lot on my mind."

I remember what she said at the Pulpitum. She wanted to hide with humans and get her head together.

"You're worried about your power."

"That's the problem." She rakes her hands through her long blonde hair. "I'm not a full monarkki yet. I need to take my crown. To do that I have to visit the Water Palace."

A jolt of realization moves through me. Lianna leaving and being at risk... That's what Silas was talking about. "On second thought, I don't think our conversation can wait."

"What's up?"

"Last night, I went after Silas."

Lianna gasps. Her skin starts to glow blue and her blonde hair takes on a sea green shade. Guess when she's upset, she goes into water elemental mode.

"And what happened with Silas?" she asks.

"I wanted to kill the guy, but he offered me a trade. He gave me information in exchange for a head start before I track down that fucker." I raise my fist. "For the record, I did not promise to let him live."

Lianna's skin gets even brighter. "What did Silas tell you?"

"Zephyr knows that you need to leave Antrum to claim your crown. He's watching all the Pulpitum."

"I'm guessing you have secret Pulpitum stations on Earth, just like you have hidden ones in Antrum?"

"Yeah. I'll get you total access, whatever you need."

"Thanks, Maxon." Her voice breaks a little as she speaks. "Everything that you did with Silas." She steps closer again. "That means a lot to me."

She licks her lips and my mind goes straight into the gutter. Or in this case, her mouth. Why didn't I kiss her before? It could have been epic. I bet she'd start off all slow and shy, and then go bad girl on me and bite down. The energy between us takes on a life of its own.

Lianna steps even closer and runs her fingers down my arm. Her touch feels so good, I want to roll my eyes back into my head and moan. I don't, though. It isn't easy.

"Did Silas cut you?" she asks. "He always kept a few special scalpels handy just in case."

"He got me once." I gesture to the side of my rib cage. "It's a small slice."

"It's poisoned, right?"

I shrug. "I know my poisons like I know my punches. This one is slow acting. I got time."

"Consider it an honor. The guy hoards his poisoned scalpels. They're incredibly hard for him to make."

I offer her a half-smile. "I'm honored."

Lianna sets her hand on my side. The feel of her sends a jolt of heat through me. "I could heal it for you right now. Just need to set my palm directly on the wound."

Okay. More touching sounds like a great idea.

"Sure, that's—"

"Maxon!" A loud female voice booms down the hallway. I don't give a crap about visitors. I was promised some skin-to-skin action.

"Maxon!" There's that voice again.

Lianna lowers her hand. "Who's that?"

"I'm not sure. There aren't a lot of people who'd barge in here, though."

"I got the idea that no one would."

"That too."

"Where are you, dear?" With that, I know exactly who's calling for me. My grandmother, Octavia, G for short. Not the kind of person that you get all lovey in front of. The energy between Lianna and me takes a major nosedive. I step away.

"Thanks for the offer, but I get hurt all the time, poison included. I'll heal up soon." I nod toward the open doorway. "Besides, we've got company."

"And who is that, exactly?"

"Someone the guards shouldn't have let in." *Only they're too big of pussies to say no.* "I'll handle this."

I reach the doorway just as G rounds into the outer hall. She's a little thing in her black gown, with long gray hair down her back. Too many thrax buy her 'sweet old granny' act. My G is sharp as a razor and twice as lethal.

"Maxon! There you are."

"G. Why're you here?" I block her from passing through the doorway.

"The guards let me in."

"That's *how*, not *why*. What's up?"

She twists from side to side, trying to see past my torso. Good thing I'm broad chested and solid as a brick wall. I shoot her a sly smile. She's not getting around me that easily. "Want something, G?"

"Stop blocking the doorway, Maxon. I know she's in there."

"How'd you find out?"

"Uther."

I shake my head. "My bad. I should've asked Ty for a memory wipe."

"Uther said to tell you that he's sorry for being a 'weasel dick.'" G makes little quotation marks with her wrinkly fingers while she says the last part. "His words, not mine."

"I guessed that part, G."

"Good. Now, step aside, my boy."

I groan like a baby. Still, I step back and let her in. Short of spontaneous human combustion, nothing will stop my G when she's on a mission. She brushes past me and into the room.

"Lianna," I say. "This is my grandmother. She has a ton of titles but I call her G. G, this is Lianna."

"So pleased to meet you, my dear." G kisses Lianna on both cheeks. "You're the Monarkki of Water, I hear."

"That's right." Lianna gives me a sly look. "One of the guys was in a chatty mood, I guess."

"Yup. It was Uther. I'm coming up with payback ideas, don't worry."

A servant appears at the doorway. "Where would you like your tea, Your Highness?"

"Over on the credenza," says G. "We've more coming."

I suck in a surprised breath. "More?"

G goes all 'sweet old lady' on me and pats Lianna's hand. "Fancy some tea, my dear?"

I'm not buying her act for a second.

"G, you didn't answer my question."

"Because I'm getting Lianna her tea."

"She didn't ask for any," I say.

"I heard it, clear as a bell," says G.

Sure, she did.

G rushes to the credenza and starts fiddling with teapots and spoons and shit. "Milk and sugar, my dear?"

"Yes, please." Lianna looks at me and smiles like a cat who just chomped down one big-ass canary. "I can't wait to learn all about Maxon."

I wink at her and mouth the words 'payback to you, too.' She sticks out her tongue at me. It should be funny, but my mind goes right into the gutter again. Her tongue is cute, pink, and hot. I picture her licking all the way up my thigh and shiver. The way my body wants this woman is something I haven't felt in a long time. Maybe ever.

More footsteps sound down the outer hall, breaking up my internal peep show. *Not good.* I step into the doorway to find Mom and Dad heading toward me. Like G, they're in full royal get-up. Dad looks like a total king with his black tunic, broad chest and graying hair. Mom looks otherworldly in her Scala robes and black over-gown. Her tail waves at me over her shoulder.

I try to act surprised. "Hey, what're you two doing here?"

"Octavia sent for us," says Mom. "The guards say she's in the library?"

"That's what they're saying."

Dad shakes his head. "Didn't think it sounded right, either. We never come to your chambers, let alone while wearing our formals."

G's sing-song voice wafts in from the library. "I'm in here, children. Who wants tea?"

Dad's eyebrows lift in surprise. "You invited your Grandmother over for tea?"

"For the record, that's a big no."

"I invited myself over," calls G. "And Maxon has a girl in here."

I pinch the bridge of my nose. *I can't believe this.*

"He does?" asks Mom.

"You do?" echoes Dad.

They both try to peer around me.

"Yeah," I say. "There's a girl in here."

"Wow," whispers Mom.

"What kind of girl?" asks Dad.

"Thrax." *Sort of.*

They start trying to peep around me, so I step back again. "Come on in, guys. Who's next? Hildy?"

"Nonsense," says G. "You know she's off building her new school in the Wastelands. Walker's coming, though."

"Walker?" I repeat.

"Yes, Walker," confirms G with one of her 'innocent old lady' grins. She waves to my parents. "Well, come on in already. She won't bite."

My parents cautiously step past me, like the library holds a mythical creature that could bolt at any second. Huh. You'd think I never brought a girl home before.

Oh right, I never have brought a girl home before.

"Lianna, these are my parents. My parents, Lianna."

They barely finish shaking hands when Walker rushes into the room.

"And Walker here's too," I add. I'm ready to introduce them when the old ghoul wraps Lianna in a big hug that lasts way too long. Like I could change the oil on my bike in the time he's got his arms around her. I've got to say something, so I try to talk without sounding like a jealous bastard.

"Huh. I guess you already know each other." My voice comes out low and deadly.

Not sure I did a bang-up job with the jealous bastard stuff.

Walker gets all gooey-eyed as he looks at Lianna. "I'm so glad to see you again."

"Glad to be seen."

"I told you that you'd make it," says Walker.

"That you did." Lianna gives him one of those smiles that should really only go to me. My hands clench into fists on their own, not that I try too hard to stop it. I'm pretty sure teatime is about to turn to shit when G claps her hands. The moment gets broken up before I do anything stupid. G's smart like that.

"Now that we're all together," says G. "We can discuss why I brought you here. I have an announcement to make." She smooths out her black velvet gown, all the better to drag out the moment. "Lianna is…" G taps her chin as if she's forgotten something. "What is your title again, my dear?"

"I'm the Monarkki of Water."

At this news, Dad puts his 'this is bullshit' face on. I should know. I wore the same one when Lianna first showed up, too.

"There hasn't been a new Monarkki of Water in twenty thousand years," says Mom.

In reply, Lianna turns blue. I'm talking hair, dress, skin, everything.

"There is now," Lianna says. "And it's me." She leans back on the couch in her blue robes, daring anyone to say shit. My parents can hardly control their smiles. They like feisty as much as I do. Maybe more.

"Trust me," explains Walker. "She's the new monarkki. Remember the girl I told you about? The one I was constantly relocating?"

Dad nods. "You said you were doing a homemade witness protection program."

Mom snaps her fingers. "She had some guy after her, right?"

"That's right." Walker hitches his thumb at Lianna. "This is who I was talking about. She's not a witness; she's the next monarkki. And the guy after her is Zephyr."

There's a long pause while my parents process this information. G has already adjusted, of course, but she's not exactly wired like the rest of us. My G runs at mental double-speed.

Dad turns to Walker. "Why didn't you say anything before?"

"Namare swore him to secrecy," explains Lianna. "She swore everyone."

"I told you as much as I could," adds Walker.

My parents share a long look, and then give each other small nods. *That means they're cool with this, which is good.* Walker's like a little God in my family. He could say Lianna's the fucking Easter bunny, and they'd buy it. Hell, I'd buy it, too. There isn't a better guy in the after-realms, which is easy to admit that now that I'm not feeling jealous as fuck.

"Since we're all together," announces G. "Why don't you tell us everything, my dear? In your own words."

G doesn't need to ask twice. "To begin with," says Lianna. "I'm from the House of Tärkein."

"Born here in Antrum?" asks G. "Because there's no record of you."

I half roll my eyes. Leave it to G to already have checked the birth rolls.

"No," answers Lianna. "I was born cloud-side in Colorado. It was just me and my parents in a little log cabin in the mountains. They wanted to be close to the elements. I don't know much about being a thrax, other than who you guys are, of course." With that admission, she gets a little blushy, which is cute.

"Where are your parents now?" asks G.

Lianna picks at the lace on her white sundress. "That part's hard to explain." She swallows and doesn't finish her sentence.

She doesn't want to talk about Silas.

What I do next is a reflex. Before I know it, I'm sitting next to Lianna and taking her hand in mine. "Want me to cover this part, beautiful?"

Lianna nods.

"Here's the deal," I begin. "Lianna's family got marked by a Class A Incarnate. He killed her parents and took Lianna for harvesting." I wrap my arm around her shoulder and give her a gentle hug. "Her parents made a trade with Silas for her life."

Lianna nods. "They agreed to go down without a fight as long as Silas promised not to harvest me until I was sixteen. They gave him the right to my life energy. The trade was sealed with black magic." She exhales a shaky breath. "It wasn't much of a trade, but we weren't in a position to argue." Lianna stares at her lap for a long time. After that, she straightens her shoulders and looks my family straight on. There's steel in her gaze. My chest swells with pride. This woman is strong.

"How did you escape?" asks G.

"Namare found me when I was fourteen," Lianna continues. "She freed me by making another trade with Silas. Namare wouldn't kill him and in turn, Silas gave up his rights to my life energy. After that, I went into training to be the next monarkki. There must have been, oh, fifty apprentices when I started. There were five when Namare transferred her power to me."

Her words seem to suck all the oxygen out of the room. Rage zings through my nervous system. To Lianna, those people were her peers. To my family and me, they're our people. Our responsibility.

G shakes her head. "We knew that the Tärkein had a high death rate, but we thought it was due to their silly practice of wandering cloud-side every chance they got."

"Zephyr killed them all, didn't he?" Dad turns to me. His eyes glisten with righteous anger. "Give it to me straight, son."

"Yeah, Dad. Zephyr killed 'em."

My father rounds on Walker. "Why weren't we told? Fifty thrax from the House of Tärkein? That's outrageous!"

"You have to understand," says Walker. "Namare was obsessed with keeping things quiet. She thought it was the only way to protect her apprentices."

Dad's mouth thins to a determined line. "I would have told her differently."

I could step in and tell my father to cut Walker some slack, but honestly, I'm pissed at Walker, too. My neck muscles clench with held-in anger. I can't believe how long this has been going on. We had no idea our people were being slaughtered.

"It wasn't that easy," counters Walker. "I had to follow Namare around for a year before she'd even talk to me. She had her own magic, too. If she got a whiff that I'd broken my word and said anything to you, I would've lost the ability to help Lianna." Walker rubs his hand over his buzz-cut scalp. "Believe me, I wanted to tell you both."

G nods. "He's right. The elementals are notoriously closed-lipped." She gestures to Lianna. "No offense."

"None taken. It's one of the things I hope to change."

Walker's voice quivers with grief. "You have no idea how hard it was not to tell you all."

Mom leans over to pat Walker's hand. "We understand that now. It's just a shock."

"Myla's right." My father sets his hand on Walker's shoulder. That's Dad's 'we're cool again' move. Walker offers him a feeble smile.

"Let's not cover old ground," says G. "What else do we need to know now?"

I lean back on the couch. "You ask me, I'd like more intel on Zephyr." I turn to Lianna. "Who is this guy, anyway?"

"Zephyr was originally a thrax in Roman times," explains Lianna. "Part elemental, House of Tärkein. His parents lived cloud-side in Greece."

"Ancient times," says G. "Lots of thrax lived cloud-side then."

"Zephyr's family got killed, but not by demons. When Julius Caesar invaded Greece, he killed off women, children, and the elderly. The strongest locals were forced into the Roman Army. Zephyr was one of those."

"Almost makes me feel sorry for the man," sighs G.

"Don't," says Lianna. "Zephyr soon found he got a thrill out of murder. He decided to become the Caesar of the elemental world."

Mom frowns. "I've seen that type before. Always looking for the next big high."

"Well, Zephyr found it, that's for sure," says Lianna. "Elemental rulers store power in stones called Kristalli. Zephyr has been using those stones to shoot up with elemental energy. Once he's done, he kills everyone around, often including his own guards."

"So, where's your Kristalli?" asks Dad.

"Hidden in my Water Palace."

The small hairs on my neck stand on alert. Something about that answer sets my inner wrath demon humming. There's trouble with the Kristalli, in the Water Palace, or both. I watch Lianna's features carefully as I ask my next question. "Is your stone safe there?"

"I'm sure it's fine," Lianna says too quickly. "Fisk is there and he's guarding it along with the rest of the Valta."

Fisk. I really don't like the way Lianna says that name.

G sets down her teacup. "I'm afraid you're going to have to translate that reply for me, my dear. I don't yet speak elemental."

"Oh," Lianna chuckles. "Elemental guards are called Valta. The Water Valta are at my palace, along with Fisk, who's their general. They're all protecting the Kristalli of Water, which can store my power." She starts fiddling with the lace on her dress again, and I know something's bothering her.

More and more, I'm getting a good read on what the trouble is. *My money's on Fisk.*

"Are you visiting the Water Palace soon?" I ask.

"Sure," Lianna answers. "I'm going tonight."

The words of Silas's warning ring in my head. If Lianna tries to leave Antrum, Zephyr will definitely make his move. There's no way I'm letting her fly solo.

"Great," I say. "I'll go with you."

Lianna shakes her head. "My people don't trust outsiders. I need to go alone."

Like hell she is.

"You don't know what you'll find at the palace," I say. "And we both know that my lightning powers can help you in a fight."

She tilts her head to one side. I grin at her for all I'm worth. She worries her lower lip with her teeth.

I'm wearing her down. I can tell.

Which is good, because if she doesn't agree, I'll have to follow her anyway. That could get weird.

"Maybe," she says.

"Hey, what's the point of being monarkki if you can't drag your favorites to court?"

She gives me a million-watt smile. "Who said you're my favorite?"

We stare at each other for what feels like a second or two. I guess it's more than that because before I know it, my parents, G, and Walker are standing by the door, waving me over.

I walk over to G first. "Must be annoying, being right all the time."

"So you admit I was correct in holding this impromptu tea?" asks G.

"Don't be a sore winner," I say.

She kisses me on the cheek. "She's lovely, Maxon. I'll hold a Ball of Welcome in her honor."

"No, you won't."

"Yes, I will. And you're not stopping me. Lianna deserves a beautiful ball gown and a handsome prince."

I shake my head. "That's not me, G."

"Poppycock." G cups my face in her hands and looks deeply into my eyes. "Are your irises changing, my boy?"

"Nah. Still mismatched."

"They won't stay that way for long, I'll wager."

I know exactly where she's going with this. If I fall for Lianna, I'll get Angelbound. My eyes will turn bright blue and I'll have power over igni. My family's been itching for this for ages, Mom and G especially. They're worried my ticker's busted and I can't fall in love. Not something I gave much thought to before, but now?

I shiver. Falling in love with Lianna would be a disaster. It's got heartbreak written all over it.

"Not going near that one," I say. "See you later, G."

Mom steps up next. "Did Octavia say something about your eyes?"

Not again.

"Cut me some slack, Mom. I'm in no rush to be the full Scala Heir." I shoot her a sly look. "Besides, I control my lightning. It's the bomb. Your igni do whatever the hell they want. Annoying little bastards."

"Language," she says.

"What can I say? I learned from the best." My mother can swear like a sailor on a week-long rum bender.

"Bye, baby." She walks off.

Next Dad steps in to give me a big man-hug. "Love you, son."

"You too, Dad."

"If you need anything for this, let your mother and me know."

"Will do."

He looks at Lianna, then back at me, and nods. I know where this is going. I'm not ready for another discussion about getting Angelbound. Too bad that Dad is as crafty as G when it comes to getting information.

I whisper so only Dad can hear. "Look, don't get your hopes up. I'm not a relationship guy. I'll help her out and set her on her way. That's all this is."

"I didn't say relationship, Maxon." He offers me a knowing look. "You did."

It takes me a few seconds to realize I stepped right into that one. *Man, I hate it when he does that.*

"Get out of here before you trick me into admitting something else."

"Of course, son." Dad walks off smiling. He's G's kid, all right.

Walker's the last in line. For a long time, all he does is glare at me. Finally, I can't take it any more.

"What?" I snap at him.

"Hurt her and I'll kill you."

I bob my head a little, considering. "Fair enough. Now make tracks."

Finally, they're all gone. I turn to Lianna. "What's next, beautiful?"

"We need to hit one of your secret Pulpitum and get to the Earth's surface. I must summon the Water Palace. To do that, I need to be near—"

"Let me guess." Stepping closer, I wind a lock of her soft blue hair around my finger. "You need to be near water."

"Right." She blushes blue again, which is quickly becoming one of my favorite sights. "I need some place where there's lots of water and no one around. A lake or beach, that kind of thing." Her blush deepens. "I guess that means another platform ride."

I play it cool, like I haven't been thinking about her sweet body pressing against me during the last trip.

"Huh, I guess it does." I take her hand in mine and nod toward the door. "Let's hit it."

11

LIANNA

$\mathcal{M}$axon and I walk along a warm Australian beach, searching for the right spot to summon the Water Palace. Foamy surf laps at my toes. Overhead, the night sky is bright with more stars than I ever thought possible. A warm and secure sensation seeps through my torso. For once, I'm not checking for wind and worrying if Zephyr'll show up. It seems impossible for anything bad to happen while Maxon's holding my hand.

"Something on your mind?" he asks.

"This is a sweet beach. How'd you find it?"

"Me and the guys came here to play as kids. You know, kick the can. Truth or dare. Capture the house flag. That kind of stuff. We were twelve and thought we were so badass for sneaking out of Antrum." He leans in conspiratorially. "My parents were tracking us the whole time, of course."

"They *let* you sneak off?"

"With a secret armed guard trailing after us, yeah."

"That's just…" I press my lips together, searching for the words. "Well, it's seems pretty loose for the thrax."

"My parents had it strict growing up. They wanted to give me more room." He lets out one of his rumbling chuckles. "Although now, they may regret it. I'm always off doing my own thing."

At those words, my mind pictures what Maxon's been doing. Or more accurately, who. Even I couldn't miss the media frenzy about him, especially when I was hiding out urban-style in Purgatory or the Dark Lands. Like everyone else, I caught the occasional episode of Royal Insider.

Maxon sure ran through a lot of women. They were all in the after-realms until someone almost went public with a sex tape. After that, Maxon only hooked up with anonymous women on Earth. The paparazzi still catch the occasional picture of Maxon with a human on his arm. All gorgeous, of course.

So on the one hand there's Maxon, womanizer extraordinaire. And on the other hand, there's me. The extent of my romantic entanglements amounts to Fisk, Fisk, and Fisk.

I'm so out of my league.

Maxon rubs his thumb along my wrist. Each movement makes my stomach do a little backflip.

I shake my head in surprise. Somewhere along the line, Maxon and I went from trying to kill each other to excessive hand-holding and staring. One side of me loves the attention. However, my sadder-but-wiser side says that I'm acting like a total tool. Right now, I'm something new and different to Maxon—a bright shiny object in monarkki form—and so, he's interested. I can't forget that Maxon's the biggest playboy in the after-realms. Once my shine wears off, he'll move on.

Don't let it go too far, Lianna. You'll only get hurt.

"This is the spot," says Maxon. "What do you think?"

Moonlight glistens on the waves in this secluded inlet. *This could work.* "You sure no one will come by?"

"Oh, yeah. No human can get within a mile of here. Ty cast a bunch of repulsion spells over the years." He gestures across the landscape. "So, will this do the trick?"

"Sure, I can summon the palace from here." In the movie of my life, that statement comes out as bold and badass. In reality, my voice squeaks with worry.

Really slick, Lianna.

Namare told me all about the Water Palace, but I've never been there. As a thrax, they wouldn't let me through the doors. I've never met most of the Water Valta, either. Now, I need to summon the palace and announce myself to the Valta. With their energy, I can claim my crown. This is what I've been training for years to do, so why do I want to run for cover?

Maxon gives my hand a squeeze. "Want to come back later?" His voice steadies me.

"No, I'll do this now." I give him a shaky smile. "Just don't let go of my hand."

"You got it, beautiful."

My mouth starts moving on its own. "It's not what you think."

He raises his brows.

"Well, it is but…" I blush something fierce. "I mean, you'll drown if you let go. Unless you can walk on water, I mean."

"Not one of my powers, no." He gives me one of his dimple smiles.

"Okay, then." I inhale a steadying breath. "We're off."

Closing my eyes, I change into my monarkki form and raise my free arm, just like Namare taught me. Instantly, a light rain pours onto the nearby surf. Within seconds, the droplets stream into the shape of two Palace Wardens. Their clear bodies are visible as shimmering streaks of water, like rain on a windowpane. From what I can tell, these guards wear heavy armor and spiked helmets. They're not easy to see, but that's all part of the elemental plan. We excel at hiding.

"Who summons us?" asks the first guard.

"Lianna, Namare's chosen apprentice." I summon blue light to shimmer across my skin, just to make the point clear. "I wish to visit the Water Palace."

The second guard glares at Maxon. "What is this human doing here?"

"He's my guest."

"I'm also far from human." Maxon snaps his fingers and a half dozen lightning bolts strike the ground around us in rapid fire. The guards outright gasp, which is mighty encouraging. I straighten my shoulders with newfound confidence. Maxon gives my hand a reassuring squeeze. I can't help but smile.

Together, we head toward the open ocean, our feet suspended on the water's surface with every step. This is another trick I learned from Namare.

Once we're well away from shore, I raise my free arm high.

"Open the gates," I command.

Before us, the water bubbles and churns. The first thing to rise from the ocean is a spire of blue stone. After that, the rest of the castle follows. It's a cone-shaped structure with ridged lines of rock that end in a single peak. It reminds me of a huge conch shell pointed toward the sky. A large arched doorway opens before us.

"Nice place you got here," says Maxon.

"Wait until we get past the door. I've only seen pictures. It's supposed to be mighty fancy."

"You've never been inside before?"

"No, elementals keep to themselves. Like I said before, it's one of the first things I plan to change once I'm officially crowned."

As we step through the main doorway, Maxon keeps up the steady rhythm of his thumb over my knuckles. It still gets my stomach flipping.

"So you know," I say. "You don't have to hold my hand once we're inside the palace."

"Not letting go, beautiful." He gives me the barest of winks. "Safety reasons, you know."

I smile from ear to ear. "Right."

We stroll into a large reception arcade made of blue crystal. The space is massive and cone-shaped, with a huge base that ends in a tiny, far-off peak. A wide walkway corkscrews along the walls. Water elementals of all kinds roam up and down this winding path. Some look like humanoid fish, while others are little more than swirls of sentient liquid with faces. They're all beautiful.

A ripple of awareness moves through the crowd. One by one, the elementals stop whatever they're doing. All turn to stare at me with amazement. Some whisper 'Your Eminence' in reverent tones. Their blue skin glows with joy. My heart warms as their happiness becomes my own.

They've been waiting for me.

A small figure races across the floor. It's a boy with pale skin, cropped green hair, and ocean-blue eyes. He wears a miniature set of the scaled armor worn by all Valta. I smile.

It's Esau.

He stops before me. "Hey."

I kneel down before him. "Hey."

"You're the lady in the waterfall."

"I am."

Up close, I can see dark marks on his skin. My voice lowers with concern. "What happened to your arm?"

Esau quickly hides his arm behind his back. "It's fine. Namare will come around to heal me."

"Let me see," I say, gently coaxing him to move his arm forward again. He does. What I see brings the sour taste of dismay to my mouth. The marks are small, striated, and gray.

"Were you playing in the Dark Lands?" The waters of the ghoul kingdom carry all sorts of disease for our kind, even when Namare was cleansing them regularly.

Esau cringes with fear. "I won't do it again, I swear."

"What is it?" asks Maxon.

I take care to keep my voice low. I don't want to frighten Esau any more than he is already. "River Pox."

"Is it..." Maxon pauses. He doesn't need to say the word 'deadly.'

I nod, my eyes stinging with grief. In the first stages of River Pox,

Esau will feel fine, apart from his rash. It's only in the later phases that the rash turns into angry, painful welts. And then?

I shudder, forcing the image of the last stages of River Pox from my mind.

That won't happen to Esau. I won't allow it.

Esau lowers his voice to a whisper. "Everyone says that Namare is gone. They don't know anything. She's coming to help me. She promised."

A voice booms across the quiet arcade. "Esau! Come here!"

Rising to stand, I survey the crowd. On instinct, my hand finds Maxon's again. Water Valta now surround Maxon and me. Their fish-like faces all look grim.

They're ready for a fight.

"Sorry, Dad!" calls Esau. He runs toward the line of soldiers, hiding behind one of the Water Valta, a spindly guy with a tentacle moustache. That must be Esau's father.

"He's sick," I say. "I can heal him."

Fisk steps out from the group, his handsome face lined with rage. His gaze moves between Maxon and me. For a long time, he glares hot daggers at our entwined fingers.

I shift my weight nervously from foot to foot before turning to Maxon. "Maybe you should go," I whisper.

"You want me to leave?"

"No."

"Then, I'm staying." He fixes me with a look of stony resolve. "Just tell me how you want to play it here. This is about getting your crown, Lianna."

Under Maxon's gaze, my shoulders straighten. He's right. Why send him away just because it makes Fisk uncomfortable? I'm the monarkki. Setting my fists on my hips, I scan the arcade in a way that I hope looks regal.

Fisk still stands across from us, immobile as if he were carved from stone. He wears his Valta armor with its blue metal scales. Signets of office mark his shoulders, holding a long, sapphire-colored cape down his back. He marches forward and pauses before us. His handsome face is twisted into an angry snarl. "You were holding his hand."

"I'm alive, Fisk. Nice to see you, too."

And there goes the regal act, right out the window.

Fisk rounds on Maxon. "And who are you?"

I raise my hand palm forward, in the universal sign for 'stop right there.' "It's my role to make introductions, Fisk." Even so, I decide to go through everything at double-speed. Something tells me I don't want these two spending lots of quality time together. "Fisk, Maxon. Maxon, Fisk."

Fisk's skin glimmers with blue light. He's really getting himself worked up. "Why do you bring a mortal among us? His presence defiles this sacred place."

Great. Fisk goes pompous and nasty, right off the bat.

Maxon hitches his thumbs into the pockets of his body armor. He's the picture of cool menace.

It's an effort to keep my voice calm. "Maxon isn't just any mortal. He's the High Prince of the thrax, the Scala Heir and…" I turn to him. "What else am I missing?"

Maxon shrugs, and even that movement is somehow threatening. "I'm second in line to the throne of Furonium." He does one of his chin-nods toward Fisk. "And you are?"

"General of the Valta," replies Fisk. "It's my job to rule the water elementals until a new monarkki is crowned." His mouth thins to an angry line. "And Lianna is my girl."

All the elementals gasp. Maxon's brows lift ever so slightly. At this point, I'd really like a do-over on the whole Fisk relationship. What was I thinking again?

Oh, yeah. Stupid hormones.

Somehow, I manage to speak in a very calm and badass voice. "That's not true, Fisk. We've talked about this. Many times."

Fisk ignores me. It's what he always does when I'm saying something inconvenient. "She's my girl, so back off." He and Maxon start a full-blown staring contest.

I groan. "Fisk."

"Make no mistake," says Fisk. "She is mine. I took her virginity."

Now, I outright gasp. "Fisk!"

Maxon's tail whips behind him in a menacing rhythm. "Disrespect Lianna again like that, and I don't care who you are. You'll regret it."

Fisk fingers the dagger at his waistline. "I'm not afraid of you."

Maxon's voice comes out as a low growl. "You should be."

The crowd gasps again, and that's when I decide that enough is enough.

I step closer to Fisk, taking care to block his line of sight to Maxon. "Are these Valta here to meet me?" My voice takes on a leading tone. "A casual 'get to know you' type thing. That's what we discussed, right?"

"Valta don't do casual when there are outsiders in the Palace," says Fisk.

"It doesn't matter who he is," I counter. "I'm here to meet the Valta and Maxon will be present as my guest."

"No," growls Fisk, and his skin flares even brighter. I've never seen him like this.

Time for Plan B.

I turn to the Water Valta. "I am Lianna, the chosen apprentice of Namare." Once again, I make my skin flare with blue light. "She gave her powers to me. I can wield the Kristalli."

"Can you?" asks Fisk. "Try to summon it."

Something in his tone sets my teeth on edge. Raising my arm, I recite the incantation to call the Kristalli. Nothing happens.

I round on Fisk. "What did you do to my stone?"

"*Your* stone?" asks Fisk. "Namare gave it to *me* for safekeeping. I'll award it to whoever I deem worthy." A muscle twitches along his jawline. "Whoever I deem faithful."

"Faithful to who?" I ask. "I've been a faithful servant to Namare. That's all that should matter here."

"Zephyr said the same words to his Valta before he was crowned, and what has happened to them? All the men killed. All the boys placed in battle before they're ready."

"How dare you compare me to Zephyr?" Now, it's my turn to glow a brighter shade of blue.

"Who should I liken you to?" Fisk's voice takes on a hysterical edge. "You're not acting like yourself. This—" He gestures between Maxon and me "Whatever it is, this pairing is insane."

"It's not what you think," says Maxon.

"We were only holding hands," I add. "You're acting crazy."

"Crazy? I saw the way you looked at him. The energy between you two. You never looked at me..." He shakes his head. "You're not trustworthy and that's all there is to it. My Valta won't take the chance."

A grumble of agreement passes through the Valta.

Fisk turns to face his men. "No crowning ceremony will take place today. Namare is gone. I don't know when we will have a new monarkki."

Rumbles of dissent instantly move through the Valta. A pang of shock twists up my throat. They all agree with him. The Valta would really rather have no monarkki than one who might treat them like Zephyr.

My surprise quickly hardens into anger. "And what the Valta want, they do, regardless of the other elementals?"

"It's our role to ensure the right monarkki is crowned."

"At what expense?" I gesture to the civilian water elementals who stand assembled behind the Valta. "Our people need healing. Their waters require fresh energy. Who are you to deny them?" The crowd quickly takes up the call.

"My father needs a cure," says one voice.

"The Lake of Dreams must be cleansed," adds another.

Esau's voice gets added to the mix. He peeps out from behind his father's leg and pulls on the Valta's armor. "But Namare is coming. She said that she'd heal me."

His father's moustache droops in sadness. "Stay back, son."

The crowd's rumbling grows louder. Excitement zings across my skin. Even if Fisk has his issues, the people want me as their monarkki.

"Silence!" calls Fisk.

The voices grow louder. I see my chance and take it.

"You mourned Namare," I say. "Respect her wishes and make me your monarkki." I turn to the Valta. "Adjourn to the Hall of Fountains. The ceremony begins now."

The time for meet-and-greet is over. These are soldiers. They understand two things: Orders and strength.

A muscle twitches by Fisk's eye. "No one commands the Valta but me." He raises his arms. "Valta, take formation!"

Soldiers appear along the winding pathway to the castle's peak. They hold crossbows. All the bolts point at my chest.

Fisk rounds on me. "Now, you go."

Deadly silence hangs in the air. I run through my options. I have Namare's power, sure. Somehow, I doubt that taking down the Water Valta in front of a crowd won't win me any points. I can't settle this with death.

So what can I do?

Quiet cries echo through the vast space. Looking over, I see Esau's face buried in his father's leg. His shoulders quake with sobs.

Suddenly, I know exactly how to handle this. Not with death, but with life.

"Cover me," I say to Maxon.

"You got it."

Leaning down, I set my hand on the crystal floor. I need to try and heal Esau. Blue light flows out from my fingertips and across the stone. The elemental power makes a straight path to the boy. There it stops.

The room seems to pause as well. Everyone stares at the sick child. My healing energy is only inches away from him. Since I'm not yet connected to my people, I can't heal him without touching him.

"See this?" I say. "I can't help this child because of the Water Valta." I fix Esau's father with a glare. "You can link me to your child right now, just as all the Water Valta could link me to my people by supporting my coronation. How can you stand there?"

Still, no one in the chamber seems to move, maybe even breathe. The energy's turning my way. A rush of excitement swirls through my mind.

"Connect me to Esau. Connect me to our people."

Esau slips his hand into his father's. "Please, Daddy?"

That does it. Esau's father sets his palm onto the floor, where my elemental power waits. Instantly, the blue light crawls into Esau's father body. His armor glows bright as the energy moves across him and into Esau. The child's skin also glows sapphire-bright.

Soft gasps echo through the crowd. Everyone watches as the dark marks on Esau's skin disappear. And for a moment, a rush of energy moves through my soul. It's the power that comes from being linked to another elemental. The truth rises from the depths of my consciousness.

Being together makes us all stronger.

I rise to stand. For someone who hates speeches, I know exactly what to say.

"We're already connected," I declare. "My energy is your energy. Your pain strikes my heart as well. We can be separated and weak, or we can join together and become strong. Fearing Zephyr will not bring you a good ruler. Linking together will. Whenever you're ready to take that step, I'm ready, too."

With that, I take Maxon's hand and head toward the door. No one moves to stop us, and I suppose that's the most I can expect at this point. We step outside. Moonlight glints off the ocean as we walk across the water. Behind us, the Water Palace disappears into the sea once again.

The calm evening waters reflect starlight and moonlight. Their beauty should be soothing. Instead, hot rage burns through my belly.

"How can the Valta be so bullheaded?" I bellow. "I will not turn into another Zephyr."

My fingers itch to do something, anything. On reflex, I conjure columns of waterspouts. They surround Maxon and me in a great circle. The liquid shoots high into the air, holds weightless for a moment, and then crashes down onto the dark ocean.

Maxon stands beside me, still holding my hand, still the image of cool. "That helping?"

"Not enough."

Giving up on the waterspouts, I summon a line of liquid bombs to explode high in the air. After that, I create a great curling wave that crashes across the ocean in a huge rolling line. The sight reminds me of the element's ultimate power. Water is eternal. And that's a very calming thought. Finally, I get my head together and return my focus to Maxon.

I hadn't been paying him much attention—okay, I hadn't paid him any—and now I'm wondering if he thinks I'm a psycho.

"So." I rock on my heels, making my toes splash in the water. "You probably have a lot of questions about that, uh, display."

Maxon tilts his head. It's like he walks on water all the time with strange women who create waterspouts and have stalker ex-boyfriends who happen to be elementals.

"What part?" he asks.

I'll skip the Fisk part for now.

"All the angry water stuff."

"Oh, I got that fine." He chuckles softly. "You're not the only one with a temper, you know."

I exhale a relived breath. "Good."

"Anything else?"

"Oh, Fisk."

Maxon shrugs. "Nah. You said you grew up isolated. I've seen his type. Makes you feel wanted. Takes advantage. You made the right call."

I shake my head. Maxon nailed that one.

"What you should wonder about is your crown," says Maxon. "How can you get it and help your people?"

I shoot him a sly look. "I thought you didn't know statecraft."

"Guess I picked up more than I thought over the years." He gives me a chin-nod. "Talk to me. What's your next move?"

Bobbing my head from side to side, I think through possibilities and next steps. "Well, getting crowned isn't happening."

"Not right now, anyway."

"Normally, I'd worry about Zephyr coming to get me. He hasn't showed, though."

"Wouldn't expect it either. Silas said some other stuff when I visited."

"About Zephyr?"

Maxon nods. "Silas said that if Zephyr's not hunting you, then he's going after the Kristalli of Fire, which is hidden in Furonium. I sent Emperor Tempest a heads up. With any luck, T will be in a good mood and want to use the attack to sharpen up his troops."

Worry zings through my stomach. "If Zephyr gets the Kristalli of Fire, then the Fire elementals will never have another monarkki. Do you think Tempest can hold him off?"

"Furor warriors are the toughest in the after-realms, and T is a great general. So, I'd say if anyone can, it's Tempest. If nothing else, he'll buy us some time. Maybe we can get some things done while Zephyr is busy."

"In that case, we should go after the Kristalli of Earth."

"Just what I was thinking. We pick up the Kristalli of Earth while Tempest keeps Zephyr busy. Where is the stone, anyway?"

"Hidden in the Philippines."

Maxon's brows pop up. "In the Chocolate Hills?"

"How'd you guess?"

"It's one of a handful of demonic dead zones. No activity there and I always wondered why. Makes sense that someone would be guarding the region. Never would have suspected elementals, though." Maxon glares at the spot where the palace disappeared under the waves. "After we're done, can I come back and beat the crap out of that guy?"

That guy being Fisk, of course.

I grit my teeth in frustration. "Only if I can watch."

Maxon lets out another rumbling laugh. "You're something else, you know that?"

"Oh, you have no idea."

12

MAXON

The Chocolate Hills… It's easy to see how this place got its name. Even in the moonlight, the ground looks brown, rounded, and symmetrical, like chocolates in a box. They're not the only sights here, either. The minute Lianna and I approached the hills, I knew we weren't alone. A pair of Zephyr's Air Valta got here first. They're already looking for the Kristalli of Earth. That's the bad news. The good news is that they don't know what the fuck they're doing. The two Valta are meandering around like they're on a coffee break or something.

When I speak to Lianna, I make sure to talk low and by her ear. Honestly, I don't need to be this close, but she smells like strawberries and it's making me nuts. You know, in a good way.

"Any more than two of them?" I ask.

"No, Zephyr's main force must still be in Furonium."

I let my lips brush her earlobe. "Can you show me where the Valta are again?" A blush crawls down her neck.

"You're trumping up reasons to keep whispering at me." She gives me an annoyed look, but her eyes are too excited for it to be real. "We're on a mission here, Maxon. Focus."

"Hey. I'm learning how to pick out elementals from the landscape. To me, they're all smoke and stuff. It's tough enough during the daylight and impossible at night." I nod to the night sky like it's there to back me up. "Need a little help here."

Lianna points across to a nearby hill. "Two Air Valta, twelve o'clock. Looks like they're keeping watch."

"Are they anywhere near the Kristalli?"

"Not at all." She taps her forehead and grins. "I've got the exact location right here."

"Good. In that case, whatever information Zephyr got, it wasn't too specific." I gesture across the hills. "So, lead the way."

Lianna walks around the base of the hills, looking from one spot to another while muttering under her breath about someone called the Etevin of Water. Seems like the guy used to visit his Earth elemental buddy somewhere nearby. All this sneaking around is giving me too much time to think about my wound from the other night. The poison's starting to hurt even more. Finally, we stop at the base of a random-looking hill.

"This is it," whispers Lianna. Kneeling, she sets her palms against the dried-out grass of the hillside. "I am the Monarkki of Water. I'm here for Terrak."

A small wooden doorway appears in the side of the hill. It swings open, revealing a massive eye. There's more to the face that's hidden inside the hill, quite possibly a whole humanoid something. With elementals, you never know. Some of those things running around Lianna's Water Palace were nothing more than a watery squiggle with an eyeball. There's also the obvious question about why a creature that big needs a door that small. I'm not going there, either. We'd be here all night.

Beside me, Lianna's shoulders slump with relief. "The Etevin's memories were right. Your name is Terrak, yes?"

"Terrak tired," says a gravelly voice. "Need to heal."

The big eye half-closes. As it moves, the moonlight reflects in funny ways. Turns out, Terrak is made of small brown gemstones. Interesting.

Lianna beams. "I'm so glad I found you."

"Terrak sick. You bring thrax for new monarkki?" Terrak lets out a yawn. "I have Kristalli. We make new monarkki. Heal Terrak. Help all Earth elementals."

I picture that sick little elemental kid back at the Water Palace. Man, that was heartbreaking. It makes sense that the other elements have the same trouble if they're missing their monarkki. My shoulders clench with rage. What a fucker that Zephyr is.

"I'm not here with a new thrax for you," says Lianna. "I came to warn you. Someone is coming to take the Kristalli of Earth. You must hide it somewhere else."

"Yes, hide," says Terrak. His large fingers squeeze through the door and set a small brown bundle onto the hillside. "You guard now."

I pick up the little package. It's a leathery sheath wrapped around what feels like a long stone.

Lianna's mouth falls open with surprise. "That's the Kristalli of Earth?"

"Looks like." The thing buzzes with an odd energy that tickles my palm. I jam the thing into a pocket on my body armor. That helps.

"No, no, no." Lianna turns to Terrak and goes nuts on him. "You're supposed to re-hide the Kristalli, not give it to me." Her skin starts lighting up, monarkki style.

"Watch it, beautiful," I whisper. "Those Air Valta are still nearby."

Terrak doesn't say anything more to Lianna. Instead he slams the hillside door in our faces, which I guess is just as good as saying 'no.' *What an elemental weasel.*

Technically he found a place to hide the Kristalli. Only now, Lianna and I have extra trouble to deal with.

Lianna presses her palms to her forehead. "That didn't work out like I'd hoped."

"Everything'll be fine." I wrap my around Lianna's shoulder. "We'll figure it out. But now, you need to turn off your glow, okay?"

Lianna looks at her skin and gasps. "Crap, I didn't even realize I was doing that." She closes her eyes and returns to her regular human form. "My bad."

"Nothing to apologize for. I like seeing you all blued up."

Her mouth slowly rounds into a smile. "Really?"

"Yeah, beautiful." I pull her in closer. It's not even conscious thing, I touch her on reflex. And once she's in my arms, it's always a rush. Lianna's the perfect mix of cut and curves. I slowly run my nose down the length of hers. This isn't the time or place for this lovey-dovey bullshit, but for some reason, I can't help it. My mouth moves closer, and she lets out one of her little bedroom moans. Those kill me.

Our gazes meet, and I know that look. Lust. Heat flares through my bloodstream.

Maybe I should kiss her once. Get it out of my system, you know? What could it hurt?

I move even closer. My lips brush against hers and damn, I'm in trouble. Her mouth is liquid soft, like I thought it would be, as well as sugar sweet. We share the barest touch and it jolts through every part of my soul. Suddenly, nothing's more important than seeing her luscious naked body, touching her bare skin, and moving inside her. The craving in my blood is like a drug. This one kiss won't be enough. I need more. I'm about to get some when a soon-to-be dead man interrupts us.

"Surrender the Kristalli," he says.

No question who that is. An Air Valta. *Damn.* My concentration is crap. What am I doing kissing Lianna when I should be hauling ass out of here?

Thinking with my dick, that's what I'm doing.

And I can't even get pissed at my dick brain. The kiss really was that good.

I give Lianna one last brush of my lips, because I'm just that stupid. Next, I turn to face the Valta. They wear Roman centurion armor and are all in different shades of gray, including their eyes. They're pretty young, too.

"Surrender the Kristalli." Both Valta speak in unison and it definitely ups the creepy factor, but not by much. These kids give off the vibe that they're used to scaring the pants off anyone and getting whatever they want without a lot of work.

That changes tonight.

"Let me talk to Lianna about that for a sec." I turn to her. Somewhere along the line, I started holding her hand again. Feels good. "What do you say, beautiful?"

"Hmm," she taps her chin like she's really thinking this through. "I say we kill them."

"What?" asks one of the Valta. "You'll kill us? With what power? We are the Air Valta. Air is supreme!"

Why do they always talk down to her? It's like that Fisk freak all over again.

"Don't disrespect Lianna." I raise my arms. A cage of solid lightning surrounds each Valta. I summon them to tilt backwards in their prisons. They end up looking like two bodies in a matching pair of lit-up caskets.

The Air Valta test out their prison, just like Lianna did in our first fight. I made their cages solid. No way to escape. Once they figure this out, the Air Valta howl like a pair of cats in heat, and then turn even harder to see.

"What are they up to now?" I ask.

"Changing into smoke forms," answers Lianna. "It's more work so they don't do that too often."

Which means I need to kill them when they're solid.

"Good to know."

And just like Lianna again, they figure out pretty quickly that their new home is one hundred percent airtight. I lean in closer to their light-ning caskets.

"I got a deal for you. Promise to smoke your asses out of here, and I'll set you free. We can forget this ever happened."

The Air Valta howl some more and start spinning themselves into whirlwinds. I have to admit, I didn't see that one coming. Lianna turned into a dainty mist, and mist pretty much floats around. Wind does a lot more damage.

My lightning containers get bashed around. The walls get thinner. The Air Valta keep freaking out and slamming harder.

"I can't hold them much longer," I say. "They only need to crack the surface and they can smoke themselves out." I wince in pain. Imprisoning these Valta is sucking up tons of my life energy and my injury's getting worse. The poison's really going to town now.

Lianna kneels and sets her palms onto the browned grass. She closes her eyes and the ground starts to shudder.

I've a pretty good idea what she's going to do, and I like it.

The Air Valta go crazy, slamming and spinning inside their prisons. It's taking all my focus to keep their lightning caskets semi transparent and solid. Pain radiates out from my side.

After that, a lot of stuff happens at once. The Valta both whirl around so fast, they crack open their prison containers. The pair of them instantly speed toward us.

Before they make it over, Lianna opens up a massive water geyser in the ground, blocking them. In response, the Valta move their windstorm to a larger scale. The geyser flattens. Wind and water splatter everywhere.

"We're going down into the geyser," Lianna grabs my hand again. "Don't let go."

"No way, beautiful."

Together, we jump into the hole in the ground. For a while, my ass gets tossed around by currents from the geyser. As long as I hold onto Lianna, I can breathe fine and nothing slams into me too hard.

We come out through the ceiling of a cavern and land in an underground pool with a splash. The water's freezing. Even though I'm wearing body armor, it feels like thousands of tiny icicles are stabbing me all over. Lianna cups my face in her hands.

"Are you all right?"

"Yeah, I still feel a breeze though." I look up. "It's coming from the hole we just fell through."

"They're following us."

"Looks like." I look around the cave. "Want to stay and fight?"

"I'd rather get the Kristalli to safety." She shakes her head. "Plus, opening that geyser took a lot out of me. I won't be ready for a big battle any time soon. You?"

"I've felt better." The poisoned cut in my side throbs with pain. "We should go."

The air currents turn gray and the Air Valta start to take shape above our heads. Time to make tracks.

Lianna grabs my hand again and pulls me underwater. Together, we swim through a network of submerged caves and passages. I've no idea where we're going. Lianna pauses every so often and closes her eyes, accessing her powers. When she opens them again, we haul ass in a new direction.

Finally, we surface in a cave where our underground pool laps against a ledge of rock. Lianna conjures up some glowing blue mist so we can see what we're doing. Hissing with pain, I hoist myself out of the water and onto the rock ledge.

Lianna kneels down beside me. "What's wrong?"

"My side."

"Is it the cut from Silas?"

"Yeah. It's taking longer for me to heal than I thought."

She tugs at the collar of my body armor. "Take this off."

I shoot her a sly smile. "Are you sure this is the right time?"

"Says the guy who kissed me with Air Valta floating around." She tugs again. "Come on, don't be a baby."

It's not easy to do. Bit by bit, I peel off my body armor and whoa, I'm a mess. My chest is covered in a spider web of black poison lines.

Lianna gasps. "How long has it been this way?"

"Not long. I tired myself out containing the Valta. Gave the poison a chance to go to town."

She slips her fingers down my torso and even though I feel like crap, her touch makes me crazy. What is it about this woman? I'm freezing cold and injured, but I'd have sex right here if she gave me the go sign.

"I can pull out the poison," Lianna says. "It's a liquid, after all. That okay with you?"

"Is it going to sap your strength?"

"Probably."

"Then it can wait."

She tilts her head to one side. "Remember how I asked if it was okay with you?"

"Yeah."

"I take it back. You look like hell. I'm healing you whether you like it or not."

A shock of hurt rips through my torso. "I won't fight you."

She sets her palms flat against my chest, closes her eyes, and changes into her monarkki self. Blue light moves on her skin and flares from her palms. Her power moves through me, charging every cell I have with light and life. My energy responds to hers. Her sapphire light dances across my skin.

"You're soaking up my powers," says Lianna. "It's your lightning. Somehow, it's compatible with elemental energy."

More blue flares across my flesh and damn, it stings like a mother. "I wouldn't say compatible. Whatever's happening, it's not good."

"Should I stop?"

"No." I grit my teeth. "Keep trying."

"But I can't stop my powers from hurting you."

I picture the lightning cages I made for the Valta. Maybe they'll help here.

"I've got an idea," I say.

"Whatever you want." Her voice is shaky, and I know her already-low power reserves are getting more and more drained.

I summon a thin sheen of lightning around my body. That does the trick. Lianna's skin brightens once again. Her power moves through me, but in a different way. The poison disappears. Strength and life flow through my veins.

"Almost done," says Lianna.

For the first time in hours, my rib cage doesn't hurt like hell. "Feels good."

After that, it feels a whole lot better.

I don't know what Lianna's doing now. It's good, though. Every inch of me feels not only healthy, but downright awesome. A delicious tension builds until something inside me snaps. Pleasure ricochets along every nerve ending I've got.

Lianna pulls back her hands. We spend a lot of time staring at each other. It feels like a few minutes go by, but knowing our track record, we may have killed an hour that way. My skin's all healed and Lianna's so mellow, her eyes are half closed.

"Was that…" My voice cracks with emotion. I clear my throat to try and get a handle on it. "Was that how it's supposed to happen?"

"No. After I healed you," she clears her throat. "Well, I think my elemental powers went a little crazy there." Lianna blushes something fierce. "I'm not really a pro at controlling them yet."

"Hey, I'm not complaining."

"No?"

"No."

She leans in until our mouths are a breath apart. "That felt…" She opens her mouth, but no words come out. Her hand slides down my torso, leaving a trail of heat.

Now, that's a go sign if I ever saw one. And hell knows my body wants her. The old me would've nailed her right here. 'Hit it and quit it,' that was my motto. This time, that'd end up with someone getting hurt: Lianna. I can't do that to her. She deserves the whole dream. Like what G was talking about. A fancy ball and a handsome prince… But a *real* one. Not me.

"Look, Lianna. I can't believe I'm saying this." I cup her face in my hands. "We can't cross that line again. I have to stay away from you. I'm broken and you're," I run my thumb along her jawline. Man, I'd like nothing better than to kiss her again. "You're so fucking beautiful, it hurts to look at you."

Another breeze strikes up.

Damn, they found us again.

Lianna stares at me for another moment, shivers and turns away. I did it again. Made her feel like crap.

"Lianna, I—"

"We need to get out of here," she says, shutting me down. Her features are all closed off and distant. Not that I blame her.

"Should we go for another swim?" I ask.

"I can't keep that up much longer." Lianna rubs her temples with her fingertips. "Maybe I can try to use the Kristalli of Earth. Figure out where the Valta are in the ground and seal them in."

"Worth a try." I pull the small case from my pocket. Power crackles through the leather bindings and onto my palm, making my skin tingle with energy. The elemental power's trying to get at me again, so I quickly hand over the stone.

Lianna opens the wrappings. Inside, the crystal is amber brown and glows brightly. She sets her fingertip onto the stone's edge. There's a crackle and hiss as her skin gets fried. Lianna pulls back her hand. "Well, that isn't going to work." She rewraps the stone without touching it. I pull the Kristalli from her hands and reset it in my pocket.

"You okay?" I ask.

Lianna closes her eyes and holds her fist against her chest. Her palms glow blue behind her clasped fingers. A few seconds pass until she opens her hands again. "I'm fine. I was able to heal myself." She lets out a long sigh. "Wish I could rest, though."

Another breeze strikes up inside the cave, and this one is super fast. Before I know what's happening, two Air Valta stand before us.

Lianna mouths two words at me. "Play along."

I nod, wondering what she's going for.

It doesn't take long to find out. Lianna falls to her knees before the Valta. "Don't seal us in here!" she pleads.

The Valta stop and share a wicked smile. "We weren't going to. We are now."

"No!" screams Lianna. "Don't you dare imprison us!"

It's a good act, I'll give her that. I've never seen Lianna this upset. The woman had the entire Water Valta army pointing their crossbows at her, and she didn't break a sweat. But this? She's missing a career on the stage or something.

Lianna looks at me out of the corner of her eye. "Help here," she mouths.

Right. I got so caught up in her act that I forgot I had a part to play.

I kneel beside Lianna, wrapping my arm around her shoulder. "Oh, my sweet, delicate flower. I know how you fear being caged and alone." I whisper in a low voice. "Too much?"

She shoots me a thumbs-up, so I crank the act up a bit.

"Guys, she's terrified of being locked up. You can't leave her trapped in here, waiting for Zephyr. Just kill us now. It'll be better that way."

The Air Valta reform by the cave's ceiling. Their gray bodies hover in space as they chuckle to each other. The two of them remind me of nasty teenagers, the kind who like to pull the wings off butterflies.

"We have orders to guard you," says the first.

"And rough you up as necessary," adds the second.

The first Air Valta looks around the chamber. "Not sure I even know how to seal you in anyway."

Lianna goes extra hysterical. "This chamber's an old mineral pocket. It's already water tight except for a few cracks." She grips my shoulders and looks at me with crazy eyes. "All they have to do is go into those cracks, break things up and align them to seal us in. Zephyr does it all the time. It would be so easy! Tell them not to!"

I pat her shoulder and turn to the guys. "Whatever you do, don't be a couple of pricks here."

They share a big grin. Oh, they're going to be pricks all right.

The second Air Valta whispers to the first, then gestures toward us. "Since being sealed in bothers her so much, we'll go with that."

"No!" cries Lianna. I think she may have burst a blood vessel with that scream.

"Good-bye fools," says the first Valta.

With a puff of smoke, the two of them slip up through a crack in the wall. A crackle sounds as they seal the opening behind them.

"Wow." I sit back and kick my feet forward. "What a couple of dumbasses."

"Zephyr kills off his Air Valta for almost any reason. Now he's got teenagers fighting for him." She rises to her feet and winces in pain. "We won't see those two again."

Something tightens in my chest. *Lianna's in pain.* I rush to stand beside her.

"You don't look so good," I say.

"I don't feel so good."

"How do we get you out of here?"

"See that crack the Valta left through?" she asks. "Zap it back open with some lightning and I'll mist my way out."

"Got it." I raise my hand and a bolt of lightning instantly strikes at the crack in the rock. Bits of stone cascade to the ground. "That good enough?"

Lianna nods. "Perfect."

"And oxygen?" If she leaves, I'll need some way to breathe.

"I'm not strong enough to summon the water needed to supplement oxygen as well as turn myself into mist." Her pretty mouth thins to a worried line. "I'm sorry, Maxon."

"You definitely got enough power to mist yourself free, though?"

"I think so."

"Then do it. Go get help quickly. I'll be fine." Maybe blue and dead from lack of oxygen, but other than that, fine.

I rub my neck, my expression lost in thought. "Remember how to get to the Pulpitum that brought us here?"

"Sure."

"Go there first thing. When you arrive, get Diana on the line. Tell her 'opus auxilium ad thrax.'"

"What does it mean?"

"It's another pass phrase, like what I used in the desert with the guys."

"Got it. What then?"

"Ask for Ty. He'll come right away."

"Can he break through solid rock and get to you?"

"Ty's an unbelievable warlock. If anyone can do this fast, it's him."

Lianna nods, turns into a light blue mist and slips away. Once she's gone, the cavern turns dark and empty. I can't even see my hand in front of my face. The silence is so complete it makes my ears ring.

I wait for what feels like an eternity before the rock wall bursts apart, showering me with small stones and debris. A dim light fills the cave. After so much darkness, it blinds me so that I can't see a thing. All I know's what I sense.

Something's coming closer. There's a short list of who could pull off that blast.

It's either Lianna or Zephyr.

Please let it be Lianna. I can't fight what I can't see. A voice sounds in my ear and thank fuck, it's a familiar one.

Nizam.

"You're a pain in the ass, you know that?" he asks. "I was about to get some action when we got your SOS."

I shoot him a sly smile. "Your hand doesn't count, Zee."

Nizam laughs as more light pours through the fractured wall. I suck in a deep breath, the best oxygen I've had in ages.

I'm free.

13

LIANNA

an't be much farther now.

I whip through the skies as quickly as my mist form allows. Ty gave me a rendezvous point to meet up with him, Nizam, and with any luck, a whole and healthy Maxon. Sure, I could have taken the wizard up on his offer to teleport me, but teleportation spells are an energy suck.

Ty needs to save his power for Maxon.

The Pulpitum seemed so close to the Chocolate Hills before. Now, it feels like ages are creeping by as I race to the rendezvous point. Did I get lost in the dark? And why did I decide to be so noble, anyway? I should have gone with Ty. Who cares if he'd be a little more tired? At least, I'd be with Maxon right now.

Besides, what do I know about Ty, really? The guy could be the worst wizard in the after-realms. My throat constricts with panic.

Keep it together, Lianna. You're almost there.

At last, the rendezvous point comes into view. The place is heavy with magic. There's a cloaking spell here.

Which means Tyberius.

I reach out with my elemental energy. It takes a few tries—and a ton of power—but I'm able to pierce through the veil of enchantment.

The first thing I notice is an ear-shattering boom. Impact waves follow, throwing me backwards. One side of a hill explodes, leaving a massive crater behind. The air turns thick with debris and dust. My senses get overwhelmed with worry and alarm.

I stumble toward the crater. Kneeling down, I grip the line of grass that marks the edge of the blast. I scan the ground beneath me. Nothing's visible through the cloud of dirt. Bands of anxiety tighten around my temples.

Where are they?

I cup my hand by my mouth. "Maxon? Nizam?"

No reply.

At least, I can still sense Ty's cloaking spell. That means Tyberius and his magic are alive. My skin glows blue with worry.

I hope he's not the only one.

"Maxon!"

Finally, a trio of figures appears at the center of the crater. It's Tyberius and Nizam. Their arms loop across the shoulders of the third figure, who stumbles along between them. My torso slumps with relief.

It's Maxon. He looks like hell with torn body armor and too-pale skin.

But he's alive.

I force my features into some semblance of calm. The trio reaches the crater's edge before sitting down beside me. Ty mutters a spell over Maxon. Bit by bit, Maxon's color improves and his mismatched irises turn bright.

He turns to Ty. "Thanks, man."

"Opus auxilium ad thrax," says Ty. "I thought we were supposed to save that for real emergencies. I could have blown a crater here in my sleep."

"Don't be such a bitch," says Nizam. He points to the crater. "That's the closest 'you' and 'blowing' have gotten in years."

Nizam and Ty keep ragging on each other while Maxon's gaze finds mine. Our mouths slowly wind into identical smiles. An odd sensation comes over me. I feel like an invisible cord stretches between us, linking us together.

"You okay?" I whisper.

He nods. "You?"

I shrug. "You scared me half to death."

"Not that much, beautiful. You still look pretty alive to me."

Nizam and Ty stop talking trash long enough to stare at Maxon. And when I mean stare, it's one of the 'he's grown two heads' variety. I haven't seen surprise like that since Maxon invited me to stay in Arx Hall.

"Hey." Nizam points at Maxon's chin. "You're smiling."

Maxon hops to his feet, his grin staying firmly in place. "Who, me?"

"Yeah, you," replies Ty.

A swell of pride moves through my chest. Considering that comment,

Maxon must not have been a happy guy lately. If he's grinning now, maybe it's because of me.

"Any news from Antrum?" asks Maxon.

"Emperor Tempest sent a message," says Ty. "Arrived just before we left."

"Let me guess," says Maxon. "Zephyr's attacking."

"How'd you know?" asks Nizam.

"We know that he's after the Kristalli of Fire," I explain. "It's hidden in Furonium."

"Did T say how they're holding up?" asks Maxon.

"Worst part of the battle's over," replies Nizam. "Good news is that casualties were low. Bad news is that the Kristalli of Fire was stolen."

"What?" I ask. "How?"

"Some little sewn-up rat thing," says Ty. "Incarnate magic, if you asked me. It even had the little rat balls to drop off a message at one of our Pulpitum."

Maxon and I share a knowing glance. No question who's sending sewn-up demon rats all over the after-realms. Silas.

My insides twist with worry. Silas's rat got the Kristalli of Fire. What a disaster.

I picture Esau. The Fire Elementals have children, too. There must be thousands in need of healing. If Zephyr gets his hands on the Kristalli of Fire, he'll drain it. No chance for a new Monarkki of Fire, ever. No hope for healing.

"Did Silas already give the Kristalli of Fire to Zephyr?" I ask.

Ty shakes his head. "Tempest's spies say no."

"Good." I exhale a relieved breath. The Kristalli of Fire hasn't been drained.

Ty frowns. "Tempest also says he lost Chimera."

"What?" Maxon sets his fists on his hips. "I practically gift-wrapped him to them. Does T know what happened?"

"Tempest didn't say," says Nizam. "But we've gotten some intel from Purgatory."

Maxon's eyes narrow. "What did Grandma Cam and Pops have to say?"

For a second, my mind gets stuck on the whole 'Grandma Cam and Pops' thing. Then, I remember my father telling me how Maxon's grandparents run Purgatory. Makes sense that they'd send him news when he needs it.

"The bottom line is this," says Nizam. "Zephyr may be protecting Chimera. Nothing solid yet, but they could've teamed up."

"I'm calling bullshit on that one." Ty shakes his head again, hard. This time, his dreads jingle with the movement. "Elementals keep to their own. Why would Zephyr team up with anybody?"

The image of Silas's face appears in my mind. "Zephyr has teamed up before, believe me."

"Still doesn't make any sense," snaps Ty.

"You're questioning Lianna on this?" asks Maxon. Ty looks away. Right now, we're all a little tired and easily pissed off.

Ty fixes Maxon with a frustrated look. "What do you want me to say, M?"

"Nothing." Maxon folds his thick arms over his broad chest. "I want you to *think*."

I should be wound up in the play-by-play between Maxon and Ty, but I'm not. Instead, I'm gaping at Maxon's chest. The way he's folding his arms, the guy looks particularly ripped. I can't stop staring, and that's downright sad. How often do I have to be rejected before I get the message? We kiss outside the Chocolate Hills, and then inside the cave. Plus, there were a million other times where we got oh-so-close to kissing, only to have Maxon back off. The guy is right. He's got some serious issues. I need to move on.

So why can't I look away?

"Why would Zephyr link up with Chimera?" asks Maxon. "The question really is, why does Zephyr do anything?"

I raise my hand school-style. "So he can get his hands on a Kristalli and get a fix."

"Exactly," says Maxon. "Clearly, he thinks Chimera can get him the other stones." Maxon gives the ground a frustrated kick. "Zephyr wouldn't be wrong to think that, either. Chimera's smart."

Nizam pulls a small envelope from inside his body armor. "This message also arrived for you."

Maxon pulls it from Zee's hand. "Is this the one from the rat?"

"Yup."

My hands twitch to grab the letter. If Silas has the Kristalli, I need to know what he wants.

Ty twists a bead nervously through his fingers. "I know you get a ton of odd mail, M. Normally, we'd chuck this away. But once we heard about the Kristalli of Fire being stolen by a rat demon, we brought the envelope along."

"That was the right call," says Maxon. He hands the envelope to me. "You want the honors?"

"Thanks." I straighten my spine and try to look calm. Inside, the terrified thirteen year old that I once was is screaming in fear. After tearing the envelope open, I read aloud. "If you want the Kristalli, here are the coordinates. Come quickly and bring my girl. Zephyr may find me before you do. Silas."

The world takes on a surreal sheen. In my mind, the Chocolate Hills become misted over in a dreamlike haze. Bit by bit, the news seeps through my consciousness. Silas is luring me back to his lair, using the stolen Kristalli as bait.

Well, screw him.

My hands ball into angry fists. I am so done with running and fearing Silas. Zephyr too, for that matter. Rage flows through my body, making my internal light flare brighter. Time was, I had to run and hide. That's over and done with. Now, I'm facing this and ending it, one way or another. I turn away from Maxon.

"I have to go. These coordinates are in England. If I change into mist, I can get there pretty quickly."

Maxon steps into my path. "Not alone, beautiful. We'll go together."

"I can't ask you to join me," I say. "You just got healed. And in any case, I need someone I trust to protect Kristalli of Earth."

Maxon hands the Kristalli to Zee. "Lock this up in my personal safe." After that, he turns to Ty. "Any more healing spells you need to cast on me?"

"Nope," replies Ty. "You're one-hundred percent healthy."

"How's that?" Maxon turns his attention back to me. "Totally healthy and no more Kristalli. Now, I'm definitely going with you."

Wow, I kind of like it when he's a little possessive and pushy. Maxon sees he's wearing me down and adds in a dimpled smile. That just kills me.

"It's settled then." Ty slips the packet into the folds of his robes and nods. "You know how to find the nearest Pulpitum?"

"I remember." I rub my forehead in a nervous rhythm. "I'm still not sure about Maxon, though." I gesture to Tyberius. "You say he's fine, but you'd lie for him, wouldn't you?"

"I'd never when it comes to my prince's health. Besides, look how happy he is. He totally wants to go kill stuff with you. How can you say no?"

Maxon bobs his eyebrows up and down. "I know you want to check me out again, beautiful." He folds his arms across his chest once more, just like he did when I was last ogling him.

"I wasn't checking you out." *Much.*

"Maybe you want a repeat on playing doctor? Make sure I'm all healthy?" He pulls on his edge of his upper body armor. "I can whip this off pretty quick."

I can't help but stare at Maxon's pecs. Warmth crawls up my cheeks. The guys start chuckling.

"Trust me," says Nizam in his rumbling basso voice. "If Maxon can flirt, he can fight."

Maxon steps in closer, invading my personal space. "You heard what the badass thrax warrior said." I really shouldn't notice how good he smells, but I do. He's so yummy.

Stay focused on the defeating Silas, Lianna. "Okay, I'm convinced."

Maxon's smile widens. "You won't regret it, beautiful."

Somehow, I doubt I will.

14

LIANNA

*M*axon and I step through a dark and deserted shire somewhere in England. Normally, I love places like this. Everything's broken down and industrial. Cracked slate walkways. Abandoned factories choked with undergrowth. Smashed-up street lamps that droop at odd angles. When I was on the run from Zephyr, I hid in spots like this all the time. Usually, they make me feel safe.

Today, not so much. Instead, a cold sense of fear creeps across my stomach.

"You're nervous, yeah?" asks Maxon.

"How'd you guess?"

"You're having trouble staying human looking." He shoots me a half smile. "Not that I don't like you in monarkki blue."

I stare down at my skin. Maxon has a point. Strong emotions like fear always make me glow. Right now, I have some serious sapphire action going on.

"Walker used to hide me in spots like this," I explain. "Normally, I'd feel comfortable here."

"I'll take your word for it. I hate these kinds of places. Class A jobs love anything industrial." He gives my hand a gentle squeeze. "Walker probably cleaned them out for you before you got anywhere near. The guy's a killing machine."

"Walker, a warrior?" I picture the tall and gentle ghoul. "That's hard to believe."

"Oh yeah," says Maxon with a chuckle. "Walker's a total badass. Killer engineer and architect, too. Your regular Renaissance ghoul." We stop outside a one-story brick building with an arched roof and shattered windows. "We're here."

I stare at the lopsided wooden doorway. Silas is in there. Images flicker through my mind. My old cage. His scalpel and bone cutters. The tiny mouse cowering against my chest. Raw terror clamps around my body, encasing me from head to toe.

Maxon seems to read my thoughts. "Chances are, he's already flown."

A heavy sense of foreboding settles on my shoulders. "Nope, he's still in there." I stare at the crooked door intently, my skin starting to flare ever brighter shades of blue. "Promise me something."

"Sure."

"We kill him first thing."

"Wish we could, beautiful. But if we do that, we'll never lay our hands on the Kristalli of Fire."

"Then we kill him right after we find the Kristalli."

"That we can do." He tilts his head. "Want to do the honors?"

My voice turns hard and rough. "So long as he's dead, that's all I care about." I step forward, push the doors open and stride inside. The moment I'm past the threshold, awareness tickles across my skin.

No doubt about it. Someone's in here with us.

Dust and cobwebs cover every inch of the abandoned weaving factory. The floor is lined with small tables, moldy sewing machines, and broken metal looms. Long strips of wire hang down from the arched ceiling. Large skeins of thread hang at the bottom of each line, their bright colors now dimmed with dirt and age.

I'd think it was cool if I didn't know what kinds of things Silas was manufacturing here.

Thwack. Thwack.

The rhythmic pounding of a hammer sounds from the far wall, followed by the sickeningly familiar sound of small bones cracking. My chest tightens with anxiety.

Oh, yeah. Silas is here, all right.

Beside me, Maxon's tail arches over his shoulder, ready to strike. I summon a dozen bullets onto my palm, each one made from super-heated water. The small blue projectiles smoke and bubble against my skin. To anyone else, they'd cause excruciating pain. To me? I barely register a tickle.

From across the room, Silas starts humming one of his mock-spiritual songs.

"Thy power is naught," Silas sings. "Surrender to thy master."

The lyrics fill my soul with boiling-hot rage. Silas is trying to use my bad memories of his evil songs to give him some kind of advantage. I suppose he expects me to cry again, just like I did when I was a powerless kid.

Won't happen this time. I'm not thirteen anymore. And I'm certainly not powerless.

With each step closer to the far wall, more anxiety and excitement zing through my system. The footfalls of my boots become overwhelmingly loud, like a drumroll before a hanging. Overhead, the long ceiling wires no longer hold sewing supplies. Instead, each line ends in one of Silas's mummified birds. I'd call it taxidermy, but that would only involve using skin. Silas's black magic goes far deeper. Memories of his terrible spells flicker through my mind. An electric charge of anger makes my skin flare even brighter.

At last, we reach the far wall. Silas sits at a long metal table, tinkering with some unfortunate dead animal. Barrels of bloody slurry line the nearby walls. The smells of rot and death fill the air. I fight the urge to dry heave.

Lifting his arms, Silas repositions the animal that he's working on. It's the head and spine of a Rottweiler. Just grown to adult size, too, by the looks of it. All this demon does is corrupt innocence. Fury courses through me. I raise my palm, aiming the boiling bullets at his head. Silas flinches but doesn't turn around.

"What do you want, my girl?" he asks.

Above our heads, the mummified crows open their eyes. A jolt of fear runs through my limbs. The birds search the factory floor, their gazes quickly locking in on Maxon and me.

Keep calm, Lianna. Stay focused.

I set my hands on my hips. "You know why I'm here, Silas."

The old demon swivels around on his stool. He looks the same as always. Balding head, bowler hat, and handlebar moustache. He inspects me from head to toe, his irises flaring red with demonic power. "It's been so long. Why don't we rehash old times?"

Maxon's eyes also flare red, only brighter. "You don't get to talk to her." He raises his hand, making lightning dance upon his palm. "Where is the Kristalli?"

Silas's mouth winds into a smile, showing off his blackened teeth. "Zephyr told me all about you, boy." He inhales deeply. "Oh, I can smell her on your skin. Strawberry, so sweet. How was she?" He looks Maxon over. "I never saw her as more than a servant. Perhaps I misjudged things. She could be a succulent concubine as well. How I'd love to take her body before I take her life."

That does it.

On reflex, I raise my palm. A dozen water-bullets whip forward and tear through Silas's chest. He leans his head back and lets out a satisfying roar of agony. His gaze snaps back to mine. Fresh menace flickers in his all-red irises.

"That was uncalled for, my girl." Silas pokes his pointer finger through one of the holes in his dress shirt. "I can give you the exact coordinates to find the Kristalli of Fire. I have my price, however."

My mouth twitches with held-in words. How much would I love to whisper an incantation and take Silas down right now? It would feel sweet, but it wouldn't get me any closer to the Kristalli of Fire. Silas watches me, his thick lips rounding into a satisfied smile.

"I remain willing to discuss terms, my girl. Magically binding, of course. You know I always keep my word."

It takes everything I have to reply to Silas without separating his head from his shoulders. "I know."

"What do you want?" asks Maxon.

"I wanted my girl's life energy. That plan ended when she became an elemental." Silas rounds on me. "Your life force is worth nothing to me now. And this one?" Silas gestures to Maxon. "He's already vowed to kill me. I know the type. He won't stop until I'm dead."

Maxon's tail whips out in front of him. The arrowhead end points right at Silas's throat. "You got that right."

Silas steeples his fingers beneath his chin. "How I'd love to kill the prince. Sadly, that would bring all the thrax on my head. I'll pass on that, thank you very much. These are my terms."

"Go on," I say.

"I don't raise a hand against either of you, and you don't raise one against me. Ever. On pain of an especially gruesome death. In return, you get the coordinates for the Kristalli of Fire."

I frown. Something about this doesn't add up.

"Why risk Zephyr's anger?" I ask. "He won't be happy when the Kristalli isn't here."

"Don't worry about how I'll position the lost Kristalli to Zephyr. Someone will die for the error. It won't be me, I can assure you."

We all stare at each other for what feels like forever. Above our heads, the crow poppets shift their weight on their wire hangers. At last, I turn to Maxon. "What do you say?"

"Your call. I'll do the deal on your say-so."

I run through my options, but every mental path takes me to the same place. There's no doubt about it. I need the location of that Kristalli.

"We accept the deal," I say. "If you give me the coordinates right now."

Silas closes his eyes and starts mumbling in Latin. I don't catch all of it. That said, I hear enough to know that he's placing a binding spell. Once Silas opens his eyes again, all our hands flare with red flame. There's a spike of pain that ends within seconds.

"Pleasure doing business with you," says Silas with a crooked smile. He gestures to one of the nearby barrels of bloody sludge. "The Kristalli is attached to the bottom of that barrel."

Rage corkscrews up my spine. "Sneak! You made it sound like you hid it somewhere else."

"I know I did. Rather clever of me, wouldn't you say? Otherwise, you might have killed me long ago. Now, we've a binding agreement." He rises to stand. "If you'll excuse me."

Above us, the birds spread their wings, showing off their long silver feathers. Or, they should be feathers. Instead, they're layers of long razors bolted together. Their clawed feet are made from rusted nails.

Maxon frowns. "I thought we weren't raising a hand against each other."

"We did agree to that," says Silas slowly. "However, that deal only includes me. My poppets can do as they like. Unfortunately for you, they like to kill."

A crow dive bombs me. I try to dodge the attack, but I'm not fast enough. The bird holds a scalpel in its claws and I know what that means: Poison. As the crow swoops lower, the blade scratches my cheekbone. Silas's poison enters my system. This is his fast-acting stuff, too. Within seconds it starts sapping my strength.

Now, I'll be limited to small strikes. Not good.

Turning on his heel, Silas runs for the back door. Maxon and I rush to follow him, but the birds are faster than we are. Dozens of them swoop down from their wires, attacking us in coordinated strikes. We're forced into defensive mode while Silas heads toward the exit.

There's no time to follow him, though. More crows dive for us, their eerie caws echoing around the factory. I kill the birds with ice darts, while Maxon summons lightning. His bolts blast through the ceiling, smashing through old desks and dusty equipment. Unfortunately, whatever black magic fuels the birds also makes them immune to these strikes. Maxon tries different lightning forms—cages, swords and shields —but the only thing that stops the birds are traditional bolts. Even then, I think it's the sound and brightness that shocks them more than anything else.

In no time, Maxon is forced to give up on lightning. Instead, he skewers the birds with his tail or tears open their chests with his dragon-scale hand. It's slow going. Still, it works pretty well.

I switch things up and summon long water whips, one in each hand. Flicking my wrists, I use the super-heated liquid weapons to slice through the birds as they close in. Before I know it, Maxon and I are fighting back to back, each of us downing whatever poppets come our way. Maxon mumbles something unintelligible. My whips slice through more birds. "What did you say?"

"I've never had a battle twin before." I can hear the smile in his voice, and suddenly, my boiling-hot rage at Silas cools a little.

"Me, neither." I test out a crisscross move with my whips and take out a half-dozen birds in one strike. "It's kind of fun. We're pretty good at this."

A low growl sounds from behind me and I freeze. A razor-winged hawk swoops close to my ear. I smash in its head with the handle of my whip. Fresh howls fill the air.

A prickly sense of fear crawls up my neck. "What was that noise?"

"Hounds." The joking tone Maxon had a moment ago is gone. With only that single word, I know we're in deep trouble.

From across the factory floor, more birds awaken from their wires. We haven't even made a serious dent in their numbers, and now we have mummified demonic hounds to deal with.

Correction. We're in *really* deep trouble.

The hounds start circling our position. Maxon calls down fresh lightning, but the dogs easily sidestep the bolts. Even worse, the strikes distract Maxon from killing poppets with his hand and tail.

A memory appears. Namare telling me to summon my elementals in case of danger. How can I summon the Valta? The last time I asked for their aid, it was face to face, and they kicked me out of my own palace. A remote summons is sure to fail.

One of the hounds gets closer. The animal is huge and could easily tower over me if it put its paws on my shoulders. Its eyes are metallic stones and its mouth has broken glass for teeth. The creature's rib cage has been cracked open and sewn back together with thick black leather straps. I shudder, thinking what Silas must have placed inside that creature to make it so evil.

The hound's eyes flare bright red as it leaps onto my shoulder, digging its teeth into my already-injured skin. Fresh pain radiates from the wound. I drop my ice whips, snap the beast's neck, and toss the carcass aside. More of my life energy goes into fighting my injuries. Less power is available to battle Silas's poppets and poison. Of the two, the poison's really starting to do me in. Black puss oozes from around my wounds. My legs feel like they're made of jelly. Sure, I know how to heal myself, but that'll take all my concentration.

That's time I don't have.

The hounds circle us as more birds swoop in for the kill. "Got any big ideas?" asks Maxon.

"I'm calling in reinforcements. Cover me."

Maxon turns and pulls me against his chest. With a great battle cry, he summons bolt after bolt of lightning to strike the ground around us. The sudden onslaught buys us some time. Leaning into Maxon's chest, I reach out with my consciousness to my people.

I am your monarkki. I need your help.

A pulse of acknowledgement moves through my mind. I could whoop with joy, I'm so excited. One of my water elementals definitely heard me.

I pull back from Maxon. "Done!"

Maxon releases me and spins around so we can fight back-to-back once more. His back shifts against mine as he takes out another hound.

"Did I get you enough time?" asks Maxon.

"I hope so."

Before me, a bright blue mist appears. Excitement tingles through my stomach.

"It's Fisk," I say quietly.

"Not sure how much help he'll be." Maxon takes out another demon bird with his tail. "You know what he thinks. We're lovers."

Quick as a flash, Fisk materializes before me. I keep working the whips to hold off the hounds, but I can't keep it up much longer. Despite the battle, some part of me registers the look of total devastation in Fisk's sea-green eyes.

He heard the last two words Maxon said.

We're lovers.

"Fisk, we're outnumbered and..." Before I have a chance to finish, Fisk disappears.

My limbs feel sluggish with disappointment. Suddenly the onslaught of demonic animals seems far too much for anyone to handle. And now? I've just managed to isolate the one person who could've helped us.

"I've enough energy for one last round of lightning," says Maxon over my shoulder. "Once I summon it, you need to run."

Well, that's not happening.

"No way. I'm staying with you."

"Well, I'm not..."

At that moment, bright blue light floods the factory. Water elementals of every shape and size cover the stone floor. Large snake-like creatures with blue scales rear up on their coils and start snapping demon birds into their jaws. Beasts that resemble a cross between bears and salamanders tear into the hounds. Fisk takes out his blue sword and dives into the center of the fighting.

These aren't professional soldiers, but they aren't nothing, either. What does it say that Fisk wouldn't or couldn't summon his own Valta?

There's no time to answer that question. More birds and hounds lunge at Maxon and me, but the numbers are back to being reasonable. Meanwhile, my rank-and-file elemental army goes to work.

Relief saps every ounce of energy from me. We may actually win this one. Suddenly, the poison in my system boils through me at a faster pace. Pain overwhelms my mind. I close my eyes and curl into a fetal position. Voices echo around me.

"Take her away!" cries Fisk. "She needs somewhere quiet to heal."

Heavy arms loop around my shoulders. I'd know that touch anywhere. It's Maxon.

"I've got you, Lianna." He kisses my temple. "It's safe now. Heal yourself, beautiful."

I close my eyes and summon my elemental power from within. Every molecule of poison inside my system becomes surrounded with sapphire light. I call more energy until every part of me is whole and healed. The poison is gone, but now I'm so tired, I could fall asleep on Silas's floor.

Bit by bit, I force my eyes to open. The first thing I see is Fisk.

Oops.

Last time Fisk saw me, Maxon was only holding my hand and Fisk had an all-out meltdown. This time, I'm cradled in Maxon's arms, only Fisk doesn't look angry so much as sad. I clench my jaw in worry. In some ways, this side of Fisk is harder to deal with, especially since I need to ask him for more help.

Now that the Kristalli of Fire and Earth are safe, it's time for me to be crowned Monarkki of Water. I need to heal my people and get connected to their energy. That way, I'll have a better chance against Zephyr. But for that to happen, the Water Valta must agree to my coronation. I must ask Fisk to get his troops in line.

Will he agree to help me?

My eyelids feel heavy as boulders. I want to sleep, but who knows when I'll see Fisk again? We must have this conversation now. Somehow, I manage to wobble up to my feet.

"You good?" asks Maxon.

"I feel fine. I just need a minute."

"You got it." He leans in to whisper in my ear. "Go get your crown, beautiful." His sweet words give me a jolt of hope.

Maxon heads off toward the barrel where Silas stashed the Kristalli of Fire. It's not very badass of me, but I'm psyched that I'm not on Kristalli duty. I spent enough time around Silas and his bloody goop.

With Maxon gone, Fisk and I start staring at each other without really staring. It's really awkward. Since I keep feeling sleepy and woozy, it's also making me nauseated.

Be strong, Lianna. Remember Esau. You need to get crowned and go to work.

I nod once to myself. Decision made. Fisk has to get his Valta on board, end of story. At this point, the only question is how I can convince him to help. A practice speech runs through my mind.

Thanks for saving my life, Fisk. And I really appreciate you not freaking out that Maxon was holding me just now. So... Can you convince all your buddies to crown me monarkki? That'd be great.

Not sure that's it, and I'm too tired to come up with something better. Best to lead off with something neutral. "Thank you, Fisk."

"Lianna, I..." Fisk stops speaking and looks away.

This is your chance, Lianna. Go for the close.

I open my mouth, but my brain gets even fuzzier with the need for sleep. Wow, do I ever want a nap. Before I can figure out something to say, Fisk disappears in a haze of blue mist.

How very Fisk of him. I'd punch him in the face if he were still here. And if I weren't so tired.

Maxon returns to my side. His mismatched eyes scan me from head to toe. "You don't look good."

"The Kristalli..." I try to say more. Sadly, my mouth doesn't want to form any words other than 'pillow' and 'sleep.'

"I got the Kristalli of Fire," says Maxon. "Dumped over the barrel and the thing was strapped to the bottom." He scoops me up in his arms. Suddenly, the world feels all cozy, warm, and snooze-worthy.

Four words register in my mind before I let myself slip into sleep.

"We're going home, Lianna."

15

MAXON

What a long-ass day. For once, I can't wait to get some sleep. Lianna's conked out in another bedroom. Now, it's my turn.

I look around and frown. My room's all modern and sleek, with a huge bed and clean white sheets. *I don't belong here.* Most days, I crash in moldy motel rooms with cockroaches and blinking neon lights by the window. I stay where the monsters are.

Some days, I feel like I'm one of them, too.

I peel off my body armor, pull a pair of pajama bottoms out of a drawer, and slip the things on. That's something else that I never do on the road. Sleep in clothing. But with Lianna around…

Hey, now.

The back of my neck tingles with awareness. Someone's staring at me. Turning around, I see Lianna standing in the doorway. She's wearing a pair of tight boyshort bottoms and a flimsy tank top that leaves little to the imagination. She looks smoking hot. I need to thank that Mistress of Cloth, whoever she is.

"What's up, beautiful? Feeling better?"

"Yeah, a quick nap was all it took. I'm working on my speed-healing skills."

I smile. A real warrior is always working on some skill, and Lianna is a real warrior. "How'd things go with Fisk? You fell asleep before I could ask you."

"He misted away before we could talk."

"And what do you think that means?"

"He knew I was going to ask for his help with the Valta, and he was too much of a weasel to say 'no.'"

"So what's your plan now?"

"Honestly, I don't know. I need a few days to get my head together. Come up with a new approach."

I raise my arms and stretch. "You can crash here if you like."

"Sure, thanks." She stares at my chest and looks away, her skin flaring a brighter shade of blue. I try not to notice that reaction. We're supposed to be just friends, after all. Still, I notice it anyway. And I can't stop myself from talking about it.

"You don't have to get embarrassed for checking me out."

"What?" She lights up even more.

"We're adults. We're single. There's no law against appreciating each other. In fact, the Furor have it down to a science." I pull back the covers on my bed.

Her mouth thins with disbelief. "Like what kind of science?"

Oh, this is too good to pass up.

I step over to stand in front of her. Her body heat warms my bare skin. She gives me another of her little gasps as I run my fingertip down her neck. I pause and pull my hand away.

Do the right thing here, Maxon.

Somehow, I find the balls to cross the room and go back to my bed.

"You didn't come here to talk about Furor lore." I slide into bed and fidget with the covers, like I give a crap about that stuff. It's easier than looking at her, though. "What's up?"

"I don't like sleeping in strange places." Lianna forces a smile. "I don't like sleeping, period."

"Your nightmares?"

She nods.

"I get it. Believe me."

"Good." Lianna anxiously twists her fingers together at her waist. "Then can I, uh, stay here? Last time, it really helped to have you nearby."

My heart starts thumping against my chest. *Love this idea.* That's when I notice how other parts of my anatomy are excited, too. Good thing I've got the covers pulled up past my waist.

Play it cool, Maxon. Remember why you put the brakes on this in the first place. Taking things too far will only hurt her.

"Sure." I slide across the bed and pat the space beside me. She slips in under the covers and cuddles into my side. With her wound against me, my senses are assaulted with sweetness. I love how her long limbs entwine with mine. The way her liquid-soft fingers rest on my belly.

How every cell in my body is attuned to her, wanting her. And if I'm being honest with myself, caring about her, too.

I wrap my arm around her shoulder. "Better?"

She sighs. "Yes, much."

"Any time."

Lianna's quiet for a minute. "Can I ask you a question?"

"Sure." I twirl a lock of her silky hair around my fingertip. "Ask me anything."

She inhales a deep breath. "What else happens in your nightmares? You said it was dark…" She swallows the rest of her words.

Normally, any mention of my time with Armageddon makes me crazy, but while holding Lianna? It's impossible to feel anything other than calm.

"You don't have to tell me," adds Lianna quickly.

"No, it's cool. Armageddon's what happened."

"The King of Hell?"

"Yeah."

She looks at me expectantly. Now, I'm getting to another part I've never shared with anyone. When I was a kid, I said I couldn't remember anything about my time in Hell. That was a lie. I've never told a soul, yet somehow, it's okay to tell Lianna. She's been at the mercy of evil, too. She'll understand instead of getting her mind blown.

I run my thumb up and down her shoulder. "My nanny Hildy was a monopsyche."

"I've heard about those. She could take over your mind, put you in a trance or whatever?"

"Yeah, it's a bodyguard technique. Protected me from pain or torture." A cold shiver rocks my spine. "But when I was taken into Hell, Hildy wasn't fully bonded to me. She couldn't protect me all the time. Every minute that I was exposed and unconnected, Armageddon knew it. That's when he'd pull me out of my prison box."

Lianna keeps looking at me. There's empathy there, sure, but something else, too. A connection. Suddenly, it's not a choice to tell her everything, it's something I *have* to do.

"Armageddon tortured me." My voice cracks with remembered pain. "Peeled off my skin. Plucked out my eyes. Beat me until I passed out." Emotion tightens up my chest. "I was a fucking three-year-old kid."

She rubs my stomach in a gentle rhythm. "Oh, Maxon."

"Afterward, he'd always fix me up and put me back in my prison box. The freak knew that my parents could see me sometimes, and he thought that hiding my torture was hilarious. Even for the King of Hell, the guy was a sick fuck."

I pull her closer. "After I left Hell, I promised myself that I'd never be at the mercy of a demon again. Now, I hunt Class A jobs like Armageddon. That's my life." I exhale a long breath. "Not much of an existence compared to some. Like I said, I'm broken."

There's a long pause before Lianna speaks again. "I understand, Maxon. Really." She's talking about more than the story. She means about us. I hoped she'd get what happened to me without losing her mind, but understanding why we need to stay friends? That seems like way too much to expect.

Can this really be happening?

"Understand what?" I ask, unsure.

"Why you're trying to protect me." She gently kisses my shoulder. "And maybe, you're trying to protect yourself, too. It's all right. I'm not going anywhere, Maxon. Whatever happens, I am your friend."

My torso warms with a feeling I'm terrified to name. She heard my story. She gets me. How unbelievable is that? It takes some effort, but I choke out three words.

"Only you, beautiful."

And that's what makes staying away from her so hard.

She gives my shoulder another kiss. "Better?"

I kiss the top of her head. "Yeah, better."

And for the first time in what feels like forever, that might actually be true.

16

LIANNA

S ure enough, sharing Maxon's bed means no nightmares.

Trouble is, it means no sleep, either.

I flip over again. Nervous energy pulses through my limbs. This is like sitting next to a chocolate cake when you haven't had dessert in ages. Hard to keep your hands to yourself.

I keep watching Maxon sleep, making note of every movement. Hey, it passes the time. I can't miss how Maxon's face looks handsome-rugged, even when he's asleep. How he arches his muscled arm above his head. How he slowly licks his full lips. Yow, I felt that last one right between my thighs.

Maybe this wasn't my best idea.

Turning flat on my back, I jam my pillow over my face. In this position, I'll either die of suffocation or fall asleep without any distractions. Either way, the sexual torture will be over. The rational part of my brain points out that actually leaving the bed would be the best solution to my problem, but rational me isn't getting lots of airplay at this point. I'm staying right where I am.

Actually, I'm pretty impressed that I was able to get the pillow over my face at all.

I inhale deeply and immediately, my huge error is clear. The pillow smells like a whole lot of Maxon. It's a mix of cinnamon, sweat, and yum. This is definitely not helping my focus issues. I pull down the pillow to find Maxon leaning over me, an amused smile rounding his delicious mouth.

"Hey," he says.

"Oh, hi," I reply, like I'm surprised to find us both in the same bed together. "You were snoozing for a while there. I thought you only slept an hour a night."

"Normally, yeah." Maxon stretches again; this time both arms are involved in the act. His muscles are so ripped, they have little baby muscles, too. I really need to stop staring one of these days.

"Running after you must tire me out," he says. His mismatched irises glimmer in the soft glow of candlelight. "Any nightmares?"

"No, you?"

"Me neither. Seems like you're good for me."

A bubble of excitement forms in my chest. "Same here."

"In that case, there's something I want to talk about." Maxon sets his hand on my hip, and I already like where this conversation's going.

"Sure."

"I won't sugar coat this. I'm broken, maybe in ways that can never be fixed. For years, my life's been nothing but demon slaying and one-night stands. That scare you?"

"It's nothing I didn't know about before. Guess the question is, does it scare you?"

"Maybe it worries me now, yeah." Maxon leans in until our foreheads touch. His skin feels warm and firm against mine. My breath hitches as his voice sounds low in my ear. "You're perfect, Lianna. Absolutely beautiful. And I want something to happen between us."

My excitement bubble explodes, sending tendrils of heat through my body.

Maxon thinks I'm perfect.

"I've been thinking about it a lot." Maxon's fingers tighten on my hip. "Maybe you want that, too."

I almost give myself whiplash nodding. *Yes.*

"Well, then." He tilts his head back and offers me a sexy smile. "I couldn't live with myself if I didn't try. How about you?"

I'm pretty sure what he wants to try here. However, my mind's a pile of overjoyed goo at this point. I need to make sure that I'm absolutely clear. If we're just sleeping together, I can't do that. I'm not the casual sex type. But if it's something more? That's another story.

When my gooey brain finally remembers how to speak, my words come out low and breathy. "Try what, Maxon?"

"Why, making you happy, beautiful." He rubs the bridge of his nose along mine. "Only you. Give me that chance, yeah?"

My mind empties of all thought, save one. "Yeah."

Maxon's lips crash onto mine. Desire flares through me and a small moan escapes my mouth.

"Damn," groans Maxon. "Your little noises drive me crazy."

I moan again and suddenly, Maxon's hands are everywhere. Taking off my tank. Sliding my boy shorts down my legs. All the while, his tongue rides against my own, fierce and rough. Desire spikes between my thighs. Maxon whips the covers off us. Somewhere along the line, he kicked off his pajama pants. Shock and desire roll through me. I've never seen Maxon entirely naked before, and every last inch of him is gorgeous. In the dim light, he soaks in the sight of my bare body, too. Bands of desire wind about us, connecting us.

"Is this…" I want to ask if this intensity is from his lust demon. I can't get the words out.

"Is this what?" Maxon leans over me, his fingertips brushing up my outer thigh. Heat rushes through my limbs. The ability to form words fails me for a while.

"The Furor," I whisper. "Different." Part of me realizes I'm talking in sentence fragments. More of me is amazed that I'm able to speak at all.

"The Furor see lust as a science." Maxon's voice comes out low, growly, and sexy. "They taught me how to focus my inner demons. Lust and wrath, I integrate both of them into my soul. Control their power. Make their experience more intense for my partner." Maxon nuzzles into my neck. "Your body is a map to your pleasure, Lianna. It starts with tracking your heartbeat. The dilation of your irises. How flushes move across your skin." His tongue flicks across my earlobe and I shudder. "You like it when I talk."

I nod quickly. *Yes, yes, yes.*

His fingers slide down my belly, circle across my hip and glide between my thighs. I gasp. He touches my heat and I'm seeing stars.

"So responsive," he says in his low voice.

I can only moan in reply.

He smiles that sexy grin of his. "And we haven't even gotten to the good stuff yet."

The good stuff. That's where I want to be.

I guide Maxon closer until his body rests atop mine, his strong arms braced on either side of my head. He slides inside me and I gasp. Time stands still as our bodies move and ecstasy mounts.

We kiss. We touch. We become one person.

Sensations multiply until it's all too much. Bliss builds through me and then shatters my soul. I arch my back as the delicious release careens through my every molecule. Maxon groans as he finds his satisfaction along with mine. Our unified motion slows, then stops. Time moves forward once again.

"Wow," I say, my voice low and husky.

A satisfied smile rounds Maxon's mouth. "Yeah."

Someone starts knocking on the front door of Maxon's chambers. Tilting his head, Maxon carefully listens to the odd rhythm of the knock. More thrax codes, if I had to guess.

He kisses my cheek. "I'll be right back."

Maxon slips out of bed and immediately, I miss the sensation of his body next to mine. Maxon pulls on a long silk robe and walks out the door. From the entry hallway, I hear low voices talking back and forth. Maxon returns a few minutes later.

"G wants me over to have breakfast."

I prop my weight on my elbow and try to look alert. "At this time of night?"

"It's early morning now." He offers me one of his crooked grins. "I'd say no, but she'd just come here." He scans me carefully. "Want to go?"

I want to say 'Sure, I'll go,' but my face muscles are so tired, it comes out as "Sue, ruff roh."

Maxon chuckles. "You get some sleep, yeah?"

I want to hit him with a cute comeback. Doesn't happen. For some reason, my mouth isn't capable of speech. Even so, the moment is perfect and peaceful. I don't know what our future holds, but like Maxon said, I couldn't live with myself if I didn't try. I mumble something else that's totally incoherent and Maxon kisses my head.

The last thing I remember is the click of the door closing as I fall asleep.

17

MAXON

I walk up to the fancy wooden doors to G's formal reception chamber. A knight stands on either side of the entrance. Both wear golden armor. Before I have a chance to greet them or even knock, the door swings open.

"Maxon, my boy!" G kisses my cheek. She's in her full-bore thrax Queen get-up today. Black velvet dress, tiara, the whole deal. She's even gotten her gray hair braided into a fancy bun.

"You look great, G."

"As do you." Her mismatched eyes get all sparkly with excitement. "You wore your formals."

"I was in the mood." Normally, I never wear my princely get-up if I can avoid it. Today, I know G summoned me here to talk about Lianna. Feels like I'm respecting Lianna to get dressed up.

G fixes the guards with a look that could melt lead. "No interruptions, do you understand?"

"Yes, Your Majesty," they say in unison. I swear they shake a little in their armor, too. G has that effect on people.

G ushers me inside. "Look who's here!" she calls.

My parents shift on G's elegant white couch. They both stare at me with bug eyes and open mouths.

"You're on time," says Mom.

"And wearing your formals," adds Dad.

"That I am," I say with a smile.

They exchange a long look, their eyebrows lifting in unison. I know that move. It means 'oh ho ho, let's hope Maxon's got himself a girlfriend.' They've been sharing this look since I was twelve. Usually, I spend a half hour telling them how they're wrong. Not this time.

I give Mom a quick kiss hello. Dad gets his traditional man-hug. After that, I head straight to where G's stashed all the food. I don't know what she does, but I swear, she gets way better grub than the rest of us. I scoop up a plate and start digging in.

G hovers by the table's end. "I suppose you're wondering why I asked you here."

"Not in particular," I say. "You want news about Lianna." I find some egg pancakes things that look pretty good. I grab seven.

"Only if you want to share," says G. "We didn't want to assume anything was going on."

"Well, something's going on." I pile on more pancakes. Damn, they smell good. I have to hang out with G more often. "What do you want to know?"

G eyes me carefully. "You went cloud-side on some mission with Lianna. Did everything work out satisfactorily?"

"Yup. We got the Kristalli of Fire and Earth. They're both in my safe." I shoot her a sly look. "Like you didn't know."

"Well," G pats down her perfectly patted-down hair. "Nizam may have mentioned something."

Nizam this time? He's joining my payback list, right next to Uther.

"How is she now?" asks Mom. "Zee said she was hurt."

"She's great. All healed up." I flash Mom a big, toothy smile. "She's in my room, sleeping."

My family gasps. Loud. I never tell them shit about the girls I'm with. But Lianna isn't just any girl. She's perfect, she's mine, and I want everyone to know it, including that weasel, Fisk. I plunk down on a nearby couch, set the plate onto my lap, and chow down.

G and my parents all take seats nearby. They stare at me like I'm a ghost or something.

"Come on," I say. "It's not like you didn't see this coming."

Mom sighs. "We hoped."

Dad grins. "I'm happy for you, son."

G stares at me for a long time. "You're serious then?"

"Yup."

"But... But..." G's face gets all blank.

Dad chuckles. "Now this is something I've never seen before. I do believe you've rendered your Grandmother speechless."

A rapid knock sounds at the door. G frowns. "I told them we didn't want to be disturbed." She gives the door another one of her angry glares. "They do this all the time."

Mom stares at the door. "Sure we shouldn't get it?"

"Absolutely not," says G. "I don't give orders to have them ignored." She rounds on me. "And you need to be careful with your heart, my boy. You hardly know this girl."

I set my empty plate aside. "Look, this might seem fast to you, but Lianna and I have had some pretty intense times. We've fought together. More than once. You get to know someone pretty quickly that way."

G's face softens. She's a warrior. She gets how intense the battlefield is. You can know someone for years and still not see their soul until you fight side by side. Her approval makes a warm feeling seep through me.

G grins. "That's good to hear, my boy."

"Plus, she gets me in a way that no one else ever has." I picture holding Lianna in my arms while telling her about my torture at the hands of Armageddon. My voice gets low and serious. "It's good. We're good. Really."

Mom's lower lip gets all trembly. This is a total Hallmark Card moment for her. "Maybe we should..." her voice breaks.

"... Talk about the ball that your grandmother is planning," says Dad, finishing Mom's thought for her. They do that a lot. Makes me wonder if Lianna and I will ever do that, too. Something in my chest gets all jittery. Finishing each other's sentences. Yeah, that could be cool.

"Quite right," says G. "We brought you over to discuss the details of Lianna's big night."

I lean back and kick my boots onto some kind of antique something. "Do whatever you think'd make Lianna happy. I'm up for anything."

Before anyone can answer, a distinctive hum fills the air. I freeze. No question about it. A ghoul portal is opening.

G pinches the bridge of her nose. "If they sent Walker in here because I wouldn't answer the door, then I'm about to be rather peeved."

Rather peeved. That's G-speak for someone getting their asses handed to them.

A black door-shaped hole forms in the middle of the reception chamber. Walker steps through in his long ghoul robes. The lines of his colorless face are drawn tight with worry. He rounds on me without saying hello.

"Why can't I get into your chambers?" asks Walker.

"Why do you ask?"

Okay, I actually have a pretty good idea why he's asking. He wants to get at Lianna. I'm in no mood to make things easier for him. The guy needs to keep his overly long hugs to a minimum.

"I must speak to Lianna. It's urgent."

"My chambers have about a hundred wards and hexes on them. You're not getting in there without me."

Walker rubs his hands over his brush-cut. The guy looks ready to explode. Could something really be wrong with Lianna? A million problems flicker through my head. She could be sick or cursed.

Mom asks the question that's on all of our minds. "What's wrong, Walker?"

"It's Zephyr," he says.

"Oh, him." My shoulders relax. "Well, he can't get to Lianna in Antrum."

"He's got his Air Valta out," says Walker. "He's given us an hour. He says that unless we hand over Lianna by then, he'll cut off the air to Antrum."

Everything turns surreal. Cut off the air to my people? Risk Lianna? This is like something out of my nightmares.

"Can he do that?" asks G.

"Yeah, he can," I say. "Some of his junior people did it in a cavern that Lianna and I were in."

Dad hops to his feet. "We can't let word get out."

"It's already out," says Walker. "People are in a panic."

"Nonsense," counters G. "Thrax won't panic about some elemental riff-raff."

I grit my teeth at the 'elemental riff-raff' crap. "Lianna's a monarkki, G. If she were threatening us, I'd worry. You get me?"

"Maxon's right," adds Dad. "Zephyr's a serious threat. Our people will never forget King Aethelwulf's war. Antrum's air got cut off and whole Houses died of asphyxiation. Antrum exists in a very delicate balance." Dad turns to Mom. "We need to calm the people. Make sure they know we have everything under control."

Mom nods. "I'll send an igni display through the cities. That always works wonders."

So does a laser light show. Not that I'll say that to Mom. We have bigger fish to fry than starting yet another 'igni versus lightning' debate.

"Very well," says G. "I'm convinced. I'll set up a command center. We need couriers running in shifts between here to Purgatory. Cam and Xav always get news first."

Cam and Xav. That's what G calls my other grandparents. Everyone else calls them Madame President and First Archangel. G turns to me. "Are you coming?"

"No, I'm staying to talk to Walker."

"Oh," G's face loses all color. "You're leaving your people?"

Frustration twists up my neck. I know what this is really about. G has liked worrying about me having a girlfriend. That said, she's not keen on my actually *getting* one. She and I have been close since I was a kid. Me settling down? It must feel like I'm leaving her.

Truth is, I am.

"I'm going after Lianna, G. Wherever it leads. End of story." I'd add that helping Lianna helps everyone, but G isn't in a logical mood.

"Come on, Mother." Dad wraps his arm around G's shoulder and leads her toward the door. "Let's leave Maxon and Walker to their talk."

Mom drops a quick kiss on my cheek. "Go kick ass and take names, baby."

I smile. Mom's the best. Within a few seconds, my parents and G are gone. I refocus on Walker.

"What's got you worried?" I ask. "Tell me everything."

Walker's all-black eyes fix me with a bleak stare. "If Lianna thinks Zephyr's after her, she'll do what she always does. Run. She'll find a new safe house, somewhere that she thinks won't endanger you or your people."

"But you always set those up for her. She wouldn't leave without talking to you, would she?"

"I'm already getting a new place ready for her. The problem is Fisk."

An electric sense of alarm charges through my brain. "What about that guy?"

"I keep in touch with some of the lesser Valta," explains Walker. "I heard that Fisk feels terrible about what happened at the Water Palace."

"Good. He should feel like shit."

"Now he wants to make it up to her. I'm worried that he'll jump the gun and get a message out to her before we can talk to her."

"What he should do is get her crowned. Once Lianna is the monarkki, she'll be connected to the power of her people. She'd have a better chance against Zephyr."

"You think he'll do that?" asks Walker.

"No," I say. "The guy's thinking with his dick."

"Are you sure?"

"I think with my dick a lot; I would know. Fisk wants Lianna back and he isn't thinking things through. He won't try to get her crowned; he'll try to get her alone. That means a safe house."

Walker steps closer to me, his mouth thinning with worry. "And that's what I'm afraid of. If Fisk tries to put her in a safe house, it won't really be safe."

I pace the room, my mind churning over this news. "Lianna's not a prisoner here. She's free to get messages or leave any time she wants."

Memories flood my head. The feel of her liquid-soft body under mine. The scent of strawberries on her skin. The rush in my heart, knowing what we were sharing.

"She wouldn't leave," I say. "Not now."

Walker fixes me with his all-black eyes. "There are a lot of confusing forces around Lianna right now. Are you willing to take that chance?"

Damn, he's right. I need to get to her.

"Can you portal me to my front door?" I ask.

"You got it." Walker closes his eyes, and a large black door re-opens before us. I stare into the darkness. My heart thumps so hard in my rib cage, it feels like it might crack.

Hell, maybe it could even break. And for good, this time.

18

LIANNA

*B*AM, BAM, BAM!

I keep dreaming about sledgehammers in my sleep. When I finally open my eyes, I realize that the sledgehammers are real. Sort of. Someone's pounding the hell out of Maxon's front door. I rub my groggy eyes. I'm still in Maxon's bed.

BAM, BAM, BAM!

"Maxon, is that you?"

BAM, BAM, BAM!

"Okay, not you."

The sleepy haze in my brain starts to clear. Maxon went off to have breakfast with his grandmother. After he left, my goal was to sleep, not have my eardrums implode.

BAM, BAM, BAM!

Holy hell, that's annoying. *Time to make it go away.* I sleepwalk out of bed, pull on one of Maxon's robes, and shuffle to the front door. I grip the handle and pause.

"Who's out there?"

"Royal courier. Open up, please."

I blink hard. *Royal courier?* Whoever this is, they must not know that Maxon's away. I'll give them the update and go back to snoozing. Swinging the door open, I find a young man standing outside. He has a small face, red hair, loads of freckles, and ears that stick out sideways from his head.

"Royal courier." He bows low. "My name is Pip."

"Pip?" My sleepy hearing must be off.

"Yes, Pip."

"Okay. What's up?"

"I bring a message."

"Maxon's not here to take it," I say through a yawn. "You'll find him with the Queen Emeritus."

Pip nervously shifts his weight from foot to foot. "No, the message is for you."

My eyes narrow with suspicion. "What aren't you telling me?"

"It's the other monarkki," says Pip quickly. "Zephyr. He's threatening to cut off our air unless we hand over some stones and..." He looks guiltily at his boots.

"And he wants you to hand me over, too."

Pip nods.

A chill of worry crawls up my neck. Last night, the Air Valta sealed off the cavern, easy peasy. If I hadn't left to get help, Maxon could've suffocated.

My limbs tremble with worry. Maxon will never hand the Kristalli over, let alone me. I can't stay here and put his people in danger. And I can't ask him to leave his homeland while it's under threat.

"How'd you learn about this?" I ask.

"The news is all over Antrum," explains Pip. "Everyone's in a panic. Our environment is very delicate, Your Eminence. If Zephyr makes good on this threat, we won't last long."

My mouth thins to an angry line. *This has gone far enough.* I've lived in fear of Zephyr for years. I won't allow him to terrify the thrax as well. "Is that what you came to tell me?"

"No, Your Eminence. I've another message for you. Telling you about Zephyr wasn't part of my orders." He shifts his weight from foot to foot. "It just slipped out. I hope you're not angry."

"I'm fine. In fact, I'm glad you told me." I extend my hand, palm upwards. "Now give me your message and you can take off."

Pip quickly sets the envelope in my hand and then races away like his life depended on it. Hell, with the threat from Zephyr, maybe it does.

I close the front door and tear open the message. The note is written in Fisk's confident script.

Dearest Lianna, I've gotten news that Zephyr is attacking Antrum. It's no longer a secure place for you. I've found you a new safe house. Let's meet at Charybdis and discuss how to lead our realm safely away from Zephyr's threat. I'll bring the Kristalli of Water. There's no time to lose; please meet me as soon as you can. —Fisk

I stare at the words. My insides coil with worry. Zephyr is attacking and Antrum's at risk. Can I trust Fisk? I pace the room and sort through the facts. Fisk risked everything to save Maxon and me at Silas's lair. Plus, Fisk trained me for years, placing his life on the line the entire time.

Maybe we've had issues, but any way I look at things, my final view is always the same: I can trust him.

And my role is to follow the elemental way. We hide from other creatures and care for nature. We don't seal off realms and murder entire populations. As monarkki, my job is to prevent this threat; Maxon's is to protect his people.

My gaze falls on the front door. I should go. Still, my soul screams that it's wrong for me to leave.

Screw elemental roles and royal obligations. Maxon and I make a great team. We'll figure this out together, right?

I turn toward the bedroom. Maybe I should just get back into bed. A quick nap can work wonders, not to mention buy time until Maxon returns. I take a few steps toward the bedroom door. From the outer hallway, a wave of worried chatter freezes me in my tracks.

"He'll cut off our air," says an older woman's voice.

"I hear the Wastelands are already suffering," answers another.

"We need to get to a Pulpitum. Run!"

An anxious shiver twists down my back. If I make the wrong call here, all these people could die.

It feels like ages pass as I stand in place, my mind locked between thoughts of the Kristalli and Maxon's warm arms.

Crap. I have no idea what to do.

19

MAXON

J rush through the door to my chambers, my heart pounding up a storm in my chest. Walker's right behind me. I wave at him over my shoulder.

"Wait here, all right?" I ask.

"Sure thing."

Walker bounces a bit on his heels, making his ghouls robes sway. He's dying to race through the South Wing and search for Lianna with me. But she could still be in bed, all naked and with that satisfied grin on her mouth. Some stuff Walker doesn't need to see. Ever.

I rush toward my bedroom. Sure, I'm moving at preternatural speeds. Still, it feels like forever crawls by until I can get down the hallway and pull open my door. My skin chills over with shock.

Lianna's not here.

My heart kicks harder in my chest. She's got to be somewhere in my chambers.

Taking off like a shot, I race through halls and passages, calling out Lianna's name like a madman. There's no sign of her anywhere. I end up in the library. A small envelope sits on the bar, right beside my favorite whiskey. I rip it open.

Maxon, I can't stay here and put your people at risk. Please get the word to Zephyr that I'm gone so he'll call off his attack. I've left with all the Kristalli and will be in touch when I can. —Lianna.

"Someplace safe? Someplace safe!" Part of me knows I'm screaming like a madman. I don't give a fuck. Lianna's safest place is with me, period.

I've got to find her before she gets too far.

I stride over to the enchanted painting. "Get me Transfer Central."

The brushstrokes on the world map reform into the familiar image of Diana. She's pale and pretty, with long brown hair and freckles. Normally, she gets all blushy when I summon her. Today, her mismatched eyes are wide with panic.

"I was hoping you'd contact us," Diana says quickly. "Are you here to stop Zephyr? Everyone says he'll cut off our air."

"He won't," I say in a firm voice.

Diana exhales a shaky breath. "Thank heavens."

"Did anyone named Lianna ask for transfer to the surface?"

"One minute." Diana starts flipping through piles of paper and leather-bound logbooks. "No one passed through by that name."

"How about the Monarkki of Water?"

Her voice lowers to a hush. "The goddess?"

"That's the one, yeah."

"She left for Pulpitum X. It just got reopened; I figured it was safe."

"Pulpitum X. That's Purgatory." Some of the weight of worry lifts from my shoulders. My grandparents run Purgatory, and they're big believers in inter-realm alliances. If Lianna steps off that Pulpitum, she's going to have a reception party waiting. Grandma Cam isn't going to let her run off after Zephyr without some explanation and protection.

"Do you want me to prep your transfer to Purgatory?" asks Diana.

I rub my neck, lost in thought. Something about this doesn't add up. Lianna's too smart to run off to Purgatory if she's in trouble. She's got to know that a new monarkki is bound to grab a lot of attention.

No, there must be something else going on.

"Diana, is there a record of her arrival?"

"Why wouldn't there be?"

"Humor me."

Diana flips through some more log books. Then, she tears through additional piles of paper. I know her answer before she says it. "There's no record of her arriving." Diana's mismatched eyes grow large with worry. "Do you think she fell off the platform?"

That kind of thing happens sometimes, and it always ends badly. But that's when a thrax is involved. As an elemental, Lianna's a different story.

"She's fine," I say quickly.

"Where did she go?"

I'm tempted to explain that she probably changed into mist form and went wherever the hell she wanted. Traveling that way will make it a lot harder to track her, which was exactly what she planned.

"Have Ty run a magical trace on her. Send the news to me at the Queen Emeritus's command center. Over and out." I wave my arm and the painting returns to its usual map image.

For a long time, I can only stand in the library. At first, my body feels numb with shock. Then the real hurt settles in.

A week ago, I didn't know if I had a heart. Now, the damned thing's shattered.

I could kick myself for being such a dumbass. Why did I go talk to G and leave Lianna alone? I should have known Zephyr would try something. I pound my fist into a nearby table. The thing smashes in two. *Damn it!* If I hadn't been such a lovesick fool, I'd never have dressed up to see G and gush about my new girlfriend.

Rage and fear battle it out in my heart. Trashing the table felt pretty good, so my tail slices a nearby club chair in half. That feels even better. After that, things get a little crazy. I tear through a few more tables and couches, then I go to town on the wet bar. Bottle after bottle gets chucked against the wall.

Finally, my soul calms enough to start thinking clearly again. First thing I notice is Walker standing in the doorway. He surveys the trashed library.

"I would've done the same thing," he says.

Some of the tension melts from my body. Walker always knows the right thing to say. Turning on my heel, I head toward the door.

"Where are you off to?" asks Walker.

"Visiting G in her new command center," I reply. "If anything happens, she'll be the first to know."

And once I know where Lianna is, I'm heading to her side. Doesn't matter what enemy she faces. Doesn't matter the obstacles along the way. Screw it all. Nothing's more important than Lianna. I see that now. She's the world to me.

I'm getting her back.

20

LIANNA

I pace around Charybdis, the dry sand crunching beneath my feet. Above me, the full moon casts long shadows across the desert floor. Any shift in the darkness quickly grabs my attention.

Is that a burst of blue mist? Has Fisk finally arrived?

But there's been no mist. No Fisk. And no question that I'm going nutso with worry.

Fisk should've arrived already, especially since I was late to begin with. It took me extra time—and some creative use of thrax transfer plat-forms—but on my way here, I stopped off in the underground caves of Charybdis. I found the stone chamber where I'd recently been trapped, and that's where I stashed the Kristalli of Fire and Earth.

A satisfied smile rounds my lips. Out of all the places Zephyr will look for the stones, the depths of Charybdis should be last on his list.

More minutes pass, and my throat constricts with fear. By now, Zephyr must know that I've left Antrum. He could show up at any second.

Don't worry. You know how to escape Zephyr. You did it for years.

At last, a blue haze forms to my left. The mist quickly takes the shape of Fisk. He's out of his general's uniform and back to cargo pants and a black Henley. His pale features are unreadable.

"Fisk." I offer him a shaky smile. "Thanks for your message."

"Everything would've been easier if you'd visited the Water Palace *alone.*"

Here it comes. Where our conversation goes to hell.

"Maxon isn't going anywhere. You need to get used to that idea."

"I'm trying." A muscle ticks along Fisk's jawline. Tension thickens the air.

"Try harder. Remember Esau? You and I both know he's not the only one who's suffering. How many are dying right now because I'm not wearing my crown?"

Fisk stares at his combat boots. "This isn't easy for me. The Valta have their concerns. They don't want a monarkki like Zephyr."

"And are you worried that I'll rule like Zephyr?" I step closer. "Tell me Fisk. Honestly."

He scrubs his hands over his face. "No, I'm not concerned about that."

"Then, why's the coronation on hold? It'll do more than enable me to heal, you know. I'll stand a better chance against Zephyr once I'm connected to the power of my people. Waiting for my coronation only helps our enemy."

"I know that. Believe me."

"Then, what are we doing here?"

"Honestly?" Fisk exhales a puff of breath. "We're trying to get past how I lost it at the Water Palace." He forces a laugh. "I guess it never occurred to me that you'd find someone else. I went a little crazy."

"A little?"

"A copious amount." He meets my gaze, his sea green eyes glimmering in the moonlight. "Since then, I've had time to think things through. The truth is this. I want you to be happy, Lianna. That's what love really is, right? Wanting someone else's happiness more than your own."

My heart lightens a little bit. Not a ton, but this Fisk is a definite improvement. He's much better than the nutjob version that I met before. Now, I need to check if the new Fisk has actions to back up these nice words.

"What about my Kristalli, Fisk? What about the Valta?"

"I want to set things right." Fisk pats his hip pocket. "I brought your Kristalli."

"Thank you, Fisk." A weight of worry lifts from my shoulders.

At last, we're getting somewhere.

"And I can assemble the Valta whenever you want. They're ready to hold your crowning ceremony."

"They are?" My breath catches. This is too good to be real.

"It took a little convincing, but they've all agreed to acknowledge you."

"Wow." My eyes sting with tears of pure joy. After so much hard work, I can finally be crowned. "Thanks again."

"Please don't say that."

An uneasy feeling creeps up my back. It's the prickle of awareness that says someone's watching us.

"Let's go to the Water Palace. The sooner I'm crowned, the better."

Fisk steps away. "One more thing, please."

I open my mouth, ready to yell my ass off if I have to. *We need to move.* Then I meet Fisk's gaze. His eyes look empty and haunted. A pang of guilt tightens my torso.

He's trying. And hurting. "Sure, Fisk. What's up?"

"I know Zephyr is attacking Antrum. You can't go back there. I found a place to keep you secure." He offers me a half smile. "So, what do you say? Are we off to a new safe house?"

"I don't know. This is too dangerous. Our people need you. I can't put both of us at risk. I'll find somewhere to hide out."

"Our people need you far more than they need me. My job is to protect you, Lianna. Please, go to the new safe house with me."

I stare at my boots. Based on Fisk's note, I knew this conversation was coming. However, it's one thing to contemplate placing someone you care about in a new level of danger. It's another thing to drag him headlong into the abyss.

Fisk steps closer. "I can't stand by without knowing you're safe. Please."

And there's that haunted look again. I'm such a goner.

"All right, Fisk. Lead on."

"Thank you, Lianna."

I'm about to follow when a harsh wind kicks up, blotting out the stars.

A half-dozen Air Valta appear in the night sky. Fast as a heartbeat, they grab Fisk and speed off toward the horizon. He struggles under their grip, fighting with everything he's got.

I take off after them, my body becoming a blur of mist. Fisk pulls out his sword and stabs one of the Air Valta in the chest. I summon a piston made of boiling water and smash another one through his face. Our group tears through the clouds, fighting and lunging as we go. Panic and rage rush through me.

Not Fisk. Not now.

More Air Valta appear. They grab my arms and legs, draining my energy and returning me into solid form. I watch in horror as Fisk is dragged off into the darkness. I thrash under the grip of the Valta, hoping that I can somehow break free. That doesn't happen. I have greater powers that I can use here. Something tells me to save them for later.

That's when Zephyr materializes. His gray Roman armor glimmers in the moonlight as he hovers before me. Fresh anger streams across my skin.

This would be the something I was waiting for.

"Hello, little monarkki."

My face twists into a scowl of rage. "Release Fisk. Now."

Zephyr pounds on his Roman breastplate. "Do you really think you can order me about?" He eyes me from head to toe. "You're nothing but a little..."

"Don't say it."

"You don't issue me orders, girl."

"Seriously? I've Namare's powers and I'm learning how to use them. Your Valta can't just hold my arms anymore and expect that to stop me."

I don't wait for a reply. Instead, I summon two daggers of boiling-hot water and hit Zephyr straight in the face. "Take that, *boy*."

With all my focus, I pull every last ounce of elemental energy from my soul. It takes a huge effort, but I'm able to overcome the magic of the Valta who hold me. My body returns into mist form. Since I'm no longer solid, I can easily slip free. Fast as a heartbeat, I conjure bands of ice to hold the Valta in place while I focus on defeating Zephyr, once and for all.

You are going down at last.

Zephyr's still hunched over, howling in pain. It'll only take him a few more seconds to heal, so I can't waste any time. Raising my arms, I summon a hailstorm to ricochet through Zephyr's body, injuring his solid body further. Zephyr heals himself quickly, but I'm just as fast to tear him apart, again and again.

I can't keep injuring Zephyr forever, though. I need help. Time to summon the water elementals. With Fisk gone and me crownless, will they answer my call?

My thoughts are so focused on summoning elementals, I barely register the air shift behind me. An oily male voice sounds in my ear.

"Excuse me, Your Eminence."

Whatever it is, it's not an elemental. And therefore, I'm not turning around to chitchat with it. "Kind of busy here."

The newcomer moves to hover before me. It's a black dragon with two heads spouting from his shoulders. A third neck-stump sits in the center of his chest. The beast's great ebony wings pump behind it in a slow rhythm. My neck and shoulders constrict with recognition and fear.

No question who this is. Chimera. I've read about this guy and his venom sacks. Him showing up here is bad news.

Chimera's appearance breaks up my concentration. Anything I've created with my powers—including the bonds on the Air Valta—now weaken. The Valta use this to their advantage. They tear free from their bindings and reach for me once again. The moment that the Valta touch my misty body, they drain my powers more than ever before. I no longer have enough energy to stay in my mist form. I am solid once again.

With rough movements, the Valta pin my arms behind my back. Pain tears across my shoulders. I twist under their grip, but it's no use. I no longer have enough energy to break free.

Now that I'm restrained, Chimera closes in. His great black wings pump the air until his two faces are only inches away from mine. Foul dragon breath warms my body. Panic electrifies my soul. Opening one of his mouths, Chimera spews green venom into my eyes.

Which one was it? Acid or paralytic?

Every molecule in my body freezes. New levels of terror careen through my mind, but I can't even twitch, let alone scream.

Paralytic it is.

MAXON

I stalk G's command central like I'm a caged animal in need of raw meat. All the pink and yellow in this place makes me want to tear my eyes out. I pause by the entrance and grip the doorjamb so tightly, the wood lets out a soft crack. G looks my way for a second, but she doesn't say anything. My G knows better than to talk when I'm like this. Instead, she starts issuing orders to the half-dozen or so folks who are running around doing damage control.

Turning around, I glare down the outer hallway. Ty could walk toward us at any second, bringing news of Lianna from his tracking spell. Since it's an emergency, Ty could even teleport right into this room. He won't, though. G considers it rude when people enter her chambers without knocking, no matter what the hell is going on. Walker's the only one who portals in whenever he wants. Then again, Walker has some serious balls.

I turn back around to find G standing across from me. She stares long and hard at my eyes.

Still mismatched, G.

Sure, I care deeply about Lianna, but I'm too broken to have it turn into more. Not that I'm having this discussion with G right now. It's all I can do to keep my staring vigil going with the hallway.

"Let's give it a rest," says G. She guides me inside the room and slowly closes the door.

"If you say so."

"How are you holding up?"

I feel and look like crap. That's what I want to say. Of course, G looks like she just stepped off the cover of a magazine. You know, if the middle ages had magazines and cover girls.

"I'm fine, G." And definitely in no mood talk about my feelings. "Mom sent her igni around Antrum, yeah?"

"Of course." A small, knowing smile rounds G's mouth. "You know your mother."

"I know the thrax. They love her supernatural light shows."

G arches her right eyebrow. "You'll command the igni one day, too."

Meaning when I fall in love. When I'm Angelbound. And I'm not having this talk, either.

A heavy knock sounds at the newly closed door. I couldn't be more thankful for a break from this awkward conversation. A muffled voice carries into the reception chamber.

"Tyberius of Striga, requesting permission to enter."

I whip the door open. "Come on in, Ty."

Ty doesn't meet my gaze. "Hey, Maxon."

The second my buddy moves past the threshold, I shut the door and push for answers. "What did you find out? Did the tracking spell work?"

Ty keeps on not looking at me. "It's a little complex."

This can't be good.

I turn to G. "Can you give us a sec, here?"

"As you wish, my child."

Once G's out of earshot, I round on Ty. "What's up?"

"Lianna jumped off the Pulpitum and went to Charybdis."

I exhale a relieved breath. "That's not so bad. We know where she is now."

"There's more." Ty's already long face gets longer. "Your parents and Walker are on the way here."

"So something else is going on? Why can't you just say it?" Ty's dancing around big news and it's getting on my nerves. "Spit it out, man."

"Zephyr's sent an emissary. He wants to talk with all the royals. You in particular."

A shock of awareness zooms down my spine. Zephyr wouldn't send an emissary unless he wanted to talk terms. And he wouldn't do that unless...

"Does he have Lianna?" All of a sudden, I'm breathless and flustered. Part of me registers that this is more emotion than I've felt in a year. More of me is beyond caring about all this emotional crap. Lianna could be in the hands of that monster.

"We don't know yet," answers Ty. "We'll find out when everyone shows up."

A low hum sounds as a large door-sized hole appears in the center of the room. Out of the portal steps Walker, my parents, and an Air Valta. I'd know this elemental anywhere. He's one of the kids who tried to seal Lianna and me into a cavern. In other words, he's a dumbass. That's good.

"Greetings," says the Air Valta. "I am Caius."

G nods toward the door. "Please excuse us, everyone."

There's a lot of bowing and "Yes, Your Majesty" as Ty and all of G's team hightail it out of the room. Meanwhile I give Caius a careful once-over. The guy has an all-gray body, baby face, and Roman armor. I tilt my head.

"You're the one who screwed up in the Philippines."

"Come again?" asks Caius.

"You let Lianna and me escape," I explain. "How are you alive?"

Caius tips up his chin. "Zephyr was merciful. He only killed—" He clears his throat, most likely to hide a sob. Suddenly, I feel bad for the kid. He's too young to be in this job.

"He let me live," says Caius.

And killed your friend.

"Look, whatever happened with your buddy, I'm sorry. I've been in battle, I know what it's like to lose someone." I fold my arms over my chest. "Now, what does Zephyr want?"

"Lianna is in Zephyr's compound," says Caius.

When I speak again, my voice takes on a deeper ring of menace. "We guessed that already, Caius. What else you got?"

"They're in deep negotiations on how to jointly rule all elementals," says Caius. "Any attempts to cease this peaceful process will be taken as an act of war. Emissaries have been sent to Heaven, Hell, the Dark Lands, and Purgatory. All have the same message." He focuses on me. "No coming after Lianna."

And leave her with Zephyr? Never.

Every nerve ending in my body zings with rage. "Negotiations? You've got to be kidding. If Lianna is with Zephyr, she's a prisoner."

Caius looks pointedly at my parents. "What is your reply?"

"There will be no official rescue party from Antrum," says Dad. "Is that acceptable?"

A breathless pause hangs in the room. Dad specifically used the word 'official.' That means I can do something on my own, assuming Caius agrees.

I love my Dad.

"Excellent," says Caius. "That's exactly what we were hoping for."

G nods regally. "I'll have my scribes put it in writing." According to G, diplomacy is all about writing stuff down. I'd rather zap a few lightning bolts, but that's me.

Mom steps in to close the deal. "You've done an impressive job here today, Caius." She grins and bats her eyes. Classic move. Mom does this all the time in negotiations. The woman can win over almost anyone with an X chromosome. Turns out, even elementals aren't immune.

Caius blushes. "Thank you, Your Highness."

"We'll finalize the agreement immediately." Mom gestures toward Walker. "Please join the Queen Emeritus and Walker in the Throne Room."

"As you command," says Caius.

With a wave of his arm, Walker quickly opens a ghoul portal. Along with G and Caius, he steps into the darkness and disappears. Once the three of them are gone, I face my parents.

"I'm going after Lianna," I say. "Unofficially."

"I know, my boy," says Dad with a sad smile.

"What can we do to help?" asks Mom.

"Nothing," I say. "This is a solo mission."

A muffled voice sounds from beyond the door. "Forget it! I'm going with you," calls Ty.

We all share a knowing smile. Ty must have cast a listening spell. I whip open the door. All the guys are there.

"Where did you all come from?" I ask.

"I might have called them here," answers Ty.

"You can't have all the battle fun without us," adds Uth.

I try to pretend that I'm pissed, but do a shit job of it. "You're a bunch of sentimental dicks, you know that?"

"Yeah," they reply in unison.

I turn back to my parents. "We have some planning to do, and then we're off."

"Be safe," says Mom.

"I can't believe you said that, Myla." Dad shakes his head. "Kick some ass, son."

"That's the plan." I speed out the door, ready to make a plan and get my girl.

Don't give up, Lianna. I'll be there soon.

22

LIANNA

I'm so thirsty, I could scream.

Only I can't.

In fact, all I can do is stare at the same stretch of blank white wall. Not that I have a choice where I look, either. Chimera's paralytic venom lives up to its reputation. It works like a charm on almost anybody. While I keep up the stare fest, the infirmary door opens with a menacing creak. I sense more than see an oily presence sidle up next to me.

"How are you feeling?" asks Chimera.

At this point, I'd love to tear the old dragon's heart out. Hell, I'd settle for being able to shift my weight or even twitch, but I can't. In fact, all I can do is make sarcastic comments inside my head.

"Ah-ah-aaaaaah," says Chimera. "You want to move again, I can tell."

You think?

"Have I told you about my paralytic venom?"

Only fourteen times.

"Works on anything in the after-realms, and I do mean anything."

Must save you money on date rape drugs.

And so it goes. Chimera's been nothing but irritating for hours.

"Ready to give me what I want?" he asks. He wiggles the Kristalli of Water, which has been strapped to my hand.

The movement reminds me for the millionth time that Fisk was the last one to have the Kristalli. I really hope he's okay.

"Come on," coos Chimera. "Charge up the stone with your power, and all this will be over."

That's so not an option. No way am I charging the Kristalli just so

Zephyr can shoot up.

Chimera taps the stone with his claw-like finger. "Not filling with power, I see."

Wow. Something we agree on.

"Ah, well," Chimera sighs. "Time for more venom."

Ugh. My stomach would heave if I could move the muscles. Every fifteen minutes, Chimera shoots another dose of his personal paralytic into my neck with a syringe. He could spit into my face too, but the nurses were complaining about getting paralyzed while they cleaned me up. So, syringe it is.

Did I mention that I hate needles?

Chimera rises to his feet, taking care to stay in my limited line of vision.

Thanks for the freak show, creep.

A pair of smiling, reptilian faces stare directly at me. They're Chimera's. The two heads have different colored scales, but both end in the same lean body. Chimera's a wily guy in a black waistcoat with matching breeches. Or at least, it's what left of a waistcoat. Since Chimera's in his hybrid form, his pair of heads have shredded the top of his outfit.

Chimera tilts one of his heads back, plunges the syringe into its venom sack and fills the glass vial with a bunch of green goop. Again, he's super careful to make sure I don't miss a second of the action. Wow, do I ever hate him.

"More paralytic, coming up."

After stepping up to my bedside, Chimera jams the needle into my throat and chuckles. My soul seethes with held in rage.

What I wouldn't give to be able to kill the old bastard, right now.

"Ready to charge up your Kristalli? All it takes is a little force of will and—whoosh—in it goes. Zephyr has given me his solemn oath that once you're drained of your powers, you'll be free to leave."

That's because I'll also be dead.

"Perhaps you think someone is coming to save you?" Chimera asks.

Hey, I'd be insane not to fantasize about Maxon busting down the door.

"I'd give up on that idea, little monarkki." I can hear the smug smile in Chimera's voice. "Escape is impossible." His clawed finger runs down the side of my face. "Why not transfer the power? You're going to die; what could it matter?"

He has a point. Hopelessness weighs down my body, heavy and cold as blocks of ice. *I don't doubt my escape is impossible.*

Still, if death is all I have left, then it matters quite a lot.

23

MAXON

I stand on the abandoned loading docks of Arx Hall. A silver Pulpitum disc glitters underneath my feet. Lianna and I used this very transfer station when she first came to Antrum. It was such a thrill to hold her as the platform rushed around.

Now, Zephyr has her imprisoned. Adrenaline kicks through my nervous system.

If that freak touches one hair on her head, I'll kill him.

I roll my eyes. *Who am I kidding?* We're about to launch a rescue mission for Lianna. No matter what's up with her hair, if I get the chance, I'm killing Zephyr.

A familiar voice breaks up my thoughts. "You okay, M?"

It's Uther. He and Ty are standing nearby, waiting to get started. We just finished the fastest planning session in the history of the thrax military. Now, we're waiting for Zee and Raj to show and we're ready to roll.

Uther raises his voice. "I said, are you okay, M?"

"Give him a minute," whispers Ty.

I rub my eyes and refocus my thoughts. "Nah, I'm good. Just thinking."

"You reworking the plan?" asks Ty.

"Nope, it's a good plan."

Actually, it's a long shot mess, but I can't say that to Ty.

In my mind, I run it through everything one more time. First step, we use Uther's phase bomb to open a doorway to Zephyr's realm. Assuming Uther's toy doesn't kill us all, then we go straight to step two, finding Lianna. So we find and rescue her. And then—if we're all still alive after that—we move onto step three, killing Zephyr. His place will be crawling with Air Valta and my lightning only does so much. That's why I'm about to send Ty to Furonium. He'll ask Tempest for help.

On second thought, calling this a 'long shot mess' is sugarcoating things. That said, it's the best plan we've got.

I turn to Uther. "Are your bombs ready?"

Uth raises two small metal boxes in his arms. "Two identical bombs, ready to go, just like you asked."

"Good man," I say. "How'd the final tests go?"

"Uh, fine." Uther stares at the floor. That's his 'I'm so guilty it isn't funny' look.

"Anything more for me than that?"

"Nope, not really," says Uth. He keeps staring at the ground. That's not good.

"So, you're sure those can punch a doorway into Zephyr's realm?"

The whole plan hinges on Uth and his bombs. It was tough enough getting into the Water Palace, and that was with Lianna at my side. And Ty couldn't even stop some random elemental lights from twinkling out of the ground. No way can he open a portal into Zephyr's backyard. Unless Uther's bombs work, this plan will stop before it gets started.

"No worries," says Uth. "These babies can open a portal anywhere in the after-realms, including Zephyr's compound." He purses his lips. "Only…"

Here it comes. There's always a catch with Uther's stuff.

"Only what?" I ask.

"We can't do it a ton."

"Define 'a ton.'"

"Well, I've been working on these bombs for months. I did one last test before I came here."

"And?"

"The space-time continuum got a little wonky."

"Wonky?" Ty gasps. "What the hell, man? You've been fucking with space-time?"

"It's not like I meant to," says Uth. "I'm a scientist. Mistakes go with the territory."

I step between Uth and Ty before they start whaling on each other. "Get to the bottom line, Uth. What's the deal?"

"Well, we can only do a few more blasts," says Uth. "Or bad things will happen."

Here we go again. You have to be super-specific with Uther.

"Define 'bad things.'"

"Oh, well…"

My voice takes on a warning tone. "Uth."

"The universe might collapse or something," says Uther really quickly. "Or, you know, it could be fine, too."

Ty shakes his head, dismayed. "That is wrong on so many different levels, I can't even begin to tell you."

Uther folds his arms over his stocky chest. "I *said* this is science, man. I wouldn't expect you to understand."

"Understand?" asks Ty. He's almost screaming, so I need to shut this convo down. I raise my hand, palm forward. Both guys go silent.

"Look, you two. Right now, all that's important is one thing." I turn to Uth. "Can we safely do two blasts?"

"Yes, absolutely."

"Good. We're using one bomb to go to Zephyr's realm, and Ty's taking the other one to Furonium for Tempest."

Uther frowns. "Why can't I take the bomb to Tempest?"

"We covered this already," I say.

"Many times," adds Ty.

Uther looks unconvinced, so I go through it again. "Tempest doesn't know you, Uth. He's only ever met Ty."

That's not entirely true. Tempest has met Zee as well. But Ty has a reputation as the best warlock in the after-realms. Dragons are big on magic. We've a better shot at getting help with Ty pleading our case.

I point between Ty and one of the metal boxes. "You know how to operate that thing?"

"Yup," says Ty. "Picture where I want to go, and then hit the red button."

"It's a really simple interface," grumbles Uth. "You could say something nice about that, you know."

That's our Uther. Still prissy that Ty bad-talked his bomb.

"Okay, fine." Ty rolls his eyes. "Nice job putting a big red button on the machine that almost blew apart our universe. Feel better now?"

Uth hands him the bomb. "Yeah, I do."

Ty holds the box like it's radioactive. Hell, it probably is. Good thing Ty has a spell to counteract that kind of thing. I lean back against the wall and hitch my thumbs into the pockets of my body armor.

"Go through the plan with me one more time, Ty."

"I'll ride the Pulpitum to Furonium and ask for Emperor Tempest." Ty's mouth presses into a worried frown. "You're absolutely sure he'll help us? Everyone else in the after-realms seems scared that Zephyr will retaliate against them. We've got no official help coming from the Dark

Lands, Antrum, Purgatory, or even Hell. Maybe we should nix this part. I should be with you guys on the strike team."

"It'll be fine, Ty. The Furor love a good fight. They practically held a party when Zephyr attacked them to get at the Kristalli of Fire."

Okay, so that answer's only partly bullshit. The Furor do like to fight, but I've no real idea if Tempest will pitch in. He's a moody son of a bitch. "Be sure to tell Tempest that our intel says Chimera is with Zephyr. That may change his mind."

Or not. T is really a wildcard.

"Got it," says Ty.

"You ready to roll?" I ask.

Ty nods.

"Good man." I cup my hand by my mouth and speak a little louder. "Activating communications system to Transfer Central. Diana, are you there?"

A sultry voice fills the stone room. "Hello, Maxon."

"Hey, Diana. I need you to send Ty here into Furonium. Make it the Pulpitum right inside Emperor Tempest's palace."

"As you command, Your Highness. Waiting on your mark."

Uther stares at the bomb in Ty's arms. The way Uth looks at that thing, you'd think Ty was stealing his baby. Well, maybe he is. I gently rest my hand on Uther's shoulder and guide him away from the circular metal platform on the floor. Uth can't be anywhere nearby when the transfer starts or he'll get mushed into road kill. Once Uther's safely out of range, I give the countdown. "Initiating transfer in three, two, one."

A burst of white light fills the room as Ty's platform takes off through the ceiling. The brightness blinds me for a few seconds, and then my eyes readjust to the dim room and torchlight.

"Will you need another transfer today?" asks Diana.

"No thanks," I reply. "Over and out."

Raj and Nizam rush into the room. Both are decked out in black body armor, like me and Uth. However, they're also loaded down with heavy backpacks. An odd assortment of crossbows and knives are strapped to their arms and legs. Jetal sits perched on the top of Raj's pack. She does not look happy about her new nest away from her master's shoulder.

Playing around in the armory again. That's Zee and Raj for you.

"You're late," I say.

"Sorry," says Raj. "We got caught up."

"I see." I make a big show of eyeing them from head to toe. It's a wonder the two of them are upright, considering all the crap they're carrying. "Think you got enough gear, guys?"

"Why?" Zee's mouth falls open with worry. "Do you think we need more?"

"Maybe we should go back," says Raj. "They got in a new shipment of nun chucks this week."

"Stay right where you are," I order. "Gear time is over. We're going to Zephyr's compound now."

Zee frowns. "How's that gonna happen?"

"If you'd been here, you'd know already," I say dryly.

Uther clasps his bomb to his chest. "This is my phase bomb. It'll open a gateway to Zephyr's compound. We know Lianna's being held there. Maxon found some old maps in the library. The best point of entry will be the forests surrounding the place."

It's a scary plan that could wrong about a million different ways, and Raj and Zee know it. Raj's eyes slightly widen with fear. Zee doesn't twitch. Then again, he's a hard-core warrior.

"What happens then?" asks Raj.

"We find Lianna and kill Zephyr. Ty is off in Furonium getting back-up from Tempest."

"Oh, I see," says Raj in a low voice. "Do you really think Tempest will show? He's a..."

"Moody son of a bitch," I finish. "I know. Hey, I'm not saying that the plan's guaranteed."

Uth smiles. "For the record, I'm really excited about this. Great plan."

"Thanks, Uth." He'd love anything that involved his bombs. "Let's get started."

Raj straightens his backpack. "We're ready when you are, Your Highness."

I freeze at his words. The guys never call me 'Your Highness' unless we're in a super-dangerous mission. And this one's got all the marks of a disaster.

Uther's bomb. Finding Lianna. Relying on dragons. Killing Zephyr.

Time seems to stop as I scan the faces of my friends. They all look set for action, and yeah, they'll follow me anywhere. Worry churns up my ribcage. We've all been in tough battles before. None like this one. I'm risking their lives so I can save my girlfriend, not protect the thrax.

"Look, guys." I rub my neck in an anxious rhythm. "This isn't an official mission. If any of you want out, now's the time to go. I won't judge you. This is all a little crazy." I laugh, but there's no humor in it. "Okay, *a lot* crazy."

A long pause hangs in the air while I wait for the guys to march out the door.

"I can speak for all of us," says Zee. "We want to do this."

My voice comes out thick with disbelief. "Why?"

More silence follows until Uther gets up the guts to speak. "We lost you," he says simply. "Like a year or so ago."

His words take my breath away. It's all I can do to stare at the wall, my face burning with shame. "And here, I thought I had you all snowed."

"That's not important," says Uth. He takes a step closer to me. "What's important is that she brought you back. You started smiling again, man. Lianna brought our friend and prince back to us. We'll do anything for her."

His words echo through my mind. For a year, I was only sleepwalking through life. Now, in the last few days, I'm alive again. Happy, angry, you name it.

She brought you back.

"She did, didn't she?" I ask.

"Yeah," says Uth. "We're not letting that go. Not for anything." He lifts his arms, offering me the small silver box. "So stop whining already and set off my bomb."

I shake my head. "You sure have a way with words, Uth."

Taking the bomb from Uther, I place the small metal box on the floor by the stone wall. In my mind, I picture the forest outside Zephyr's palace: A creepy place filled with bare white trees and waves of choking smoke. I lean over the box, hit the red button and wait.

It doesn't take long.

One wall of the stone chamber crumbles in on itself. Gray smoke pours into the room, covering the floor. Beyond the open wall, tall white trees stretch out into the murky distance. Long and bare branches reach up into the night sky like bleached skeletons.

Uther jumps up and down. "It worked! It really worked!"

I pat him on the shoulder. "Nice job, man." I gesture to the other guys. "Let's move out."

Zee and Raj answer in unison. "Yes, Your Highness."

As I step through the wall, my boots move from hard stone onto the soft earth of a forest floor. Tall trees surround me as I make my way toward our first objective, the outskirts of Zephyr's compound. Behind me, the others march over the same low pile of rubble and follow my trail. The moment we're all secure inside Zephyr's lands, the Antrum wall reforms, trapping us in the realm of air elementals.

A spark of excitement flares in my chest. For the first time since Zephyr threatened Antrum and grabbed Lianna, I can actually do something.

The four of us hike in a rough line through the darkened forest. Every step sounds like a drumbeat in the quiet night. Smoke hovers up to our knees. A sickly sweet smell fills the air. Makes me want to puke if I think about it too much.

The rustle of wings sounds nearby. Jetal lets out a squawk.

A pair of crows lands on an empty branch right above our heads. Acting in unison, Raj and Zee point their crossbows at the birds.

"Hold your fire," I say. "Let me get a closer look."

I approach the crows. The guys follow slowly behind me. There's not a lot of moonlight. Still, I can see that the birds have stone eyes, razor-sharp wings, and rusted nails for claws. Both of their rib cages have been cracked open, then sewn back together at an odd angle using leather strips. Bits of mangy straw peep out from the needle holes.

"What the hell are those things?" asks Zee.

"Cross between taxidermy and zombie, far as I can tell. It's the work of a demon warlock named Silas. Class A job."

The joy in Raj's tone is unmistakable. "You think he's nearby?"

"No doubt." I scan the darkened skies. "Let's hope Tempest gets here first, though."

"Why?" asks Zee.

"I took an oath not to harm Silas. Long story."

Zee frowns. "Think it applies to us, too?"

"Yeah, I'd assume so. Let's just say that Silas is a crafty demon and I'm not willing to risk you guys being on the wrong side of his spell." I stare at the birds a bit longer. Their stone eyes shift, looking each of us over in turn. "These are scouts. You guys have fire bolts on you?"

"Yes, Your Highness," say Raj and Zee together.

"Take them out."

A second later, Raj and Zee fire off their weapons. A quick zing sounds in the air, and then the crows go up in smoke. Raj and Zee exchange a high five.

"That was easy," calls Raj. From his backpack Jetal lets out a happy caw.

"Keep your voices down," I say. "There are more of them."

Uth stares at the smoldering bird carcasses, his head tilting from side to side. No doubt, he's calculating how best to blow them up going forward. Gotta love Uth.

"How many more of these birds do you think there are?" asks Uther.

"Lots." I reply. "Remember the Scarlet Horde?"

"Yup."

"More than that."

"Cool." Uth pats down the pockets of his body armor. "I brought a ton of mini-grenades. They'll be perfect."

"That's good news, Uth." I scan the skies. Everything's clear, both of crows and dragons.

Damn, I hope the dragons get here first.

We march along through the darkened forest. More of Silas's crows appear in the trees. Raj and Zee have a grand time striking them down, but there are only so many flaming bolts that they can shoot without a magical refill. We need Ty here and soon. More and more, I'm wondering why I sent away my only wizard.

At last, the outline of Zephyr's compound appears through the trees. It's a series of huge concrete blocks, each about one-story high and without windows. Some wooden structures peep out from behind them, but they're far off in the distance.

Lianna's in one of those buildings. The thought sends fresh adrenaline coursing through my system.

There isn't time to analyze the view. A figure steps out from behind one of the thick tree trunks. It's a girl, or what's left of one. She's in a nurse's uniform, only the white cloth is all mucked up and torn, showing her upper rib cage. Like the crows, her chest has been cracked open and re-sewn together. Her eyes are smooth black stones, while her legs are those of a panther, not a human. Long daggers have been tied to her hands with more strips of leather. She's the perfect mix of speed and lethal power, all wound up with magic and taxidermy.

Now, I've seen some sick demonic shit in my life, but Silas just hit a whole new level of awful. My blood boils with fury. This human was a nurse, like the ones I met back in the club on earth. When I took those ladies for ice cream, they told me all about how they loved helping people heal. Soldiers, especially. And then this demon abducts someone like them. Hatred charges every muscle in my body.

Sure, I gave an oath not to hurt Silas. That doesn't mean I won't find a way to kill him anyway.

"Silas!" I call. "Get out here. Now."

The old demon steps out from behind another large tree trunk. Probably hiding back there so he can quietly cast the spells that direct his poppets. Moonlight outlines his handlebar moustache and bowler hat.

"Hello, Maxon," says Silas. "I'm here to thank you."

"For what, exactly?"

"You gave your oath not to kill me, so Zephyr has given me the task of destroying you. He'd do it himself but he doesn't think you merit the effort. Seems two of his most junior Air Valta locked you and your lady love in a cave without too much effort."

"They didn't see me at my best." I raise my hand so lightning can dance across the palm. "I still have a few surprises for you."

"I'm sure you think so," says Silas. "However, I've a few of my own as well."

Within a heartbeat, the forest fills with Silas's horrible creations. Hundreds of crows fill the branches of nearby trees. Mutilated bears, dogs, and wolves line the forest floor. Undead humans—patched up with body parts from other animals—slink out from the shadows.

There are hundreds of them, and only four of us. I scan the skies. No sign of Tempest or Tyberius.

We're so fucked, it isn't funny.

"Quad formation," I call. The four of us move into a loose square, our backs to each other, our faces turned out to the zombie army.

Silas smiles, showing a mouth of black and broken teeth. "Attack!"

All at once, the creatures come at us. I summon a column of lightning down from the sky. It scares back some of the larger animals, but the birds easily avoid the strike. The humans couldn't care less. The ones with animal legs vault over the other cowering creatures and leap for our heads. I take them down with my tail or, better yet, my dragon-scale arm.

Silas watches the action from the sidelines, and damn, he's getting pissed. Raj and Zee are still using their distance weapons. Although they're out of cross bolts, they've simply moved onto throwing daggers and short bows. They haven't had to get out to their hand-to-hand gear yet, which is good.

The problem is the damned birds. Without any fire bolts left, they're back to being a bitch to kill. Uther can blow them up with his mini-grenades. The blast radius is small enough. Even so, things get messy. Plus, Uth has to maneuver around to get at them, leaving him exposed for attack. Long story short, I keep having to stop what I'm doing to prevent some souped-up zombie from slicing Uth into mincemeat. Makes it harder to down the baddies who're coming after me.

Out of the corner of my eye, I see Silas smile as some wolfhound with broken glass for teeth tries to take a chomp out of my shoulder. It's the arm covered with dragon scales but still, half my upper body armor gets torn off. Gripping the hound by its jaws, I tear the thing apart and toss it aside. Instantly, a black bear with silver armor takes its place. Moonlight strikes the beast's armor and I get a better look at what Silas has done.

That's not silver armor. It's layer upon layer of long razors, the ends bolted together. The thing's like a zombie lightning rod.

Beautiful.

I raise my arm and summon a trio of lightning bolts straight into the bear's skull. The creature bursts into flames and falls to the side. The break in the battle gives me a chance to check out my buddies.

They're not doing well.

Uther's back got clawed by some sewn-together mix of human and wolf. Raj and Zee are down to their short-swords. All of them are missing body armor. Their exposed flesh is a patchwork of gashes and blood.

We don't have much longer.

Another crow swoops in past me, its rusted nail claws scraping across my neck. A razorblade feather makes a gash along my jawline.

"You see?" says Silas. "My birds will get you. I knew they would." He gestures to the skies. "And now, more are coming."

As I glance up, I'm only half aware of another rabid hound sinking its teeth into my arm. This is the one without dragon scales, and whatever Silas put in these creatures for teeth hurts like hell. I rip the creature off, snap its neck, and lift my gaze to the night sky. It's darkened over, and not with clouds.

Something is flying across the horizon and in such numbers, it's blotting out every star.

Please let it be dragons.

An angry chorus of caws sounds above me. My heart sinks.

Not dragons. That's the sound of a murder of crows. Damn.

A humanoid monster attacks my arm. This one's a cross between man and bear. My tail punches its head. After that, I kick the beast squarely in its belly, launching it into the forest. Unfortunately, two more bear-human hybrids quickly take its place. I steel myself and pull a fresh dagger out of its holster on my thigh.

I'm not going down without a fight.

The human poppets prepare to lunge when a new sound freezes them in their tracks. This time, it's not the caw of crows. It's a roar. I could fucking cry, I'm so happy.

The dragons are here.

My limbs become charged with energy and hope. "Tempest is here, guys! Get back in a quad."

The four of us limp into our back-to-back formation once again.

More caws sound from the darkened skies. This time, the birds sound frightened. Bursts of golden fire appear above our heads. Only one kind of dragon does that particular battle move. The Kathikon, Tempest's personal guard.

In other words, the best of the baddest warriors in the after-realms. Thank Heaven.

Dragons land all around us. The dry and blackened trees quickly burst into flames. Some of the Furor tear through the forest in their dragon forms. Their long tails slam through enemy and tree alike. Other dragons move into a hybrid state where their skin is fully covered in dragon scales. They grab poppets, tearing them apart with glee.

Only one dragon changes into a full human. Tempest. He's broad shouldered and tall, with strong bone structure and wavy black hair. He's wearing some kind of tricked-out heavy black armor. His eyes, normally brown, are slitted length-wise like a lizard's and glow red with demonic rage. Tempest has a tail like mine. As he steps along, it sweeps behind him, taking out Silas's monsters left and right.

I've never been happier to see anyone in my life.

The fight moves to wherever the dragons are, which means less trouble for me and the guys. Still, in our weakened state, it's trouble enough. Raj is leaning against Zee, hardly able to stay upright. Uther's body armor is shredded. His exposed skin is covered in bruises and blood.

Silas decides that now is the right moment to join the fight. He stalks toward me, unknowingly stepping right into Tempest's line of approach. Silas stops when we're only inches apart.

"No attempt to strike me down?" asks Silas. "Such a pity. It would cause you extraordinary pain to try and break our black magic bond. And I was so looking forward to watching you writhe."

I meet his gaze straight on. "You're still going to die, Silas."

"You can't kill me. You made a magical vow."

"I know I did." I nod toward Silas's shoulder. "Tempest didn't, though."

Turning around, Silas sees Tempest looming over him. The Emperor's slitted eyes are bright red with rage. He leans his head back, and black dragon scales crawl up his neck. The glow of red fire peeps out between the scales.

Tempest opens his mouth and releases a stream of red flame straight into Silas's face. The Incarnate howls in pain while Tempest's tail slices Silas in half, brains to balls. The demon falls over, dead. A warm sense of satisfaction blooms through my chest.

Goodbye, Silas.

Tempest's face returns to his human state. Our gazes meet and we share a half-smile.

"Tyberius seemed to wonder if I would come to your aid?" he asks.

His English accent somehow goes perfectly with his lizard eyes and badass armor.

"Well, you can be a touchy bastard sometimes."

"And you're an awful lad that I keep meaning to remove from my line of succession. Next month, for sure."

"You always say that."

"I always mean it."

A moan sounds from beside me. Spinning around, I find that Raj has collapsed. None of Silas's creations are left nearby, but my buddies are a mess. Tyberius races out from the trees.

"The dragons set me down near you," says Ty while panting for breath. "Then I got lost in the battle. Finally, I had to cast a locator charm and…"

"You can tell the story later," I say quickly. "These guys need your help."

Ty finally pauses enough to see the guys. Uther and Raj are now lying on the ground, passed out. Zee is kneeling with his eyes rolled up into his head.

"I've got to teleport them out of here," says Ty.

Tempest nods. "Do it now. My troops are still flying in, so the portal's open."

Ty frowns. "Once I teleport them, I'll be wiped out. These injuries are serious. I won't have enough magic to save them."

"Take them to my palace," says Tempest. "The Hexenwings can help you."

"Thanks, T." I pat Tempest on the shoulder and turn to my friend. "Get them out of here, Ty."

Tyberius raises his arms and starts chanting. For a few seconds, a light purple mist surrounds him, Uther, Raj, and Nizam. A loud crack tears through the air and then they all disappear. I stare at the spot for a few seconds.

"I hope they're holding up," I say in a low voice.

"You've other things to worry about, lad."

I turn to face Tempest. "Like what?"

He points to the white figures that are now filling the forest.

Air Valta. Hundreds of them.

"We can hold them for a while," says Tempest. "Get out of here and find your girl."

"I don't know where she is."

"I caught a scent on that demon," Tempest nods toward the charred body of Silas. "Elemental and antiseptic. He was near your monarkki.

They must be holding her in one of the infirmary buildings. I saw them on the flight in—wooden structures along the back of the compound."

"Thanks, T." I turn on my heel, ready to sprint away.

"Oh, and Maxon?"

I pause. "Yeah?"

"I scented Chimera there, too." Tempest's eyes flare red. "He's mine."

"Understood." I take off at a run.

24

LIANNA

*A*t last, I can move my eyes. No more staring at the same spot on the infirmary wall.

Hallelujah.

Chimera's paralytic is finally starting to wear off a little. These moments are rare. Normally, Chimera gives me more than enough venom ages before I need it.

I'm still thirsty as hell, though. They won't give me water in case it strengthens me enough to escape. Good thinking, actually.

A pair of elemental heliae float-walk into the room. They're the nurses of this place. The heliae have super-long necks, hollow sockets for eyes, and long silver hair that hangs down to their waists. Their skinny arms sport an extra set of elbows, so they can grab a syringe and stick you before you have time to realize what's going on. I learned that one the hard way.

"Treatment," says the first heliae. He speaks in a slow, rough howl that reminds me of harsh winter wind. "Chimera."

Not a chatty bunch, the heliae. This is his way of asking why Chimera isn't here to jam more venom into my neck. I'd say there's no rush, but I can't speak yet.

"Audience," says the second. This one's a woman; I can tell because her winding-sheet robe covers her from shoulder to ankle. Her voice quivers with fear. "Zephyr."

A spark of hope ignites in my soul. I know what that shaky voice means. It's the same one all the heliae use when Zephyr's temper is up. Half the infirmary is packed with air elementals that Zephyr hit or hurt.

One guy got his legs torn off for addressing Zephyr as *Your* Eminence instead of *The* Eminence.

Man, I can't wait to get out of here and kill that monster.

Fresh voices sound in the hallway. The heliae gasp, turn into their smoke forms, and drift silently away. That can only mean one thing.

Zephyr's coming to visit.

I hear him talking outside my room. "Silas's work in the forest is an utter failure," says Zephyr. "I need every Air Valta there to clean them out."

If I could smile, I would. Maybe I'd even cheer, too. Sounds like Silas is in trouble.

A new voice sounds from the hallway. "And what do you wish of me?" That one's Chimera.

"What I always want," says Zephyr. "Your venom. Her powers."

"Before we discuss this, there is another matter I wish to raise. Perhaps I can be of more use…"

"Silence! You said you were an expert in torture." Zephyr's voice takes on the roar of a cyclone. "So, why must I watch over you like a child? You know what I expect of you. If the girl transfers her power to that Kristalli, I'll continue to keep you safe from Tempest." I hear his fist pound the wall with each word. "That is all."

"Then, I shall do as The Eminence commands."

"At last." A whoosh of air follows those last words. Zephyr is gone.

Chimera growls under his breath. "That monarkki needs a strong general to keep him in line." When Chimera speaks again, he raises his voice. "You there. Heliae."

"Sir."

Chimera starts rattling off commands at the heliae. My mind can't focus on his words. Instead, the mention of 'general' has my thoughts returning to old paths of worry.

Fisk.

Once again, I wonder what happened to my friend. With any luck, all Zephyr wanted was the Kristalli of Water. Once he had the stone, Zephyr should've let Fisk go.

A long creak sounds as the door opens, jarring me from my thoughts. Heavy footsteps tromp across the floor. Chimera's here. He's in his hybrid human-dragon form, so his two necks sway as he steps to my bedside. Chimera lifts my right hand, examining the Kristalli that's still tied to my palm.

"The stone's dark," he whines.

And it'll stay that way.

"You're incredibly stubborn." Chimera paces along the back wall. "Zephyr says that I should torture you. Pull out your nails. Punch in your eyes. Elementals heal so quickly, you'd feel an exquisite sort of pain."

What I wouldn't give to flip him the finger right now. And then maybe scream and run for cover. That torture stuff would suck.

"Then again, you *are* a warrior." Chimera's voice lowers an octave. "For one such as you, there are more effective means of delivering pain."

Icy fear trickles down my spine. He's right. Namare trained me to handle physical torture. She always worried that Zephyr would capture me and do his worst. On the other hand, Chimera seems like the type who likes mental torture. Not something I'm familiar with.

"Last chance," says Chimera in a sing-song voice. "Transfer your powers back to the Kristalli and I will kill you quickly. You'll get no such promise from Zephyr."

My mind races for a way out of this mess; I come up empty. With a flash of realization, I know that I'm about to die. At this point, my only choice is *how*.

Do I go while giving Zephyr what he wants?

No way. After all these years, I can't give the evil freak anything. If holding back the Kristalli is the only victory I can have over him, I'll take it.

Chimera leans across the base of the bed. His reptilian-slitted eyes stare directly into mine. "Oh, no. You can move your gaze. Let's fix that, shall we?" He smiles at me for a long moment, and I know another needle is coming my way.

And so it does.

Chimera drags out the process of filling up another syringe and then pumping it into my neck. Once he's done, he steps into my frozen line of vision, his pair of lipless reptilian faces winding into ever-wider smiles. "Let's get down to business, shall we?" As always, his heads speak in unison.

A cold bead of sweat slowly dips down my back.

What's he planning to do, exactly?

Chimera waves his scaled hand before my eyes, ensuring that my gaze is once again locked at a certain spot on the wall. Whatever he has planned, it requires that I can't look away. Fear twists my insides.

"It seems I can't convince you to transfer your power," Chimera says with a dramatic sigh. "And I very much need Zephyr's help. You see, my son is causing all sorts of trouble and I'd much rather be scheming against him than wasting time with you. So, I've decided to bring someone else in... An expert in changing minds."

Chimera drags a chair so it's placed directly in line my sight.

Terror overwhelms my mind. All I can think about is the chair and empty stretch of wall. This is some kind of performance for my benefit.

Chances are, it won't be pleasant.

Chimera bangs on the door. "Bring it in!"

A pair of heliae haul in a pale figure. With a great heave, they set the lifeless form onto the empty chair. My skin crawls with grief and horror.

It's Fisk.

And he's dead.

The man I once loved has his throat torn out. Ligaments and bone protrude from the open wound. His beautiful sea green eyes stare at me, while his mouth rounds into a silent scream. Tears stream down my face. Everything in me wants to turn away from this sight, but I can't. And the worst part of all? *I'm* the reason his life's over.

This is torture. Pure. Raw. Unthinkable.

I don't consciously will it to happen, but the Kristalli in my hand glows with a pale blue light. Fisk's empty eyes seem to plead with me to join him in the next world. We'll reunite in friendship, free of pain and loss. My fears were right, all along. I was never strong enough to be the monarkki. Now, I crave a simple end to my useless life.

Chimera promised me a swift death. I hold onto that thought as my power slowly seeps away. I'm vaguely aware of raised voices somewhere in the infirmary.

Zephyr must be at it again. More heliae are about to die.

I brace my soul for the screams that inevitably follow one of Zephyr's rages.

They don't come.

Instead, there are rushed footsteps in the outer hallway. The heliae sound frantic. I focus on their wispy voices.

"Evacuate."

"Warrior."

"Front door."

My thoughts freeze. Zephyr sent all the Air Valta to the forest. So who's trying to break through the front door?

A thrill of realization moves through me. Maybe Zephyr wasn't fighting Silas after all.

Perhaps Maxon is here.

As soon as the thought strikes my mind, I dismiss it. There is no rescue from an elemental realm. Zephyr only allows those he chooses into his compound. Maxon couldn't have found a way in, could he?

Another heliae voice reaches my ears. "Thrax."

Pure joy zings through me. A thrax warrior in Zephyr's realm? It must be Maxon.

Chimera has the same thought. He bolts to his feet, races to the door, and pulls it open. "Come here, you."

"Yes?" asks a heliae.

"I heard someone speaking of a thrax. Who is here?"

"Warrior." The heliae's voice quivers with fear.

Chimera speaks slowly and with a menacing edge. "What's the name?"

"Maxon."

I sense more than see Chimera dragging the heliae into my room.

"You know how to use a syringe?" he asks.

"Yes," answers the heliae.

In my peripheral vision, I see Chimera open a supply drawer and pull out a fresh vial. He plunges the needle into his throat, draws a full dose of green paralytic venom and then sets the syringe into the heliae's hand.

"Inject her in fifteen minutes," orders Chimera.

"Evacuation," says the heliae. "My people."

"You're not going anywhere." Chimera voice comes out a low growl. "Stay right here with her."

"You stay," replies the heliae. "Zephyr says."

"Blast Zephyr!" roars Chimera. "Prince Maxon and I have unfinished business. No one cuts me and lives." Chimera bolts from the room, leaving the heliae waiting and silent.

A full minute passes before the heliae lets off a string of odd words. I don't need to speak air elemental to get the gist. The heliae is cursing out Chimera. With a dramatic swoosh of his extra-long arms, the heliae resets the syringe back into its drawer and slams it shut.

"My people," hisses the heliae. "Evacuate."

As the heliae leaves the room, a great crash sounds from the far side of the infirmary. An unmistakable noise follows—the happy gurgle of water as it tumbles from a broken cistern.

I sense the clean liquid as it flows under my doorway and beneath my bed. Hope lightens me, body and soul. Maybe I can cleanse myself with the fresh water, just like I cleansed Maxon in the cave.

Only one way to find out.

On my command, the water in my room transforms into mist. A blue haze surrounds me, soaking into my skin. I focus on each molecule as it moves through my body, asking it to remove the harmful venom.

Seconds tick by, then minutes. At last, the process works. My skin flares blue with glee as I move my eyes once again. Soon, I can twiddle my fingers and toes.

This is happening. If I can move, I can escape.

A new voice rings in my ears, chilling me over with cold despair.

"Where is he? Where's Chimera?"

It's Zephyr. And man, does he ever sound pissed.

I focus my energy on the fresh trickle of water nearby. More and more, I ask it to rise into my body, clearing away Chimera's paralytic. Next, I can move my legs. After that, my shoulders are mine to control as well.

Meanwhile, light footsteps speed down the outer corridor.

Zephyr.

If he reaches the door before I'm fully healed, I'm in deep trouble. I can't fight back. I can't even scream. He'll whisk me off somewhere and find a new minion to torture me.

My eyes widen with comprehension. He may even take the task upon himself.

A thin tendril of smoke pours in from under the door. Zephyr is coming inside. With aching movements, I force myself to stand up. The ordeal is exhausting. There's still too much poison in my system, but I can't give up. Before me, the smoke starts to gel into a human shape.

I'm almost out of time.

That's when it hits me. If I can change my appearance to resemble my old thrax self, why not try something else? Sure, Namare never changed herself to look like another creature. That doesn't mean it can't be done. And that syringe is still sitting in the drawer...

Zephyr's body becomes solid and complete. He stares at me carefully, his fingers playing along the scar on his cheek. I fight the urge to gasp. In the rush, I'd forgotten all about my precious Kristalli of Water. I must have dropped it in the bed.

"She's gone?" asks Zephyr.

I nod and try to look terrified. It isn't hard. I can't talk with a windy voice like a real heliae, so hopefully that'll be enough for Zephyr.

"Chimera failed," he adds.

More nodding.

"Where is her Kristalli?" Zephyr asks slowly.

I shrug and gesture to the mattress.

Fast as a heartbeat, Zephyr rifles through the bed, tearing apart pillows and blankets in his search. After a few seconds he pauses, holding the Kristalli of Water high. He wraps it with a bit of leather and sets it into a holster at the waistline of his Roman armor.

I'm out of time.

Racing to the other side of the room, I yank open the drawer and pull out the loaded syringe. Twisting about, I stab the needle into Zephyr's neck, quickly pressing down the plunger to inject the paralytic venom. He feels the prick of the needle and roars with anger.

"How dare you?" Zephyr spins, his arms outstretched and ready to throttle me.

I stand motionless as a statue, frozen in terror. One thought echoes through my mind.

Please let this work.

Zephyr's hands brush my throat. After that, they stop. For a few precious seconds, his mouth tries to form words. He can't. Instead, Zephyr tumbles to the floor, paralyzed. His eyes stay fixed on me, while his mouth hangs open in a snarl.

Raising my arm, I conjure an ice sword into my right hand. "This is for Namare." Raw rage sends my energy levels skyrocketing. Gritting my teeth, I slam the frozen blade into Zephyr's belly. It's a perfect strike, just like Fisk taught me.

I summon another sword and raise it high. "And this is one's for Fisk."

Before I lower the blade, a dragon roar fills the air.

Chimera.

My arm freezes with fear. Maxon is somewhere nearby. What if Chimera finds him?

Dropping the blade, I force myself into mist form. This shift takes a ton of energy even if I'm at full power, and right now I'm definitely not. I give myself an internal pep talk and hope like hell that it works.

Hurry up, Lianna. You have to find Maxon.

25

MAXON

I stand on the cobblestone courtyard before one of Zephyr's infirmaries. There are a shit-ton of these places around here. I could search for days and not find Lianna.

Good thing I found these kids instead.

A couple of Air Valta boys stand guard at the infirmary door. It's obvious they know where Lianna is and won't say anything. Stubborn little guys. I've been negotiating with them for too long already. Hell, I called down enough lightning to smash down three trees and burst up a cistern. At least, the kids are softened up now. Dragon roars are now carrying in from the battlefield, so that's helping to loosen them up, too. One more round of threats and they'll be ready to talk.

"Where is she?" I ask.

The kids look at each other, their eyes wide with terror. Neither replies.

"Last warning." Raising my hand, I summon lightning to crackle across my palm. "This one isn't going into the trees, guys. I'm out of time."

"She's inside this building," says the first kid quickly. "Last room on the left."

"Good work," I say. "Now go hide. Things are about to get nasty." The kids disappear in a puff of smoke.

I kick down the front door and race into the infirmary. The place is half deserted. Worried heliae carry wounded elementals out to safety. None of the injured are Valta, though. I picture my Furor allies back in the woods, fighting off the Air Valta. Anxiety constricts my temples. I hope they're okay.

One battle at a time, Maxon. Focus on Lianna.

Turning on my heel, I race down the main hallway. My gaze stays locked on the last door on the left. Lianna's room.

Almost there.

My chest warms with a mixture of hope and excitement. Is she still in her room? Will she be all right? I'm only a few yards from her door when the unexpected happens.

The entire wall of the infirmary bursts open.

It's Chimera, and he's in his full dragon form: A massive body covered in black scales.

At least I lopped off one of his heads back at Charybdis. Less to worry about now.

Chimera's two remaining heads swivel on their long necks, tearing through the wooden walls like tissue paper. I grit my teeth, disappointment and rage battling it out in my nervous system.

I was almost to Lianna.

Chimera's long, powerful limbs flex down into crouch, ready to pounce. I mirror the movement, keeping my tail high above my shoulder.

Chimera launches at me, his dual jaws snapping at my head. Venom-laced saliva drips from his long pointed teeth. Pushing back with my legs, I jump right at him. The arrowhead end of my tail plunges through his dragon scale hide right at the top of his rib cage. Once I have a good catch, I use the momentum to tear a line down his torso. I land in a roll on the courtyard grounds, one thought on my mind.

Nothing cuts through dragon scales like dragon scales.

Chimera sits up on his haunches and lets out a howl of fury. The cut isn't deep enough to kill the old bastard, but I'm sure it hurts like hell. Chimera's bulk twists around to face me. He stomps through the remains of the infirmary wall and onto the courtyard, the venom sack on one neck puffing out as he moves.

Right neck. That means acid venom.

I dodge for cover behind a cluster of trees that line the cobblestone yard. A blast of yellow acid hits the trunks, melting them into the ground.

That was Chimera's volley. It'll take him time to work up another venom shot.

Now, it's my turn.

Rising to my feet, I summon bolt after bolt of lightning. Some slam straight into Chimera, shocking him and giving me time to close in.

Once I'm near enough, I leap toward his throat, loop my legs around his neck, and spin until gravity has me hanging upside down. After that, I go to town on his neck. Using my scale-covered hand and tail, I punch into the venom sack, rapid-fire style.

Chimera lets out another big roar. The bare trees shimmy from the force of his cry. I cling to his throat as Chimera tosses his injured head from side to side. For a while, I keep my grip. Soon, the movement tears me free. I fall onto my back with a thud. Chimera's wounded head hangs at an odd angle, unable to focus or speak.

Good. His second head is unconscious. One down. One to go.

Chimera's final head focuses on me. This is the one that spews green paralytic. Opening its jaws wide, the mouth releases a stream of venom straight toward my face.

Nice try, asshole.

I roll out of the venom's strike zone. With a low hiss, the liquid slams into the ground beside me. I leap upright, jump onto Chimera's back, and race along his spine scales.

Paralytic head, here I come.

I speed up the thick neck. My tail arches over my shoulder, ready to spear its arrowhead end straight through Chimera's last functioning skull.

That's the moment Chimera decides to take flight.

The dragon's huge black wings spread wide, beating in a regular rhythm. I'm tossed onto my ass. Leaning forward, I grip the larger scales with my hands, while my tail plunges through the skin for a better hold. Chimera spirals up and up in a corkscrew motion. Clouds whiz by us. The air turns cold. My vision starts to blur with dizziness.

Chimera pauses mid-flight to change direction. For a second, I feel weightless. After that, Chimera swoops down toward the ground. He keeps flying in a corkscrew motion, only faster this time.

I get dizzy as fuck and lose my grip.

For a while, I tumble through the air. My heart hammers away in my chest. Somehow I'm able to twist onto my side, which is the best way to hit the ground when you fall.

It still sucks when I slam into the earth, though. There's a bone-crunching crack, too. I try to get back on my feet. Every part of me screams with the effort. It's all I can do to look up and see Chimera dive-bombing toward me. The jaws of his last conscious head are wide open, ready to spew paralytic at me.

My mind runs through options and implications. At this speed—and with my injuries—I won't be able to run away. I can't cower, either. It's not in me. I glare at Chimera as he swoops closer. My eyes flare demon-red with rage.

Chimera opens his mouth; the venom sack on his neck flexes as he prepares to douse me with paralytic. I keep my gaze locked with his.

Somehow, somewhere, I'll get you for this. Maybe as a damned ghost.

The paralytic spews from his jaws, ready to engulf me.

But it doesn't.

Instead, the venom freezes into a hard lump and tumbles onto the ground. Chimera does the same. His skin prickles over with frost. He loses control of his wings and crash lands not far from me. His last head rises up, ready to spit more venom. Before he can, the frost along the length of his neck thickens.

Chimera becomes frozen solid.

I grin from ear to ear. Freezing dragons means someone's nearby.

Lianna.

Sure enough, a blue haze forms. The mist solidifies into Lianna's lovely body. Moving as quickly as I can—which isn't too fast—I wrap my arms around her and hold her tight. Makes my rib cage scream with pain, but I don't care.

She's my heart and she's come back.

26

LIANNA

$\mathcal{M}$axon's heavy arms wrap around me, making me feel warm and safe. I nuzzle into his neck and instantly relax. His voice is a sweet growl in my ear.

"How are you holding up, beautiful?" He leans back and I almost fall over. My legs are still jelly after so much time under the paralytic.

"You can't stand up straight," Maxon wraps his arms around me once more, only more tightly this time. "So I guess that's my answer."

"Chimera put too much paralytic in my system; I'm having a hard time cleaning it out." I slide my arms around his waist. "How about you?"

"Got a little banged up back there. Chimera decided to take me for a ride and drop me."

"I guess he did some damage to us both."

"I'd be in worse shape without your flash freeze." Maxon leans back and fixes me with his mismatched eyes. "Thanks for saving my ass."

"Well, I *am* partial to your ass."

He chuckles. "Good."

My gaze shifts to Chimera and my skin glows with rage. "He made me stare at Fisk's body. Sat it right in my line of vision."

"I'm so sorry, Lianna."

When I speak again, my voice comes out low and deadly. "I want to kill him. Now."

"That's not an option, beautiful."

"Why not? Don't you want to kill him?"

"Fuck yeah. Look, he hurt you and it's taking everything I have not to rip his last two heads off. But I made a promise to Tempest. The Furor are fighting the Air Valta for us right now. In return, they want Chimera. Alive."

An idea forms in my mind. Chimera has two heads. That's one more than anyone really needs.

"Alive eh?" I ask.

Maxon shoots me a sly grin. "Yeah. Tempest wants Chimera to serve trial for crimes against his people." He taps his chin dramatically. "But it's probably a lot easier to try someone who can't spit paralytic venom in your face."

"Good point," I say.

With a snap of my fingers, I send a fissure through the ice in Chimera's body. From across the courtyard, a long crack forms in one of the dragon's necks. For a moment, his paralytic head wobbles, then it falls to the ground with a heavy thud.

"Nicely done," says Maxon. "Only one head left. Now, we need to get you out of here. Can you mist away?"

"Zephyr's probably dead, so I should be able to manage it."

"Probably dead?"

"I might have drugged him with some of Chimera's paralytic and then stabbed him in the stomach."

Maxon lets out a low whistle. "Have I told you you're perfect?"

"Yes. But don't stop."

"Good. If Zephyr's down, then it's definitely time you left."

"No, it's time *we* left. With Zephyr out, I may be able to open a gateway for both of us."

Maxon eyes me carefully. "Nah, you should go alone. I can't leave until I'm sure Zephyr's history."

"In that case, I'll check on Zephyr with you. Last time, I had to leave before I was sure he was dead. But if Zephyr's still alive, then I want to help kill him."

"You're not killing anything. You can hardly stand on your own."

I roll my eyes. "And you're half dead from fighting Chimera."

Maxon purses his lips, considering. "You're not leaving without me, are you?"

"Not a chance."

"Well, then." He gives me one of his crooked smiles. "How do we leave together?"

"I'll need some help. Let me show you."

Turning away from Maxon, I raise my right arm. A small waterfall of bright blue liquid materializes before us. Within seconds, an image forms in the shimmering water. It's a view into the Hall of Fountains. Once again, Esau appears.

"Lianna! You're here!"

His happiness is so contagious that I smile. "What are you doing there?"

"I'm waiting for you. Dad said I could. Everyone told me that you'd come back with Fisk, not show up in the Hall of Fountains, but I said they were wrong. You'd want to talk *our* way."

Maxon hides a smile. "Looks like you've a boyfriend there, Li."

"She's not my girlfriend!" says Esau. "That's gross. Are you ready to become the monarkki, Lianna? Do you want me to get all the Valta? They'll come if I ask them. General Fisk explained everything." Esau lowers his voice. "Dad said Fisk acted like a deuce-bag to hit on you when you were so young. The guy's like three hundred."

I can't believe my ears. "Deuce-bag?"

"I think that's what he said. Anyway, are you ready to get crowned?"

"Not quite, Esau. I do need you to summon the Valta, though. Bring them to the Hall of Fountains as quickly as you can."

"All right," says Esau. He races away screaming. "Hey everybody!"

In no time, the Valta fill the massive space. None of them ask me about Fisk, and I'm not going to volunteer the information. That's something best said in person.

Esau's father steps forward. I remember him from his long droopy tentacle moustache. "I'm Johtaja. What do you require of us?"

For a moment, it's all I can do to soak in his words. *What do you require of us?* I'm not crowned, and yet Johtaja is treating me as his monarkki. A sunny sense of pride spreads through my chest. Trouble is, it's quickly overwhelmed by a cold wave of fear.

Zephyr could show up any second.

"Johtaja, I need your strength, and that of all the Valta. Remember when I gave my power to your child, back when I first visited the Water Palace?"

"I was so disrespectful then, Your Eminence—"

"That's not important now. All that matters is the connection that took place. I need to find that again, but this time, it needs to be with all of you. I'm trapped in Zephyr's realm without enough power to leave. If you can connect your elemental energy to mine, I may be able to turn this fountain into a gateway for escape."

Johtaja nods briskly. "As you command, Your Eminence." He leans his head back and lets out a long set of calls that remind me of whale song.

Within seconds, the Valta are hovering in the air, their bodies aligned into a diamond formation.

"On my mark," commands Johtaja. "We send our energy to Lianna." He bows his head and raises his right hand. The other Valta do the same. "Now!"

All of a sudden, elemental strength pours into my body, over-whelming my mind. I feel frozen in place. At last, a voice breaks through my inner haze.

"Are you all right, Lianna?"

It's Maxon.

My voice quakes when I reply. "I think so."

"Focus, Lianna." Maxon links his fingers with mine. "You can do this."

I stare into his mismatched eyes and my spine stiffens with resolve.

This will happen. I'll get us out of here.

Keeping my gaze on the waterfall, I reach toward it with my left hand. Fresh power flows to me from the Valta. My body fills to bursting with energy and light. Blue luminescence cascades into my fingertips, turning my skin even brighter. Excitement churns through me.

We're really making this work.

Suddenly, the waterfall starts to disappear. Instead, a gateway opens directly into the Hall of Fountains. I lean forward, stopping right before my fingertips pass through what was once cascading liquid. Now, I feel nothing there.

I push further.

My hand touches the warm air of the Hall of Fountains. The scent of seawater rises to greet me.

We're so close.

More Valta appear below. Additional power flows through me. I tighten my hold on Maxon's hand.

"You ready?" I ask.

"Whenever you are."

Acting in unison, we both stare down into the open gateway. Maxon and I share a nod. Moving as one, we crouch down and prepare to jump.

The waterfall vanishes.

"Oh no," I whisper. "The gateway closed."

We're out of time.

Lifting my gaze, I see Zephyr standing across the courtyard. The light on his gray skin pulses with rage. His Kristalli crown becomes blindingly bright. My skin prickles with fear.

"On second thought," I say slowly. "I think we may get to kill Zephyr anyway."

Maxon cracks his neck from side to side. "Good."

Zephyr glares at Chimera's frozen form. The monarkki's mouth twists with disgust. "Fool! I never should have trusted you with such a simple task." Turning away from Chimera, Zephyr raises his arms. "Air Valta, to me!"

Tendrils of smoke instantly appear on either side of Zephyr. Two Air Valta take shape. Both are young with battered armor and lines of exhaustion on their faces.

Only two Valta come to Zephyr's call? Clearly, the Furor are having fun. That's good for our side.

Zephyr lets out a howl of rage. "More weakness! Where are the rest of your kindred?"

My mouth falls open with shock. If this were my Valta army, I'd leave the rival monarkki and thrax warrior alone so I could go help my own people. The enraged look in Zephyr's eyes says he couldn't care less about the Air Valta. Instead, he rounds on Maxon and me. "Attack!"

The two Air Valta speed toward us. Fortunately, there's plenty of water nearby, thanks to the broken cistern from Maxon's battle with Chimera. I summon liquid whirligigs—pinwheels of water with the bite of a circular saw blade. With a shout, I launch them at each of the Valta. The impact sends them careening into the forest, their Roman armor sliced open.

Meanwhile, Zephyr turns to the shattered remains of the infirmary building. He creates towering cyclones of wind. The broken floorboards and bits of wall are quickly engulfed in the storm. The debris spins at mind-blowing speeds as it whizzes in our direction. Once the projectiles cross the open courtyard, Maxon zaps them with lightning. The hunks of wood explode in fire. White ash cascades over the courtyard. The nearby forest erupts in flame.

Suddenly, a pair of cyclones slams into me. I glance at Zephyr. That wasn't his handiwork; the Air Valta are back. My body's tossed against a burning tree trunk. Flames singe my spine and bite into my watery body. I try to move, but the Air Valta flank my sides. They've created ropes of fast moving air that bind me in place as tightly as steel.

Through the smoke, ash, and flame, I stare up into the skies, hoping for the Furor will appear. They don't.

Instead, the Air Valta tighten the bindings around me, making the fire burn more deeply into my body. None of the life-giving water from the broken cistern can reach me through the blaze. My waning powers are sapped, and all my abilities go into simply regenerating my flesh. My watery skin peels and reforms, becoming papery and dry. Pain like I never could have imagined rushes through me.

A heavy sense of doom drives into my soul, as harsh as the charred tree branches that dig into my body. The truth becomes crystal clear through the miasma of agony. The Air Valta are formidable enemies. The Furor are still occupied fighting them. No one is coming to save us.

I search for Maxon. In between the thick gusts of smoke, I see him grappling with Zephyr in the center of the courtyard. Maxon distracts Zephyr with pinpoint lightning strikes as he drives punch after punch into the monarkki's gut. Even as I bite back pain, I can't help but marvel at the speed and accuracy of Maxon's attack. He's a tough warrior. Maybe we'll get out of this yet.

Zephyr curls forward, tumbling onto his knees. Despite the hurt, I feel a jolt of elation. Maxon has Zephyr down. Now, the Air Valta will have to choose between fighting Maxon and holding me captive. They can't do both. Soon, we'll be free.

Only we're not.

Zephyr raises his head, leaps to his feet, and slams his skull onto Maxon's. The Kristalli of Air breaks apart. Half of it falls onto the courtyard's cobblestones; the other half attaches itself to Maxon's chest. My world freezes as I watch Maxon claw at the stone, his face writhing in agony.

Oh, no.

It's just like back in the cave, when I tried to heal Maxon. He somehow took in my elemental abilities. Now, the Kristalli of Air is digging into his rib cage. There's no doubt in my mind. It will kill him.

Maxon's expression hardens with resolve. He calls down more lightning. This time, Zephyr wasn't expecting a counter-strike. Maxon catches him unaware. The bright bolts slam into Zephyr's solid form, sending him tumbling to the ground.

My body stills with anticipation. Finally, Zephyr's knocked out.

Unfortunately, so is Maxon.

Maxon lies unmoving on the courtyard stones. Anger, pain, and terror churn through me.

Not Maxon. Anyone but Maxon.

I roar with rage. *Maxon will not die while I stand by and watch.* Closing my eyes, I tap into some last reserve of elemental energy. A final burst of power charges my limbs. I tear through the bindings that hold me in place. Quick as a heartbeat, I cast two great icicles, one for each of the Valta. They don't see the attack coming, so they're unprepared. That means they're in solid form, not smoke.

Much easier to kill.

I skewer both Valta through the chest. My icicle blades meet heavy resistance as they slice through the guard's flesh. The pair of Valta crumple over, dead.

Gritting my teeth through the pain, I limp away from the burning forest, making a path toward the courtyard and Maxon. As I step along, fiery splinters spike into my bare feet. I don't care. Zephyr lies on his side, injured but still dangerous. It doesn't enter into my mind to worry. All I can see is Maxon's immobile form. Blood pools around him. Half of the Kristalli of Air burrows into his chest. I hobble toward him as fast as I can go, tears of rage and fear streaming down my ash-covered face.

Not Maxon. Anyone but Maxon.

MAXON

I lie on the courtyard grounds like a corpse. Somehow, part of Zephyr's Kristalli attached itself to my chest. Damn, it hurts like hell. Tiny prongs of stone burrow into my rib cage. Questions burn through my brain, but the pain's too intense to really think things through. Still, I keep asking them, over and over.

Why did the Kristalli do this? Is it some trick of Zephyr's?

Pain sears my lungs as the Kristalli digs deeper. On instinct, my fingers tear at the stone, trying to yank it out. It doesn't budge. Somewhere through the haze of shock and hurt, my mind's able to focus on one thing—the reason why I'm here in the first place.

Lianna. What happened to Lianna?

Wincing through the pain, I force myself to move and inspect the courtyard. Lianna slowly limps toward me. She's safe and alive, so at least that's going right. The two Air Valta who were holding her are now impaled on tree trunks. Their heads sag forward onto their punctured chests.

That's about as dead as you get, right there.

I make a quick scan for Zephyr. He's lying on his side, curled into fetal position. The other half of his broken Kristalli lies nearby. The stone keeps pulsing with light, but Zephyr's not moving.

I hope to hell that he's dead, or close to it.

Another jolt of pain sears through my nervous system. This time, the hurt isn't coming from the tiny prongs driving into my chest. Instead, agony radiates throughout my body. This isn't regular pain. I've been around enough crazy supernatural crap to know this is something else.

It's power. Elemental power.

I try to think through my situation, but misery keeps me trapped without answers. Surges of hurt run through me in waves. With a low moan, I move onto my knees. My body curls forward while my hands press at my temples. Every inch of me radiates agony.

Across the courtyard, Zephyr's arm twitches. Damn, the bastard's still alert and alive. He grasps for the other half of the Kristalli; the stone attaches itself to his hand.

What's going on here?

Fresh surges of power and pain careen through me. I let out an anguished howl. More elemental energy tears through my system. The flesh on my arms and legs begins to smoke and bubble. I've been in tight spots before. Nothing like this, though. Reality hits me like a physical punch.

I'm about to die.

At last, Lianna crosses the courtyard. With jerky motions, she kneels down beside me. She's hurting, too. I want to ask her if she's okay. The words can't get past my gritted teeth.

Lianna's voice comes out all calm and sweet. "Do you remember the cave, Maxon?"

I manage a half nod.

"You were poisoned. I tried to heal you and you took in my power instead."

Another small nod.

"That's what's happening now. Somehow your powers align with elementals. Stuff got mixed up in your fight with Zephyr. You're taking in the energy of the Monarkki of Air." She lifts her hand to brush her knuckles down my cheek. The touch helps me focus. For the first time since this stone glommed onto me, I'm able to think beyond the torment.

Lianna's right. I got a taste of her power in the caves and used light-ning as a buffer. That slowed everything right down.

I hiss out two words. "Thanks, beautiful."

With all my focus, I summon a sheath of lightning to surround my skin. At first, the brightness is pale and weak. Soon, the power grows. Within a few seconds, the shield is strong enough to block whatever the fuck the Kristalli is doing. The hurt lessens. My head clears.

"That's it." Lianna gently kisses my chin. "You're doing it."

The power of the air element starts to seep away from me as well. Pain drains from my body. Without the weight of agony in my limbs, I can breathe deeply again. My thinking becomes clearer by the second.

My focus immediately snaps to Zephyr. We need to kill that guy and get the hell out of here.

Zephyr lies on his side about twenty yards away. I release a relieved breath.

"He's still down," I say to Lianna.

"Can you stand?" she asks.

"Can you?"

Lianna chuckles. "Now, I *know* you're feeling better."

We both try to rise to our feet when shit goes downhill, fast.

Zephyr's started to move, too.

The Kristalli on his hand glows with energy. A ripple of fear moves across my limbs. My now-clear mind can easily see what's happening.

As I release air power, Zephyr takes it back in.

Damn.

Pressing his palms against the courtyard stones, Zephyr hauls himself up to a sitting position. Not good. The more power Zephyr gets back, the more Lianna and I are screwed. Neither of us is in any condition to fight him at full strength.

What happens next isn't a thought-out thing, but when it comes to a battle, sometimes there's only reaction. You just do. And now, what I'm doing is removing the lightning shield from around my body. I can't let Zephyr get back to full strength.

Instantly, white-hot hurt shoots through every nerve ending I've got. This time, it's even worse than before. Still, accepting the elemental energy does the trick. Zephyr howls in pain as his Kristalli dims.

Lianna leans forward, her gaze meeting mine. "Maxon, stop!"

I shake my head. "If I stop, he kills us both."

From the opposite side of the courtyard, Zephyr moans and bitches as he flips over and starts belly-crawling toward Lianna and me.

Man, I hate that guy.

"I am The Eminence!" growls Zephyr. "You both will die."

Lianna tries to drag me away, but she can barely stand up. I grab her hand.

"You need to go," I say. "Find Tempest. Be safe."

"I'm not leaving. There must be something else we can do." Her face lights with an idea. "There's something you haven't tried."

I see where she's going with this. "I can store the power in the stone. See if my lightning will keep it from Zephyr, too."

"Can your lightning power do that?"

"It can try."

Closing my eyes, I realign the lightning shield around my body. Right away, it focuses the elemental energy into the Kristalli. My pain lessens. The Kristalli shimmers with a pale gray light.

"It's working," says Lianna. "Keep going. Move all the power you can into the Kristalli. Zephyr will be weak as a human."

With every ounce of will inside me, I order more energy into the stone. The Kristalli grows brighter. I glance over to Zephyr. His part of the Kristalli has stayed pretty dark. The bastard keeps crawling at us, though. He's only ten yards away now.

Lianna raises her hand, summoning some kind of frozen spear. The second it appears, pain racks my nervous system again. I howl in anguish.

"Step back," I say to Lianna. "Your power's mixing with Zephyr's."

Lianna moves away. That doesn't do dick to stop the hurt. She lowers her hand. The ice spear vanishes.

"You should take him down," I say through clenched teeth. "I can handle the pain."

"I'm not doing that until you've moved more power into the stone. I don't know what releasing my energy will do." She runs her fingers along my neck. Her touch is soothing. "It won't be long now, Maxon. You're doing it."

"No, beautiful. *We're* doing it."

Never thought I needed a battle twin, but I need her.

We're working together, turning this shit around. Yeah, my head feels like it's about to explode. Still, my body's no longer screwed up in agony. And although Zephyr keeps belly-crawling toward us, he looks like total shit. His Kristalli is almost dark, and his body's all banged up and bloody. If he's dumb enough to keep coming, then Lianna and I can make mince-meat out of him when he gets close.

I look into her eyes.

Damn, I love this woman.

And with that, everything goes to hell.

A cool sensation pools behind my eyes and I just know my irises are flashing blue.

Lianna tilts her head to one side. "Are you okay, Maxon?"

Sadness weighs on my heart like a block of cement. I want to tell her no, I'm not okay. In fact, I'm pretty sure that I'm fucked.

"Are my eyes glowing?" I ask.

"Yes."

"What color?"

"Blue." Lianna's fingertips brush beside my eyes. "What does that mean?"

"Means I'm getting Angelbound."

"What?"

"I love you, Lianna. My powers are changing. No more lightning for me. I'll get control over igni."

As much as anyone can control igni.

"I don't understand. You can't change, not now."

"Not my call, beautiful. It's happening."

After that, the crazy music starts in my head, just like Mom said it would. A pretty children's choir for the light igni, which is the power that sends mortal souls to Heaven. Next I get the screeching voices of the dark igni, which is the energy that condemns spirits to Hell.

My abilities over lightning start to fade. I do everything I can, but it's like trying to cup water in my hands. The droplets simply go; there's nothing I can do about it. The reality hits me like a punch in the gut.

I'm gaining power over igni, same as my Mother did. That means I'm losing my control over lightning, which is the only thing keeping me alive right now. Without that lightning shield, Zephyr's energy will go to town on me. I don't stand a chance.

Bit by bit, my lightning-shield disappears. Instead, tiny bolts of sentient light—the igni—start swimming around my body. They move in little schools like fish. I've seen igni a million times as they move around Mom. I never seriously pictured them anywhere near me.

A thin hope sparks in my mind. Maybe these igni can still protect me from the power of Zephyr's Kristalli.

A heartbeat passes. Then two.

At three, it happens.

Zephyr's elemental power slams back into me. Agony like I've never known rips through my soul. It's like every inch of me is being torn apart. My skin bubbles and smokes once again. Black puss oozes from my veins.

Lianna gasps in horror. "No!"

Zephyr sees his chance and makes his move. Jumping up from his crawl-mode, he body-slams Lianna. Rage overtakes me despite the agony. I lunge forward, knocking Zephyr down. Lianna leaps back towards us, wraps her hands around Zephyr's skull, and twists the fucker's head right off. There's a satisfying crack as Zephyr's spine snaps in two.

The Monarkki of Air is dead.

Fuck yeah.

With Zephyr gone, the power that was stored in his half of the Kristalli now slams into my nervous system. I grit my teeth in agony.

Lianna rounds on me. "You have to stop it."

"There's no way to do that, beautiful."

More igni whirl around me. All I know is agony and their childlike voices. They sing a bunch of nonsense and do whatever the fuck it is that they want to do, just like I always said they would. More of my flesh starts to smoke and peel away.

Lianna grabs some bandages from the infirmary. She wraps the long strips around my body, trying to keep all of me together. Somehow, that's the worst part of this. That she's trying so hard to save me when we should be saying goodbye.

"Don't waste your strength," I say. "Whatever happens to me, happens."

"No, Maxon." She wraps another bandage around my forearm.

"Go find Tempest. Please."

Bright blue tears stream down Lianna's face. "I'll find a way to save you." Her voice breaks with grief and fear. "I refuse to let this happen."

Once again, the igni take charge. They wrap around Lianna, pulling her away. She tries summoning all sorts of water magic. None of it goes past the heavy column of brightly lit bodies swirling around her. It seems my new Scala powers and I agree on one thing: Lianna can't waste her energy on the impossible. This transition is going down and she needs to stay away. Most likely, I'm dead.

Who am I kidding? I'm totally dead.

The pain and process takes over. I tilt back on my knees, my arms thrown behind me. Smoke burns through my skin and digs into muscle and bone. Pain blots out every other sensation. My vision starts to dim.

This is it. I'm going down. One last thought hits me as I'm completely torn apart.

I'll die here, but at least Lianna will live.

28

LIANNA

*F*inally, the little lightning bolts release me from their hold. I stumble forward, my legs numb with shock. In my mind's eye, Maxon's last moments replay over and over. He kneels on the courtyard. His body curls backward. The skin on his torso turns black and bubbling. Hunks of his flesh are torn away. His beautiful face contorts in pain.

Maxon literally gets torn apart, the tiny pieces of his flesh carried off in smoke.

It can't be real.

Losing my footing, I fall forward. It hurts like hell but I don't care. All I can focus on is reaching the spot where Maxon last lived. I crawl across the courtyard, my chest aching. Somewhere in the recesses of my mind, I register that the Air Valta are carting away Zephyr's lifeless body. It's a hollow victory.

At last, I reach the place where Maxon fell. I sit back on my knees, just as he did. This was where he pulled his final breath. My parents and Namare are gone. Now Maxon is too. My chest aches with loss. Warm tears roll down my cheeks and off my chin. They dot the smooth brown stones beneath me like so many raindrops.

Perhaps I weep for hours, minutes, or days. There's no telling. Time has little meaning for me. Eventually, a hand rests on my shoulder. I look up, seeing Tempest. He seems indomitable in his heavy black armor. I wouldn't have thought he mourned Maxon, but his eyes are rimmed with red. Maxon was second in line for the Furor throne.

"He gone," I whisper.

"I know," says Tempest. "I'm so sorry."

I can only repeat myself. "He's gone."

Tempest's voice is mild. "They want to know if you're leading them now."

"Leading? Who?"

"The Air Valta."

"Aren't they all dead?"

Tempest shakes his head. "We just held them down until the battle was over. They're now the released prisoners of a very short war."

For the first time, I notice dozens of Air Valta standing behind Tempest. They should look tough in their Roman armor. Instead, their young gray faces are lined with despair.

"You're the last monarkki, Lianna. The Air Valta want to know if you're their ruler as well." Tempest pats my shoulder before pulling his hand away. He moves to stand behind me, giving me some breathing room. "What should I tell them?"

"I don't know." It's hard to speak through the knot of grief in my throat. "I need a moment to think."

Silence follows. The Air Valta continue to stare at me, their all-gray eyes wide with worry. Zephyr was cruel. Their desire for a wise ruler is a living thing. It tugs at my heart.

Maybe I have the strength to lead them. Maxon might have wanted that.

Someone calls my name again. "Lianna?"

"Wait, Tempest. I need more time to decide."

Tempest steps back into my line of vision. "I didn't say anything." He tilts his head. "Did you hear something?"

"Yes, I thought you said my name."

The voice speaks again. "Lianna."

I hop to my feet, my skin flaring blue with excitement. "Did you hear that?"

Tempest frowns. "I heard nothing."

"That voice. I thought it was…" I shake my head.

Stop now, Lianna. You're imagining things. How could it be Maxon?

It happens again.

"Lianna."

A ripple of awareness runs through the Air Valta. They exchange curious looks. I round on them, every particle of my consciousness on alert. "Did you hear it, too?"

A handful of the Valta nod slowly.

"There's a voice on the wind," says one of them.

Now the cry is loud and unmistakable. "Lianna!"

Before me, wisps of smoke drift into the shape of a man. The form is so thin and transparent, it could be a trick of the eyes.

But it's not. This is Maxon. He's alive. Somehow, he survived.

A crazy dream comes alive in my soul. I've seen those wisps of smoke before. How they start as winding tendrils and then transform into a human shape. It's what happens every time an air elemental appears.

Could Maxon have become an air elemental, too?

For a fraction of a second, Maxon's body comes into clearer focus. His arms reach out for me.

"Maxon!" I strain toward him. Our fingertips almost brush. At the last second, he turns back into smoke and drifts away. My soul aches with loss and longing.

I don't know what happened to him. I don't know if I can ever find my Maxon again, let alone touch him. I don't know, and I don't care. Something that looks like Maxon is leaving and he's not going alone.

In the blink of an eye, I transform into mist and follow.

29

MAXON

hat the fuck is going on?

One second, I was kneeling on the courtyard in Zephyr's compound. My body had never known such pain. The next thing I know, I'm yanked away on a vicious gust of wind.

My mind gets assaulted with so much stuff, I can't take it all in. One place after another tumbles past me. Even worse, I don't just see stuff. I'm part of it, too. First, I'm a summer wind that rolls down an empty city street. Then, I'm a storm tearing across the Himalayas. And finally, I'm a stream of air driving through a jet engine. This is insane.

Did I die and go to Hell?

No way. I've been to Hell. This is something else.

So what's happening to me?

The answer's almost clear when—whoosh—I'm carried away on another blast of wind. This time, I'm a gust that slams into skyscrapers. Whips through pinwheels. Touches the upper layer of the atmosphere. My mind starts to keep pace with the constant changes, and that's when the truth gets both obvious and nasty.

I've become an air elemental.

Screw Zephyr and his Kristalli. All I wanted to do was protect Lianna. Now, I've no clue if she's safe and I'm stuck whipping around. Pangs of worry spin through me, whatever 'me' is anymore. I've no clue how to control this shit. I try to focus. Come up with a Plan B.

No such luck.

Before I can string a strategy together, my consciousness gets yanked in a new direction. This time, it's an ocean-bound hurricane at night.

The thing is one vast mess of tall waves, lightning, and wind. My mind gets tossed around like one of the dumbass ships trying to navigate this storm. All the twisting around isn't helping my concentration.

One thing does help, however.

Now that I'm over the ocean, there's an unmistakable aura in the air. Even though I'm being spun around like crazy, I can't miss the sensation. Damn, I'm not even sure what to even name it. Energy. Magic. Elemental power. Whatever it is, it's bringing her closer.

Lianna.

Is she really here? Is she all right?

Man, do I need those answers. I try like hell to take some kind of human form. That's not happening, so I do the next best thing. Scream for all I'm worth.

"Lianna!" My voice comes out rough with excitement and fear.

Please let her hear me.

Little by little, a hazy shape appears on the storm. It's her. The hurricane winds whip through her hair and long robes. Still, she appears perfect, strong, and beautiful: Lianna, my blue-skinned goddess. Watching her, I can only think about what I said to her.

I love you.

Sure, saying those words got me into this mess. My lightning powers changed into Scala stuff and ended up getting me killed or shredded or whatever happened to me. Even so, I can't regret the feeling. After Armageddon, some part of my soul was broken and should have stayed that way. But she fixed it. Actually, *we* fixed it. Maybe I only had that feeling for only a minute or two. That's enough.

No, that's everything.

A warm sense of joy moves through me and that's when I realize it—I have a body again. No way am I missing this chance. I may be a gray and smoky blob, but I'm here. The wisps of smoke that are my arms reach for her. Seeing her helped me take solid form again. If I can only touch her...

"Lianna! I'm here!"

She turns toward me. "I'm trying to stop the storm." Her face is the picture of bone tired. "It's so strong."

"No time for that. Hold onto me."

I set my palms onto hers and whoa, I didn't see that coming. Some kind of elemental charge moves through my soul. It doesn't feel bad, necessarily. In fact, I'm pretty sure this rush was why Zephyr ran across the after-realms trying to suck off other monarkki. It's a huge wallop of energy, though, and that's not what I was expecting.

My limbs start to disintegrate into the windstorm.

Damn, I'm losing it.

"Can you hold back your elemental energy?" I ask. It's hard to howl over the crazy winds.

"Yes, I think I can."

Lianna reaches for my hands, her fingers trembling. The storm lashes against us both as we hover above the churning waters. We're getting tossed about, making it harder and harder to connect. My body is almost completely faded now, but I'm not giving up. Not on her. Not on us.

"Come on, beautiful." I move the wisp of smoke that is my hand toward hers. "A little farther."

Finally, her fingers brush mine. There's no elemental power rush this time, either. Almost instantly, I take solid form. My skin is now the same dove gray that Zephyr's was. I wouldn't care if it came out plaid with green polka dots; I'm solid once again. I fold Lianna in my arms. Peace and joy swirl through my soul. The storm slowly dies down, leaving Lianna and me as two solid points in the night sky, holding each other close. I rub her back in soothing strokes.

"You okay, beautiful?"

"I'm so tired," she says. "I couldn't figure out how to control the storm."

I kiss her cheek. "You did great."

She meets my gaze and smiles. "No, *we* did great."

And since that's the truth—and my life tends to change on a dime—I decide that now is the perfect time to kiss her.

So that's exactly what I do.

30

LIANNA

I watch Maxon pace across his makeshift bedroom. The place is pretty sparse. A mattress on the floor. Gray concrete walls. A metal folding chair. Believe it or not, this is one of the nicer rooms in Zephyr's old compound. Not a shocker, actually.

Two weeks have passed since we killed Zephyr, and we're both still recovering. Right now, Maxon practices changing from elemental into human form. Half the time he hits one state or the other, he forgets to add clothes. I'm watching from the room's only chair.

Needless to say, I'm enjoying myself immensely.

A knock sounds at the door. Maxon changes back into his elemental state. In this form, he wears gray body armor. His skin has a light gray tone as well, although his eyes have stayed a searing shade of blue.

A warm sense of affection blooms through my chest.

That's my blue, right there.

Maxon pauses by the closed door. "What's up?"

I can't stop the smile that rounds my mouth. I love how Maxon doesn't do all the formalities of court.

"It's Viktor here. I'm your new general. I was wondering if you were in need of any assistance."

"I know who you are, Viktor." Maxon says with a sigh. "I'm the same as I was fifteen minutes ago." The Air Valta keep checking on Maxon, like he'll disappear or turn back into a thrax. Can't blame them, though. Maxon's a precious commodity now.

He's agreed to become their new Monarkki of Air.

That said, if there's some kind of special clingy disorder for elementals who just lost an evil monarkki, then Maxon's Valta have it.

Excitement seeps into Viktor's voice. "Does that mean you need something?"

"No, it means that I'm still perfectly fine, thanks." A long pause follows as Viktor quietly steps away from the door. Maxon turns to me, his mouth winding into an all out grin. The sight makes me gooey inside.

"That was Viktor," he says.

"I noticed."

This is when I also notice that my ass has fallen asleep. To restart my circulation, I go into mist form and hover for a while.

Maxon's forehead crinkles with concern. "You sure you should be going misty?"

I shrug. "I'm trying to get my endurance up."

"It's too soon, beautiful. You shouldn't overdo it."

"Says the guy who's practicing changing forms and refusing any help from poor Viktor. Give the guy a letter to take to the post office or something. Sheesh."

"Oh, Viktor will be fine." Maxon changes back into his thrax state. This time it should be jeans and a black Henley, but he forgets his shirt again. *Nice.* "How was that one?"

"You forgot something."

"My shirt?" He offers me a sly look. "The way you keep ogling my chest, I didn't think you minded."

"I don't. You forgot your tail as well, though."

"Good call." Maxon snaps his fingers, and his tail reappears behind him. "That's better."

"Do you miss it? Your demon side, I mean."

"A little. It was integrated with the rest of me, though."

"Because of your Furor training."

"Right. So now, I feel a little off. Still, I feel like me, if that makes any sense."

"Hope you haven't lost any skills."

I didn't mean for that reply to come out sexy, but it sure did. The way Maxon raises his eyebrows, though, I can't say I'm bummed that he got the wrong idea. Or the right one, depending on how you look at it.

"Want to do an experiment, beautiful?" He prowls toward me. "Right now. You and me. I bet it'll be so good as elementals, we won't be able to speak." He leans in until his mouth is above my ear. "And you know how I like to talk."

Before I have time to respond, his left arm slides around my waist while his right curls into my hair. His mouth is right above mine, and yow, do I ever want him to kiss me.

"You know what I like about being an elemental?" he asks.

I'd try to speak, but all the energy that would normally fuel rational thought has gone south. I can only manage to shake my head.

"Clothes." Maxon nips my earlobe. A shudder of want moves through my core.

"Hmm?" Not sure that's an answer. Not sure I care, either.

"We can make them disappear with a thought." His fingertips glide up my belly, sending a ripple of desire through my center. "Especially these blue robes of yours. Make them disappear, and we could be skin-to-skin in a matter of seconds."

So I do just that. Maxon eyes me and sucks in a heavy breath. That's pretty satisfying.

"Your turn," I say.

Maxon gives me one of his dimpled smiles. More yum. More gooey-ness. "I like that it's my turn," he says.

Another knock sounds at the door. I grit my teeth in frustration.

I'm going to kill that Viktor guy.

"That's enough for one day, Viktor," calls Maxon.

A voice answers, and it's not Viktor. "Open up, my child."

I know that tone. It's Maxon's grandmother.

"Damn, G. Give me a minute."

"Are you ill?" she asks through the closed door. I can picture her mouth pressed by the doorjamb, her wrinkled lips drooping into a frown.

"I'm fine, G. Hold your horses."

Maxon conjures his jeans and T-shirt back on, checks his tail, and then inspects me as well. Evidently, neither of us is missing clothing or limbs, so Maxon steps over to the door and swings it open.

A lot of hugs and hellos start up as Octavia enters the room, followed by Maxon's parents. They've been visiting regularly and we're all getting downright friendly with each other. Of course, Octavia's still pulling together a huge ball for me. Now, it's to celebrate my coronation. At least, that's what she says it's all about. I'm pretty convinced that it's more of a 'Maxon has a girlfriend and we actually met her' kind of thing. Even so, I'd be lying if I said I wasn't excited. I missed every prom and dance and club experience growing up. This will be great.

Octavia moves to stand in the center of the room. "Let's review seating charts, shall we?" She pulls out a sheath of papers from seemingly nowhere.

Maxon's Mom leans against a nearby stretch of concrete wall. All the color drains from her face. Maxon rushes to her side.

"You okay, Mom?"

"Your mother is fine," says Maxon's Dad. He may be in jeans and a T-shirt, but he still looks like a King as he pulls his Queen into his arms. He whispers to his wife. "Do you need to lie down?"

"A nap might be good."

Looks like Maxon and I aren't the only ones who'd rather be doing something else.

I plunk down onto the metal folding chair and let out a huge sigh. "You know what? Maxon and I were practicing all day."

"What kind of stuff?" asks Maxon's Grandmother.

"Elemental, uh, things."

Not my best lie. Hopefully, it'll still do the trick.

"We're pretty tired, too." Maxon quickly moves to stand at my side. "I think we could all use a break." He gives G one of his patented smiles. "You set up the seating chart, G. We trust you."

Octavia scans the room, her eyes narrowed suspiciously. "If you insist."

"We do," says Maxon. He's got his 'I'm not arguing about this' face on. No one pushes him when he's like that, even Octavia. Maxon opens the door and ushers them outside with lots of thank-you's and kisses.

Once they're well and gone, Maxon summons Viktor. The guy is so excited to have an actual task, he could burst with pride.

"Yes, Your Eminence?"

"No disturbances for the next twenty four hours. I need to you to guard my door with your life."

Viktor's face brightens. "As you command, Your Eminence."

Maxon closes the door and turns to me. A sneaky light shines in his eyes.

"What are you thinking, Your Eminence?" I ask.

Now, I know exactly what's on his mind, but I do love to hear him say it.

"Remember when you tackled me outside Charybdis?"

"Mm-hmmm."

"I think we should do that again." Maxon runs his finger along my neckline. "Only naked."

"All right," I say slowly.

And as Maxon predicted before, that's the last word either of us utters for a long time.

31

LIANNA

*M*axon and I stand on the same stretch of Australian beach where I first summoned the Water Palace to confront Fisk, one month and a million years ago. An impossibly blue sky arches over us. Palm trees sway in a gentle breeze that Maxon summoned. I'm still getting used to the idea that wind means good stuff—like Maxon approaching—versus imminent death.

A good problem to have, I think.

Behind us, a hundred Air Valta line the beach. Their gray bodies shimmer in the morning sunshine. When Maxon's looking at them, they wear faces that are placid and supportive. But when he turns away? They scowl for all they're worth, mostly at me.

Maxon leans in to whisper in my ear. "Don't think I don't notice."

"Notice what?" I ask with mock innocence. "That the Air Valta loathe the idea of crowning us both at the Water Palace?"

"Yeah, that." Maxon's careful to keep his voice low. "Zephyr drilled it into my people's heads that Air is the ultimate element. It's not. We're all brothers and sisters. That's why you and I are getting crowned together in the Water Palace."

"I get that concept, sure." I look at him out of my right eye. "Do you really think that idea will stick with the rest of them, though?"

"Oh, I got a plan." Maxon winks. "You ready?"

"Sure thing."

I take his hand in mine and set out on a trek across the water. This time, we don't need to hold hands, considering that Maxon can float as smoke if he likes.

We stroll across the ocean for a time, the Air Valta following behind us. Once we reach a fair distance from shore, I raise my right arm.

Like before, the Water Palace comes bubbling up from the water. I visit all the time now, so you'd think that this shell-shaped castle wouldn't leave me gaping in awe anymore. But it does. Every time.

Once the palace is fully visible, the front door swings open. Maxon and I march through, hand in hand. We pass the reception arcade and head right into the Hall of Fountains. The place looks especially lovely today, with blue lights dancing through the waterfalls that line the space. A few hundred Water Valta stand in a rough circle on the chamber floor.

We move into the center of the room. The Air Valta follow, mixing in with their water counterparts, just as Maxon ordered them to. Once everyone is in place, Maxon's first to speak.

"Air Valta, connect to your brothers and sisters." In response, all of Maxon's people raise their right arms, placing their palms onto the shoulders of a comrade in arms. Viktor rests his hand on Maxon's shoulder.

That's my cue.

"Water Valta, connect to your brothers and sisters."

My soldiers do the same, reaching out their right arms and placing their palms onto the shoulders of another Water Valta. Esau's father rests his hand on my shoulder. With that, the connection to our people is complete. If I could look down from the ceiling, I'd see an intricate snowflake of gray and blue bodies.

The ceremony is ready to begin.

Raising my arm, I summon the Kristalli of Water to appear in my palm. Maxon does the same with the Kristalli of Air. We both lift our stones high. I've practiced this particular move for years. Many times, I've raised this stone in preparation for battle practice.

Today, I lift it to change the Kristalli into my crown.

Excitement strums through me, like my inner life is a musical string that's just been plucked. Maxon and I share a small smile that's full of hope and promise. After that, we speak together.

"Who names us their monarkki?" we ask.

The crowd replies in unison. "The Valta."

Blue and gray light dances around the room as one by one, the Valta's bodies glow with emotion. Their feelings pass through their connected bodies, compounding as they go. Soon the full weight of their sensations slams into me. There's love, support and—if I'm being honest—a little fear, too. My Kristalli fills with their emotion and power, growing brighter by the second. Maxon's does the same.

My Kristalli juts out small prongs into my hand, extending, contracting and pricking into my flesh as it begins climbing up my arm, shoulder, neck, and cheekbone. From there, it creeps around my temples, taking the shape of a crown.

Across from me, Maxon's Kristalli is making the same journey. The power of his Valta is changing his people's stone into a crown. I smile so hard, it feels like my face could break.

Once our new crowns are firmly in place, the Valta lower their arms and fall to their right knee. Again, they speak in unison.

"Our monarkki."

Suddenly, I sense the water elementals in my realm. In my mind's eye, I see them all. Young naiads frolic in lakes, their long blue hair steaming over their naked bodies. Rain golems pour moisture into the clouds, their great blocky shoulders carrying huge vats of glowing liquid. Ocean guardians patrol the depths, their long seaweed cloaks flowing behind them.

I see and sense my people. Joy, pain, peace, and worry... All their feelings move through me as my own. We are no longer separate. I connect to their consciousness and speak to them through my soul.

I will fight for you, heal you, and help you. I am your monarkki. Together, we will be strong.

Across the after-realms, I sense water elementals everywhere bowing onto their right knee. They speak to me in a voice that rings through eternity.

Your Eminence. We are yours.

A part of my essence finally clicks into place. It's like some piece of me was always missing, and now I am whole. I turn to Maxon.

"I feel my people," I say with a smile. "Do you?"

"Yeah." He returns my grin with one of his own. "We've got a lot of work to do." He leans in and whispers in my ear. "Together."

I do my best Maxon impression, keeping my voice low and my mojo controlled. "Yeah."

We share a grin and then return our attention to the Valta. They clearly want a speech, and that still isn't my strong suit. I frown.

"Want me to go first?" asks Maxon.

I'm about to take him up on that, when suddenly, I know exactly what to say. "Nah, I got it."

"That's my woman." He kisses me gently on the cheek. Warmth and love radiate from his touch. I turn to face the crowd.

"I don't give speeches much," I begin. "Well, at all, really. I can't begin without saying that I wouldn't be here without some very dear friends. Namare rescued me. Fisk sacrificed everything to keep me safe. And you all have connected me into your power. Together, we will heal our world."

A pulse of energy hangs in the air. I totally nailed that speech. Or at least, I'm pretty sure I did. Either way, I'm feeling good.

Maxon winds me into a deep hug as his voice sounds low in my ear. "Good work, beautiful." He kisses me, brief and sweet.

Too soon, our kiss ends. Now, it's Maxon turn to scan the crowd of faces. What will he say? Will he leave his warrior-self behind and go all statesman on me? Not that I mind that but... Okay, I would totally mind that. Maxon and fighter are one and the same to me.

Maxon rubs his stubbled chin. "You're all warriors, so I'll do you the honor of being direct here."

A small grin rounds my mouth. That's my guy, all right.

With pointed movements, Maxon positions me so my back rests against his firm chest. His solid arms wind around my waist. A fluttery feeling starts up in my rib cage. I do love it when Maxon gets possessive. "There's been a lot of bullshit around here about which element is the best. That ends today. You make Water your enemy, you make me your enemy. Everyone understand?"

The Air Valta nod silently, their gray eyes large with surprise. A realization moves through me me as well. *This is the moment Maxon whispered about on the beach*. Now that he's monarkki, he's making his play to end Zephyr's policy of one element being first.

That's my guy, again.

"Now," he says. "You all play by the rules and we're good. No one's number one anymore. No one gets hurt because of that shit anymore, either. We're all a team now." His voice lowers. "I know this is a big change for you. It'll be weird for a while. Hell, it took me some time to adjust to the idea of having a battle twin, too. Trust me, once you're there, you'll never go back." He turns me around to meet my gaze, and all the love and respect in the after-realms gleams in his eyes. My skin glows with joy.

He'll never go back.

"You got anything to add, beautiful?"

"No, you said it perfectly."

"Good." He leans forward, nuzzling into my neck. "Now, since you already got your tiara on and all, how about we head off to Antrum and finish getting ready for your party?"

Crap, I almost forgot. Octavia's throwing me a ball tonight.

"Sounds like a plan," I say.

We're still holding hands when we walk away from the Water Palace, and that's what's I call a good day.

32

MAXON

I step around the floor of the Golden Ballroom, bored out of my damned skull. Lianna's not here yet, and I know why. Octavia's spending a million years making my woman ready for tonight. And why? She already looks beautiful.

Plus, I miss her.

There, I admitted it to myself. The guy who needs no one except a good demon to kill now misses his woman. I shrug. When the woman's Lianna, that's a good thing.

G spots me prowling in the shadows, so she comes over to chat. As she steps closer, I can see her black velvet gown and shit-eating grin. Finally, G got to throw her 'my grandson got a girlfriend' ball. She steps up beside me and surveys the crowd.

"How are you enjoying the festivities?" she asks.

I shrug. "You know how I am with formal stuff."

"That I do." G grins.

"It'll be better when Lianna shows. When are you releasing her from the girlie brigade?"

G shoots me a sly look. "My Ladies in Waiting know you call them that, by the way."

"They got no complaints with me."

I know that because they tell me that all the time, mostly while hitting on me. I'm not into cougars, so I've never been tempted to take them up on their offer. Not that I'll tell G a word about it. She'll flip her lid.

"Suffice it to say that Lianna will be here soon." G freezes in place. "What the?"

"Is something wrong?"

"They brought out the enchanted sculptures too early. The magic will wear off before the first dance." G pats my forearm. "Excuse me."

As G steps away, Mom and Dad approach my hiding spot. A small crowd of courtiers and hangers-on trails behind them. My tail arcs into battle stance over my shoulder. I hate courtiers. People should fight with knives, not words.

"Hello, son," says Dad. We do our man-hug thing.

"My baby." Mom's voice breaks with emotion. "My sweet, sweet boy."

Normally, Mom gets weepy faster than anyone I know. Lately, she's been on a hair trigger.

The courtiers create an ad hoc circle around us, chattering about Lianna, the ball, and how excited they are to have a royal elemental. I'm glad they're all pumped about my new state, but five minutes of their love is usually all I can handle. Tonight, I've had to listen to them for hours. It's getting on my nerves. Some courtier starts chattering about my new Kristalli crown and I've officially had enough. I raise my hand.

"I'm talking to my parents now." All the courtiers stare at me with open mouths. "Alone."

They don't budge. On reflex, I start calculating how to take them all down. Mom fidgets uncomfortably. She hates royal events almost as much as I do.

Dad catches the vibe. His face takes on that King look he gets sometimes, mostly when he's feeling protective. And these days, there's only one thing *really* sets off his protective side. Mom.

Huh. Something's definitely up with her.

"Excuse us," says Dad. Two words never sounded so powerful and threatening. The courtiers take off like a small bomb exploded nearby.

Once they're well out of earshot, I carefully scan my parent's faces.

"So, what's going on?" I ask.

Mom twists her hands nervously at her waist. Whatever's happening, she needs a little time to talk about it.

No problem, I can wait.

"Have you seen Cissy and her girls?" Mom asks quickly.

Cissy is Mom's best friend from growing up in Purgatory. She's also the Diplomatic Senator. She and her husband have six girls, all part lust demon. I dated the two oldest. And by 'date,' I mean the relationship lasted all of three hours. Mom doesn't know this and I want it to stay that way. So, I avoid them at all costs to keep the peace. They're beyond clingy.

Mom keeps looking at me, waiting for the answer. "Well?"

"I saw them tonight." *From a distance.*

Dad slides his arm around Mom's waist. "Cissy and her girls are fine." He shoots Mom a sly smile. "Zeke is great, too. Why didn't you ask about him?"

"Must've slipped my mind," she says with a chuckle. Mom and Zeke never got along, although these days, Mom feels that six girls is some kind of karmic payback for Zeke being a player in high school.

Dad nuzzles closer to Mom and changes the subject. At least, he changes the subject as far as Mom's concerned. Dad and I continue a hidden conversation about Cissy and her daughters.

"Did you see Hildy?" Dad asks me.

Those are the words that come out of this mouth. The look in Dad's eyes says 'I totally know you nailed two of Cissy's girls.'

I shrug, which is my way of saying 'hey, I'm a guy.' Out loud, I say, "Yeah, Hildy and I talked for an hour. Her school's going great."

"Lots of *legal issues* with that school," says Dad. "You ever put yourself in situations like that?" Translation: Am I going to have trouble with Cissy on this? Were any of the girls underage?

"No way. You know my system, Dad. I'm all about keeping it legal."

Mom's eyes narrow. She's starting to see through our shit, which isn't good.

"What are you two boys talking about anyway?"

I put on my most winning and innocent smile. Mom is a sucker for dimples. "Dad and I were chatting about Hildy's new school for monopsyches. She built it in the Wastelands without Anton's permission. The Earl's having a hissy fit but she won't tear it down. Dad's acting as legal intermediary."

"I'm changing a few laws so she can keep the school," explains Dad. "I told you about that last week." He kisses her forehead. "Your memory's a little tricky these days."

Which is totally true. Another reason to get the full story out of Mom.

A long pause hangs in the air. I'd hold my breath now, if I still needed to breathe. *Will Mom drop the Cissy conversation?*

"Oh, that's right," says Mom. "You did mention the legal troubles."

And she's moving on. This is my lucky night. I decide to push it.

"So, what's going on, Mom?"

My mother blushes, which is something that I've seen about three times in my life.

"We didn't want to say anything until we were certain," she says.

"About what?" I ask.

Dad beams from ear to ear. "You're going to have a baby sister."

"Really?" I raise my brows. "You're too old for another kid. I mean, I know we've got an extra-long lifespan and all..."

Mom raises her right brow. "Keep talking like that, and I'm liable to get insulted."

"No, I mean... That is..." I scrub my hands over my face.

You're babbling, Maxon.

"Here's the thing," I say. "I thought Mom couldn't get pregnant. There can only be one Scala and one Scala Heir, and I'm the Heir."

"And you lost that job when you changed into an elemental," says Dad.

"Exactly," says Mom. "You practically threw a party when you found out the igni weren't coming back, remember?"

I rub my chin. "Uh, I forgot about that."

"You did?" Mom's face gets all pale and worried.

"I've had other stuff on my mind, Mom."

Plus, igni get on my nerves. Once I knew I didn't have to deal with them, it's like I automatically erased them from my memory.

Mom turns to Dad. "Do you think he's fully recovered from his change to an elemental?"

"He's fine," says Dad.

Mom keeps going. She's on a roll.

"Maybe you suffered some kind of brain damage." Mom raises her hand up to my face. "How many fingers am I holding up, baby?"

Dad lets out a low chuckle. "Give Maxon a minute. He'll put two and two together."

"Yeah. Let's do what Dad said."

I stare at them both, trying to process this news. Mom's right. There isn't a Scala Heir anymore so it makes perfect sense that a new one would be needed. And who better than Mom and Dad to bring up the new Heir?

All kind of warm and happy now bubble up through my chest. "I'm going to be a brother!" I wrap Mom and Dad big hugs. "This is great news."

And speaking of karmic payback, Mom and dad deserve some of the positive variety. My parents got a major shaft when I was abducted. This time around, maybe they can have a typical parenting experience. Well, as typical as you get when you're supernatural thrax royalty.

"Glad to see that you're excited, son."

"I should've guessed this would happen," I say. "The igni worship Mom." I shoot her a sly wink. "When they got in my head, half of what they said was about you."

"And what was that, exactly?" she asks.

"Hell if I know. It was a lot of nonsense with your name thrown in every so often."

Mom all-out laughs, which is one of my favorite sounds in the world. "That's the igni, all right. They have lots of opinions on the baby, too."

My brows lift with interest. "Like what?"

"Her name," explains Dad. "They want her to be called Portia."

At this moment, my grandfather Xavier leans over my shoulder to pop his head into the group. "Hello, everyone!"

"Pops!" Now, Dad's not the only one smiling from ear to ear. I'm beaming, too. "I thought you and Grandma Cam couldn't make it."

"One advantage of being an archangel," says Pops with his toothy grin. "You can tell the other angels to reschedule conventions and they go along with it, no problem."

Grandma Cam bursts into the group and kisses my cheek. "Your grandfather cancels things and then I have to reschedule them. We have our system down to a science."

No surprise, there. The pair of them have been running Purgatory for years.

"I've been thinking," says a still-smiley Pops. "The after-realms need monarkki for Fire and Earth."

Not sure where this is going. Knowing my grandfather, it's a short list of places.

"Yeah, Pops?"

"Well, the easiest way to create new monarkki is for you and Lianna to start a family."

And that would be one of his favorite places. Grandkid-ville.

"Don't push it, Pops. Lianna and I haven't known each other for very…"

I freeze mid-sentence. There's more for me to say here. Really, there is. Still, I can't get another word out. That's because Lianna's finally shown up and damn, she looks gorgeous.

My family says a bunch of stuff about her, but I don't hear them. There are people around Lianna, complimenting her blue gown and long blonde hair. I don't see them, either.

There's only her.

I march up to my woman, wrap my arms around her, and kiss her with everything I've got.

"And hello to you, too," she says with a smile.

"You know how to dance?" I ask.

"Wasn't part of classic monarkki training."

"Damn." I lean into her ear and speak in a growling-whisper, which I know drives her crazy. "I need my hands on you." I nuzzle into her neck and her hair smells fucking awesome. How does she do that? Take a bath in strawberries or something?

A smile sounds in her voice. "I'm supposed to meet the thrax nobility. Your grandmother was most specific."

I scrub my hands down my face and admit the truth to myself. Yeah, G is right on this one. The thrax are taking my change in status pretty well, considering I'm technically no longer thrax. This night is about getting them used to Lianna and me as elemental rulers.

And about my surprise for Lianna, too. But that'll have to wait.

I steel my shoulders and slap on a half-hearted smile. This is what G calls the 'royal expression' and it's what we're supposed to use at formal stuff.

"Let's do this," I say.

Lianna stares at me for a long minute. "Why do I have the sneaking suspicion that you have something else up your sleeve?"

"Because I do."

Her mouth opens, ready to ask a slew of questions, so I whisk her off to meet the Earl of Striga.

And this is the first rule of Furor seduction: Anticipation makes everything better.

Lianna meets all the earls and nobles. The guys come by too, and we gab it up. They all look great, fully recovered after the battle with Zephyr. The night passes pretty quickly. As formal balls go, it's one of the best. It may have something to do with Lianna being at my side, too. Actually, it has everything to do with her. I could hang around watching paint dry and it would be fun if she were with me. Before I know it, the herald announces the end of the evening.

Lianna scans the room while worrying her lower lip with her teeth. Not sure I like that look. "What's wrong, beautiful?"

"Walker never showed up."

"Oh, that."

"You know where he is?"

"Yup." I pull Lianna close to me again. "You ready for your surprise?"

He gives me one of her dazzling smiles. "Absolutely."

We head off to one of my hidden Pulpitum and take a quick ride up to the Earth's surface. For sentimental reasons, I pick the station near Charybdis. We step outside into the darkened desert, and Walker's waiting for us, his long black ghoul robes fluttering in the breeze. When he spies Lianna in her crown, his face glows with happiness.

"Lianna," says Walker. "You're the monarkki at last."

"Thanks to you." She wraps him in a big hug. "Wish you could've been at my crowning."

"Me, too," he replies. "However, I understand why it was a closed event. The Valta had enough to adjust to, what with it being a double coronation and all. Allowing outsiders in would've put everyone on edge."

"You were there in my heart," she whispers.

Now, I don't want to be a jealous little bitch here, but I can't help it. The hug and happy chatter are lasting way too long, so I step closer and rest my hand on Lianna's shoulder.

"That's enough of a hello, don't you think?"

Walker backs off, a sly look in his all-black eyes. "Why, you jealous?"

"Hell, yeah. Besides, you're here for another reason."

Lianna playfully swats at Walker's shoulder. "This better be good. I can't believe that you missed my ball."

"Oh, it's good," says Walker as he opens a portal behind him. After linking hands, we all step into the darkness. Seconds later, we reappear at the top of a black volcano in Hawaiian islands. Portal travel is sweet.

I cup Lianna's cheek. "You okay, beautiful?" Although I like portals, some people get dizzy. Plus, any excuse to touch Lianna is a good one.

"No, I'm good."

Lianna steps around, taking in the view. It's nighttime here too, with a sea of stars wheeling over our heads. Far below, the ocean rolls over a beach of black sand. Nearby, the red mouth of the volcano lights up the night sky. I set my hands on my hips, thinking the same thought as when I first found this place.

It's perfect.

"So this is what you've been up to?" asks Lianna. "Hanging out by volcanoes?"

Walker winks. "Something like that."

I slip my arm about her waist. "Ready for your surprise, beautiful?"

Lianna bobs a little on the balls of her feet. "Sure."

Walker snaps his fingers and a crystal palace appears above our heads. Starlight glistens through the milky-white stone. It's three stories high with lots of spires and towers. Walker said women like stuff like that. Lianna stares at it for a long minute, her mouth falling open.

"You don't like it?" I ask.

Lianna tries to talk, but she starts crying instead. Fuck, I did something wrong. This was supposed to be perfect.

I exchange a defeated look with Walker. We've been working on this for months.

"Sorry, beautiful."

She speaks through sobs. "No, Maxon. These... Are... Happy... Tears."

"So, you're crying because you're so *happy*?"

More sobs. "Yes."

I smile my face off. "That's good news, beautiful."

That's as far as I get before Lianna's mouth is on mine and we're a tangle of limbs on the warm green grass. When I come up for air, I wave Walker off and he has the good sense to portal away.

Lianna finally comes up for air, too. "It's so lovely. Is it for me?"

"It's for us, actually. This is what Walker's been working on. This place is the perfect mix of earth, sky, fire, and water. It's our joint castle."

I don't want to scare her off, but I made sure there was lots of room for kids, too. Pops was right about the Monarkki for Fire and Earth. Lianna and I really need to do our bit there, eventually. Of course, there's lots of time for that.

Lianna gives me another teary smile, and this time, I know exactly what it means. She's happy. Time to go for the close.

Before I lose my nerve, I fall onto one knee and pull out the royal betrothal jewels. They've been burning a hole in my tunic all night. I meet Lianna's semi-stunned gaze.

"What do you say, marry me?"

Lianna tilts her head, confused, and I realize I may have jumped the gun. Lianna's lived her life in a cabin. Plus, I have no idea what elemental traditions are for this. Who knows if I made the right move?

"Is that what elementals do?" I ask quickly. "They get married?"

Shit, I should know this stuff.

The confusion drops away from her face. "Yes."

I raise my brows. "So, which question were you answering?"

Her smile turns so bright, it's dazzling. "Both of them."

Lianna's body literally beams with joy. Gray light shimmers across my skin too.

She said yes.

"All right." I set the necklace, earrings, and rings on her. "I didn't think it could happen, but you look even more beautiful now."

She slips her hands in mine. "So, is the palace ready for inspection?"

"It's built out in some parts."

"Is there a bedroom yet?" Her skin starts to glow a different shade of blue, and I'm definitely liking where she's going with this.

I act all cool. No need for her to know how much I want to tear everything off her right now. "The bedroom's just a floorboard and some tarps."

"Never too early to test it out, though."

"Yeah."

Acting in unison, Lianna and I change into our mist and smoke forms. Together we rise up to the palace gate. Happiness radiates through my soul. This has been a crazy long journey, one that started with torture in Hell and it ended with a castle in the sky. It wasn't an easy road, but it brought me to Lianna.

And given the choice, I'd do it all again.

She's worth it.

EPILOGUE

LIANNA

SIX MONTHS LATER

*M*axon and I march toward a metal skyscraper. A shiver rolls across my shoulders. Like an oversized knife, the steel building cuts into the countryside—a weapon against nature itself. The promise of a storm hangs in the air; maybe that's why no one's around. I shake my head. This place is more than quiet. My elemental sense pops another thought into my mind.

It's dead.

I hug my elbows. "What do the humans call this land again?"

For the record, I've researched this particular building for months. But where it fits on a human map? That gets squishy. Hey, I just transformed into the Monarkki of Water. There's a lot to track.

"By location, do you mean state, county or city?" asks Maxon. He knows his human territory cold.

I tilt my head, considering. "State."

"We're in Pennsylvania."

I roll the name around in my mind. *Pennsylvania.* Such a strange word. Then again, this is Earth. Mortals do all sorts of odd stuff. Like macramé. Tap dancing. Or baking potato chips with perfect zigzag patterns. Why? Most of the time, I don't bother to wonder. This case is different, though. Simply put, I must understand what happens inside this metal building. Leaning back on my heels, I gaze upwards. Twenty stories of burnished steel tower above me. No windows. All shiny metal.

A glass panel stands by the building's front doors. I soak in the familiar words etched into its surface.

DEX. The Department of Elemental eXplorations.

Nervous energy zings through my body. For months, my naiads—powerful water sprites—have been falling ill. At first, it was only a small group. I healed them easily. But all water connects, and so this plague spread quickly. Through research, magic and some oracle action, I traced the illness to its ground zero.

The DEX building.

In just a few minutes, Maxon and I have an appointment with the humans inside. In other words, this morning marks our first real chance to look around, ask questions, and with any luck, get some answers.

A realization hits me. I grew up in a cabin on the backside of nowhere. I know zero about being a regular human. Smoothing the folds of my skirt suit, I turn to Maxon. "Do I seem like someone who works for the mortal government to you?"

"And a beautiful one at that." Maxon then straightens his tie. Both of us wear dark suits today. In reality, we've only reformed our elemental bodies to appear as if we're sporting human outfits. Which means that Maxon's only *pretending* to fix his tie. *Good idea, actually.* The movement helps sell the illusion that we're mortal.

Maxon gestures across his suit. "How about me?"

"You look very…" I pause. *What would a human say?* My eyes widen as it hits me. "You look quite professional."

Maxon winks. "Thank you."

Excitement pours through me. *We're really doing this.* Straightening my shoulders, I turn and face the front door. Like the rest of the building, it's a solid sheet of metal. Gripping the silver handle, I prepare to pull. Thunder rumbles through the air.

I pause.

All of a sudden, the rain clouds whirl more violently. A storm is about to strike. All around, the world darkens. An electric pulse moves through my torso. The gurgle of rushing water fills my mind—it's a sound that only I can hear. All of which leads to a single thought.

Oh, crap.

No question what's happening. *Another elemental approaches.* Since I'm the Monarkki of Water, I know exactly *who's* heading this way as well.

I sigh. "Kyo is coming."

Kyo is my second in command, what we call a majordomo. She manages the day-to-day stuff while I tackle the big problems. Like DEX.

She also has the gift of foresight, which helped pinpoint this spot in the first place.

Maxon narrows his eyes. "Should we go inside?"

"No, she'll just follow." This has happened before, by the way. Nothing like a flash rainstorm inside a building to freak out the mortals.

Boom!

Another ear-piercing roll of thunder shakes the air. Sheets of rain pour down. Although the storm is heavy, every drop carefully arches away from me and Maxon, leaving us dry. The rough outline of a woman's face appears in the cascade before us.

"What are you doing here?" asks Kyo. As the rain intensifies, her face becomes more defined. High cheekbones. Bow-shaped mouth. The elaborate, looping hairstyle of a nineteenth century geisha. "You're holding a major healing tomorrow morning," continues Kyo. "Six naiads." She emphasizes the word *six*. Normally, I heal one naiad and then sleep for hours. Six is a big deal.

"I'll still heal them." I gesture toward the building. "But I need to work the problem, Kyo. Whoever's hurting my elementals must be stopped."

"You take too many risks," she snaps. "It's beyond time you took care of yourself. *Six months*, Lianna."

"I know." Mostly because we have this discussion constantly. *Six months* marks how long Maxon and I have been engaged. Yet in all that time, we've made zero plans for our wedding.

"You're sweet to worry about our personal stuff," says Maxon.

"But it's wasted energy," I add. "Maxon and I are basically immortal. There's plenty of time."

"Namare always said the same thing," she counters. "*I'll live for eons; my personal life can wait.* Namare thought there would be time to find a partner. Start a family. That never happened."

My throat tightens. I still miss Namare. And yes, Kyo might have a point.

With inhuman speed, Maxon moves to stand between me and Kyo. "You're upsetting Lianna. It's time to go." The way Maxon snarls those last four words, I'm shocked Kyo doesn't take off in a pouf of rain.

"I'm the Majordomo of Water," declares Kyo. "I'll leave, but only if my monarkki demands it."

"Look, I get that you worry." On reflex, I fidget with the door handle. Nice carved metal. Odd the things you notice when things are turning uncomfortable. "But Maxon's right. It's time to go."

"For now," says Kyo slowly. Little by little, her face merges back into the heavy raindrops. For a moment, I can make out the shape of her eyes, then nothing at all. The storm slows. Soon the only sign of rain are rivulets of water on the cement walkway. The sky brightens. No question about it.

Kyo is gone.

I shake my head. "Why did we appoint majordomos again?"

"Because we can't track all four elements without help."

Two words stick in my head: *for now.* "You heard what Kyo said."

"I did."

"And you know what that means."

Maxon nods. "She's calling in reinforcements."

In this case, *reinforcements* means Kyo's contacting the majordomos for the other elements. Things could get awkward. Our four majordomos like to pester us in shifts; a wedding is their favorite topic. A sly gleam lights up Maxon's blue eyes. "I could always call in Mother, you know."

Maxon's mom is rapidly becoming my favorite person. "That would be something."

"She'd kick all their elemental asses, easy."

"Not necessary, but I do like the visual." I chuckle. "Besides, I get why the majordomos are obsessed with our wedding." To the elemental world, Maxon and I getting married means stability. Plus, our children are bound to be powerful monarkkis. No one currently rules earth and fire, so that's a big need. An image appears in my mind: a pair babies made from rock or flame. Instantly, my body stiffens.

Parenthood. What an overwhelming thought.

All of a sudden, this steel building seems to tower even higher. I drop my arm from the door handle. "Maybe we should just go home."

Maxon moves closer, pausing when our gazes lock. His blue eyes are wide with sympathy. "I get the concern. But you've been working non-stop on this for months. Healing naiads. Tracing the problem to DEX." He nods toward the building. "Your plan is brilliant. Our identities are set. An appointment awaits. This took weeks to set up. Going inside today is the right thing to do."

"Maybe we should wait until dark and *turn elemental.*" That means taking our forms as mist and wind. "We can try to sneak in again."

"We've done that a dozen times already. Whoever built this building, they know more about our kind than they should."

Which is true. Normally, I can go misty and get in anywhere. But no matter what Maxon and I try, we can't break into DEX. No one knows how to block elementals. It took weeks—and special contacts from Emperor Tempest—to get us false identities and invitations inside.

"I meant what I said." Raising his hands, Maxon cups my face with his fingertips. "You're brilliant. This plan is solid."

Reaching up, I clasp Maxon's wrists. "But all that talk from Kyo. You know what she really means. We need to get married. Have a family."

With gentle motions, Maxon runs his thumb across my bottom lip. His touch sends a pleasant shiver through me. "And so we will ... when the time is right. Besides, Kyo always brings up the wedding whenever she wants you to stop doing something."

My eyes widen. "Like when?"

"Like yesterday, when she wanted you to stop researching DEX."

"It was two in the morning." Not sure why, but I feel protective of Kyo.

"Then two days go, when she didn't want you healing anyone new."

"Only because I'd already cured a naiad that day."

Maxon sniffs. "And Kyo takes forever to find your sick naiads. Each time you ask her why, she pulls the wedding card. You back down every time."

I purse my lips, thinking this through. "Damn, you're right. She's like *the girl who cried wedding*." I narrow my eyes. "What do you think she's up really to?"

"Nothing bad." Maxon shrugs. "Mostly, Kyo wants her lovely monarkki to slow down." Leaning in, he presses a petal-soft kiss across my lips. The touch of his mouth against mine launches a whirl of emotions.

The burn of desire.

Rock-solid determination.

The feather-light pull of hope.

"But what if things go wrong today?" I ask. "We've no idea what's inside this building."

"That's part of being us. Surprises happen. We improvise. It all works out in the end." Maxon's voice lowers to a rumble. "But the important question is this—what do *you* want?"

"Multiple things." Slanting my mouth across his, I deepen our kiss. There really is nothing better than the play of my tongue against Maxon's. "To be honest, some of those things involve you being naked."

Maxon gives me the hint of a smile. "How about at this very moment?"

I consider the question. Not sure how Maxon does it, but I always feel better after he showers me with some kisses and chatter. A minute ago, I was ready to fly home. But now? Not so much. When I next speak, there's no question in my voice.

"Let's find out who's poisoning my naiads."

Maxon's expression blooms into an all-out grin, complete with dimples. "My beautiful warrior."

"Right." A sense of pride heats my chest. Turning toward the door, I grip the handle once more.

We're going in.

2

MAXON

*L*ianna and I step into a boxy space that's covered in dull gray walls. It's also empty.

As in no furniture.

No *be happy in your work* posters.

Not even a person standing around.

I take in a deep breath—or what passes for it now that I have no lungs —and sift through the air particles inside me. Totally stale. No humans have walked into this space for months.

Odd.

Suddenly, the walls flare to life. Turns out, they aren't regular panels. Nope, these are huge monitors. One second, everything is dim. The next moment, all four walls radiate white light. A woman made of silver appears on the screen before us. She's like a faceless Barbie doll, only one that's made of metal. Gotta be honest. This kicks up the *freak factor* in here.

A smooth female voice echoes through the room. "Greetings." I'm guessing the silver chick speaking, although it would help if she had a mouth. "I am the Government Elite Entity Nine Alpha. GEENA for short." Her voice carries a little metallic echo. "You must be Doctor Gusty."

"That's me," I say.

Note to self: The next time Tempest makes us fake identities, make a point to ask the dragon emperor to open a freaking thesaurus. As aliases go, *Doctor Gusty* sucks ass.

GEENA turns to Lianna. "And you're Doctor Flume."

Lianna nods. "Correct." My girl shoots me a half-lidded gaze. This is her *snarky face.* It means one thing. She's not happy with her name situation, either.

"You brought no armaments," says GEENA. The way she says those words, it's not really a question. I inspect the walls once more, wondering about those hidden cameras. Are there scanners embedded as well? Probably.

"Of course not," I say smoothly, because it's the truth. Tempest insisted that we wouldn't get inside with any weapons, even if I only brought my baculum. As always, the old dragon was spot-on.

"Welcome to you both," says GEENA. "I'm here to provide you with a tour of our facilities for your purposes in…" Her face flickers. "Requesting additional funding for our efforts."

"That's right," I say. But even as the words leave my mouth, something feels mighty *wrong.* Over the years, I've both lived and memorized miles of demonic facts. A beast with seven heads? Fought that. A snake meanie that changes size? Read four books on the topic. But when it comes to high tech, I only know the basics, like how to use a cell phone. Super computer stuff like GEENA? No clue.

All of a sudden, that feels like a big miss.

A sense of unease winds through me. I scan the walls more carefully. There must be super-strong sensors in here. Otherwise, how does GEENA know where to look at us? Which is a pretty cool trick. And it makes me wonder: what else is this place packing?

If Lianna is worried, she doesn't show it. "Before you give us a tour, I'd like to start with some basic questions. What do you do here, exactly? Manufacture chemicals?"

"No," replies GEENA. "We're a storage facility."

That's unexpected. I figured this place was a huge office building. Lots of little desks and junk like that. But storage? This structure is way too high tech for that.

"What are you storing here, exactly?" I ask.

"It's easier show you, Doctor Gusty." She looks to Lianna. "Doctor Flume."

A mechanical whir sounds. A panel wall rolls up, revealing a corridor that leads inside the building itself. GEENA steps into the hallway, although she really doesn't step anywhere. It's just that the image of her on the monitors walks from the screens in the lobby onto the ones in the corridor. As she 'walks' into the hall, the walls there light up as well.

My brows lift. This is some strange stuff. Human governments don't develop crazy tech like this, as a rule. I rest my hand on the base of Lianna's back as we follow GEENA into the hallway. The passageway ends with a waist-high metal gate. GEENA gestures to the corridor's end. "This way," she instructs.

Lianna and I follow her direction, but I can tell my woman isn't happy about it. Lianna's body turns arctic cold. It's one way my woman shows worry or fear. My own element churns inside me, like dozens of tiny cyclones are spinning within my torso, ready to break free. Together, Lianna and I stroll toward the hallway's end. All the while, my elemental instincts scream at me.

Something about this wrong.

Even worse, I fear this place threatens my Lianna.

3

LIANNA

*M*axon and I reach the end of the hallway. There, we pause by the gate. It takes a moment for my vision to adjust to the dim light.

What I see turns my world upside down.

Before me looms a large and open space. Like the inside of a chimney, it stretches far above. All the walls have the same dull gray look that lined the outer hallway and lobby. Clearly, this place holds more monitors. But that's not what shocks me. On the floor below, huddled in a corner, there sits a naiad. And not just any naiad, but Avonlea, the most powerful water sprite of her clan.

They captured her.

I scan her body. Normally, Avonlea is blue-skinned and lithe as a ballet dancer. Her long silver hair usually hangs to her ankles. My heart sinks. Small patches of scraggly hair now cling to her skull. A white film dims her once-bright eyes. All her skin oozes the same greenish pus that's been spreading through other naiads. Poisoning them. Cold rage swirls within my soul. I grip the metal railing before me. The steel immediately frosts over from my touch.

Inside the containment chamber, the gray panels come to life, flaring with white light. GEENA appears again. Only this time, the projection of her stretches twenty stories tall—the entire length of one wall panel. Her metal arm gestures toward Avonlea.

"Do you see that puddle of water?" asks GEENA.

"Puddle?" I meant to ask that as a question, but the word comes out as more of a snarl. Maxon rests his hand on my shoulder. It's a comforting move.

"The small green puddle in the corner?" clarifies Maxon. "That's how it *appears to you*, right?"

Maxon's words cut through my icy rage. That's right. Unless you're an elemental, Avonlea would look like nothing more than water.

"Correct," says GEENA. "That's water sample Q43. And yes, that puddle is more than it appears to be. Let me demonstrate. First, we'll apply our chemical spray."

Down by the metal floor, images of nozzles appear on the walls surrounding Avonlea. Then, the metal cones stretch out from the wall.

They become real.

At this point, I should be shocked that pictures on a monitor screen can transform into something physical. But I can't. All I can focus on is how Avonlea cowers in the corner, her shoulders heaving with silent sobs.

My poor naiad. Sprites like Avonlea giggle when a stream gurgles. They laugh as sunlight dances through water. Their joy seeps through to humankind, allowing everyone to enjoy nature's beauty in all its forms. And now, she's tortured for being different.

"This chemical mixture should turn Q43 into vapor," adds GEENA.

The metal nozzles spit a black haze above Avonlea's head. She coughs, her hands grasping at her throat. Tears stream down her cheeks.

"As you can see," says GEENA. "Sample Q43 remains liquid. That shouldn't happen." She rolls her eyes. "You've no idea how many chemical mixes we went though before we found this particular reaction."

When I speak, my voice comes out low and deadly. "I'm starting to understand."

"Excellent," says GEENA. "It took our agency decades simply to create a scan that could separate Q43 from regular liquids. Then we had to locate this particular sample and contain it. All these steps needed to take place before we could start testing. And the tests themselves have taken ages to create. That's why we're low on funding. We need more investment in order to continue our research."

"How much have you spent already?" asks Maxon.

"This facility has required sixty years and three-point-seven trillion dollars. We've only begun to test this thing and its capabilities."

"She's not a thing," I declare.

If GEENA detects the rage in my voice, she doesn't show it. "*No one* knows what Q43 is, Doctor Flume. That's why we need more funding. Here's another example."

This time, the images of long metal rods appear high above Avonlea's head. Once again, the pictures become real. Four actual devices now point at Avonlea.

"Watch this," says the massive version of GEENA.

Lightning coils along the metal rods. For a long moment, the bolts crackle and twine together. Then all four devices let off thin cords of energy and power. All the lightning bolts strike right at Avonlea.

My sweet naiad screams.

"Do you see this?" asks GEENA. "After that blast, this water should have evaporated completely. But it doesn't so much as ripple under the lightning."

Maxon rubs my back in soothing motion. "We see it," he says. "That's enough of a demonstration."

"Just let me show you what happens with more power. This is the best part."

The four rods now flare more brightly. The bolts of lightning turn searingly strong. Avonlea screams and bursts into a cloud of vapor. Green haze fills the chimney-like tower. My elemental sense knows what's happening.

They're killing her.

This time, my words come out as a howl. "No! Stop!"

The lightning ceases. All four devices retract into the wall. Avonlea lays on the metal floor, unconscious. I barely notice how GEENA returns to her regular size.

After that, she steps out of the wall.

Just like the metal devices, GEENA has become real. I should be worried. Surprised. Something. Instead I only feel numb. It's all I can do to stare at Avonlea and not weep. When GEENA speaks, it's like I'm trapped in a dream or something. I can hear her words, but I can't focus on them.

"Why Doctor Flume," says GEENA. "You're blue."

"It's an illusion," says Maxon quickly.

But it's not. I often turn blue when I'm overwhelmed.

A sensor orb appears on a nearby wall. Like everything else, it starts off as an image and then becomes real. A moment later, the orb flares to life, sending a grid of white light across my body. GEENA steps closer. "In fact, you're the exact same color that Q43 was when we first brought it in." GEENA raises her hand so that her palm faces toward me and Maxon. "Perhaps we should take a closer look at you, too."

Black mist shoots out from GEENA's palm. The haze tightens my throat. Waves of pain shoot down my body. I grit my teeth, fighting the hurt. What GEENA does is no longer important. *I must connect with Avonlea.* Crouching, I focus my powers on the naiad below.

"Avonlea," I whisper.

My naiad opens her eyes a crack. She gives me a thin smile. A rush of water sounds in my mind. That means one thing. Avonlea is trying to communicate with me. I hear her hoarse voice in my head.

"Narragansett River."

I nod. "The Narragansett River," I whisper. "Your sisters are there. I'll take you to them. I promise."

Avonlea closes her eyes once more, confident that her monarkki will save the day.

Trouble is, I don't know how I'm getting out of here myself, let alone taking Avonlea along.

4

MAXON

*F*rustration swirls through me. Lianna's in pain. I must get her and that naiad out of here. But how? I scan my surroundings. Shit keeps appearing out of the freaking walls. Who knows what else is coming? I've fought enough demons to know that understanding your opponent is key.

Trouble is, I have no idea what I'm up against.

GEENA tilts her head. The orbs set into the nearby walls now flicker white grids across both me and Lianna. "Neither of you are scanning like humans. You're more ... like Q43." More black mist hisses out from GEENA's palms.

In some ways, the chemicals from GEENA don't effect me. This stuff is designed for water elementals; my power comes from air. But the moment the dark haze reaches Lianna, she screams in pain. Her agony tears through my consciousness. Two thoughts spin through my mind.

Save Lianna.

Make them pay.

Reaching forward, I grasp the railing that separates us from the chimney-like prison.

"Stop," cries GEENA. "Everything in here is precious."

"Good." I round on her. "Now watch me level it."

"Altering headquarters," states GEENA. "Alerting headquarters." Her electronic voice now carries a note of hysteria. "Request guard support."

The steps for escape appear in my mind: Tear up the hallway ... Prevent anyone else from coming in to help ... Then take Lianna and her naiad to safety. And if I can destroy this whole place in the process? Good.

I nod once to myself, my scheme set. I don't know everything this building can do, but that goes both ways. These DEX clowns have no idea what I'm capable of.

Time to end this.

Cracking my neck, I take one of my elemental forms. For what I have to do, it will be far easier as a monarkki. One moment, I'm a guy in a suit. The next, I'm a humanoid who's made up of gray swirling mist. Tightening my grasp on the railing, I yank it out from the floor with ease.

GEENA gasps. "Stop!"

Rising up, I fly down the corridor, using my metal rod as a make-shift baculum. The steel tears through the monitor walls. Tubes and wires pour out of the gashes. Sparks arc into the air. When I reach the corridor's end, I tear the largest opening yet.

Then I fly inside the wall.

Once within the panel, I coil my power into a small swirl. The greatest air storms can appear out of nowhere. That's what I do now. With a great surge of energy, I expand into tornado size, whipping out pipes and cords as I go. I'm vaguely aware of something biting into my skin, but I'm too jacked up to care. The debris slams into the wall, sending it crumbling onto itself. I whip out from the building's interior to reenter the torn-up corridor.

Just as I planned, the hallway is now blocked off. No one's coming in here to catch me and Lianna.

At the opposite end of the hall, GEENA stares at me, her head ticking at an odd rhythm. Looks like I screwed her up as well. Good for me.

"How…" GEENA spasms. "How…"

"I don't know much about tech, but I do know one thing. It's buggy as hell. Break one thing and it all falls apart."

GEENA crumples onto her knees. Too bad about that. I was looking forward to fighting her. Ah well. Something for another day.

Flying forward, I scoop up Lianna into my arms and then zoom into the prison space itself. All the wall panels flicker with massive images. The rolling countryside. Lines of formulas. Plans for GEENA. It all moves too fast to track, which is a shame. At some point, I'd like to know what's really happening here.

No time for that now.

Swooping downward, I expand my body so I'm five stories tall. That way, I can hold both Lianna and the naiad in one hand. Trouble is, being this large this lessens my power. The more concentrated I am, the more I can do. Still, there's nothing for it.

Looking up, I inspect the ceiling. If this building is like most, then that's my easiest exit point. Raising my massive fist high, I fly with one goal.

Bring down the roof.

My fist slams into the ceiling. The metal panel shifts, but doesn't break. Before, I'd felt some vague pain when blocking the corridor. Now that hurt comes back in force. Something injured me before.

I slam into the ceiling once more. A long crack tears across the metal. It's progress, but not enough. Meanwhile, some guards in silver armor appear at the base of the prison chimney. They're moving quickly and assembling some kind of gun. I suppose it was too hopeful to think I destroyed their only access route.

Alarm rattles through me.

We have to get out of here, fast.

I slam into the ceiling a third time. Then fourth. With each push, my powers grow weaker.

This isn't working.

In my hand, Lianna stirs. Her eyes open. She quickly takes in her surroundings. With a great roar, my woman turns full elemental. She seeps into the crack above us. I grin. Another thing I know about tech? It doesn't react well with liquids.

A moment later, a great rrrrrrip sounds as the ceiling is torn off by a powerful typhoon. Blue sky arches above. Below us, one of the guards calls out.

"It doesn't matter if the weapon isn't ready. Fire!"

Lianna and I fly away from the building. The naiad stays safe in my hands. As we zoom off, a great ka-BOOM sounds from what was once the DEX skyscraper.

Now, it's a pile of rubble.

Couldn't happen to a nicer place.

5

LIANNA

*M*axon, Avonlea and I whip across the skies. To the humans below, the three of us look like nothing more than fast-moving clouds. I've told Maxon where we're headed, since he's Mister Maps.

The Narragansett River.

It feels like days pass before we reach our destination. In reality, it can't be more than a few hours. The three of us touch down onto a deserted stretch of forest. Thin trees line the clearing, their branches heavy with emerald-colored leaves.

Maxon still carries Avonlea in his massive size. A few seconds later, he shrinks down to his regular human form. Avonlea lays unconscious in his arms. Maxon gently sets my naiad onto the forest floor.

I kneel beside Avonlea. There's a still a dark green tinge to her skin. Fortunately, I've healed this particular illness before. Leaning forward, I set my palms on either side of my naiad's head. Closing my eyes, I focus on the elemental energy inside me. The power swirls within me, liquid bright and strong. My torso lights up blue. I then send the energy down my arms and into Avonlea's body.

Maxon kneels beside me as I keep working. Little by little, the green ooze seeps away from Avonlea's body. Her skin transforms into a healthy blue. Minutes pass before Avonlea opens her eyes.

"My Monarkki," she whispers. "Thank you."

I lower my hands. "I only wish I could have reached you sooner."

"You came in time," says Avonlea. "That's what's important."

Nearby, a fresh downpour of water droplets appear. Soon, the liquid takes the shape of a woman in a blue kimono. Kyo. My Majordomo of Water can choose any form, but she selects the look of a geisha from hundreds of years past.

Kyo steps closer. "You almost got yourself captured."

I rise. "Yet Avonlea is free and healed."

Kyo narrows her eyes. "What will you do now?"

"Avonlea has sisters. I must check on them."

"No, my Monarkki." Avonlea shakes her head. "My sisters are well. You healed them days ago."

"I'd rather not trust to that." Perhaps it's the energy rush of exploding that DEX building, but I feel fit and alert. Normally, a healing tires me. This time? Not so much.

Kyo steps closer. "Please." She gestures to me and Maxon. "Both of you need to rest."

"Why?" Rising, Maxon gives Kyo the side eye. "You're up to something."

"Even monarkki have their limits," counters Kyo. "The two of you appear exhausted."

Now, I stand and work a *side eye* as well. There's something suspicious going on here. "We're fine."

"That's far from true." Kyo lifts her chin. "And I'm not the only one who thinks so."

My brows raise. *That's a surprise.* Kyo never exaggerates. Pausing, I give Maxon a careful once-over. He looks healthy as always. That said, maybe I'm off. Who knows what those chemicals from GEENA do to you?

Maxon tilts his head. "Maybe we should call it an early night."

I frown. "But I worry about Avonlea's sisters." Yet as I say those words, they come out as more of a question than a statement.

"You're not going anywhere," counters Kyo. She stomps her foot. "Come out, Tiny."

Tiny is the Majordomo of Earth.

Maxon and I share a sly look. We both suspected that Kyo would call in reinforcements. Here it comes.

The ground rumbles as a series of round-ish rocks pop up from the earth. None of them are larger than an egg. The stones quickly line up into a humanoid form that's only two feet tall. Tiny. He takes his small rock fist and proceeds to punch his own face. This is standard stuff, by the way. Once Tiny's walloped himself, his smooth rock face is shatters into sand. The tiny particles then take the shape of large eyes, a button nose, and a cherub-mouth.

Tiny really is cute.

"Bad bad," says Tiny. His voice is high pitched, like a cascade of small stones.

"You mean we look bad?" asks Maxon.

"Bad bad," replies Tiny. That's basically a *yes*.

At two thousand years old, Tiny is a baby by elemental standards. Sadly the earth element is so inert these days, Tiny's the only one who could help us out as majordomo.

Tiny slams his rock fist onto the ground. "Wakey wakey!" he cries. A fissure opens up in the earth. Flames lick out from the break. Soon the fire takes the form of a hand, which then grips the earth, hoisting the rest of itself out of the ground. And what appears? A bulky humanoid formed of molten lava.

Bubba, the Majordomo of Fire.

Now, this guy may look like a big bad fire demon, but he's really a total softie. "You two have me worried sick," whines Bubba.

Maxon and I exchange yet another look. Concern fills Maxon's blue eyes. Bubba always gets to him.

Before I can answer, none other than Ziggy lands in the clearing. As a badass wolf with wings, he's the Majordomo of Wind. In truth, his full name is actually Duke Zigismund of Östliche Winde. Maxon says the flying wolf takes himself too seriously, so we call him Ziggy. I think he likes it.

"Zis is unacceptable," says Ziggy in his crisp German accent. "You two look horrible." Ziggy rounds on me. "Mostly you."

I turn to Maxon. "They aren't giving up, are they?"

"Not a chance." Maxon steps to my side and whispers all low and growly in my ear. "Besides, it wouldn't hurt to have some alone-time. Right?"

My man makes a good argument. A small smile rounds my mouth. "In that case, it's time to improvise. Let's go."

After saying our goodbyes, Maxon and I retake our elemental forms and whoosh off to our crystal castle. I wish I could say that we had some hot and heavy alone time, but what happened was a deep kiss followed by a heavy sleep.

Turns out, I was more tired than I thought.

6

LIANNA

runch. Crunch.

Odd noises wakes me up from my rest. Opening my eyes, I see that I'm cuddled into Maxon's shoulder. His chest rises and falls in a steady rhythm. I blink hard, trying to shake the drowse out of my head. Clearly, Maxon's here and resting. So what's the noise all about?

Crunch. Crunch.

Rolling over, I find a small rock face peering at me over the mattress. It's Tiny.

"What's up?" I whisper.

Tiny lets out a low *shh* noise.

I nod.

With hobbling steps, Tiny lurches toward the bedroom door. I slip out of bed, careful not to awaken Maxon. Summoning my elemental powers, I change from a nightshirt into jeans and a T. Moving silently, I follow Tiny down the outer hallway to our living room.

Then I pause, surprised by what I see.

It's not the room's decor that shocks me. Like the rest of our house, the living room is a sleek space that's decorated in all white everything. What gets me is who is here.

Myla Lewis, Maxon's mother.

I grin my face off. Rushing over, I fold her in a big hug. Leaning back, I look to her stomach. She's six months pregnant now, and her bump has barely begun to show.

"It's so good to see you," I whisper.

Myla beams. "Surprise," she says, also in a low voice. "You're getting married today."

My mouth falls open. "What?"

"Marriage. You and Maxon. Today."

I tilt my head and try to process this news. I'm getting married today? How does that work, exactly? "You shouldn't have done this."

"I didn't. The majordomos got together. All you have to do is show up."

Tiny hobbles over, pointing at Myla's swollen belly. Then he gestures wildly at me.

Point made.

Myla rolls her eyes. "Are you bugging Lianna about having children?"

Tiny nods.

"That's supposed to be my job," says Myla. She returns her focus to me. "Well, what do you say? Are wedding bells ringing?"

For a long minute, I think things through. It's true that when it comes to marriage, Maxon and I have done nothing the last six months. And clearly, the majordomos have been scheming on this for a while.

Is this wedding day?

Energy zings through my limbs. I could actually marry Maxon today. The more I think about it, the more I love this idea. When I next speak, it's an effort to keep my voice low. "Consider me sold."

With that, I start toward the door. After a few paces, I realize a key problem. Myla and Tiny aren't following me. Turning around, I find the pair of them staring at me, speechless.

"What?" I ask.

"Don't you want any details?" retorts Myla.

No question about this one. "Not a bit. Surprise me."

"Good." Myla bobs her brows up and down. "Because I wasn't going to tell you anyway." She hooks her elbow with mine and whispers one last phrase. "Let's go."

And so we do.

7

MAXON

I open my eyes and find Lianna's gone. Sitting up, I rub my neck and scan the all-white bedroom. Where's my woman, anyway? Lianna loves to sleep in.

Slam!

The door whips open and four figures rush inside: Ty, Zee, Raj and Uth. The guys surround my bed with looks that can only be called *shit-eating grins.*

I shake my head and laugh. These guys never stop by in the morning. That's weird enough. But there's more strangeness going on. All my buddies are wearing their formal best, including their crowns. Technically, these guys are all princes in their houses. I'm the High Prince, meaning that I outrank them. Even so, my buddies rarely wear their crowns.

Something is definitely strange here.

"What's all this?" I ask.

"You're getting married today," says Ty simply.

My eyes almost pop out of my head. "What?"

"Your majordomos set it up," explains Zee. "They think you haven't been taking things seriously enough with Lianna."

I blink hard, trying to process this news. A wedding? Today? Can't decide if that's a good thing or not.

"If you don't want to get married," says Uther. "I can blow it all up."

Now I don't doubt that Uther would figure out some way to make things explode. "Thanks, Uth, but no explosives."

Uther sighs. "If you say so."

As the moments pass, my thoughts clear. Lianna is my woman. I want to marry her, end of story. Which means having a wedding today is really her call. "Does Lianna know?"

Raj nods. "As of two minutes ago. The majordomos set everything up, including having us act as your wake-up call."

Uth straightens his crown. "And we're already dressed up."

I shake my head. "I noticed that."

"What, you have different ideas for who'll be your best men?" asks Zee in his rumbly voice.

I rub my chin, thinking this through a little more. If Lianna is on board, then there's no question. And there's also no debate about who'll be at my side. "No, I think you guys would be great."

"Want to know all the details?" asks Uther. "I can explain the best points to use explosives, if you're curious. It doesn't have to ruin anything. I can help things look great."

I can't help but smile. Uth is such a character. "Look," I begin. "If the majordomos set things up, then I'm sure they considered the whole explosion thing. Really, Uth. Don't blow anything up."

"But I can explain everything, at least," says Uther.

"Does Lianna know all the details?" I ask.

"Nah," says Zee. "She wants it to be a surprise."

"Then that's what I want, too."

"So, is that your way of saying *yes*?" asks Ty.

"Didn't I do that before?" I ask.

"You said you wanted us as your best men, but not if you'd do this today," explains Raj. And per usual, he's right.

"In that case, let me clarify." I give my buddies a mock-salute. "I am officially on board for this mission."

Ty lines up along the wall and starts the traditional thrax roll call. "Tyberius of Striga, ready!"

Zee rises to stand beside him. "Nizam of Horus, ready!"

"Uther of Acca, ready!"

"Raj from Kamal, Ready!" His hawk Jetal caws in agreement.

At this point, another figure steps in the doorway. *Dad.* My father nods. "King Lincoln, ready." His face softens in a warm smile. "I'm proud of you son."

"Thanks." All of a sudden, my body feels positively light with excitement. "Let's hit it."

8

LIANNA

I stand on the edge of a large clearing. According to Myla, the mortal name for this place is Oregon. Majestic pine trees frame the grassy space, their prickly branches reaching up to Heaven. The wind carries a green and crisp edge; a pale blue sky arches overhead. On the ground before me, rows of stone benches stretch on for ages. A single aisle cuts down the center.

That's my aisle.

It's really happening.

I'm about to get married.

I scan the rows before me. My chest warms with the sight of so many familiar faces. I count Octavia, Camilla and Xavier. Walker's here in a tuxedo—who knew that was possible? Dignitaries from all four elements are here. So is Hildy, Tempest, and a ton of nobles from Antrum. Someone even set up a temporary Pulpitum station nearby.

King Lincoln—I can't yet think of him as Dad—steps to my side. He's in his traditional thrax best, meaning a tunic, crown and boots. Since it's a special occasion, both he and Myla are also wear long capes as well.

"Are you ready?" he asks.

Lincoln is walking me down the aisle. And the fact that he asking that question? The ceremony is about to begin. At the end of the aisle, there's an arch made of flowers and everything. There stands Maxon with his buddies behind him, all in their thrax formals.

An electric mixture of excitement and terror churn through me. On reflex, I check my dress. Like the suit I wore to the DEX building, this isn't a real garment. I've just created the illusion of a pale blue gown with a sweetheart neckline, princess waist and bell-shaped skirt. I even summoned a bouquet of blue roses to match.

Everything looks fine, which should be comforting. It's not. Instead, my body feels woozy with anticipation.

Twisting about, I scan behind me as well. Myla's ready , too. She'll process behind me as my matron of honor. Plus, I've asked all the major-domos to march as well. Sure, it's not the traditional definition of brides-maids, but when has anything in my life been typical?

Lincoln tilts his head. "Do you need a few minutes?"

My eyes widen with shock. *That's right. He asked me a question.* "I'm ready to go, Lincoln. I mean, Dad."

"Perfect." Lincoln offers me his arm. I wrap my hand about his elbow.

That's the cue for things to begin.

Great clouds materialize above. The white shapes twist into the form of four massive frigates as the air element joins the celebration. Fresh figures appear on the vessels.

Angels.

Lines of angelic singers step up to the edge of the elemental ships. Their wings gleam in the early morning light as they launch into an cappella version of Pachelbel's Canon.

I sniffle. Okay, that's gorgeous right there.

The ground rumbles as great fissures open on either side of the audi-ence benches. Now the earth elementals are getting into the act.

Hiss!

A massive water spout erupts from one side of the congregation. The liquid spins through the air before landing in the fissure on the opposite side. One by one, great arches of water form over the grounds, creating a kind of cathedral for me and Maxon.

That's the water element.

I sniffle again, and this time there might be a tear or two involved. The majordomos really went all out.

Bright red light flares across the clearing. Crackling noises fill the air. Beside each liquid arch, there now appears a line of fire. The light of red flames shimmer and dance through the blue waters.

The fire element is here.

My feet seem to move on their own as I begin my procession down the aisle. The choir's song swells over the audience. Avonlea and her sisters wave as I pass by. I catch Octavia drying her eyes with her finger-tips. Walker hands her a handkerchief. As I process past Tempest, the dragon winks. Beside him, Hildy shoots me a thumbs up. Xavier and

Camilla sit up front, their arms wrapped about each other. Both are beaming.

The Queen of the Angels, Verus, appears in the skies. With slow motions from her wings, Verus carefully descends to land right behind the arch of blue flowers. The choir's song grows louder than before, then falls silent. Looking around, I realize that I've somehow reached the end of the aisle. Lincoln kisses my cheek; I turn to Maxon. The clearing turns quiet and solemn.

Maxon looks me over from head to toe. "You look beautiful," he says, his blue eyes glistening.

I shake my head. "I can't believe this is happening. It's not what I expected at all."

Maxon shoots me a knowing look. We have an ongoing joke between the two of us that says, *nothing in our lives ever goes to plan.* I'd call it a family curse, but it's not always a bad thing.

"Dearly beloved," intones Verus. "I was the one who married Xavier and Camilla. After that, I joined Myla and Lincoln. Today, I am thrilled to unite Maxon and Lian—"

"Oh, fffffffudge," grumbles Myla. She stands to my left, her hands braced on her knees. A bead of sweat rolls down her cheek.

I set my hand on Myla's shoulder. "Are you all right?"

Lincoln steps forward from the first row of benches. "The baby," he whispers.

I look down and, sure enough, Myla's stomach is now nothing less than massive. Maxon told me about his birth. Myla didn't show so much as a bump and then—BAM!—she was nine months pregnant and giving birth.

Myla's eyes flash red. "I am not ruining this wedding."

Lincoln kneels beside her. "Yet you remember what happened last time." His voice is all things soothing. "You're about to have a baby. Fast."

"No one freaking touch me," snaps Myla. "My son is getting married right now. I mean it."

"This is an important ceremony." Verus twists her hands by her chest. "It shouldn't be rushed." She reaches for Myla.

Maxon's mom speaks through gritted teeth. "Touch me, Verus, and you'll be the Queen of the Dead People."

Okay, that's just a little but funny. Maxon and I share another sly look before my fiancée takes my hand in his.

"This is us, right?" he asks.

And in that moment, I know exactly what he means. "I believe this is the part where we improvise." I turn to Verus. "What's the speed version of this ceremony?"

Verus catches on right away. "Maxon, do you take Lianna?"

"I do," says Maxon.

"Argh!" cries Myla. "I'm trying not to swear here, but fffffffffudge this hurts."

"Lianna, do you take Maxon?"

"I do."

Verus waves her hand. White flame flashes on my ring finger, but it doesn't hurt or burn. That's *angelfire.* When the flames vanish, a simple golden band shines on my ring finger. Looking over, I find that the same has happened to Maxon as well.

"I now pronounce you man and wife," pronounces Verus.

Myla waves at me and Maxon. "You two go enjoy your reception." She looks to Lincoln. "And you..." She hisses in another pained breath. "The royal infirmary."

Fast as a heartbeat, Lincoln scoops Myla into his arms and races down the aisle in the opposite direction. Within seconds, both he and Myla are inside the tent that marks the temporary Pulpitum station. A flash of light beams through the entrance flap as they are taken off to the finest doctors in all the after-realms.

I return my focus to Maxon. "You're about to be a brother."

"But first, a husband," says Maxon. "Right, Verus?"

"Of course," says Verus. "I forgot the most important part. You may kiss the bride."

So he does. And it's marvelous.

MAXON

*A*s Mom ordered, Lianna and I hit the reception. Eventually. First we have to make sure that my mother is okay. Good thing both the reception and infirmary are in Antrum.

The waiting room to the royal infirmary is a plush space with lots of cushy chairs and snacks. Unlike my birth, this turns out to be a slow labor. Dad talks me and Lianna into visiting the reception. Which we do.

Note to self: never lock my buddies, booze and a bunch of recently-healed water naiads into the same room with a deejay who loves disco They literally tore up the dance floor.

What I remember from the reception are more images than memories. There's Pops in his golden armor, wings on display, waltzing with Cam (after the disco got yanked.) Walker and Hildy whispering in a corner. G laughing by the punch bowl. I don't see Tempest, but T's become a wild card at parties. A while back, the emperor of lust and wrath decided that the opposite sex was off the menu. The guy's basically become a monk.

We say our hellos and high tail it back to the infirmary. That's where the best images stick into my mind. Mostly, I'll never forget the moment Dad stepped into the waiting room with baby Portia in his arms. Lianna got all teary, and to be honest, I did too. My little sister is simply the cutest. Portia is all big eyes and chubby cheeks. She gives out those toothless smiles where you can't tell what made the baby so happy, you're just so glad they're grinning. In fact, the whole scene really gets me so caught up, I step out into the hallway to catch my breath.

That's where I find Tempest. He's all cut lines in his tuxedo. Not a lot of guys can pull off a cravat, by the way, but T manages. Maybe it's the British accent.

"How's the baby, mate?" asks T. There's a gleam in his eyes that I can't quite place.

"Portia's adorable."

T takes in a long breath. It's like he's bracing himself for something. Although I can't imagine what that might be. I've seen T take down a pack of Class A demons without so much as batting an eye. All this puffing with worry is not my bud.

"What's up?" I ask.

"Portia. Is there a birthmark by her eye?"

That's a surprise, to be sure. Leaning back on my heels, I think through every moment of meeting my baby sister for the first time. "Yeah, there's a mark. How'd you know that?

Closing his eyes, T lets out a long breath. "Wild guess, mate." When he opens his eyes again, T's pupils have turned into reptilian slits. That means one thing. His dragon side is close to the surface. "You won't be seeing me for a while."

I take a half-step backward. "What do you mean?"

"I'll be staying in Furonium."

"How long?"

"Years. Seventeen, maybe eighteen."

My thoughts reel through this news. Sadly, there's so much work Lianna and I have to do, and not a lot of elemental activity in Furonium. "I'm not gonna lie; that's a bummer. I won't see you so much, but I get it. You're the emperor of the dragon lands. There's a lot going on."

"Something like that," says T. "Plus, I can only see *you* for a while, mate. Not your family."

Damn, T is acting really strange. First, the emperor of lust swears off all women. Now, T plans to hide out in his homeland and stay away from my family. "What's up? Anything I should know?"

"Decidedly not. Go enjoy your wedding night." Tempest whistles as he steps away. Actually whistles. I've seen the guy drunk and surrounded by no less than six dragon ladies, and he didn't let out a note. This is definitely strange. In the back of my mind, a little voice screams that the reason here is obvious. But it's been a big day. I'm not even putting together obvious shit at this point.

Lianna steps out into the hallway. "Hey."

"Hey. The strangest thing just hap—"

But Lianna doesn't let me finish. Instead, she wraps her arms around my neck, guiding my lips to hers. Our kiss deepens. Lianna even wraps her legs around my waist while scratching the back of my neck. That sends me over the edge.

I want her.

Leaning back, Lianna breaks the kiss. "You were saying?"

"That Tempest just had the most amazing idea. Let's go home and enjoy our wedding night."

Which is exactly what we do, and not only for that night but for many afterwards. You see, after seeing baby Portia, Lianna and I want a family of our own.

Can't wait.

-The End-

The adventure continues in PORTIA, book two of the Angelbound Offspring. Read on for a sample chapter!

ALSO BY CHRISTINA BAUER

PORTIA

The adventure continues with PORTIA! Read on for a sample chapter!

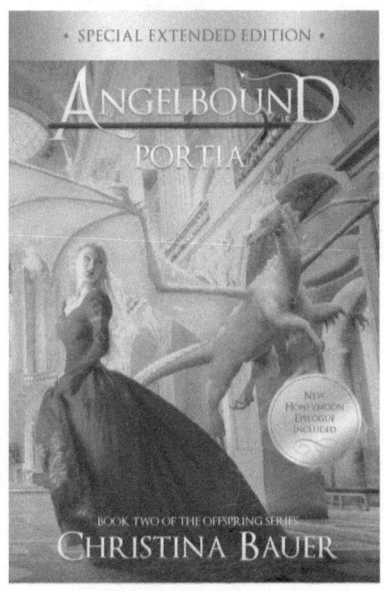

ANGELBOUND

Revisit ANGELBOUND, the kick-ass paranormal romance with more than 1 million copies sold!

LINCOLN

Enjoy Lincoln's perspective with the Angelbound LINCOLN series!

FAIRY TALES OF THE MAGICORUM

A modern fairy tale that *USA Today* calls a 'must-read!' Check out WOLVES AND ROSES!

DIMENSION DRIFT

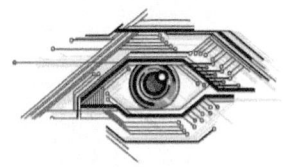

A kick-ass heroine + a swoon-worthy prince + an all-girl heist = the DIMENSION DRIFT series!

BEHOLDER

Medieval mages ... Slow-burn love ... And heart-pounding action! Check out the BEHOLDER series!

PIXIELAND DIARIES

PIXIELAND DIARIES tells the story of sassy pixie Calla and 'her' elf prince, Dare.

I am so late.

My heart beats at double speed while I rush down a marble staircase in the Ryder Mansion. If I were a doll, I'd be Action Librarian Barbie, The Super-Late And Extraordinarily Stressed-Out Edition. I glance at my watch and cringe. My lecture on *Magic Across The After-Realms* should've started twenty minutes ago.

The President of Purgatory waits for me at the bottom of the stairs. Her mouth presses into a thin frown.

"Portia, you're finally here," she says. "We were getting frantic."

The President's known for being tough on crime, corruption, and well, everything really. But she's also my grandmother. When it comes to family, Gram's a softie who worries like crazy.

"So sorry, Gram. I got caught up."

Her eyes widen with alarm. "It's your Firmament spell, isn't it? You've been working on that non-stop."

The magical Firmament is what holds the after-realms together. Void demons have been attacking it for years. My spell will show the damage. Worst case scenario? All the after-realms could fall apart. Question is, will the catastrophe hit in six months or six hundred years?

My stomach twists with dread. My intuition tells me it's closer to six months.

"When do you think you'll finish the spell?" asks Gram.

"Any day now."

"That's excellent news. We'll finally know if danger is imminent." Her face beams with pride. "My brilliant grandbaby. After all the years of hard work, you must be thrilled."

I try to muster up a smile; I can't.

"Something else is wrong," says Gram. "What is it?"

I try to play it cool, but I can't stop the splotches of red that appear on my cheeks. "I was, uh, talking to someone before."

Gram lowers her voice to a hush. "Was it a boy?"

My heart sinks. Technically, it was a boy. In reality, it was a disaster.

Trouble is, I should be a man killer. I have all the ingredients. I'm nineteen years old, not terrible to look at, and a princess to boot. Plus, I'm part Furor dragon, which means that I should have supernatural powers over lust and wrath. But I'm the opposite of a man killer. More of a man frightener.

Gram's features soften with concern. "Please tell me what happened, honey." It's the 'honey' that gets me, every time. "Did you really talk to a boy?"

"Maybe."

"Oh, Portia!"

"Please try not to make it a thing. It didn't go well."

Gram stares at me expectantly. Her face is so open and understanding, I can't help but spill my guts. "I've been having flirty conversations with this guy, Alex, who works at the dry cleaner. But it was all by phone, you know? He never saw me. And I never wrote my real name on any of the slips, so he didn't know I was…"

"High Princess of the thrax and the granddaughter of the President of Purgatory?"

"Yeah, that." I anxiously shift my weight from foot to foot. "Anyway, today I needed to pick up my suit for the lecture. So, I decided to go in person." Alex looked adorable through the store window. He had blond hair, tawny brown eyes, and a sweet lion's tail. "Once he saw me, he freaked out and ran away." I spent an hour moping on the couch. Not my best morning.

On reflex, I brush my fingertips across the black tribal markings near my right eye. These are why Alex panicked. My marks frighten everyone. I've had them since birth. There's no hiding them. No removing them. And no avoiding what they mean. One day, I'll transform into one of the Void. A weight of sadness settles into my bones. "I should have expected it."

Gram gently guides my hand away from my eye. "Someone cast that spell on you, am I right?"

I nod.

"Then, there must be a way to break it. We'll never give up." She lifts her chin defiantly. "And you're a marvel. Only nineteen years old, and look how much you've learned about magic. There's a way to break this thing and you'll find it."

I try to force another smile. It doesn't happen. Normally, Gram's pep talks work like a charm. But I'm not feeling it today. "You know me. I'll get my head together. Alex threw me off, that's all."

"Oh, honey. I may be old as dirt, but I remember talking to boys. How you look? It can *feel* very important when you're young. That's all an illusion." Gram sets her fist over her heart. "It's what's inside that counts."

Here it comes. No one gives a better 'be yourself' lecture than Gram. Most days, it works great. But today, all I can picture is the terror on Alex's face. Sure, we'd totally connected on the phone, but did that make any difference once he saw I was Marked? Not at all. "Gram, I wish people saw what's inside. I really do."

"Listen to me carefully, Portia. I'm a quasi-demon. Your grandfather's an archangel. According to our DNA, we should be enemies. But when I look at him, I don't see an archangel. I see Xavier. That's love, and that's what you need. I'm not saying it'll be easy, honey. I'm saying that you're worth it."

Gram takes my hands. Though her fingers are slim and dainty, her touch is firm as steel. "As a matter of fact, nothing worthwhile is easy." She gives my hands an encouraging squeeze. "But I know my grandbaby. You're a fighter."

I offer her a sad smile. "I can barely hold a dagger."

"That's not what I mean and you know it." She steps away and releases my hands. "Now, be honest with me. If you're too upset for today's lecture, you can cancel."

I stare at the closed door. If I walk out now, I know where that path leads. More hiding out in my penthouse, reading books, and practicing spells. *Alone.* I straighten my shoulders. Some risks are worth taking. "All right, Gram. Let's go."

"Now, that's my girl."

Gram and I walk down the hallway and into the packed ballroom. My body goes on high alert. Everything seems to warp and lengthen, like I'm looking through a fun house mirror. The tall French doors seem to tower impossibly high. The crowd's chatter echoes in odd ways. And all the faces somehow multiply by the second. I wipe my sweaty palms on my tweed skirt.

Why did I agree to this again?

If the full room makes Gram nervous, she doesn't show it. With an effortless grace, Gram steps up to the podium and speaks into the microphone. The crowd instantly quiets.

"Good afternoon, everyone. Welcome to our monthly lecture series for diplomats…"

As Gram does her introductory stuff, I scan the space and try to dampen my rising panic. The audience includes representatives from all five lands of the after-realms. There are angels from Heaven, quasi-demons from Purgatory, and ghouls from the Dark Lands. There are even a few full-blooded demons here, although they're all flanked by guards. And finally, there are a handful of demon-fighting thrax from Antrum. That's my father's side of the family.

"And now, it's my sincere joy to introduce our guest speaker." Gram gestures to the few thrax in the room. "Some of you already know her as Princess Portia, heir to the throne of Antrum. But I see a different side of this young woman. My granddaughter is one of the foremost experts on the different types of magic used across the after-realms."

Gram shoots me a proud glance. I inwardly cringe. No question what's coming next—Gram loves to talk about how smart I am. It's not my favorite topic.

"Portia has been named to the Angelic Council for Academic Excellence," says Gram. "She tested out of the human equivalent of high school and college at the age of thirteen. She was also awarded the Golden Pentagram for achievement in witchcraft. Portia is the only spell caster known to have mastered all forms of Level One magic."

Gram leans in toward the microphone, her brown eyes glittering with delight. She's on a roll now. "You know, this reminds me of a story."

Reminds her of a story? Kill me now.

"My granddaughter's nineteenth birthday was just last month. Portia always makes a big book donation in honor of her birthday, and you know what? My granddaughter has given more than five thousand books on magic to Purgatory's libraries. Many of them are rare editions."

Gram shoots me a friendly half-wave. I try to grin back, but it might look like I have gas pains. The more Gram talks, the more I want to kick off my heels and run for the hills. I don't do attention. Period.

Before I can make any real escape plans, Gram ushers me to my place at the podium. "Therefore, without further ado, I present the Princess Portia."

Gram bows slightly and steps away. My heart thumps so hard, I feel the beat in my throat. I stare blankly into the crowd.

You can do this, Portia. You've been practicing your speech for ages.

"Canopic jars," I say in a full voice. "Does anyone know how they work?"

Evidently no one knows, as the room stays deadly quiet. My skin prickles with anxiety. This is not going well.

Thankfully, all my rehearsing pays off. My mouth starts moving on its own, following the familiar course of my presentation.

"Canopic jars were used by humans in ancient Egypt. We use them in the after-realms, too." I lower my voice to a conspiratorial whisper. "Only unlike humans, we don't fill the jars with body parts."

A few chuckles echo through the crowd. My confidence rises. "Canopic jars are best used as supernatural batteries. Energy goes in and gets doled out slowly over time. The Firmament uses this principle, too." Some confused looks appear in the audience. I frown.

Oops, I may have lost them there.

"How many of you are familiar with how the Firmament works?"

A few people raise their hands. Most look even more confused. "The Firmament is an invisible magic network that holds the after-realms together. At the heart of this system, there are four Sacred Trees." I pick up the glass of water sitting atop my podium. "Think of this as a Sacred Tree. The water inside is Firmament magic. It slowly evaporates over time, feeding the roots and branches that connect all the after-realms."

I scan the audience. The confused looks have disappeared. My confidence soars. With that, I launch into a detailed explanation of the magical underpinnings of the after-realms. The more I talk, the easier it gets. After a while, it's hard to tell how much time's gone by. I don't really mind, though. Now, I'm the one who's on a roll.

I lean closer to the microphone. "There are four magical researchers who've done serious work on the Firmament. Two of these have theories I find useful."

Gram slips up to my side, her face all smiles. She gently nudges me away from the mic. "My, that does sound interesting. Sadly, I'm afraid we're nearly out of time."

My brows lift with surprise. "It's already been thirty minutes?"

"You've been up here for almost an hour, honey."

An hour? I can't believe it went by so quickly. The audience looks sleepy and dazed. My heart sinks. Maybe that last bit on magical researchers was too much. I turn to Gram and speak from the side of my mouth. "What do I do next?"

"Perhaps you can take a few questions?" suggests Gram.

At these words, about a hundred hands zip up into the air at once. Gram gestures to a cute kid with a mop of ginger hair. "How about we start with this young gentleman?"

The boy bounces on his seat with excitement. He appears so sweet and harmless—all messy hair and freckles—that I take Gram's suggestion.

"How about you?" I point to the boy. "What's your question?"

The kid hops to his feet. "Where's your tail?" As he speaks, the boy twists his own lizard tail between his fingertips. "Did it get cut off or something?"

A jolt of anxiety hits my bloodstream. The fact that I don't have a tail really worries the general quasi population. "No, I was born without a tail."

Some members of the audience shift, uncomfortable in their seats. I can almost see their commentary hovering above their heads in cartoon-type thought bubbles. *Real quasis have tails, end of story.*

I worry my lower lip with my teeth. I need to lighten the mood here. I inspect the boy and guess why he asked the question in the first place. "But I bet I know someone who can lose their tail and regrow it."

The kid's eyes go big as saucers. "Yeah, I can."

At this point, the boy looks totally adorable. The crowd lights up with happy faces. Some photographers crouch-walk closer to the boy, all the better to get a good shot. Flash bulbs go off like fireworks. My heart lightens. At last, a front-page picture that won't make me cringe.

"Thank you, Princess," says the kid.

I smile from ear to ear. This is totally working. Without thinking, I gesture to the man who's next in line, his arm held high in the air.

"How about your question, Sir?"

The guy rises. "Roy Cotter, Purgatory Enquirer."

My heart sinks to my toes. This creep is one of those reporter-stalkers who follow me around looking for tabloid headlines. They always print the same stuff—how any second now, I'll turn into a demon, launch my secret plan, and overthrow Purgatory's government. Not that I blame the quasi population for being jumpy. We had a demonic diplomat who seemed harmless—that would be Armageddon—and he ended up leading a marauding army through Purgatory.

Roy stares at me eagerly, his dark eyes glittering with excitement. How could I have missed him? He's tall, bony, and has a scorpion's tail. Not easy to forget.

"When will you turn into a Void demon, Princess?"

Gram leans into the microphone. "You know our official stance on this topic. My granddaughter has had a spell cast on her. She has some unfortunate marks. That is all."

I press my lips together, hard. It's all I can do not to scream the truth into the microphone. I am Marked for the Void. And worse than that, those monsters are destroying the after-realms. It's only a question of when.

Maybe I can just say one little thing.

I raise my pointer finger. "Actually, when it comes to the Void—"

Gram grips my hand tightly, stopping me. A warning flashes in her brown eyes. I know that look. She doesn't want me talking about the Void and the Firmament. Not yet, anyway. We need to know if it's an imminent threat.

Roy glares at me, a challenge in his eyes. In the past, I've always agreed with Gram about holding off on the Void news until we had more specifics. But today, the truth bubbles up inside me, dying to get out.

"What do you say, Princess?" asks Roy. "Are you Marked for the Void or what?"

"I'm not here to disagree with the President," I say carefully.

"Ha! That's what we call a non-denial denial... Which means that you *do* think you'll turn into one of the Void. Come on, we all know it."

His words hit me like fists. *My tragedy is his next headline, nothing more.* My heart feels hollowed out and empty.

Gram sets her hand on my shoulder, gently pressing me away from the podium. "My granddaughter is not responding to that ridiculous accusation."

Normally, this is the part where I stiffen my spine, shut my mouth, and tough it out. That isn't happening this time around. Instead, something snaps inside me. There's almost an audible ping through my soul. Suddenly, I'm sick to death of concealing everything that I am. The guy wants an answer? He'll get one.

I lean into the mic. "No, I've got this."

"If you're sure, honey."

"Positive." Fresh rage corkscrews up my spine as I scan the audience. The anticipation turns so heavy, you could cut the air with a chainsaw. "Am I Marked to transform into a Void demon?" I drag out the moment for extra emphasis. "Absolutely."

A chorus of gasps fills the room. It's a satisfying sound.

"Perhaps we should end questions now," says Gram.

"With all due respect, Madame President," counters Roy. "The people of Purgatory have a right to know what's happening with your granddaughter, especially since you let her run wild." His mouth twists into a sneer. "We know what happens when a full-blooded demon goes free in Purgatory."

More anger spikes through my soul. "Worrying about full-blooded demons is a waste of time. The real threat goes beyond Purgatory."

The crowd gasps once more. Roy rocks happily on his heels. "Knew it! You're planning to conquer the after-realms. It's Armageddon all over again. This, my friends, is why full-blooded demons always have an armed guard."

Rage jolts through every muscle in my body. *How can he be so blind?* "You're focusing on the wrong thing!" I pound the lectern for emphasis. "I've researched this every way you can think of, and the fact that I'm Marked isn't what's important." The audience stares at me, dumbfounded. "This is a sign. Someone's warning us about the Void."

Worried chatter breaks out through the crowd. Roy's features brighten. He just got the scoop of a lifetime and he knows it. "Is that an official statement? You're turning into one of the Void and know about their plans to attack."

Rage seethes under my skin. "The Void are tearing apart the Firmament that holds the after-realms together," I say. "That's as official as it gets. Whether or not I'm one of them doesn't make any difference."

Gram wraps her arm around my shoulders. She's the picture of smooth. "For the record, my granddaughter is an expert on magic, not a representative of the government of Purgatory. If she has reason to believe that the Void are a threat, then I'm sure she has the documentation to support her claim. However, that does not mean that threat is immediate."

Roy starts to talk again, but Gram simply raises her hand and speaks in a deadly soft voice. "That's enough. I realize the quasi are wary of full-blooded demons. That's why I've supported the Senate's regulations on keeping them guarded within our borders. But to extend this scenario to my granddaughter is simply unacceptable." Her tone says that this is not up for discussion. "The lecture is over. We'll now retire to the gardens for more refreshments."

For the first time, I notice a series of servants standing by the French doors that line one wall of the ballroom. Acting in unison, they motion the crowd to step out into the gardens. The audience leaves so quickly, it's like a gunshot went off in the ballroom.

Gram pulls me aside and kisses my cheek. "That was a solid step forward, honey."

I lift my eyebrows in disbelief. "That was an all-out catastrophe, Gram."

"Give it time. Today, the quasi people saw that you're impassioned about their welfare. They didn't see a demon; they saw a young woman with a good heart."

Her words soothe my frazzled nerves. My anger cools, only to be replaced by a hot wave of embarrassment. "I'm so sorry I let loose on the Void. I know we agreed to keep it a secret."

"It's fine." Gram stiffens her spine. "More than fine, actually."

"What do you mean?"

"We're way past due to start messaging this to the general population. Xav's been on me about it for ages. I just wish we knew the timeline we're looking at."

"I'll finish the spell soon. I promise."

Gram sets her palm on my cheek. "You've such a good heart. Whoever cast that spell on you, they knew what they were doing." She runs her fingertips along my marks. "There's no one better to find out what's happening with the Firmament."

Warmth and pride seep through my chest. "Thanks, Gram."

"Why don't you take a break first? Xav told me that he found you some new magic books."

My eyes widen with excitement. "The medieval alchemy series?"

"That's the one." She gives me another quick peck on my cheek. "They're on the desk in his office."

"I'll stop by right away."

"Great idea." She makes shoo fingers at me. "Now, take the rest of the afternoon off. You deserve it."

Gram walks away while glad-handing everyone in sight. Turning on my heel, I beeline toward my grandfather's office in the Ryder mansion.

Alchemy books, here I come.

~

End of Sample

Order PORTIA, book two of the Angelbound Offspring today!

APPENDIX

IF YOU ENJOYED THIS BOOK...

…Please consider leaving a review, even if it's just a line or two. Every bit truly helps, especially for those of us who don't *write by the numbers,* if you know what I mean.

Plus I have it on good authority that every time you review an indie author, somewhere an angel gets a mocha latte. For reals.

And angels need their caffeine, too.

ACKNOWLEDGMENTS

If you're reading my freaking acknowledgements, chances are, I should thank you for something. So, for the record: you are awesome, dear reader.

That said, huge and heartfelt thanks must go out to my husband and son for their rock-solid support. Being an author means a lot of early mornings, late nights, long weekends, and never-ending patience. You two are the best guys in the universe, period.

After that, I must thank the extensive network of reviewers, friends and colleagues who helped me build my writing chops in general. Gracias.

Finally, deep affection goes out to my late, much loved, and dearly missed Aunt Sandy and Uncle Henry. You saw the writer in me, always. Thank you, first and last.

ABOUT CHRISTINA BAUER

Christina Bauer thinks that fantasy books are like bacon: they just make life better. All of which is why she writes romance novels that feature demons, dragons, wizards, witches, elves, elementals, and a bunch of random stuff that she brainstorms while riding the Boston T. Oh, and she includes lots of humor and kick-ass chicks, too. Christina lives in Newton, MA with her husband, son, and semi-insane golden retriever, Ruby.

Stalk Christina on Social Media

Blog:

http://monsterhousebooks.com/blog/category/christina

Facebook:
https://www.facebook.com/authorBauer/

Instagram:
https://www.instagram.com/christina_cb_bauer/

Twitter:
@CB_Bauer

VLOG:
https://tinyurl.com/Vlogbauer

Web site:
www.bauersbooks.com

COMPLIMENTARY BOOK

Get a FREE novella when you sign up for Christina's newsletter: https://tinyurl.com/bauersbooks